THE REGICIDE REPORT

CHARLES STROSS

orbit-books.co.uk

ORBIT

First published in Great Britain in 2025 by Orbit

1 3 5 7 9 10 8 6 4 2

Copyright © 2025 by Charles Stross

The moral right of the author has been asserted.

All characters and events in this publication, other than those clearly in the public domain, are fictitious and any resemblance to real persons, living or dead, is purely coincidental.

All rights reserved.
No part of this publication may be reproduced, stored in a retrieval system, or transmitted, in any form or by any means, without the prior permission in writing of the publisher, nor be otherwise circulated in any form of binding or cover other than that in which it is published and without a similar condition including this condition being imposed on the subsequent purchaser.

A CIP catalogue record for this book
is available from the British Library.

ISBN 978-0-356-52467-2

Printed and bound in Great Britain by Clays Ltd, Elcograf, S.p.A.

Papers used by Orbit are from well-managed forests
and other responsible sources.

Orbit
An imprint of
Little, Brown Book Group
Carmelite House
50 Victoria Embankment
London, EC4Y 0DZ

The authorised representative
in the EEA is
Hachette Ireland
8 Castlecourt Centre,
Dublin 15, D15 XTP3, Ireland
(email: info@hbgi.ie)

An Hachette UK Company
www.hachette.co.uk

orbit-books.co.uk

*For everyone who's ever had to sign
the Official Secrets Act*

PART ONE

PROLOGUE

Hello, diary.

My name is Bob Howard, and this is my workplace journal. It's classified TOP SECRET BORING, BIN BEFORE READING, and it really *is*, so if you've read one of these journals before you can skip this entire chapter, which is just background bullshit.

My name is Bob Howard, and I'm a mid-level officer in the British Government Security Service that guards the United Kingdom against magical threats to the realm. I've been working here for nearly two decades and going by my pay grade I should actually be about a third of the way up the senior civil service promotion ladder, but instead I've got unique responsibilities of my own (ahem: I wear a pair of dead man's shoes inherited from my former boss and predecessor, Dr. Angleton). I'm a troubleshooter: the kind of trouble I shoot comes with tentacles and magic attached.

Maintaining a workplace journal is a requirement for all employees tasked with active operational roles. It's a measure intended to help retain institutional knowledge in the event of the unexpected death of the diarist, namely yours truly. I'm not sure how useful this is in practical terms: I do so much codeword clearance work that I'm pretty sure nobody short of a Senior Auditor is cleared to read this. Hell, I'm not sure *I'm* cleared to read it.

(Anyway, dying in the line of duty has only happened to me a couple of times, and it didn't stick. But I suppose it's more fun than dreaming up new and creative ways to lie on my time sheet, so here we are.)

Let me start with a word about my agency. We are—or were—Q-Division SOE (nicknamed the Laundry, because during the war we worked out of offices above a Chinese laundry in Soho). We are Her Majesty's Occult Security Service, and we've been grappling for some years with a contingency codenamed CASE NIGHTMARE GREEN.

So. Here's what you need to know about magic: feel free to skip ahead if you've heard it all before.

Magic is a side effect of computational processes that you can perform using your brain, a computer, a pocket calculator, or even a *Magic: The Gathering* card deck. (MTG is Turing-complete: its rules are sufficiently rich and complex to emulate any other abstract computing system.) The paradox of CASE NIGHTMARE GREEN is that the more magic there is, the easier it becomes to do magic. More brains? More sorcerers. More computers? More thaumaturgic processes. It's a doom loop, and it's been getting doomier and loopier ever since microprocessors showed up in the early 1970s.

This century, there are more than ninety microprocessors for every human being on the planet, with billions more manufactured every month. The effect on magic snowballs, so much that superhumanly powerful and inhumanly malevolent entities—let's call them Gods—have been trying to move in and squat the collective subconscious, because they find brains and computers tasty to snack upon. We've beaten some of them back, but our luck ran out eighteen months ago in the worst disaster the UK has suffered since the Second World War: the elven invasion of West Yorkshire. With the walls between the worlds thinning, a sorcerous combined arms brigade retreating from a magical world war in another universe popped out of the dream roads in Malham. And then they attacked Leeds.[1]

You can't cover up a five-digit death toll in the third most

---

1. To *alfär* eyes Leeds was the obvious capital of the British Empire: it's right there in the middle of England, where else would you put a capital city?

populous city in England. King Arthur was supposed to come back and save the Britons in their hour of greatest need—there's a frankly bizarre contingency plan called FORLORN AVALON that I read a year or two ago—but Art isn't answering the red telephone these days. So who're you going to call next?

With the agency in disgrace, a deadly dangerous religious cult called the Golden Promise Ministries got far too cozy with the government. We—what was left of the Laundry, after the then Prime Minister shut us down—were on the ropes: so in order to keep fighting, our high-ups struck a Faustian bargain. Instead of letting the cult sacrifice us all to their alien god, we invited in one of its rivals: Fabian Everyman, political supervillain and living avatar of His Dread Majesty N'yar Lat-Hotep, the Black Pharaoh.

After neatly cleaning the clock of his rival cultists, Mr. Everyman stormed to victory in a surprise by-election, was elected leader of the Ruling Party by unanimous acclaim, threw a snap general election, wiped out the opposition completely, and established himself as the head of a government called the New Management. All in three months flat. *Oops.*

In the aftermath of the first conquering army to rampage on English soil since 1688, and the subsequent brain-worming of the British government by minions of the Sleeper in the Pyramid, petitioning a greater power to tidy up our toy chest seemed like a proportionate and reasonable response. But once Nanny gets her feet under the table it's not up to the children to dictate when she leaves: and this particular nanny, better known as N'yar Lat-Hotep, the Black Pharaoh, was now the Prime Minister.

So we went from being an organization dedicated to keeping the eldritch horrors out, to being an organization dedicated to serving one.

Instant existential crisis, right?

*

Here is a necessarily incomplete list of important points that didn't occur to our departmental executive until it was much too late:

- An avatar of an Elder God manifesting in the person of a politician might possibly have an agenda of his own and might be sufficiently competent at finding allies, or at least adoring cult members, to win the largest general election landslide victory since 1945.
- The UK, as Lord Hailsham famously remarked in 1975, is an elective dictatorship.
- Consequently, such a politician might be a bit harder to control than a merely human Prime Minister.
- One of the most fundamental rules of Applied Computational Demonology is "do not summon up anything you can't put down in a hurry"; the avatar of an Elder God is pretty clearly something along those lines.
- This particular avatar of an Elder God turned out to be immune to: bell, book, and candle; bullets; blackmail; botulinum toxin; bribery; bombs; back-bench plots; banishment; and (worst of all) bureaucracy.
- Not only are we unable to banish the Prime Minister, every entity we are aware of who might be able to do so is *even worse*.

It turns out that when an organization like the Laundry accidentally finds itself doing *the exact opposite* of what it's supposed to do, its members can respond in at least three different ways. The psychology of how human beings behave during a crisis sheds some light on this: sinking ships, house fires, plane crashes, alien invasions, that sort of thing.

In general, during an acute emergency, only about 10 to 25

percent of people will react appropriately—that is, by taking effective action.

Humans are social animals, and they take their behavioral cues from the other people around them. They know how they're supposed to behave on a ship or airliner, or in a shopping mall, so that's what most people do—even when things are going sideways around them. They pay no attention to the flames or the waves lapping at the upper deck windows or the gunshots in the concourse. They just sit tight and assume that somebody will sort it out.

Uncertain and confused people hesitate, and that's how they turn from potential victims of disaster into *actual* victims. Hesitancy afflicts 60 to 80 percent of people in an emergency, and accounts for most of the deaths.

Which brings me to the final 10 to 15 percent, who realize something bad is happening but who drive right past the turn-off to Safety City and floor the accelerator all the way to Panic Attack, where they then increase the death toll by adding themselves to a fiery multi-metaphor pile-up.

What has happened to the Laundry since the New Management came in isn't an acute crisis but an ongoing state of emergency. And we've all been flailing around in it for months now. I'd like to be able to tell you that highly experienced civil servants who have spent their entire careers facing down tentacle monsters can handle themselves better than civilians in a crisis, but I'd be lying.

The organization is still here, and is back in roughly the same shape it was before the previous government dissolved it. We're the same people, doing the same jobs in some of the same offices. Same paperwork, same pay grades, same beige paint on the walls, same dire coffee.

But about 75 percent of our staff are in complete denial. Eating, sleeping, writing reports, dealing with minor diabolic infestations, attending meetings—it's the same job, right? They're still shopping at IKEA and Tesco, picking up the kids after school, budgeting for a family package holiday over the school vac.

They pay no attention to the chrome and steel gibbets at Marble Arch, rattling with the skeletonizing corpses of priests who sold their souls to the wrong god. They block out the blood-robed hierophants of the Black Pharaoh, droning their imprecatory prayers at the enemies of the Prime Minister. They refuse to see the sullen coffles of sacrificial victims winding their way toward the altar in Westminster Abbey, where they will be beheaded with Excalibur reforged.[2] And they pay as little attention as possible to the horrors in the background on the *Nine O'clock News*.

Sociologists call this normalization of deviance: deviation from correct or proper behavior becomes normalized if it's allowed to persist. And the vast majority of our staff don't notice anymore.

(Another 5 to 10 percent are on long-term sick leave, huddling under the duvet and gobbling prescription meds with both hands. I can't say I blame them: even if their reaction is less than helpful, at least they recognize the severity of the situation.)

And that leaves just 10 to 15 percent of us who recognize that the plane is on fire, the ship is sinking, the Joker's minions are out of the Asylum and sweeping the mall with automatic gunfire, and it's up to us to save the day.

And despite knowing all this, I'm still not sure which category I'm in . . .

---

2. The original Excalibur was gifted to the Kingdom of Sicily by Richard the Lionheart in the twelfth century. Its badly rusted remnants were recovered last year by a crack team of combat archaeologists from the British Museum. Subsequently it was melted down for scrap and remanufactured as a thaumically active component of several execution swords by BAe Systems under contract to the Post Office and Fujitsu. The Prime Minister is a fan of Henry VIII . . .

THE REGICIDE REPORT 9

Mo is reading over my shoulder, and she thinks I've taken it for granted that you know about magic—about what we do at the agency, not card tricks and stage magic—so I'm going to backtrack a bit.

I usually cover this stuff in my *Applied Computational Demonology: 101* introductory lecture, but this isn't a classroom and there's no exam, so you can skip to the end of this chapter if you already read about this stuff in *New Scientist*. (Go on, I dare you.)

We live in a multiverse. There is a transfinite number of parallel universes, created and destroyed by merger whenever quantum indeterminacy brooks multiple outcomes. Mathematics—in the most abstract sense—underpins the quantum multiverse we experience. There's a deterministic substrate below the Planck scale: the reality we experience appears to be a buggy full stack simulation. Because we've learned how to exploit some of the bugs in reality, acts of symbolic logic manipulation allow us to pass messages to localized entropy-reversing entities in other domains of the multiverse: for convenience we will call these entities "demons." We can ask them to do things, and they respond reasonably predictably, that is, almost invariably deterministically. We call this process "magic."

Of course, when doing deals with demons you want to use the simplest possible constructions, to minimize the risk of a sorcerer's apprentice scenario (or, as we in the comp. sci. sector call it, an unterminated loop). And you hope like hell that you never attract the interested attention of a greater demon—one with a mind of its own—because they don't necessarily stick to your instructions.

Now, I'd like you to imagine you're trying to design the simplest possible program for an extradimensional entity. You're writing code for a very stupid imp—on the order of Maxwell's Demon—that can read an instruction from an input, write an output, and execute a very limited number of tasks ("put this electron into an excited state," "pause," "resume," "halt and catch fire" . . .) with extreme rapidity and absolutely no discretion. It's not exactly Microsoft Excel, so how much can you do with this?

Everything, as it turns out: the basic abstract model of all computers everywhere, a Universal Turing Machine, only needs four basic instructions and a unidimensional storage tape of infinite length to carry out any computable process. The full set of opcodes for our physical reality is only a bit more complicated than Intel's 64-bit instruction set. But—and here's the catch—just as it takes a lot of steps to write a PC operating system, it's the same with magic.

If you want to do spells, you're going to have to start by obtaining a degree in computer science. Then you need to forget everything you've learned about how *actual* computers work and start over again with a wildly different abstract machine architecture. Then you need to learn how the whole rigmarole of software engineering methodologies, test harnesses, and teamwork apply to demonology before you write your first "hello, imp" invocation. And that's the *safe* way to do magic.

Of course, there's an unsafe way to do magic. Nervous systems like brains are *also* computational substrates, and it turns out there are thoughts you can think—unnatural, spiky thoughts that make your eyeballs catch fire if you get them wrong—that get the attention of some of those extradimensional listeners. If you manage to get a handle on how to do this without emulsifying your brain or transmuting 1 percent of the carbon nuclei in your body into silicon (which, believe me, is an explosively bad idea), then you can get the demons to obey you *just by thinking*. You don't even have to draw diagrams in blood and annotate them in abstract syntax notation! It's wins all round! Except that doing magic in your head can attract several types of microscopic parasites from the dungeon dimensions—variously called eaters or feeders in the night or V-symbionts—which bite microscopic chunks out of your gray matter because they find human sorcerers tasty.

THE REGICIDE REPORT 11

Being brain damaged by alien parasites causes a condition called Krantzberg syndrome, alternatively Metahuman-Associated Dementia, which is the leading cause of death or early retirement among ritual magicians. (It also accounts for the tendency of every computer running Windows to blue-screen at the most inconvenient time—if you wondered if they could sense your desperation and choose the worst possible moment to crash? You were right.)

Some mages avoid succumbing to cortical bit-rot, but that's not great either. I mentioned V-symbionts: they're magical parasites that confer handy benefits on the human mage who hosts them, in return for the host helpfully introducing them to other victims, who eventually die of cortical bit-rot by proxy. We have a special term for these mages: we call them "vampires" (or, in bureaucratese, PHANGs).[3]

Not everyone who thinks spiky thoughts realizes they're doing magic. You might have noticed the headlines about so-called superheroes and supervillains? These are autodidact magic users who grew up on a diet of Marvel and DC comics and are acting out their adolescent power fantasies while the parasites drive them insane. (Or worse, they're autodidact magic users who are copying the comic fans inaccurately—which makes them dangerously unpredictable.)

It's possible to design a ward—a protective shielding amulet—that keeps the eaters out of your head. Again, the agency provides these to approved government-licensed superheroes, field agents, and practitioners. It's rumored that they even leaked a flawed version of the schemata on the darknet, "Anarchist's Cookbook" style, so that would-be supervillains would create wards for themselves that signal FREE ALL-YOU-CAN-EAT BUFFET HERE rather than saying NO EATERS ALLOWED.

Now, as to the reason for CASE NIGHTMARE GREEN:

---

3. Photophobic Hemophagic Anagathic Neurotrophic Goons. I think. I can't give you a hard and fast definition of the acronym because it's classified.

it turns out that reality exhibits subtle caching behavior so that, as magic becomes more prevalent, it increasingly enables algorithmic processes to proceed to completion in linear time. The more computers there are, and the more brains there are carrying out computational processes, the easier it gets to repeat a set process. It's not something that our classical computers can take advantage of, but it's a force multiplier for quantum computers—and also for mages and monsters and things that go bump in the night. We are hurtling toward a sorcerous singularity: and if you've been wondering why we're suddenly drowning in Elder Gods and Lovecraft's nightmares, this would be why.

And all this is by way of leading up to an explanation of what I do for the government.

Now, some more about me: I'm Bob Howard, and I'm a specialist.

I started out as an ordinary computational practitioner—doing sorcery by means of software. But two years into my deployment on Active Operations, I got cross-wired with an entity known as the Eater of Souls. It was an example of what used to be called demonic possession: a group of incompetent cultists tried to sacrifice me in order to control the Eater, not realizing that he was already incarnate. Upshot is, I carry the Eater of Souls around in my head but I'm still Bob . . . I think.

The other human previously bound to the Eater of Souls was my former boss Dr. Angleton, but he died during a security incursion I still have nightmares about years after the event. So I'm now its sole living avatar. Am I still Bob Howard, now with extra magic mojo? Or am I a hungry ghost dreaming that I'm him? I dunno. Mo, to whom I've been married for over nine years now, thinks I'm still him. I mean, me. But Mo is a mite uncanny, too, ever since she relinquished her violin made from undead human bones in return for a *really disturbing* superpower. And that was before she got a ringside seat at a boss fight between godlike entities at Nether Stowe House, which by rights should not have been survivable—at least not by a merely human bystander. Who cares? (I still love her, I'm pretty sure she loves me, too. The family of sorcerers that sacrifices together stays together and all that. I just try not to think too hard about it.)

My uncanny status comes with some perks. I'm immune to K syndrome: the Eater of Souls eats any feeders who come near me. I'm also immune to PHANG syndrome—I've been bitten, the V-symbionts that tried to chow down on me died. Go, me! (I try not to think too hard about the fact that I'm the bogeyman vampires warn their brood about.)

I have other duties—troubleshooting, like I said—but the biggest threat besetting the agency is beyond me, namely the New Management itself. Maybe I was responsible for the biggest zombie-raising in Western Europe this century, but I'm *still* not in the same weight class as the PM.

And then there's the little problem there's only one of me.

The power of a bureaucracy lies in its ability to throw more interchangeable bodies at a problem. Unfortunately rock star necromancers don't scale—and that's what I am. Here's your analogy: most magical practitioners are four-year-olds running around the playground wearing dad's threadbare dressing gown, pointing a stick at people and shouting, "Bang, you're dead!" *I* am skulking around the woods in urban camo with a loaded L85 service rifle. And then you get to the Black Pharaoh, who can tell His artillery corps where to point the big guns.

Anyway, this is all a long and involved lead-up to the story of why Iris Carpenter—the PM's chief of staff—tapped me for the operational side of the investigation into the first assassination of a reigning monarch since the Middle Ages. And the explanation of why SOE Q-Division, also known as the Laundry, no longer exists. Also why Westminster Abbey is being rebuilt, there's a giant Aztec-style skull rack at Marble Arch, and I've been pulled off operational duties for the indefinite future, stuck here in a cubicle in the basement of the archives, writing my memoirs.

Let the fun begin . . .

DEATH BY BUREAUCRACY

Things they never taught you in Sunday school: even after the apocalypse, there will still be committee meetings—and attendance is mandatory.

Well, they *may* have taught you that. My parents didn't send me to Sunday school so I don't really know what they teach there. What I do know is that the apocalypse happened on the evening of Saturday the 17th of May, 2014, during a party at Nether Stowe House in Buckinghamshire. Things got slightly out of control: half the Cabinet was brain-wormed by extradimensional hypercastrating parasites, and in the resulting reshuffle Fabian Everyman[1] became our new Prime Minister, leader of the New Management.

To say this upset the Civil Service would be an understatement. And I am, for better or worse, a Civil Servant. Hence the committee meetings. (It's what we do best.)

So here I am, sitting in Conference Room D7 on a rainy Tuesday afternoon in mid-January, trying not to doze off while Vikram Choudhury drones on about our assigned roles and responsibilities in the current operational plan for this event—his voice is quite remarkably soporific when he's reading from the minutes of a previous meeting. I mean, even Jim Grey is channeling the spirit of Alex in the aversion therapy scene from *A*

---

1. Living avatar of N'yar Lat-Hotep, the Black Pharaoh, His Dread Majesty, Supreme Lord of Chaos, etc.

Clockwork Orange, looking for all the world like his eyelids are being held open with surgical steel clamps—

"—Dress code is strictly black suits, white shirts, black ties, and a black armband. Dresses, skirts, or trouser suits for the ladies, also black; hats with veils optional. In other words, full formal mourning wear or mourning dress uniform where applicable for the two weeks after LONDON BRIDGE is announced. After the funeral, retaining the dress code is advised for the remainder of the month but may be relaxed if absolutely no public-facing duties are required. Footwear—strictly no sandals. Bob. Bob? Are you still with me?"

I blink helplessly. "What about trainers?" I ask, because I know the answer but I'm a glutton for punishment.

"Definitely no trainers"—Vik looks horrified that I'd even ask—"you do own a pair of black dress shoes, don't you?"

I cringe slightly. "Not currently, no," I reply. I had a pair, but a couple of months ago our cat committed an act of unspeakable feline desecration against them for some obscure slight, and I haven't replaced them yet.

"Buy a pair, break 'em in, then store them in a plastic box against the day—God Save the Queen," interjects Gerald Lockhart, his tone so witheringly dry that I imagine the rain outside freezes from sheer terror for a few moments. Strictly speaking Gerry needn't be in this briefing for middle-managers like me—he's Director of External Assets, he has minions to delegate to—but I suppose LONDON BRIDGE briefings show up on his monthly matrix: it's as inescapable as taxes.

Operation LONDON BRIDGE, the cause of this afternoon's tedious recap of dress codes, is the operation that will be activated when Elizabeth Alexandra Mary, better known as Her Majesty Queen Elizabeth II, dies. She's 88 and in just one more year she'll have beaten Queen Victoria to the gold medal for longest-reigning British monarch. So of course we have contingency plans for Operation National Granny's Funeral, and the older she gets the more portentous and elaborate they become, because the Palace has a neurotic compulsion to be seen to be licking the coffin handles. Hence this annual wankfest we're required to attend instead of working—

"Bob?" Someone is waving a hand in front of my face. "I think he's catatonic—"

"—Smelling salts—"

I force myself to inhale deeply through my nose, breathe out, breathe in again (thereby avoiding a yawn that would have given the game away), and try to look alert. "Yes?" I ask.

Vikram leans toward me. "We were talking about your shoes, Bob."

Jim Grey glowers. "They've got to go." (Which is okay for him to say, he's a cop and gets to wear shit-kickers the whole time.)

"There's nothing wrong with my trainers," I say defensively, flipping my phone face-up to unmute it and check if there are any notifications important enough to get me out of this purgatory.

"They're different colors," Jim accuses me. "And you've got a red one on your right foot and a green one on your left. Do you even sail? They're back to front!"

"Yes, but they're the same make and style," I reply. "And I alternate daily! It's called wear leveling."

Pinky chirps up: "If someone would assassinate the Queen it would put us all out of Bob's sartorial misery!" (*See, I knew someone would take my side.*) "At least until the next monarch croaks," he adds.

"Not helpful," Gerald says repressively, then glances at his watch. "Kindly stop wasting our time, Bob, some of us have homes to go to."

"I'll shoe shop this weekend," I promise, hoping the concession will put an end to the footwear nonsense and we can move on to ensuring that the black crepe in the stationery cupboard isn't time-expired. (As opposed to, say, planning how to get the necromantic horror that currently passes for a Prime Minister out of 10 Downing Street.) But right at that moment my cursed phone takes matters into its own metaphorical hands and barfs a series of alerts that will undoubtedly spice up my week, because I had to fuck around and find out.

See, it's not that the messages themselves are in any way interesting, but the notification sound? It's *that* sound sample. What can I say? Pinky, Brains, and I were in the pub after work last night and after three pints of Landlord it was mildly amusing to see who twitched when it went off, and neither of my idiot co-conspirators stopped me. And it would have been fine if I'd set it back to the default chime when I left.

But I didn't. Which is why the sudden flurry of help desk notifications on my phone sounds like a stream of incoming Grindr chat alerts. And when I glance up I meet a very irate pair of eyes, and cringe as I realize that I've accidentally outed the head of External Assets.

Do not meddle in the affairs of senior civil servants, for they are quick to anger and will drown you in paperwork, as J. R. R. Tolkien probably wouldn't have admitted in public—he would have known better than to inadvertently out a head of department. But then, I never claimed I was smart enough to invent Middle Earth, did I?

As it happens there were no immediate consequences from my god-awful choice of alert sounds. Nobody in the meeting acknowledged Gerry's brief expression of shock, or my own contrition as I muted my phone and apologized. It was like the silent but deadly fart that lingers in a stuffy room, denied by all. So by Friday I was beginning to think I'd gotten away with it—but at 4 p.m. Outlook threw a meeting notification at me:

Monday, 9 a.m.: Secure Briefing Room 14, MR Building, discuss sensitive new assignment with Iris Carpenter.

THE REGICIDE REPORT   19

Iris was my line manager some years ago, until that one time when she tried to sacrifice me. She doesn't work for the Laundry anymore: but after her stretch in Camp Sunshine she received an official pardon then prospered alarmingly. These days she's the Prime Minister's Chief-of-Staff, and so far above my pay grade I need to bring an oxygen cylinder to meetings. (Rumor has it that her handbag rates motorcycle outriders.) She's a political animal, and by animal I mean the kind with venom sacs and stingers: I try not to attract her attention if I can avoid it.

Our bad history aside, Iris and I have a degree of mutual respect for each other's abilities. She's a coldly ruthless management shitweasel and evil sorceress with a mind as twisty as a seven-dimensional Möbius strip, but to be scrupulously even-handed, she probably thinks I'm a Generation X slacker unfairly gifted with powers that make me the necromantic equivalent of a walking neutron bomb. And the hell of it is, we're both right.

For her to be visiting our offices—even the executive suite, five minutes' walk from Downing Street—is slightly horrifying. Especially if it's to have a quiet word with *me*.

So on Monday morning I report to Secure Briefing Room 14 in Mahogany Row to hear my doom.

("Don't worry, she won't put you in charge of LONDON BRIDGE," Mo reassured me over breakfast. "She likes to play with her toys so that they last longer, not run them over with a steamroller.")

We're meeting in a boring office building off Whitehall that Laundry senior management was moved to six months ago. It is distinguished from other secure briefing rooms in that there are thaumaturgic containment grids on all the surfaces—walls, floor, and ceiling. If you die of shame while they're hauling you over the coals, your ghost isn't allowed to leave until it's been deleted by Payroll *and* exorcised by Janitorial Services.

"Come in, Bob. Long time no see." Iris gives me a fey smile. She looks slightly haggard, as if she's been on the go continuously since midnight Black Mass on Saturday. (For all I know, maybe she has?) She's upgraded her wardrobe for Downing Street to tailored black business suits and heels, so I'm feeling outgunned from the get-go. "I ordered coffee," she tells me. That is a surprise: it implies I'm not in immediate disfavor. "You still take it white, no sugar?"

"Yes, thanks." I stifle a yawn. "I don't think I've seen you since . . . was it last month's break-out session? How have you been?"

"I've been good." Her smile fades into a mild frown. "I'm running divisional meetings here this month because His Nibs wants me to monitor you lot personally, and Number Ten is an eighteenth-century rat's nest—no occult security at all—and my office there is being rebuilt. So you can find me right here every Monday from nine to one, at least until all the fires are out and the restructuring is under control. My door is, as they say, open. How's Mo doing these days?"

We make small talk for a few minutes but I barely register it because I'm in a state of mild cognitive dissonance. Iris is normally the model of self-assured professionalism. For her to be feeling the pressure, or less than on top of her game, is disturbing. And for her to take time out from biting the heads off delinquent cabinet ministers to make idle chitchat with little old me is unprecedented.

"—Which brings me to why I wanted to see you. I get reports."

I clear my throat, desperate to cover the fact that I zoned out for a second or two just now. "Is this about Gerry? Because I can explain—"

"Not my circus, not my monkeys. Just remember to mute your phone in future: oh, and Gerry *really* likes his Speyside single malts. No, I wanted to see you about something else. Forecasting Ops have flagged up a sensitive upcoming contingency, and I'm putting together a tiger team to deal with it. There will be an investigatory phase which you might be useful for, but you're a particularly good fit for containment if events develop as prophesied. So this is your advance notice that you're going to be drafted."

My alarm bells are ringing so loud that my phone is about to scold me for exposing myself to damaging noise levels. (The New Management likes euphemisms: *containment phase* is usually code for *kill them all, god will know his own*.) So of course I Do The Stupid and ask: "What kind of forecast is this?"

"We—" she begins, but then pauses as the VISITOR lamp beside the door flashes. We wait while our coffee delivery arrives. (Rank has its perks, I see: we're getting the good china from the executive dining room.)

After the door closes and locks, she continues. "Forecasting Ops has received credible indications of a threat to the Crown. They read the entrails and said the immediate threat level is low right now, but it rises to near-certainty in about six weeks— right around the first anniversary of the snap election."

"By the Crown"—I pick my words carefully—"do you mean the Queen, or His Dread Majesty?"

Iris's cheek twitches as she replies, "Yes."

"Oh," I say, feigning enthusiasm: "I *love* ambiguity."

Later that week—gift-wrapped apology bottle of whisky notwithstanding—I am experiencing the full brutality of Gerry Lockhart's revenge. It didn't take long for him to point a new assignment at me, and it's an absolute masterpiece of bureaucratic evil. The worst part? From the outside it looks like a promotion.

FLASHBACK:

"Bob," says Jez Wilson, who I technically outrank but can't ignore because she's kinda-sorta Iris Carpenter's successor (minus the dark priestess bit), "I've got a niche role opening up and

Gerry passed me your name, I hope you don't mind? It's good for about one day a week for the next six months, strictly desk liaison stuff, needs someone fairly senior to stick on the org chart but it's not public-facing and doesn't involve a lot of boring paperwork."

And because I'm a nice guy I nodded politely and said, "Do go on."

BACK TO THE PRESENT:

That conversation is why I'm trying really hard not to bang my head on the desk or turn the idiot in the chair opposite me into a midwife toad.

"You'll understand if I find this all a bit much to swallow," the man-sized specimen of *Alytes obstetricans* snarks patronizingly. His name's Allen Stephenson and he's on the planning approvals board of Birmingham city council.

"Next you'll be telling us the moon landings were real!" his companion simpers. This is Laura Jones, who is a grand panjandrum in municipal waste and recycling outsourcing management.

We're sitting in an office in Birmingham where I am surrounded, outgunned, and in some cases outranked, by an office full of middle-ranking local government managers, all of whom share the peculiar delusion that magic isn't real. I've been sent here to disillusion them, and it's not going great. It's like trying to deliver a lesson on celestial navigation to an audience of flat-earthers. Excuse me; Sorcery Skeptics, Demonology Denialists, the salt of the earth: hence the codename for this boondoggle, MUGGLE WONDERLAND.

These people did their research on the internet: watched the YouTube videos Penn and Teller released explaining how they stage magic tricks; read op-eds debunking palmistry, astrology, and witchcraft in *Scientific American*; binged on *MythBusters* episodes . . . they're hardcore unbelievers. Under normal circumstances this would be a good thing—we don't need a Civil

Service run by conspiracy theorists—but these are the days of miracle and wonder, as Paul Simon sang. Lives could be lost if the authorities refuse to believe their eyes when a necromancer targets Sutton Coldfield cemetery, or a supervillain raids the Jewellery Quarter.

I manage not to roll my eyes. "I'm not talking about stage-magician magic, sleight of hand or trickery that relies on distraction. When we use the term 'magic' we're doing so in a technical sense to describe resonance effects—"

"Oh! Oh!" Marissa McCoyle presses the back of her wrist to her forehead like a fainting Victorian ingenue: "The vibrations! Can you feel them? There's something coming through!" Ms. McCoyle is the deputy director of libraries and adult education. She has a master's degree in education and an MBA, and she thinks she's here to take the piss. "Really, it's not news that the new Prime Minister is up to his eyeballs in mystical bullshit but we don't need that here—"

I smile and blank her out, because informing her that His Nibs is talking about reintroducing the criminal offense of Lèse-majesté would not contribute anything positive to this circus (even though it's true). Besides, I'm trying to think of a suitable demonstration that won't result in me being up on a disciplinary notice tomorrow morning—I knew it'd be a tough audience going in, but this is some above-and-beyond denialism. At least nobody's called me a fraud yet.

"Is that all?" I ask after Ms. Jones titters something about knowing how to deal with rubbish in her department. I look around: "Have you got it out of your system yet?" I stand up and stretch, then wrestle my cuffs back into position because I'm not really used to the whole suit thing. "I assure you, it's just as real as the maniac who animated the Bull Ring bull last month and took it for a ride around the Grand Central site—"

Ms. McCoyle interrupts again: "That was just a viral marketing event for the latest New Avengers movie."

"No it wasn't." *Right, that's it*, I think, and before I can work through all the possible ways this can go wrong I utter a phrase in Old Enochian, a language that was never intended for late morning local government meetings—the air actually turns blue for a couple of seconds, the pale aqua of liquid oxygen shimmering in the corpse-light of an ancient white dwarf star. The walls of the conference room fade into translucency, laying bare a desolate, frosted landscape beneath the bowl of a black sky. It's pierced by the merciless pinpricks of stars seen without the protection of a caul of atmosphere as the full moon floats high above us, its pockmarked silvery face carved into the likeness of Adolf Hitler by unspeakable ancient powers. "Like I said, magic is *real*, and it's what my department deals with. Or do you think I smuggled a planetarium into this meeting room in my pocket?"

The illusion is actually a reified memory of mine, from a very unpleasant experience—a visit to another timeline or pocket universe via the ghost roads, a world where the Second World War had ended in a pyrrhic victory for the Third Reich. The Birmingham Skeptics Society don't need to know the background deets, or feel the bone-deep cold of a world refrigerated to the temperature of high noon on Pluto, but they do need to smell the coffee. I snap my fingers and the illusion vanishes, leaving me with their undivided attention.

"There are other universes. We use resonance effects to access them, and the bleed-through between different versions of reality lets us manipulate stuff in this realm more or less at will. But there are consequences—take that world, for example. I was there about fifteen years ago"—give or take a year or two because who's counting?—"and it's lifeless and barren, all the heat sucked out of it by monsters that live in the darkness behind the walls of the world."

I sit down again. "You don't know about this stuff because the agency I work for, and our foreign counterparts, have spent decades papering over the cracks. But it's impossible to keep the lid on tight anymore. Something equivalent could happen here.

So, look, I want you to take it on trust for now that there's a *very specific thing* we refer to as magic, and it's not to be confused with card tricks and pulling rabbits out of hats on stage. It's a real problem, like asbestos wallboard in the school estate, and we need to deal with it. And to make matters worse there are jokers out there who will call anything they don't understand magic, and you need to be able to tell whether—"

Which is precisely when my phone emits the nuclear attack air raid siren screech that means *big trouble ahead*.

BEHOLD THE TRUE HORROR OF GERRY LOCKHART'S REVENGE:

There are roughly 450,000 people in the British Civil Service at present. That's not including the million and a half in the NHS organizations and the third of a million in the military and the police. We operate on a gargantuan scale, and doing so coherently is an immense challenge.

When you're dealing with roughly two and a half million people a certain amount of nonsense is inevitable. At any given time, a couple thousand of them will be undergoing an acute psychotic break. Another ten or twenty thousand will have joined one bizarre religious cult or another—from the relatively mild, like Seventh Day Adventists, through the reality-disconnected, such as the Fully Automatic 24-hour Church of Elvis. (At least two dozen will have fallen down the rabbit hole of call-the-PREVENT-hotline stuff like the Cult of the Mute Poet.) Maybe 10 percent of the population are flat-earthers, another 20 percent are young earth creationists, and don't get me started on how many of them worship the royal family.

Then you come to the Laundry, and the revelation in the media that magic is real and we have, in fact, spent half a century working to suppress it—hey, it's an actual government conspiracy! A real one! Men In Black going door to door near *you*!—

and we've spent so long educating our highly intelligent civil servants to disbelieve conspiracy theories that, now we're owning up to one, *they won't listen to us.*

When a secret government agency confesses to a conspiracy, people often refuse to believe the confession.[2] It doesn't matter how much supporting evidence you provide if it doesn't reinforce their existing beliefs. This is especially true when what you're confessing to is a half-century-long coverup of something even more bonkers than usual—secret Cold War bases on the moon, vampires run the banking sector, that sort of thing. So

---

2. Let me give you an example:
Back in May 1982, during the Falklands Conflict (a few years before I was born), a Royal Navy nuclear submarine, HMS *Conqueror*, became the first (and hopefully only) nuclear-powered attack submarine to engage another warship with torpedoes. It fired on and sank the Argentinian heavy cruiser *General Belgrano*, which might or might not have been steaming toward the Falkland Islands (it was changing course hourly at the time). More than three hundred sailors died in the incident, and it made a big stink because if the *General Belgrano* had been outside the UK's maritime exclusion zone around the islands at the time of the sinking, which had been ordered by Margaret Thatcher herself, that would have been illegal.

Anyway, one thing led to another and in due course a conspiracy theory emerged: that the *Belgrano* had not been heading into the exclusion zone at the time of the sinking, and that the relevant pages in the log book of HMS *Conqueror* had been destroyed to cover up a PM ordering the navy to commit a war crime.

To this day there are people who believe the conspiracy theory about the Iron Lady deliberately ordering a mass murder and then a coverup involving the murder of anti-nuclear activist Hilda Murrell, even though the truth was declassified thirty years after the event and is much stranger.

It turns out that the log book of the *Conqueror* was censored to cover up an entirely different incident two months after the *Belgrano* sinking! HMS *Conqueror* had been assigned to Operation BARMAID, a cold war spy caper in which the submarine snatched a Soviet-towed sonar array right off the back of a Polish spy trawler in Soviet territorial waters, using a top-secret cable-cutting device. The logbook was censored right afterward just in case a Soviet mole in the Civil Service found it in the archives. And this real explanation only came to light when Operation BARMAID was declassified thirty years later.

now the requirement for a coverup has passed, and we need the Civil Service to work with us, we've run head-first into the unpalatable truth: about 30 percent of our own people refuse to believe anything we tell them.

Jez asked me to be part of our outreach team, visiting outlying offices to explain the facts of life to the skeptics, and muggins here was stupid enough to say "Sure." And that's why I now spend a day a week in meeting room hell.

Welcome to Gerry's revenge!

I pick up my phone, despite the dirty looks and exasperated sighs from around the conference room in Birmingham. It's a work call, with a high enough priority to override my *do not disturb* filter.

"Mr. Howard? Duty Officer here, please confirm."

"I'm in a meeting—"

"Please confirm."

"Um. Oxtail, Antelope, Brimstone. Over to you."

"Sideboard. Teapot. Excalibur. You have a flash priority call from Mr. Choudhury, please hold."

(Swearing ensues, then I make my apologies to the room: a minute later I'm crouching in a supplies cupboard just along the corridor.)

"Bob? Are you secure?"

"I am now. I'm supposed to be conducting a MUGGLE WONDERLAND training seminar—"

"—But you're in Brum, am I correct? City council headquarters?"

"Yeah, visiting Council House. What's up?"

"You need to get down to the lobby right away. A police armed response unit will pick you up in the next five minutes. There's a metahuman incident in progress at a comic book shop on Queensway and you're the nearest asset we've got to ground zero."

I swear. (A lot.) "Isn't this a job for TPCF? The Home Office heavies? You know who I am, right?"

"TPCF teams one and two are currently out fighting fires in Lancaster and Fishguard and can't make it back in time. Your assistant"—Peter-Fred—"is in remedial diversity awareness training this morning. The Duty PHANG can't handle it because daylight hours lock-down, the other H-list officers are variously on annual leave, off sick, or busy, and the Queensway situation hasn't escalated to major incident *yet* so we can't assign an OCCULUS team."

(I sigh.) "Okay, I'm moving, I'm moving. What do you mean by *yet*?"

"There are Daleks."

Oh God, and by God I mean Shub-Nuggirath, the Stoat of a Thousand Young, it's one of *those* incidents.

"It's a comics shop siege," Sergeant Samson sums up succinctly when I pile in the back of the police BMW. His driver, Constable Nobby (he hasn't told me his name and I've been reading Pratchett last thing at night so that's what I'm calling him) floors the accelerator and hits the lights and siren. "Some saddo wanted his latest fix and wouldn't take no for an answer." (It's Thursday, comic release day is usually Tuesday. Don't ask why I know this: I could tell you, but then I'd have to kill you.) "When the owner asked him to leave things turned weird."

I manage to strap myself down between tire-screeching corners as I grapple with the conundrum of an armed siege in a comic shop. "I was told Daleks were involved? Is this a prank?"

A Gatso camera double-flashes our numberplate from behind as we accelerate. "That right there was half an hour of extra forms to fill out after end-of-shift so I sincerely hope not, sonny." More screeching tires. "Whoever's responsible will be getting a piece of my mind. You're with the X-Files crowd, you can sort it out."

"Daleks," I prod.

"Awright. Sitch is called Andromeda Bookshop, they do books and comics, and apparently they've got a *Doctor Who* exhibit running. Saddo is holding the owner and two or three members of the public hostage with a couple of Daleks from the BBC props department"—he's interrupted by a burst of radio fuzz—"he wants his copy of the next issue of Squidbob Shartpants or whatever *right now* or he's going on a rampage in the Bull Ring Centre."

"But Daleks?" *Daleks aren't real!* a part of me is screaming.

"Oh yeah, he animated them and it turns out that makes them *really angry* and they exterminated the hell out of a red pillar box before we could clear the street. So there are more MOPs sheltering in place."

Sounds like I've got a rogue animator on my hands—a powerful one if he's making constructs with firepower. Or maybe he's an invoker? "Fuck my life," I mutter.

"Fuck your life indeed, sonny," the sergeant says affably. "We've got AROs on site backed up by SFO snipers at each corner but it's anybody's guess how effective they'll be against robot Space Nazis. It's up to you to handle it."

"Sounds like I'm going to need specialist support. Let me make a call," I tell him, then get on the blower to the Duty Office.

BACK TO IRIS'S BRIEFING . . .

"Forecasting Operations can't give us anything specific because an adversary is fuzzing the probabilities. They're getting hit with haruspicy countermeasures, oracular paradoxes, nonlinear invocations, all sorts of stuff that point to a top-rated occult operations agency. Anyway, the threat—when it shows up—will need to be investigated, and the adversary needs to be told to fuck off with extreme prejudice before His Dread Majesty notices and gives it His *personal* attention, thereby generating an international incident and much screaming from the Foreign Office. He's planning something for the anniversary and He will be *most* displeased if His elbow is jogged."

Threats against Her Majesty the Queen are an everyday occurrence. Nutters: we have them. The police deal with them when needed.

Threats against the Prime Minister also come up regularly, but are not a problem for the police: anyone stupid enough to get in the PM's not-a-face generally leaves only a greasy smear on the ground.

But I doubt I'd be sitting in a securely warded briefing room if this was a *normal* threat.

My heart is down to periscope depth and still diving even before she adds, "It needs to be done without making visible waves. It's probably the neighbors, and we don't want to give them the impression we can't take out our own trash."

"Oh boy," I say faintly.

Mention of the neighbors puts this particular threat *well* beyond the frontier of normal and deep into *yikes* territory, because the neighbors most likely to pull this kind of stunt are our US counterpart agency, the Black Chamber.

While the US and the UK are theoretically allies, a better fit would be frenemies: the USA acquired many of the British Empire's former possessions at gunpoint, and in the occult sector the mugging is still ongoing.

Anyway, they've had the knives out for us ever since His Dark Majesty sent a team into Washington, D.C., in February last year to kidnap—er, rescue—the President, who they were planning to sacrifice because an unharvested head of state is an *amazing* store of *mana*, magical energy accumulated through worship. The Pentagon Ringwraiths are extremely peeved, and our relations with them are chilly at the best of times, so some kind of counterattack is totally in their wheelhouse.

A thought occurs to me: "Are any of the YELLOW OLYMPIC team available?" I ask, "I mean, the survivors?" YELLOW

OLYMPIC was the operation in D.C. "I mean, they've gone up against BC operatives and survived, and Officer Friendly alone would make a huge—"

Iris makes a cutting gesture. "Sorry, Bob, Jim is unavailable."

"He's unavailable? Why?"

Iris looks momentarily uncomfortable. "Almost all the team who weren't already vampires came back as PHANGs. As for the others—" She pauses. "Given your history I assume you don't want to work with the crazy *alfär* mage, either." Iris is right: Yarisol of the Host, the anomalous *alfär* sorcerer Mhari dragged along on her caper, is bad news.

Iris stands, clueing me in that it's time to leave. "I have another meeting to get to. Meanwhile don't get too far ahead of the eight ball just yet. I'm assigning you to ops, but you'll be working under an Auditor—in case you have to go head-to-head with senior executives in the course of the investigation—and they'll be reporting directly to me." So I'm going to be in charge of operations but number two on the org chart? Whoopee, all the work and none of the credit. I can hardly wait. "I'm going to read them in next. Anyway, this is just your initial heads-up: enjoy your coffee." And with that, the meeting's over.

If this is how my week is starting, surely things can only get better?

Ten minutes after leaving Council House the police car I'm sitting in has slowed to a comparative crawl. (Say what you will about police drivers, but even they aren't crazy enough to play chicken with trams.) And I'm on the phone to the situation room and back-office support the Duty Officer has scared up for me.

"I need to know exactly what items besides the two Daleks they've got in the exhibit," I explain. (There's nothing like a rogue Cyberman or unaccounted-for Auton to ruin your day.) "In particular, is there a TARDIS in the shop? And if so, is it a

BBC prop or just a cardboard cutout?" (I have the beginnings of a plan.)

"Let me just loop in someone in the Beeb's publicity team and get back to you, sir," says the support officer, who is irritatingly bright-eyed and bushy-tailed for a Thursday morning. "Is there anything else you need in the meantime?"

I pinch the bridge of my nose. I manage to bite back *a sonic screwdriver*: this is not the time for inappropriate humor. "What's the ETA if I ask for an OCCULUS team?"

"Unit One is already en route from Hereford, but they're at a standstill on the M5—there's heavy congestion from a multi-vehicle RTA earlier this morning. They'll be at least an hour."

Fuck it. "Okay, you go talk to the BBC, I'll hold."

I lean back and try to close my eyes as Nobby drives us up onto the pavement to get around an inconveniently parked Amazon delivery van. "Any joy?" asks Samson.

"OCCULUS is a support unit for this sort of incident, looks like a generic Fire Service command vehicle except it carries a specialist squad of Territorial SAS operatives." (Well, they used to be that—they've got a different name now—but the tiger doesn't change its stripes.) "You may not have worked with them before but they're used to working with you guys. Once they get here they'll take point and your job then is strictly support and mop-up. But this time they're snarled up in a jam on the M5 because, I say again, fuck my life."

I'm interrupted by my phone again. "The shop is currently hosting a traveling exhibit of *Doctor Who* props including two original model Daleks, an older TARDIS mock-up, and a cardboard cutout of the latest Doctor and his companion (this year that's Peter Capaldi and Jenna Coleman). Apparently the owner has friends in high places at BBC Wales. OCCULUS are rolling again but traffic is slow to clear, so ETA is still an hour and a half. Mr. Choudhury says to be aware the press are taking an interest so please keep it low key?" (Translation: no explosions. So that rules that out.)

Finally—*finally*—ten minutes and half a kilometer later, we pull up behind a mob of police vans and barricades parked at one side of a dismal dual carriageway. To our right, a row of offices and retail storefronts curve toward the Bull Ring. It looks to be one of those brutalist smash-and-grab raids on our historic architectural heritage that were all the rage in the 1950s. There's a weird shortage of moving vehicles and pedestrians—not too surprising, under the circumstances—so when we pile out onto the pavement the first thing I do is ask my minders, "Right, where's the nearest hotel?" just as I see a sign for a Radisson Blu further up the street.

"Not so fast, son . . ."

In my experience the three stages of any positive interaction with the police are: suspicion, incredulity, and a good old-fashioned briefing. (Or, if you're interacting with them negatively, a good old-fashioned beating.) This time around I get hustled straight into the third stage, courtesy of a very annoyed chief inspector who clearly doesn't approve of bizarre bookshop bandits. Especially when they're accompanied by screeching cyborg Space Nazis who shoot up innocent law-abiding pillar boxes. So I get my ears pinned back by a very irritated Inspector Angel, who, unlike the sorcery skeptics in the council offices, is fully up to speed on supernatural crimes and is having none of my shit. "You're that clown off *Newsnight*? I know your type! Understand this—I want a clean takedown, no casualties, no injured bystanders or hostages, no property damage, and definitely no fucking zombies. Can you do that, son? Because if not, if you can't match those targets, I don't want you on my patch—you're just another distraction and I've got six of those already."

I do not roll my eyes at Inspector Angel: he's got a twitchy eyelid and a taser and this is something like the fifth metahuman-associated incident in Brum so far this year. "How about this: I get you in through the back door and we can take a look? I'll update the OCCULUS team who're inbound, then if it's safe you can neutralize the, uh, overenthusiastic fan. If it's not safe, then we sit tight and wait for OCCULUS. Does that work for you?"

Angel crosses his arms angrily. "There is no back way in or we'd have been through there faster than a TWOCer on the Aston Expressway—"

I hold up a finger: "As it happens there *is* a back way in—for my type. I can get you inside. Want to tag along?"

"Jesus Fuck, this I have got to see . . ."

Fifteen minutes later I'm wearing a helmet, a stabby, and a set of borrowed overalls that don't fit very well as I lead Angel and a posse of tooled-up SFOs into the hotel.

The front desk manager smiles at us glassily. "How can I help you?" she asks, trying not to stare at the firepower on display in her lobby.

"Which way to the laundry?" I ask. She points at a door bearing the mystical sigil STAFF ONLY. Right. "Okay, follow me," I tell Angel.

"Hey, there's no way—" I hear one of the AFOs begin, then I push through the door and we're into the familiar drab service passageway and—

—I hold up my warrant card and squint as I think my way through a soft spot in the structure of reality and—

—Break through into hotelspace, the manifold of passageways that connect every hotel everywhere (and ever) in space and time. It's a patch of the hyperdimensional manifold that spiritualists and some ritual practitioners call the Other Side, and we mostly call the dream roads or the ghost roads, and it connects liminal nonresidential spaces where transients bed down. I'm not kidding; if you get lost in a chain hotel in Birmingham and take the wrong turn you could wander for hours before you come out in the Trump Hotel in Chicago, or the Grand Hotel Budapest. Or, as I intend, you exit into—

—A different kind of twisty infinite manifold of passageways and spaces, dimly lit with dangling tentacular ductwork, blue-tinged lighting panels, and curved interior walls. It's almost as if we're walking through the intestines of a biomorphic machine, rather than the crew quarters of—

"—Fuck me, is this the TARDIS?"

I hold up a hand and stop. "The TARDIS doesn't exist," I tell my escorts. "This is an expression of the collective subconscious, made real by viewers' beliefs in the TARDIS." A cult TV show that has been running since before I was born can accumulate some serious *mana*[3] along the way.

"We're dealing with a powerful animator here, one who can turn plywood-and-aluminum shells with sink plungers into plausible Daleks." Most animators are kids, and mostly they animate Barbie dolls and Playmobil minifigs, that sort of thing. Alien invasions, not so much. "But that's a good thing for us, because the shop also has a sound stage TARDIS in its exhibit, and I can tap his mojo to make it sufficiently real to serve our purpose." It's not real enough to actually function as a spacetime ship, but it's plenty real enough to hook up to hotelspace via the back door. "From here on, keep your voices down—I've no idea how good the sound insulation is, and we're nearly there."

A left, another left, a right, and then we're crouching just behind one of the archways leading onto the mezzanine level that circles the TARDIS control room. The front door is closed, so I tiptoe down the steps and peer at the hexagonal central console. Up close there's a slight whiff of PVA glue and polystyrene, and I can see that the display screens are painted on. The nearest one is a green screen, which is just too bad—it means I can't magic up an external camera view of the shop. Inspector Angel waves off his troops and now he follows me down to the plywood floor, which creaks slightly under his weight. The shadows cast

---

[3]. *mana*—occult power in a form that can be stored and used by a ritual practitioner—is a side effect of belief.

by the indirect lighting make a death mask of his face, and for a moment I'm not sure whether I should be more afraid of the rogue metahuman outside the door or the feral copper inside it.

Angel surprises me by saying, "Right, son. How d'you want to play this?" Apparently I've earned some Brownie Points for getting him this far. He's not exactly deferential, but he's not snarling at me anymore.

"Er—" I run out of planning. We're standing inside a life-size mock-up of a TARDIS control room ten meters across that somehow also exists as a one-and-a-third-meter-wide, two-and-a-half-meter-high Police Box inside a books and comics shop. There are no windows, and opening the door seems inadvisable. "Are you any good at eavesdropping?"

"Watch me," he says, holding his G36c out of the way as he crab-walks toward the entrance.

It turns out that the door is made of plywood and wishful thinking. It's lined with low density foam but there are gaps so we can hear everyone in the shop quite clearly. And it doesn't sound great right now, because our suspect is clearly so far out of his tree the squirrels are sending out search parties. And also—

"Why don't you have *Annihilator*? I want my *Annihilator* order! It's on my pull list and it's two days late and I want it right now!" shrieks the perp, his voice cracking horribly midway through. "Also, where's my *Hellboy*?"

"Fuck me," Angel mouths silently, "he's a kid!" Any copper above the rank of sergeant is to some extent a political animal and I can hear the gears whirring in Angel's head as he realizes we have a Problem.

I shrug: What can I say? "It's your call."

The kid is over the age of criminal responsibility so the plod can arrest and charge him, but shooting him will go down like a lead balloon unless he's actually killed someone, not just sent his angry killbots to shoot up a postbox. So the job just got a whole lot tougher.

Someone—not the boy—says something which I don't catch, because my attention is on the inspector (who has safed his big scary gun and is fiddling with his taser). It seems to upset our perp because now he screams—and I cannot believe I am recording this blatant *Girl Genius* rip-off—"Fools! I will destroy you all! Ask me how! Go on, I dare you!"

I hold up a hand in Angel's direction and toe the door open. Then I hold out my hands to show they're empty and step through—

NEW PAGE six panel grid, three rows.
Panel 1: Long shot: Scene is a view through the window of a bookshop. Bookcases stretch away into the background from an open area at the front of the store. A handful of terrified bystanders sit on the floor by the counter at one side, hands on their heads. Opposite the counter is a life-size TARDIS. Bob, wearing a rumpled suit, stands in front of the TARDIS. He looks a little like David Tennant with a hangover. He's facing SPIZZ.
   Bob (thought bubble): Oh fuck me, he's just a kid.
   Bob: "Yeah, go on. Tell me how?"
Panel 2: Detail on Spizz. He's a skinny 12-year-old white boy wearing joggers, cheap trainers, and a hoodie. He's having a growth spurt so his sleeves don't reach his bony wrists. He holds his arms up toward the hostages but is looking at Bob in surprise. His hands are glowing and surrounded by whirls of occult energy.
   Spizz: "Da fuck are you and how did you get in here?"
   Bob: "I'm the Doctor! I've been in the TARDIS all along."
Panel 3: View from window display again. Spizz steps back and turns to point his scary glowy hands at Bob but his posture is defensive. We can't see his face in frame but we can see Bob and Bob does not look impressed.

Spizz: "I want my comics!"

Bob: "We got the message. Your comics are on the way."

Panel 4: Wide angle from the back of the bookshop looking out at the protagonists. The back of the TARDIS is at one side, and beyond the window, on the left, we can see police barricades with an Armed Response Team crouched behind them. They're facing something just outside the right of the frame.

In the foreground we see Spizz facing off with Bob, and both of them have glowy hands now.

Spizz (screaming): "Not good enough! I want them now!"

Bob: "Let me sort it out for you—"

Panel 5: Same view from back of shop. Outside the shop window, the police are shooting at a DALEK which is entering from right of frame. In the foreground Spizz is throwing down with Bob. Both their hands are extra glowy and surrounded by swirling vortices that suck in the background image like whirlpools.

Dalek: "Exterrrrrrmin—"

Police: "DakkadakkadakkaPEWPEW"

Spizz: "DIE, EARTHLING SCUM!"

Bob: "Not today, kid."

Panel 6: Same view. Beyond the window, the police are unloading some heavy firepower and the DALEK has bullets emerging from its back. The DALEK is returning fire and one of the cops is falling over, smoking and skeletonized by its exterminator.

In the foreground, Spizz is facing off with Bob, oblivious to ANGEL emerging from the TARDIS to shoot him in the back with a taser.

Insp. Angel: "You're fucking nicked, my lad!"

Bob: "Leave the Daleks to me."

DON'T CALL HARRY

"I can't believe you, of all people, are asking me to organize this," the assassin complains.

She stirs a sachet of white powder into her coffee as the older man sitting across the cast-iron outdoor table shrugs. "Who better?"

"I thought you people all swore an oath to defend the Crown?"

"Oh, we absolutely did." He stares at her hand, avoiding her gaze. "But these are not normal circumstances."

"Indeed."

The assassin glances at the TV screen on the shelf beside the board with today's prices. A blast of steam from the coffee range drowns out the sound, but it appears to be showing rolling twenty-four-hour news coverage of . . . something royal? The Queen, waving a white-gloved hand, with a fixed half-smile on her face. A Royal Air Force helicopter on a lawn, men and women in uniform saluting. A talking head in a conservative suit—probably a royal correspondent describing the monarch's visit to a hospital or school. "Not that you can tell from the TV news."

"We've been trying to keep everything out of the news since the lid blew off in Leeds." The older man sighs. "There's no going back." He is in his late fifties or early sixties, in good physical condition for his age: he dresses like an office worker, possibly in management or sales, and his gray suit is clearly tailored to fit. The only sign that all is not well is his expression. His gaze is the distant stare of someone who's been forced to bear witness to things better forgotten.

The assassin sips her latte thoughtfully. She, too, wears a tailored suit. With her cloud of black hair, high cheekbones, and abstracted air of efficiency she could be a corporate solicitor, or perhaps a very senior executive's assistant. Appearances, as in her companion's case, are deceptive. "So," she finally speaks, "it comes down to the Queen. How exactly is this meant to work?"

The man in the gray suit chooses his next words carefully. "*Mana* accumulates in any object of adoration. As we saw during the American crisis the President isn't just a politician with a job, he's the embodiment of the faith in the presidency held by a third of a billion people. Philosophies, work: so do gods. Some maniacs a few years ago even tried to *make* one via a role-playing game. Basically egregores—any shared belief that takes on a life of its own—can serve as a *mana* capacitor."

The assassin nods. "So that's where the Queen comes in."

"Exactly. Royalty is the oldest and strongest egregore; the US Presidency is just an eighteenth-century knockoff of the king-emperor, after all.

"Now, Her Majesty has been queen regnant over thirty-two sovereign states for sixty-three years. The United Kingdom, Canada, Australia, and New Zealand are the best-known, but there are a bunch of others, even today. She's the monarch of a hundred and fifty million people currently, and reigned over a couple hundred million more until a few decades ago."

"Are you saying she's the biggest repository of untapped *mana* on the planet?"

The man in the gray suit tilts his head in thought. "Not quite. Belief in the British monarchy is rather weaker than the fervor surrounding the US presidency. The Pope is ahead of either of them, as are the most popular strains of Islam. Nationalism works, too. But. But." He taps the table. "Her Majesty is the most powerful resource available to *this* nation, and the Prime Minister means to keep her safe, until there is no longer any risk of her power being harnessed to dislodge him.

"The Evil Vizier Pattern is a classic, and he is well aware of his potential starring role in it if it isn't deflected. So he has a countermeasure in progress to lock down the threat by explicitly not overthrowing the Queen, which is why he hired the Professor."

He drops a memory stick beside the assassin's coffee cup. "This contains everything I've been able to discover so far about Operation FAIREST. It seems to be based on sections of the Aarne-Thompson type 709 archetype: interment in a glass coffin in a death-like state. It's intended to stop her *mana* field decaying, and keep her alive indefinitely so she can be rolled out for ceremonial occasions like the State Opening of Parliament. As she's the head of the Church of England she's to be stored in the crypt of Westminster Abbey. Alongside her predecessors."

The assassin drops the USB stick in her bag. "I find this rather hard to credit," she says mildly. "How is his Dark Majesty going to pull this off?"

The man in the gray suit waves vaguely at the front window: "The diagnosis will be something unspecified but horrible and degenerative that the Royal Medical Household hasn't got a handle on. Nobody wants the Queen to die, so when it's announced that we have the technology to put her in a state of magical suspended animation the disinformation campaign will spin up. There's a private intelligence firm who work with the security services and they've been tapped to run the campaign: bunch of Old Etonians called Cambridge Analytica, solid chaps. The Establishment protects its own, and you don't get much more own than the Queen.

"Anyway . . . the chief royal physician has just retired and the Palace has been handed a replacement by Downing Street—the Professor. He'll be playing the organ, and you're the accompaniment—for one final recital. You know the Professor's usual price: for a genius, he's childishly predictable."

"By His grace." The assassin gives him a sharp look. "Why didn't you just have your PHANGs turn her?"

The man in gray tilts his head thoughtfully. "Can't inoculate her with an attenuated strain, the PM would smell it immediately and take her over. But practicalities aside, can you imagine how the PM would view an immortal—and extremely popular—vampire queen whose will he couldn't seize? Especially as PHANG syndrome is protective against the adverse side effects of ritual magic . . . no, it wouldn't do at all. The gloves would come off immediately, he'd drain her himself and damn the consequences. There wouldn't be time to train her to fight back, so she'd go down in the first round. King takes Queen."

"Oh. Oh dear."

"And if by some miracle she prevailed we'd then have to explain to the public why the Queen has contracted extreme photophobia and acquired a taste for Type O Negative."

The man in gray stares at his empty mug in a brown study. "Anyway, that's where we've come to."

The assassin shakes her head again, more in despair at the situation than in disagreement. There is an almost imperceptible wobble in her voice. "What a mess."

"For what it's worth, I take full responsibility. It happened on my watch, just a series of unfortunate events. The cards fell in exactly the wrong sequence. So here we are."

"Well!" The assassin takes a shuddery breath as she stands. "You want me to destroy the Crown in order to save it. Right. I'll be in touch when I've read this. Getting the band back together to perform at a royal funeral?" She shakes her head in disbelief. "Until then—" She offers her hand, and after a couple of seconds the man in the gray suit accepts it.

"—God save the Queen."

MEANWHILE, IN 10 DOWNING STREET:

"We suppose you're wondering why We invited you to tea today," says the Prime Minister, the faintest impression of a smile hovering in front of His head.

Mo nods cautiously.

Interviews with the PM are always disturbing. It isn't just His face, or the lack thereof: it's the way it feels as if He's playing multidimensional chess, and she is less a player than a pawn in an incomprehensible game.

"Of course I'm curious," she says, then forces herself to sip her Darjeeling and await illumination at His pleasure.

"Dominique," He says: "Dr. O'Brien." The intangible dancing feet of a thousand graveyard millipedes raise gooseflesh on her arms. "Please don't hide your light under a bushel. You are at least a bishop in this game, and your husband a knight. Played skillfully, you are at least as powerful as a queen."

Mo puts her teacup down. She is secretly proud that it doesn't rattle, not even slightly. "It would help if I knew what game we're talking about," she comments. *And whether I'm one of the players or one of the pieces*, she adds silently.

"GOD GAME RAINBOW, of course." The Mandate smirks knowingly. It's a codename Mo is cleared for but she still cringes to hear it on the lips of one of its subjects. "The earlier game plans are all obsolete now, however: the players are almost fully engaged, with only a few surprises and omissions."

"Omissions?"

"Your agency successfully blocked the Sleeper, so GOD GAME BLACK is in abeyance for the time being. We are not inclined to adopt an adversarial stance toward Our servants, so GOD GAME GREEN is canceled. As for GOD GAME RED, Ms. Murphy successfully kicked that one down the road for a while. So one might summarize the score at halftime as one–nil, with a promising outlook for the second half." He projects a Cheshire Cat smile, a suggestion of facial flexure that hangs in the air in front of Him. "One is reasonably content. But there is much to do."

The PM leans forward, telegraphing confidence and engagement: "Q-Division has done a sterling job until now, but is not up to dealing with the challenges We foresee going forward. As a subdepartment within the Ministry of Defense, the Laundry performed tolerably well until the business in Yorkshire." He sniffs. "But the new emerging challenges extend well beyond the reach of the MOD. There is an *unbelievable* amount of work to be done before the New Management is secure. The agency's previous remit does not include treatment of demonic possession via the NHS. Or amending the legal system to take account of persons who continue to exist after metabolic—as opposed to legal, or spiritual—death. Let alone the social security system, or the Department for Education! We face a herculean task of modernization throughout every branch of government, and it will require new legislation and direct Ministerial supervision."

He sits back and raises His teacup.

Mo grapples with the scale of what the PM is describing. "You're talking about growing the Laundry into an entire government department?" He nods, so she continues: "A, what exactly? A Ministry of Magic?"

The event horizon in the armchair across from her smiles affably. "It won't be called that," He says. "Mind you, the Laundry is in a surprisingly good starting place at present. It's overstaffed and bloated by normal civil service operational metrics—something to do with providing usefully monitored make-work assignments for anyone who survived a close encounter with things that go bump in the night, One gathers? Normally gross overstaffing is bad, but there is an available cadre of initiates with civil service experience who can be reassigned to other agencies. As for the Laundry's existing focus, that will be addressed by the new Department for Existential Anthropic Threats, which will be co-equal with the Ministry of Defense and the Home Office. Its mission to defend the state against threats from within and without, a kind of paranormal Department of Homeland Security."

Mo works through the acronym and stifles her immediate

reaction. "You're really going to call it DEAT? Why not just add an H at the end?"

"Because, my dear, it's not about protecting Humanity."

He puts His cup down. "The Bill creating DEAT will be one of the highlights of the Queen's Speech at the next opening of Parliament. So that you know where you stand—the Audit Commission will continue to operate as currently, but upgraded to supervise the new department. Your immediate supervisor, Dr. Armstrong, will receive a promotion: he's going to be the first chief secretary to the Minister of DEAT. You will replace him as Senior Auditor. You'll have a budget and you'll be responsible for recruiting your own staff, just as you did when you set up TPCF. Everything will be on a larger scale. But none of this will happen for at least six months, and remains in strict confidence for now. For the time being, you'll begin shadowing Dr. Armstrong and familiarizing yourself with his responsibilities. He has been informed of the reorg and will mentor you."

In strictest confidence, from the mouth of a godlike being who can set your brain on fire just by wishing it so, is a synonym for *beyond top secret*. Mo nods, and hesitantly asks, "Is there anything else?"

"Yes." The Black Pharaoh produces a new smile, a thing that once unseen can never be forgotten: "Certain troubling forecasts have recently come to Our attention, and Mrs. Carpenter is setting up a team to address them. Iris has tapped your husband to lead the POISON APPLE committee that will handle cleanup if events, ah, eventuate. I'd like you to oversee the team on behalf of the Audit Commission, just to set My mind at ease—I think you are the best person to keep Robert focused and on track. Iris will brief you in due course."

"What kind of forecasts are we talking about?" Mo asks as she stands.

"A terminal prognosis for the head of state, Dr. O'Brien."

He tips His head toward her, beaming like a skull. "The Queen is dying: she just doesn't know it yet. Your first call tomorrow is the head of the Royal Medical Household. And on that note"—He rises—"we're done here."

Buckingham Palace is a classic case of home extension overshoot.

Back in the early eighteenth century, George III bought a modest three-story town house as a private retreat for his wife. Then he began remodeling it. George IV continued the renovation, meaning to create a small, comfortable home. Construction continued fitfully throughout the nineteenth century. Queen Victoria couldn't stop building extensions and gardens. Edward VII added decorative bits. Edward VIII wanted a swimming pool. George VI needed a bomb shelter. And so on.

Today, there's a post office, a helipad, a jeweller's workshop, more than ninety offices, bedrooms for 200 live-in staff, a bank ATM in the basement, secret evacuation tunnels, and an entire department just to keep the clocks wound.[1] It's a million-square-foot office complex, public museum, art gallery, and the world's most exclusive hotel: 52 bedrooms, heads of state only.

The royal family actually occupies a small private suite in the north wing when they're in residence (usually they're elsewhere). The Palace prefers it that way: having the royal family around is an inconvenience. Royals get underfoot, clutter the place up, attract even more tourists than usual (and tourists are the bane of a smoothly functioning office complex), and have unreasonable expectations of service. And the Palace does not exist to serve.

---

1. There are over 600 clocks in the building, some of them very fragile and valuable.

It's a bureaucratic institution: it exists because *someone* has to keep all the clocks wound.

To visit someone who works in the Palace, assuming you have an appointment, you first have to find the right entrance. Which is not the one the tourists are using. Mo follows her phone's directions along a narrow street with an office block on one side and a row of gift shops on the other. This brings her to another road, across from a featureless brick wall. Over the top of the wall she can just glimpse a long, low building with arched windows: part of the stables. She checks the time. Turning left she crosses the street and follows the wall until she comes to a set of solid-looking gates fronting a courtyard. The gates are closed, but to one side there's a town house, with an entryphone besides its front door.

Trying not to pay attention to the cameras watching her, Mo pushes the button and waits. After a moment there's a crackle. "Please present your ID."

Mo reaches inside her suit jacket and pulls out a badge on a lanyard. "Dr. O'Brien, here to see Professor Anton Phibes. I have an appointment at noon."

A few seconds later the door buzzes and she steps inside.

The town house is part of the palace complex, for Buckingham Palace has expanded over time to absorb an entire neighborhood, like an amoeba happily feeding on a raindrop full of protists. The front room Mo finds herself in is dominated by a security checkpoint with metal detector archway, X-ray belt, and a reception desk with a uniformed officer on duty. But there's no queue, the cop is extremely polite (deferential, even), and she's through the next door in barely a minute. Minus her phone, laptop, front door keys, and handbag (all of which go into a secure luggage store).

"This way, ma'am," says the usher, and he opens the inner door for her—the frame is clearly reinforced—and leads her through a narrow, very plain corridor to an armored back door that opens onto a gravel path running along the back of a row of brick buildings. "You want the third door on the left, Staff Reception. They'll point you in the right direction from there."

It's your worst workplace bad dream: you're running late for your first meeting on a new job, but you're lost in an office warren with eight hundred rooms, there are no signs, everyone is too busy to stop and give you directions, and you can't phone ahead to apologize for being late because your phone was confiscated. All you need to complete the nightmare is to be naked from the waist down and taking an exam you haven't studied for.

It's not quite *Mo*'s worst work nightmare, because highlights of her career include being kidnapped by tentacle monsters, fighting vampires, and getting caught between the avatars of two gods having a throw-down. Workplace performance appraisals don't even make the top ten, not least because Mo has never had a negative one. But she is somewhat out of breath by the time she finally finds an office door bearing the name "Dr. Thompson."

This is not the man she's looking for, but the receptionist assured her that Dr. Thompson was Professor Phibes's predecessor as the Queen's Honorary Physician, and they'd replace the name plate any year now. It's a sinecure for a *very* eminent doctor. Because the medical household is a microcosm of the Royal Household, which resembles the rest of the civil service the way an irate seagull resembles an Airbus, the Professor she's about to take tea with is actually a Baron, recently elevated to a seat in the House of Lords by order of the Prime Minister Himself. And the most interesting thing about him, in Mo's opinion, is how absurdly thin his dossier is.

Mo knocks. "Come in," calls an oddly fluting voice. It sounds as if its owner is speaking through a kazoo.

She opens the door. "Professor Phibes, I presume?"

Phibes smiles as he stands and offers her his hand: scar tissue from extensive burns and subsequent corrective surgery make a battlefield of his face, so that she can't tell if he's snarling or welcoming her into his lair until he speaks. There's something ineffably disturbing about his demeanor that goes beyond the scarring: Mo has a lot of practice at telling operatives apart from ordinary citizens, and Phibes feels dangerous. "Doctor O'Brien from the Security Services, I presume? Not a medical doctor, then. Come in, come in, have a seat—how do you take your tea?"

It takes Mo a couple seconds to realize that Phibes's voice is coming from a box on his desk. She smiles politely as she shakes his hand. "Milk, no sugar. I'm a PhD, not MD, I'm afraid: Number Theory, with an MPhil in computational musicology on the side. Thank you for meeting with me at such short notice."

Disfiguring injuries apart, Professor Phibes is a very distinguished-looking fifty-something fellow. He has both the silvering hair and gravitas that are essential for his position here, and his dove-gray morning suit is apparently palace-appropriate workwear: everything about this institution is oddly antiquated, and Mo feels as if it ought to smell of mothballs and furniture wax. "I'm sorry to be the bearer of bad news, but we—by 'we' I mean my department—are investigating a credible threat to Her Majesty, and we need your cooperation on this matter," Mo states.

The Professor's gaze sharpens disturbingly. "A security threat? Does it involve a member of the medical household?"

"Not as far as I am currently aware." Mo sips her tea. "You know what my organization deals with. One of our more frustratingly unsystematized units, Forecasting Operations, deals in precognition—they predict and head off undesirable events before they happen. I say 'frustratingly' because quality control is sorely lacking, the theoretical aspects give cosmologists nervous breakdowns, and their actual methods are non-replicable. Other governments have their own counterparts, and sometimes they deliberately mess with us—they can interfere with each other. Unfortunately FO has issued a warning concerning Her Majesty's health. They assigned a high probability of her undergoing a serious decline in the three-to-six-month time frame, although they can't explain why—or what the diagnosis is—and there is some suggestion that a rival agency is jamming them deliberately. Hence my inability to state whether it's a security threat or a health scare. It could be anything from an assassination attempt to cancer."

"Well, I can do something about that!" says Phibes. "As you surmise, cancer is one possibility, given Her Majesty's age. I can't discuss Her Majesty's medical state with you without obtaining her informed consent, and what you've given me isn't sufficient to disturb her peace of mind at this point, but I assure you we monitor her health closely."

A shadow crosses his face. "She *is* eighty-nine years old, and next year she'll be ninety. The absolute record for female longevity is one hundred and twenty-two years, but it's extremely unlikely for anyone to make it past one hundred and fifteen. So I think we'll almost certainly have a different monarch in 2040. But her mother made it to a hundred and one, and Her Majesty is in good shape to equal or surpass that, so: God save the Queen."

"God save the Queen," Mo echoes, entirely unironically. She drains her teacup and sets it down. "I'll send you a memo with everything I can disclose, and I'll update you as we learn more. I'm putting together an investigatory team in case it's something like thallium in the teapot—"

"—Or polonium-laced soup, ha ha!" Phibes seems to find the idea unaccountably funny.

"—Yes, or that. Hopefully Forecasting Ops just sprang a false positive on us and I'll be able to give you an all-clear in due course, but for now please keep an extra-sharp eye out for chronic poisoning or early stage cancer. Or anything else. And you *will* let me know if you find anything."

Mo stands.

Professor Phibes shakes his head as he, too, stands: "I'm afraid that won't be possible. Confidentiality—"

Mo smiles tightly. "That wasn't a request. I'll have the Prime Minister instruct the Privy Council: I'm sure they'll see things my way! Good day, Professor."

After her meeting at the Palace, Mo grabs lunch at the nearest Pret a Manger, then heads back to the office. She catches up on her secure email—stuff that can't be routed over the public internet—then attends an afternoon meeting with Trust and Security to go over their quarterly outcomes, but her head's not in the game. So she makes an executive decision to goof off productively: she reschedules her final meeting of the day and heads down to the subbasement secure thaumaturgic test suite.

The suite lies behind a security barrier and a cast-iron door inlaid with protective sigils. The floor, walls, and ceiling are concrete reinforced with horrifically expensive silver-alloy rebar: there are cold iron containment grids on all exposed surfaces. An outer vestibule contains secure computing terminals that talk to servers running esoteric monitoring software; also equipment lockers and emergency telephones. But the test suite itself is an empty white cube four meters on a side, starkly illuminated and chilled to goose-flesh-raising temperature by air conditioning. It is featureless, except for the scorch marks on the floor and roof. And this is her happy place.

She leaves her jacket and handbag in a locker, then dons protective goggles, elbow-length gloves, and a lab coat dyed gray-black with silver salts. She fills a special-purpose bag with necessary equipment, then she steps over the boot barrier and enters the vault.

Taking a stick of chalk laced with a disturbing and unusual pigment, Mo crouches and begins to sketch out her frustration on the floor.

She doesn't blame Phibes for his reticence. His patient's health goes beyond mere medical confidentiality and well into national security territory—but it still feels as if she spent the morning banging her head on a wall. Normally a Laundry warrant card would get her supine compliance anywhere in Whitehall.

Mo finishes the outer circle of the main summoning diagram, then steps outside it to draw in a smaller protective circle for the summoner. Writing in the safety parameters is almost instinctive—she's been doing this for years—but when it's time to go back to the summoning circle she pauses and makes herself double-check everything. For the past couple of months she's been working her way up to more dangerous power levels. Now she's ready to test it on a fully-embodied Class Three emanation.

(A Class One emanation is a minor eater. If you don't take precautions it'll chew holes in your gray matter and it might possess you, thereby causing you to drop dead on the spot, but it's completely mindless and not terribly effective. Class Two emanations are an order of magnitude more powerful and they're used by the Night Shift to animate Residual Human Resources—zombies, to the uninformed. A Class Three is not something amateur necromancers should be allowed to mess around with: they have theory of mind and even when they're locked inside a decaying corpse they're dangerous. An unbound one is a lethal threat to an exposed human, capable of possessing their brain. Don't ask about Class Four and above: the power and malice go up exponentially.)

Back in the lobby, Mo picks up the phone. "Facilities? What have you got waiting for me?" she asks.

"You're practicing already, ma'am?" The voice at the other end sounds young: also taken by surprise. "The paperwork says you're due to check out unit 61 at five o'clock for destructive testing, but it's only four fifteen."

"Yes, I started earlier than I expected. Is 61 ready yet?"

"I'll just check. Please hold."

Mo waits, just a little impatiently, while the security officer does whatever it is that security officers do when a senior sorcerer asks to check out a Harry nearly an hour early. Finally: "You're in luck, ma'am, 61 is ripe for you. Er, I mean, ready. For decommissioning, that is." In a secure test suite, nobody can see you roll your eyes. "I'll walk him round momentarily. I'm supposed to remind you not to damage the servos and armature? Les gave me an earful last week after one of your colleagues got a little overenthusiastic. And we need a tissue sample afterward for the coroner to sign off on."

"Understood. I set up a safety ward in here—if you've got ten minutes to spare, you can watch for yourself?"

"Great! Hey, is it okay if I take photos?"

One of the signs that you might be growing old is that security officers look young enough to be your children. As Mo's fortieth birthday is receding in the rearview mirror, she feels a slight twinge of something—not regret exactly, more accurately world-weariness—as a girl in a blue uniform and surgical mask pokes her head into the lobby. She appears to be barely out of her teens. "Miss? Er, ma'am?" (Mo's demeanor triggers a high school flashback in kids these days.) "I've brought you your Harry!"

"Thanks." There is a whirring and clanking from the corridor outside. "What's your name?"

"M—ma'am! Angela Cortez, Security Ops Two!" Cortez attempts to stand to attention. She's short, bubbly, and entirely too enthusiastic for a day like this, but Mo manages to summon up a smile from somewhere.

"At ease! I'm Dr. O'Brien. You can call me Mo." Behind Cortez, the whirring and clanking resumes, accompanied by a scraping noise as if somebody is pushing an empty filing cabinet along the bare concrete floor. There is also a stench, rapidly growing stronger, that even the HEPA filters in the air conditioning can't overcome. "I see what you mean about Harry 61 being ripe . . ."

Cortez steps away from the entrance. "Oh, there's a boot barrier? Good thing I came along: 61 is bad at stairs!" As she speaks, Harry 61 enters the lobby.

Laundry site security relies heavily on Residual Human Resources: zombies, to everyone else. They're what you get when a low-level eater gets bound to a human cadaver. You do not want to let an RHR touch you because the eater can jump bodies via touch, much like a high-tension electric current. Mo—and Ops Two Cortez—wear wards, grounding devices that protect them against having their minds eaten: random intruders are not so fortunately equipped. RHRs are dead, by definition, and after a few days they begin to rot. The turnover is high, and horror movies to the contrary, embalming fluid and mummification don't help.

Sixty-one is an RHR nearing the end of its service life: a Harry. A Harry is an animated skeleton straight out of a Ray Harryhausen movie. The decaying RHR is debrided almost down to the bone (maggot baths are involved), then Tech Support wires it into a motorized steel exoskeleton to keep it moving. The eater anchored to the skull controls the exoskeleton through a rat's nest of electronics and keeps it shambling around terrifying the civilians for a few months longer.

Eventually all good things come to an end, and 61 is stinking up the subbasement intolerably. It's time to banish the eater animating 61, recycle the Raspberry Pi and the motors, have the coroner sign off on the mortal residue, and indent for another body.

"That's the main containment grid." Mo points at the large circle she prepared. "I want you to park 61 inside the inner circle. It's very important that 61 is *completely* inside, and that the diagram is unbroken and unsmudged. Can you put it there?"

"Sure! Do you mind if I video it for our YouTube channel?"

Mo bites her lip. There is an official agency YouTube channel these days, and the New Management is big on demystifying the ineffable for shits and giggles. Still, it strikes her as a terrible idea for numerous reasons. Finally she delivers her mildest reply: "You know, decommissioning an RHR isn't entirely safe. You might want to watch it on CCTV instead."

Cortez looks at her appealingly, all big eyes and innocence. "But I'm warded! And the CCTV in here is ancient and there's no output to capture"—because it's a classified site: letting randos plug memory sticks into the feed would be a security hole— "Are you sure I can't stay and watch?"

Big brown eyes *and* she's barely more than a kid. Mo shrugs. "I want you inside that smaller circle at *all* times. You will be inside it before I start, and you will remain inside it until I say the words *all clear*, even if the fire alarm goes off or you need the loo. *Don't* let any part of your body cross that line or you will die: it will take quite a while, and it *will* hurt all the time you're dying. Do you understand?"

"I got that! I had to do a Manifestation Security refresher last month, I've seen the, uh . . ." She trails off. Obviously she's alluding to the workplace accidents showreel all new security personnel are required to sit through. "But there's only room for one of us in there! What about you, miss? Is it safe for you to be out there?"

Mo lets it all hang out for a moment: "That's what we're here to find out."

"What? But—"

"Look, just park 61 right there, all right? Inside the containment where it can't get at us. I'll be fine, I'm warded too." *And I have extra protection*, she adds silently. But Cortez has no need to know about Mo's special sauce.

Cortez looks doubtful, but raises the battered Xbox controller with a pentacle duct-taped to it and maneuvers Harry 61 into the magic circle. The motorized skeleton stinks abominably and lurches as it moves—the left patella is crumbling, some of the metatarsals in the right foot are hanging by a sinew, and the collar bone is fractured—but she has it going where she wants.

"Okay, hold it right there." Mo squats and reviews the annotations on the grid for a third time, making sure that she hasn't left anything out and the necessary guardrail lines are all clear and unbroken. After she's satisfied with them, she checks the safety circle around Cortez.

She tries to ignore the coldly hostile and utterly inhuman mind locked inside the jail of decaying meat and bone watching her from inside the circle. Cortez's presence is a lively spark of warm humanity inside the figurative bars of the magical shark cage. She's pulled out a shiny new iPhone 6 Plus and is fiddling with the camera, framing Harry for the viewers.

"I'll be ready to go in about two minutes," she tells Cortez.

"I'm good here!" The security guard smiles as she pokes at her phone screen. Mo returns to the lobby area and types up a report on her setup. When she returns, things are just as they were. Well, almost: Harry has turned to orient toward her. For a dead guy he looks disturbingly aware. Luminous tendrils of light shine in the depths of his eye sockets: *Who were you, anyway, when you were human?* Mo wonders. (The New Management seems to have a bottomless supply of corpses for experimental use these days.)

"Okay, ready to go," says Mo, nerving herself. "And we are live in three, two, one—"

Because Harry 61 is looking directly at Mo, she sees the apprehension on its fleshless grinning face, awareness of its own end turning its aura black as she opens her mouth and speaks in a tongue that predates humanity. There's a bare metal instruction set beneath the operating system of reality, and sufficiently powerful sorcerers can program it directly: Mo knows this microcode. "*Go,*" she utters in Old Enochian, and throughout the test area un-life comes to an abrupt end.

The skeleton collapses inside its motorized gibbet cage. Small bones disarticulate and fall through gaps in the armature, clattering to the floor. The writhing light in the eye sockets disappears. Finally, the joint motors, reacting to a sensor reading, whirr as they lower the charnel assemblage to the floor.

"Wow." Cortez's voice is hushed. "Was it that simple?"

"*Don't move!*" Mo snaps. Banishment isn't always instantaneous, and a wisp of malice remains. It twirls in the air like smoke from an extinguished candle, invisible to a non-sorcerer's eyes. Class Threes are sufficiently self-aware that escape attempts are a very real problem, and if this one anticipated its decommissioning it might have—

There. Outside the containment grid there's a thin spot in the universe. Mo can feel such things, with a new and disturbing sense that only really emerged after she survived the Non-Survivable Incident at Nether Stowe House.

"Don't move," she repeats. "It's not gone." The Class Three is still hanging around like a stale fart in the quantum foam beneath normal spacetime. It's angry—or as angry as a consciousness with no brain and no glands can be—and it's looking for a new body to steal. It's out for revenge and it's not trapped inside the two-dimensional magic circle right now. "*Are* you?" she says, glaring at the twist in spacetime.

The PA system emits a crackle of static, then an eerie hiss of white noise.

"Of course not, because then this would be too easy." Mo snorts. Then she glances at SO.2 Cortez. Angela is standing inside the safety circle, phone still pointed at the fallen Harry, but every muscle is rigid. Mo can see the whites of her eyes, shining with terror. Shit just got real. The disembodied eater is not only uncontained, it's infiltrated the protective circle: the only thing keeping Cortez alive right now is her standard issue necklace ward, which is smoking because it wasn't designed to protect against a Class Three for long.

"*Attend me!*" Mo snaps in Old Enochian. She crab-walks around Cortez's safety cell toward the wisp of malice hanging in the air. "*Attack me, not her! It's me you want!*"

For a split second Mo flashes back to a night in a hotel in Amsterdam, tentacular appendages coming out of the wallpaper to wrap an icy chill around her. For a moment she relives the frozen terror and sense of helplessness as she sees a hole in space opening to suck her in. But she knows what to do now, and she's one of the most powerful sorcerers Mahogany Row has trained up in the past three decades. That night lies twelve years in her past. She's spent every month since then training for some asshole extraterrestrial to try it again, to drag her shrieking into a back alley nightmare and feed to satiation on her horror and despair—but this time she has a black belt in necromantic self-defense.

Mo draws a deep breath, and on her exhalation she utters a deplorable word. It hangs on the air, shimmering like the end of all things, unbearable and growing in power until she inhales once more, and draws it back inside to drown it in silence.

"*Ohh,*" Cortez moans, staggering but somehow keeping a grip on her smartphone. "I, ugh, I don't feel so good. Is this normal?" A drop of blood rolls from one nostril, then her eyes droop and she collapses. Mo manages to catch her just in time. She's still breathing, which is more than can be said for Harry 61, who is a pile of crematory ashes and a red-glowing, half-melted cage inside the containment grid. The ceiling, meanwhile, has acquired another scorch mark.

"Let's get you next door and have a sit-down while I call the first aider," Mo tells her. She pulls Cortez's arm over her shoulder and tries to stand. "You can stop filming now, the show's over."

Which is entirely true. There's no way in hell Public Relations will allow that particular footage to go up on the organization's YouTube channel.

"We're done here."

Paperwork: we hates it. Especially when it's the kind of paperwork that sneaks up behind you with a cosh and forces you to do a full debrief on an impromptu joint operation with the police about a major incident in which shots were fired. Thankfully nobody was seriously injured: animated cardboard Daleks exterminate suboptimally. Spizz is under arrest in hospital recovering from a tasing, questions are being asked about Inspector Angel's robust approach to youth crime (which would come as a surprise to precisely no one who knows what happened in Sandford), and I only avoid being cornered and interviewed by the media by hiding in a cleaning supplies closet.

The upshot is, my assigned day of convincing skeptics that magic is real has been wasted, it's nearly eight o'clock when I get home, and I'm going to spend tomorrow morning meeting with a Professional Standards jobsworth and an Auditor, even though West Midlands Police have already got everything down in triplicate.

At least I have my phone. I warned Mo I'd be late so she's already eaten. When I slouch through the living room door with my microwave meal on a lap tray I find her curled up on the sofa with a half-empty glass of wine and the cat: that's when I realize I should have poured myself a glass of wine, too.

I park my arse in the armchair and hunch protectively over my beef bourguignon before Spooky can teleport across the room. (He's a cat. I swear they're like the weeping angels from *Doctor Who*: close your eyes for an instant and when you open them again your dinner is in the feline digester.) I chow down as fast as possible because I missed lunch, thanks to Kid Dalek. Mo has registered that I'm hangry so she leaves me to it until I sigh and put my tray on the coffee table. "How was your day, dear?" she asks, with a secretive smile that suggests she has a very good idea how it was, but is leaving me room to vent.

"My day? Let me tell you all the ways—" I stop so abruptly I nearly swallow my tongue. "Nah, I'll still be going tomorrow if I get started. How was yours?"

"I swear I spent it all in meetings with time wasters." Crow's feet appear at the corners of her eyes. "Nearly got lost on my way to a lunchtime off-site which was a complete waste, and I only got back in time to snatch half an hour in the lab. So. How about you, again?"

"I think"—I check the time and reach for the TV remote—"it's top of the hour. Mind if I put the news on?"

She rolls her eyes: "If you must—"

"—No, really." I pull up BBC News 24 and there it is, the Birmingham Bull Ring with a smoldering Dalek behind crime scene tape. "Ah, dammit."

"Is this a"—her gaze sharpens—"Bob, was that you?"

The newsreader chirps up: "Drama in Birmingham today as teenage supervillain lays siege to comic shop with animated space robots! Dramatic scenes as armed police evacuated the center of—"

I switch it off again. "Dammit."

"*Bob*. What have I told you about—"

"—I had a choice: go help the police fight Daleks, or spend the day arguing with a room full of magic denialists. What would *you* do?"

She puts her empty glass down. "That calls for a refill," she says, and fetches an extra glass and another bottle of wine. She pours and raises her glass to me: "To escaping from meetings with time-wasters."

"To that!" I take a mouthful. It's the cheap Sainsbury's Bordeaux, but it's not bad: medium dry, tastes of dead grapes. (I'm trying to develop a palate, don't harsh me.) Then I do a double take. "Who did *you* escape from?"

"I had a very frustrating argument with a rather creepy doctor—he was right about medical confidentiality but I'm still going to have to get the Cabinet Office to overrule him—then decommissioned a rotter in the subbasement. It was scheduled for the dump—one leg was falling off—but anyway, it turned out to be a Class Three—" (I fail to freak out only because she's explaining this over a glass of wine.) "—It turns out my technique works fine, but an eager chipmunk from Security wanted to video it for the YouTube channel and her ward was time-expired. She's spending the night in hospital for observation until the brain swelling recedes."

"You did the"—I wave my free hand in a vague circle—"thing? Without a fiddle?"

"I don't have the fiddle anymore," she retorts. "It went back to Carcosa!" Banished, and a bloody good thing, too: that bloody violin once tried to kill me.

"So you talked it to death. With your larynx."

She raises an index finger: "It was a one-word kill." She looks both smug and shaken, as she should be.

"Wow." I drink some more wine until I'm sure I've got a lid on my anxiety. "That's quite the exorcism."

She looks at me sharply, then her face softens and she asks, "When did we get so bad-ass?"

"Some time after . . ." I trail off. Mo takes another mouthful and strokes the puddle of black fur in her lap. Spooky buzzes sleepily, then stretches a pawful of fluffdaggers toward her knee. (Spooky, in case you're wondering, is just a cat. According to the vet he's female: Mo has so far resisted my attempts to rename her Stabby on account of her favorite form of social interaction with humans.) "It began about six years ago?"

She shakes her head. "Eight. That's when they gave me Lecter." The bone violin.

"Huh. That works. It's about when I got entangled with . . . you know." The Eater of Souls, an unfortunate spiritual infestation I ended up with when the Cult of the Black Pharaoh tried to sacrifice me in an attempt to summon it, not realizing it was already bound to my then boss, Angleton. (There's a school of thought that Bob Howard died and I'm just the Eater of Souls wearing his body and memories like a skin-suit, thinking I'm still him. It's nonsense, of course, but if I was an undead horror pretending to be me that's exactly what it—I mean, I—would say, isn't it?) I discover that my glass is mysteriously empty, as is the bottle on the coffee table.

"I think I'd better"—I do a double take when I realize it's past ten o'clock and I have an early start tomorrow—"I'd better have a quick shower."

"I wonder what happened to Lecter?" Mo asks as I carry our dirty dishes out. And I shiver, because that's a question I hope we never learn the answer to.

At the same time that Bob and Mo are killing a bottle of wine and trying not to scare each other with their workday anecdotes, the assassin pushes a buzzer beside a dusty storefront on a busy shopping street in the 4th arrondissement of Paris. The Centre Pompidou looms at the far end of the road, but it's late and the crowds thinned after the shops closed. Tourists and locals wander between restaurants and bars, but nobody is paying attention to the shadowy doorway.

After a minute, someone shuffles toward the door. A light flickers on inside, and the resident calls, "Go away! We're closed."

The assassin buzzes again, tapping out A-R-T in Morse code: short-long, short-long-short, long.

A moment later a deadbolt rattles, then the door swings open.

"You're late," a short, angry cactus of a woman snaps at her.

"Eurostar delays." The assassin pushes the door shut with one gloved hand, then follows the shopkeeper down a narrow tunnel between racks of music scores and shelves of sequencers, amplifiers, keyboards, and less scrutable boxes with MIDI interfaces. At the back of the shop the owner leads her past a curtain into a cramped room with a dragon's hoard of stringed instruments. "Is it ready?"

"I don't know, are *you* ready?" The shopkeeper is offensively blunt. "I want it gone: I don't want it in my shop another minute." She bends behind a counter, wheezing and swearing under her breath, then lays a nylon carrying case on the counter.

The assassin carefully unzips the carrier to inspect the violin. It's made of a yellowing ivory-like substance, bonded together from numerous strips and scraps. To those who can sense magic, a shimmering heat haze of malice seems to boil off it, like the radiation flux at Chernobyl after the B reactor blew its top and sprayed fallout over half of Europe. The radiation then was so strong that bystanders could feel their skin prickling with the healthy warm flush of radioactive decay. The evil intent emanating from the open instrument case is so powerful it's a wonder that milk isn't curdling and the catacomb occupants rising within a five-kilometer radius.

"Well, that's quite something, isn't it." The assassin produces a compact digital thaumometer and carefully scans the instrument. Instead of clicking or beeping the sensor emits an angry high-pitched whine, like a mosquito's hatred-driven death throes. If it was a Geiger counter the assassin might expect to spend her last living weeks in a hospital bed while clinicians document her death for the medical journals. Luckily this isn't radioactive decay: the assassin and the shopkeeper are both warded, and the back room is surrounded by containment grids. But it's still alarming.

"Hello, you," says the assassin as she delicately touches a gloved fingertip to the instrument's body. It's not the first bone violin she's met, although it's by far the most powerful, and it purrs in anticipation at her touch.

"Not in here, imbecile!" snaps the shopkeeper. "Take it away first, why don't you." She grumbles on in like vein for almost a minute, casting aspersions on the assassin's sanity, probity, genealogy, and common sense.

"As you wish." The assassin closes the case and zips it shut. It's clearly the real thing—not that the luthier would be stupid or ignorant enough to cross her. "An Erich Zahn original. I played one of its siblings . . ." It was a gift from the Doctor. She still has it, but it's much weaker. That one lacked the Hilbert-space pickups made by Leon Theremin himself. It was un-hacked and pristine. This one—with an instrument this powerful, who needs amplification? The mind boggles. "Do you have the full provenance?"

"Do I look like a moron?" The old woman snorts. "Dr. Mabuse himself commissioned it, using raw materials sourced from the medical facility at Dachau. Being taken in possession of one of these instruments would have earned you a date with la Guillotine right up until Mitterrand abolished it! Do you think he bothered with receipts?" she shrugs, and for a moment she looks haggard. "I just want it gone."

"Your fee." The assassin turns the case over and adjusts the shoulder straps—it can be worn as a backpack—then hands the esoteric luthier a silvery coin.

"A moment." She whips out a monocle and peers at it. It bears an Elder Sign on one face and a spiral of hieroglyphs on the other: "Yes, that suffices." The coin vanishes into her pocket. Rather than money it's a token accepted by an obscure private bank in Basel. In conjunction with a codeword and a number, it will give the bearer access to a strongbox. "Now go on, get out, these old bones won't stand forever and my supper is waiting."

"A pleasure doing business with you." The shopkeeper watches her through narrowed eyes, half-anticipating a foolish and futile attempt to silence her on the way out: but this customer isn't stupid enough to betray her. The shopkeeper has powerful protectors, and the only thing that can really hurt her these days is daylight.

"Don't forget to leave a Yelp review!" she sings out as the assassin opens the door.

ALL GOOD DOGS GO TO HEAVEN

The following Monday morning, the Prime Minister visits the Palace for His weekly audience with the Queen.

One of the peculiarities of the British political system is that the Prime Minister—the chief executive of the government—is nevertheless a subordinate, who is regularly called to the boss's office to report on what her government is doing.

The PM's role is as a supplicant, for Her Majesty is the landlord and the PM is merely a tenant: the PM is summoned to brief the Queen and to answer her questions. In the opposite direction, the Queen has seen governments rise and fall, and wars start and end: she is more than happy to discreetly steer a Prime Minister through crises she's seen before, because when it comes down to it, if the PM fucks up, it's her property that gets damaged.

There's a format to these talks. Her Majesty meets with the PM in one of the official reception rooms—usually a small drawing room with armchairs and a side table. Tea and refreshments may be served, depending on how welcoming the Queen feels toward her visitor of the hour. (No refreshments: she wants to keep the meeting short. No visitor seating: oh dear.) No staff are present (a footman and a butler wait outside the door), no notes are kept, and gossip is strongly discouraged.

At least that's how the British constitutional system works in normal times. When the PM is a regular politician and the

Queen is the crowned ruler they advise and serve. But under the New Management things are slightly less clear-cut, and the Queen is clearly not comfortable with the current PM, much as a paralyzed caterpillar is not comfortable with a parasitic wasp injecting eggs into its abdomen.

"Good morning, Your Majesty!" says the grinning spectral presence in the doorway. Elizabeth smiles by reflex, managing to suppress the cold shudder His presence inspires.

"Enter," she says. She gestures at the chair opposite: "Please, have a seat. I regret I can't stand—"

"That's entirely understandable," says the Prime Minister, with a small and perfectly eerie chuckle. "None of us are as spry as we used to be, alas!" And He's right. Even though she doesn't usually feel the full weight of her eighty-eight years, something about the Right Honorable Fabian Everyman MP makes her feel ancient, the weight of centuries pressing down on her. *His* centuries, she supposes. It's difficult, keeping up the pretense that she doesn't know exactly what He is, but she's been briefed by ashen-faced civil servants. And all she can do is grin and bear it, like the caterpillar.

"Thank you," says the Prime-Minister-shaped Thing sitting in the armchair opposite. "I'm happy to be of service, Your Majesty." A sardonic grin flutters across the blind spot fronting His head.

She rings for the butler. "Would you care for tea, Prime Minister?" At least there is comfort to be found in small, familiar rituals.

The formalities take a couple of minutes, during which neither of them feel much need to talk. A trolley is rolled in, a silver tea service is ceremonially arrayed on the side table, and a silver platter bearing her favorite shortbread fingers is proffered. "A gift from Balmoral," says the Prime Minister, "I thought you might appreciate it." It's the sort of kind gesture a cunning monster might use to lend the semblance of humanity—even the butler seems appreciative.

The Prime Minister pours tea for her, and gets it absolutely right even though He has never asked her how she takes it. She sips and nibbles a biscuit, and the PM gives her a brief recitation of this week's government program. Another small cabinet reshuffle is in the cards—*House of Cards*, she thinks as He outlines His tentative plans. (The Black Pharaoh is very hard on Home Secretaries, this one only lasted two months before her breakdown.) "It's hard to find high-functioning psychopaths with both the administrative track record and enough self-restraint to present a veneer of humanity, what?"

The Queen blinks. "Oh, really?" *Have you met Andrew?* she thinks.

"I have a few strong contenders but they're not seasoned yet," He explains: "Patel, Badenoch, and Braverman will go far, but they need more experience. Truss—" He snorts, almost giggles, then changes the subject.

"Whuff?" A canine rump leans heavily against the Queen's ankle.

"Candy!" she chides sharply. The dorgi—a corgi/dachshund cross—looks up at the Queen adoringly and dribbles crumbs on the eighteenth-century Axminster.

"I'm *terribly* sorry, Your Majesty," says the footman, looking appalled. "She escaped from the Corgi Room while it was being cleaned and she nipped me when I tried to leash her, hence the bribe."

The Prime Minister points the front of His head at the errant pup. "Candy," He says, His voice an echo of a distant thunderstorm, "return to your basket *immediately*."

The dog glances up at him, utters a chastened whine, and slinks away.

"What did you give him?" asks the Queen.

"A shortbread finger—"

She nods. "Don't do it again. Next time, ask James to deal with her."

The footman bows and retreats, still bowing. The Prime Minister's eyebrows might be raised, if He had any such. "She's on a strict diet," says the Queen, unsure why she's explaining herself.

"I quite understand." He sounds amused. "Dogs will be dogs."

That is something—one of a very few somethings—that they can agree on.

The Queen eats another biscuit—they're very more-ish—and asks the PM about His choice for the Ministry of Justice portfolio. It's going to be Braverman: a barrister and a highly ambitious politician the PM is training up for a senior role. (Pay no attention to the rumors about the necromantic rituals she conducts at dead of night in Middle Temple: the eldritch horror knows his own.)

After another twenty minutes the Queen is done, and so are the biscuits. The PM hasn't touched His: a pity. "Thank you," she says, putting down her empty teacup. "Was there anything else?" she asks pointedly.

"I believe that's everything, Your Majesty." The PM rises and bows to her; she stands and dismisses Him.

"I'm done," she tells the butler, and he rolls his trolley over to the side table to clear up the tea and the uneaten biscuits. At a guess the shortbread won't make it back to the pantry uneaten: the butler is a skinny fellow, on his feet all day.

"I'll check on Candy," he murmurs, then he bows and removes the detritus.

Neither of them notice the peculiar tarnish speckling the silver platter.

Mo is in her office, checking her secure email (which requires a wired ethernet connection and a circle of deconsecrated salt around the laptop, before the firewall will even consider letting anything through) when her land line rings.

She picks up. "Dr. O'Brien here, Audit Office. How can I help you?"

"Dominique, this is Iris. I see from your Outlook that you have a free slot between eleven and one today. Please block it for me."

Mo sits up. "Can do. You want anonymity?" The internal phone line is reasonably secure against eavesdroppers, but the departmental Outlook calendar used for meetings can be read by all sorts of intelligence officers, thaumaturges, and their mid- to upper-level managers. "Audit business?"

"Yes."

"Okay, consider me available. Is this a lunch date, or should I make alternative arrangements?"

Iris hesitates a moment. "We can do lunch," she agrees. "I'll book us into the Director's Dining Room, then swing by and collect you after my last interview of the morning."

"Jolly good," Mo says briskly, then hangs up. Iris Carpenter is not her favorite person, to put it mildly. Nobody who tries to murder her husband is ever going to make her Christmas Card list, even though Iris was only following orders from, it transpires, the current Prime Minister. Awkward. But the PM said *frog*, so Mo will obediently hop when ordered and listen to the witch, and she might as well get a meal out of her in the process.

Dining Room D is a small fistula off to one side of the staff refectory—a necessity, for it takes half an hour to leave and reenter the security cordon if you want to eat out. The single table in the middle of the room is set with stiffly starched linens, crystal glassware, and silver cutlery, thoroughly warded. The waiter is a relatively well-preserved Residual Human Resource: dead men tell no tales, after all.

Today they're serving posh pub grub: minestrone soup followed by Cumberland sausage in gravy with mash and steamed vegetables. But there's a passable Sauvignon on the side, and as Mo picks at the main course Iris signals for a top-up. Obviously she prefers her prey well-lubricated. Finally she says, "I suppose you want to know why you're here?"

"POISON APPLE, I suppose." Mo stares expressionlessly. "Are you Maleficent or Grimhilde in this remix?"

"Very funny." Iris's smile doesn't reach her eyes. "You asked Emma in HR to assign you a PHANG or two and someone from Forecasting Ops. Unfortunately Dr. Schwartz and Ms. Brewer are unavailable, but as it happens I have two alternates in mind for you. There's just one problem—they were both part of the YELLOW OLYMPIC team and came back from D.C. infected with the wrong strain of V-symbionts."

The Nazgûl employ PHANGs too, but unlike the free-range maths vampires the Laundry employs, the Nazgûl are into selective breeding of nonhuman assets. They cooked up a slightly attenuated strain of V-parasites, the extradimensional symbionts that give thaumaturgists and mathematicians a power-up in return for regular blood meals. Nazgûl symbionts are weaker, easier to install in warm bodies sourced from the prison-industrial complex, and easier to mind control—but they're not much better than zombies with superspeed and a taste for blood.

"If they're infected with the wrong strain . . ." Mo pauses.

"Not anymore, they aren't." Iris shrugs. "There's no cure, but He has a technique for reinfecting them with a more useful lineage."

"So they're ours, now? Not Nazgûl meat puppets?"

"Well, they wouldn't be much use to us if they belonged to the Black Chamber, would they?"

Mo nods. "So who are you talking about?"

"Well, that's the thing. You need Forecasting Ops input, and it so happens that when the Nazgûl bagged Derek the DM—"

"*What?*" Mo is halfway out of her chair before she catches Iris's smirk. Derek is one of the most powerful precognitives the Laundry has ever discovered. "Derek was in the field with YELLOW OLYMPIC and *got caught*? In which universe is that not a disaster?"

"Stop right now." Iris raises her wine glass. "He was unconscious for most of it right up until the prisoner exchange. The Black Chamber didn't get anything useful out of him before

His Majesty replaced his V-symbionts. Whole blood transfusion, very pricey." She winces slightly, does a double take at the red liquid in her wine glass, and puts it down. "Anyway he's recovering from having his carotid chewed on, but he'll be out of rehab soon and he's eminently qualified for your team, so he's yours. But Derek's not really the problem."

"Problem." Mo doesn't like turning into an echo but Iris is doing a very good job of keeping her off-balance.

"One of the other new PHANGs has special needs." And now Iris pulls a face.

Mo swallows her exasperation: "Who is it?"

"It's Pete"—the Reverend Peter Russell, D.Div, PhD in theology, friend and occasional consultant to the Laundry on matters relating to Christian apocrypha—"he's taking his new dietary requirements really badly. I want you to take him on for POISON APPLE and see if you can fix him. Think of it as the quid pro quo for getting exactly what you want." Iris smiles brightly, then stands. "See you later." And she leaves, without waiting for a reply.

No plan survives contact with the enemy, or in this case, Human Resources, in a ghastly pincer movement with External Assets. EA say who we get from the roster of heavy hitters: they get to sign off on all PHANG assignments. Which is why we aren't getting Dr. Schwartz and the All-Highest of the Host of Air and Darkness, who are a package deal and also reasonably hard to break.

Instead we're getting Derek the DM, who was on our gimme list for the planning team but isn't exactly James Bond, and Pete, who is an actual fucking Vicar. I mean Jesus, *why*?

Pete's supposed to be in an office in London, writing reports on absurd apocrypha. He's almost a civilian—he's a part-timer with a parish to run, married with a toddler. How was he even exposed to hostile PHANGs in the first place?

When I finish swearing Mo fixes me with a glare that could scorch concrete and says, "You know this is all your fault, right?"

"I—well, fuck." She's right. "Fuckety-fuck. So where is he now?"

"Not at home, obviously. He's out of hospital, in some kind of safe house with PHANG-specific affordances. It's not safe for him to see Sandy and Elinor yet"—Elinor is their year old—"except for video calls."

"Fuck."

"Language, Bob." Mo doesn't say that because I'm swearing but because it's getting repetitive. Nothing annoys her quite like tedious repetitive swearing, unless it's drum machines.

"Swive, then. What kind of safe house?"

She sighs. "How well do you know the banksters?"

"The—oh. Which banksters do you have in mind?"

Flashback time: You can catch the V-parasites that cause PHANG syndrome by doing the Wrong Kind Of Magic in your head, or by knowingly engaging in brain-curdling mathematics. A team of magically illiterate quants—physics and maths PhDs working in the market analysis arm of an investment bank owned by an elderly vampire—fell victim to it while testing a new visualization algorithm. Some of them survived: we made them a job offer they weren't allowed to refuse. Of those, a couple took to it like ducks to the proverbial pond. But others were less, shall we say, adaptable. So arrangements were made for keeping them alive because vampires are not in fact soulless monsters, they're people just like us, and tomorrow it could be one of us in the frame.

Now, I had the misfortune to be the bloke who uncovered the vamps in the bank. So I have some relevant experience.

"Facilities runs a halfway house for PHANGs in Upminster. It started out as a normal employee house but they added special affordances: blackout blinds, a secure porch, fireproof panic room in the cellar. A live-in house master keeps the baby vamps in line. Pete's rooming there for the time being, along with Dick—who is on probation *again*—and Derek, when he gets out of rehab."

I get sidetracked. "House master? What is this, type O positive Hogwarts?"

"Focus, Bob. Right now the house mistress is Janice. I know you've met her: she tried to throw you through a wall, didn't she?"

"Yes. Ugh." I shudder. "She'd keep them in line alright." Janice: devops person, has purple highlights and an undercut, was semiserious about martial arts before she turned PHANG. She's probably a sixtieth Dan black belt by now. "Wait, who else did you say lived there?"

"Dick." I can't tell if she's swearing or naming him. "You remember Dick?" (Dick is the sleazeball vampire who got put on a performance improvement plan for fucking the residual human resources.) Mo sighs deeply and her gaze turns inward. "I propose we visit Pete after work. If he's murdered Dick we can help him dispose of the body: nobody in HR needs to know."

The District Line at rush hour isn't my favorite thing, but it gets us there just before sunset. "What would you like for dinner?" Mo asks as we walk toward the vampire safe house.

My stomach rumbles. "South Indian?" I suggest, absolutely not because we just passed a restaurant advertising all-day thalis.

"Hmm." She pushes an entryphone buzzer and shows her face to the camera. "Capital Laundry Services—" The lock clicks open and I follow her into the daylight-free porch.

Janice is waiting in the living room. If you discount her pallor—which is normal-for-goth—you could mistake her for any other thirtyish, no-nonsense IT contractor on her day off. "Mo." Pause. "Bob." Pause. "What brings you here?"

"We're here to see Pete," Mo says.

I clear my throat. "We're told he isn't doing well. Thought he might like some friendly faces."

For a moment I think I mis-stepped and she's about to rip my face off and piss down my throat: but Janice slumps slightly, then shrugs. "Yeah, I think he would." She glances at Mo. "How well do you know him?"

"I was matron of honor at his and Sandy's wedding." Mo elbows me: "This one helped organize the stag night."

"How is he doing, really?" I ask. "I know he was turned against his will, then there was some sort of prisoner exchange and Him Upstairs replaced his V-symbs with the local strain? Er, unclear on the details, but I can't imagine he's terribly happy with any of that." I scratch my head, then glance at the doorway to make sure he's not lurking on the threshold. "In fact, I'm half-surprised he didn't go for a noonday stroll."

"*Bob.*"

Mo elbows me again, but Janice nods.

"Yeah: you and me both, but he takes the 'suicide is a mortal sin' line seriously. Listen, before you go upstairs I'd better check that he's not been pouring his rations down the drain again. If he's starving—"

Mo stands up. "We're both immune to V-symbs," she says, as I say, "He won't hurt us."

Mo continues: "If it helps, think of this as an intervention, not a visit." By rights I ought to be petrified right now—blood bags shouldn't party in a Phi Alpha Ng house—but humanity is something I only see in the rear-view mirror these days. As for Mo, she's an Auditor, which means she's got the root password to the fuckery the Laundry oath of office installs on our gray matter.

"Top of the stairs, second door on the right," Janice says grimly. "I'll be right here if you need me."

Mo and I head upstairs.

It is a fact that most assassins need a regular day job to support themselves: they can't make ends meet with the stabby side hustle alone.

THE REGICIDE REPORT 75

Unless they live and practice their calling in a violent hellhole where mass murder doesn't make the front page news, there is almost never enough work to keep an assassin busy. So, much like the state executioner, the assassin is an occasional contractor. England's last hangman was a pub landlord who, once in a while, nipped out after closing time to pull a different lever from the beer engines. And today's assassin has just arrived on the Eurostar from Paris. She's on her way to Maida Vale Studios because that's where the BBC Symphony Orchestra is recording this week, and music is her main line of work.

In addition to broadcasting and recording concerts for the BBC, the orchestra performs regularly at the major London venues—including the Proms concerts held in the Albert Hall. Although she isn't a full-time member of the orchestra, the assassin is a conservatory-trained violinist, and often fills in when a member of the regular string ensemble is unavailable.

The assassin read the background dossiers the Senior Auditor provided, including the history of Operation Freudstein and the disaster at the Last Last Night of the Proms. And she also knows why it was necessary. Because that very reason is rattling its chains in her violin case right now.

The violin has been whispering seductive lies in the back of her skull ever since she collected it in Paris. Unbearable falsehoods that could only be worse if they were true. She is aware, thanks to her briefing, that Dr. O'Brien carried this occult parasite around for years—as did Dr. Armstrong, O'Brien's predecessor. And she's carried a white violin of her own in decades past—but that was a child's practice instrument beside the Stradivarius from Hell.

There's a difference between reading about something and experiencing it for yourself. And just six hours of carrying this damnable violin has left her numb with horror. It's an undead nightmare in a backpack, a white and osseous doom. It makes her skin crawl. As soon as she gets to the studio she rushes to the instrument room, desperate to stash it inside a warded cupboard. It will, she hopes, be safe behind burglar alarms and a powerful containment grid. As soon as she's secured it she padlocks the door and flees. It's still only half-awake, but she feels like if she spends too much time close to it her mind will melt like a candle at a nuclear test.

Before she collected Lecter she'd thought the reports of its potency were overblown, but she can't kid herself anymore: she is not in fact a top-rated government sorcerer. She's been many things—heiress, nurse practitioner, classical violinist, personal assistant to a haunted genius, assassin—but she's not Dr. O'Brien.

Unfortunately Dr. O'Brien is personally known to the Prime Minister. There's no guarantee that she hasn't been subtly Renfielded, compromised by a cranial rootkit installed at such a low level that even her oath of office might not override it.

The assassin is an External Asset who was unofficially retired from the field several years ago—kept on the books, but given no missions, *don't call us, we'll call you*—she was probably passed over as insignificant. When she was reactivated a few weeks ago it came as a big surprise. Who could have imagined that? Unless, of course, her retirement had been part of a contingency plan laid down years ago . . .

Quite how the Senior Auditor has retained sufficient autonomy to ordain acts of high treason is a mystery. But the Senior Auditor also arranged for the Black Pharaoh to take over the government in the first place. Obviously you do not sit down and do a deal with the living avatar of an Elder God unless you have done your homework well in advance, and triple-checked your work.

The assassin has heard rumors of a program called Continuity Operations, and received the clear understanding that this is real Death-Before-Disclosure stuff. Quite what purpose Continuity Operations serves is unclear to her, and that's probably for the best. You can't betray what you don't know, after all. But she suspects—you don't have to be a Brain Genius like the Organ Master to see this coming—that her assignment is part of some sort of scheme to kneecap the New Management.

She intends to go through with it—it's a goal she supports—but she's not stupid: she's looking to secure an escape route, and is prepared to drop everything and run for her life at the first sign that the Black Pharaoh has noticed the egregore is waking up. As for her former lover, he's more than capable of looking out for himself. (Only the substantial payout for a successful mission could induce her to work with him again.)

Meanwhile: the string section is due to practice tomorrow morning. She won't be playing either white violin, but there's a perfectly serviceable Cremonese instrument she can carry to and from practice on the tube without worrying unduly about insurance. (Her story is that she has a vintage Guarneri del Gesù as well, but it's with a restorer.) When it's time to play for real she'll be wearing Dr. O'Brien's face.

And then hell will be loose on Earth, for the strings of the King in Yellow are back.

Mo knocks on the bedroom door. Nothing happens for a while: we exchange a look, then she knocks again.

After about a minute I start to get twitchy. And Mo has begun to shift her weight from one foot to the other. I touch her arm: "Allow me?" I ask, then I open my inner eye.

Normally the inner eye stays firmly shut—there are too many people out there and seeing their souls gives me a headache—but I need it now. There is indeed someone alive inside the room, a mind surrounded by the numinous susurration of eaters (or in this case, V-symbionts). Which is a relief; it means he hasn't topped himself. But he feels oddly dim, dark even. Pete is depressed.

I nod at Mo. "Go on," I say, so she opens the door and steps inside.

It's pitch-black in Pete's vampire lair, the lights out and the windows firmly shuttered. My first impression is that it stinks, the peculiar sourness of unwashed clothes and despair of someone sheltering in their room like a wounded animal hiding in its den, waiting to learn if it will live or die.

"Pete?" Mo's voice is low and gentle. "I'm going to turn on the light now. You should close your eyes." Then the light goes on.

You've probably seen student halls of residence or a house in multiple occupation. Perhaps you're also familiar with the hangover aftermath of exam finals and a three-day bender? Or with students who, due to stress or illness, go into a doom spiral of depression? Well, this is like that, only Pete isn't a student. He's a responsible adult with a PhD, a motorbike, a wife, and a toddler. Part of his job is providing pastoral care to people going through horrendous shit, giving them the steadfast nonjudgmental support they need without batting an eye or showing any sign of stress. Which makes his own meltdown all the more horrific.

Pete is curled up on top of an unmade bed with a pillow clamped over his head. He's fully dressed apart from his shoes and one sock. There are fast food wrappers, drained beer cans, and bottles of cheap spirits all over the carpet. (PHANGs need to eat and go to the toilet just like the rest of us: the mandatory blood meals are an unwelcome extra.) Judging by the smell, one or more forgotten snacks have crawled beneath the bed to die.

"Pete." Mo touches his bare ankle. "Are you awake?"

A sound trickles from under the pillow.

"I'll be back in a sec," I say, and head downstairs. To Janice: "Where do you keep the cleaning supplies?"

By the time I get back to Pete's room Mo has gotten the pillow away from him and she is sitting on the bed with his head on her thigh. She's talking quietly but he's not replying. I get busy collecting the rubbish. I have to remember to breathe through my mouth; I refuse to even look at the door of the en suite bathroom until I've got the bedroom under control.

"—We only learned you were here today, which is why we're visiting. Your phone's going to voicemail, have you left it somewhere? I wanted to call Sandy, but we thought we should get the story from you first. How bad is it?"

Pete groans quietly. "They turned me."

"We heard." Mo rubs his shoulder. I'm glad it's her: I'm not great at this kind of emotional labor so I stick to collecting cans—I remember too late to upend them over a dead coffee mug in case they're not completely empty—then get down on my knees and start searching under the bed.

"I thought I understood. I mean, I was with Brains and Derek and Yarisol—she was wearing Iris Carpenter's daughter's face—and that was horrible enough, but then I got bloodshot. Yarisol killed the shooter and the symbionts used the link to take me as a replacement host."

Holy crap, I think. Mo strokes his hair: he's shaking like a frightened dog in a thunderstorm. "What about Derek?"

Pete shudders. "I don't remember." (I tie off the first waste sack, then start filling another.) "It was—have you ever had the kind of nightmare where you're a passenger as somebody else moves your body around like a meat puppet?"

I clear my throat: *Eater of Souls here.* Mo doesn't spare me a glance.

"It wasn't a nightmare," he says dully. "He, it—whoever it was—made me attack Derek and bite his throat. I *fed* on him. It was awful. But it was also wonderful and that's when I knew I was damned, even before Mhari brought the Black Pharaoh to me and He turned me again."

It comes out in fits and starts. Pete has a degree in social work. On top of that, he has a PhD in theology. He reads Aramaic, Classical Greek, Latin, and motorcycle maintenance manuals. He's absolutely *not* a knuckleheaded biblical literalist: he's an academic who lectures on how the current consensus bible contains various pieces of second-century Jesus fanfic, how Genesis contains bits of three different incompatible creation myths, not to mention the badly erased traces of Jehovah's wife Asherah (before she got scrubbed out of the Bible by the patriarchal priesthood).

He's blessed same-sex marriages in his church, and got an earful from his bishop. So for Pete to start throwing around words like *damned* is pretty alarming.

"There's no way out," he mourns. "Can't kill myself, Sandy and Elinor would never forgive me. And my parents. Everyone who depends on me." (He sobs quietly.) "It's a mortal sin, but that's kind of beside the point when you're already damned. But I can't carry on like this either, because the blood is the life."

I ran the numbers years ago, when I was on the OPERA CAPE committee: V-symbionts rely on their host to find them a succession of victims. A healthy but abstemious PHANG can't help but drain 150 quality-adjusted life-years from their victims every twelve months. Two entire lifetimes, in other words. If the PHANG refuses to feed, the V-symbionts turn on them instead . . .

The hell of it is that PHANGs are potentially immortal. We don't know for sure, but Old George and Basil Northcote-Robinson (both very dead, and good riddance) were turned at least two centuries ago. They must have drained four hundred victims between them. Almost certainly more.

"Even if by existing I can be a net force for good in this world—which is pretty fucking unlikely, given I'm a vampire—I don't want to watch Sandy and Ellie grow old and die. But I can't turn them either! That would compound the sin. It's an actual living hell on Earth."

He sits up a bit, and gets his head out of Mo's lap, which is a promising start, but if you could bottle the despair in his voice the Met would buy it by the gallon to spray at demonstrators.

"Well, this is all very depressing," I say with deliberate emphasis—Mo glares at me—"but can I tempt you downstairs for pizza, while we run the washing machine and brainstorm what to do in the short term? I mean, the *really* immediate short term? Because I can't imagine Sandy's very happy about you hiding in your Fortress of Solitude, and I can absolutely guarantee that Elinor is too young to understand. And also, we might just have an ulterior—"

"—Bob, now is not the time—"

"—*Motive* because we've been given a job to do and tag you're it for the team?"

Suddenly my back is rammed up against the wall and a vampire is baring his centimeter-long canines at me and hissing. "Did you not hear a *fucking* word I said?" Pete's grabbed me by the throat but he's not actively trying to throttle me, and when I look past his shoulder I can see Mo rolling her eyes at me as if to say, What did you expect? And also, ew, Pete's breath is caustic.

"Yours is a Giardiniera with Romana base and a side of Bruschetta Originale from Pizza Express, right?" I squeeze out. "This late it'll take an hour to get here, just time for a shower and a shave first while we run the hoover over the carpet, eh?" Behind Pete Mo is performative-dancing *facepalm* with a side of *you suck*, but Pete's pupils aren't in beast mode and he's not sniffing my jugular, so I think he's still in control. "After you've eaten I'll set up a FaceTime call with Sandy and Ellie because when did you last talk to them? Also we can order in dessert—tiramisu, right?—and make coffee. Work can wait . . ."

Pete drops me. "You are an ass—I mean, a very naughty boy," he says, surprisingly mildly for someone who just had me by the throat. He huffs, almost a laugh, and I swear his canines shorten visibly. "I'll listen once I'm fed and I promise I won't make any decisions while I'm hangry. Okay?"

I tip Mo the nod as Pete turns toward the bathroom and she nods back, then slips downstairs to ask Janice if there's an untouched blood ration in the kitchen fridge. And then we'll see. Right?

It's Thursday afternoon, and Candy is sick.

The royal pups lead a pampered, albeit regimented, life. There are currently five residents in the Corgi Room at the Palace: the two elderly corgis, Holly and Willow, and three dorgis—royal corgi/dachshund crossbreeds—including Candy.

Each dog has a wicker basket of his or her own, raised above the floor to avoid draughts. In the morning they're fed a breakfast of specially baked dog biscuits, prepared to a royal recipe; for high tea they dine on fresh rabbit or beef in gravy, prepared by a gourmet chef. Each dog has a bowl bearing its name, and they're trained not to raid one another's food. There is no longer a permanent vet in residence for the dogs, but two of the veterinarians who work with the horses have a secondary specialty in canine medicine. Someone visits the Corgi Room every week, or more frequently if called in—like today.

"I really don't know what's wrong with her," the royal dog trainer tells the vet. "She seemed a bit quieter than usual after evening exercise yesterday but I didn't think anything of it. No diarrhea or other digestive troubles. But this morning she was off her food completely—refuses to touch it, didn't want to mess with Vulcan's either. Whiny and subdued, refused to get out of her basket at first. And now . . ."

The vet watches the dog out of the corner of her eye to avoid agitating her—the dogs pick up on human unease—but there seems little point. The other corgis are outside, exercising with two footmen. Meanwhile Candy lies in her basket, breathing in shallow pants, clearly not paying attention to anyone. She's four years old and normally a rambunctious troublemaker—but not today.

"How long has she been like this?"

"Since I came on duty. Eight this morning? I coaxed her out of bed but then she sat down and refused to go anywhere. I tried again after lunch and she just fell over. Not play-dead roll over, it was clearly serious. That's when I sent for you."

"Right. Sorry it took me so long to get here, this is worse than Reception said. Has it progressed?"

"I . . . think so? Slowly, though, no seizures or anything obvious."

"I think—" This time the vet looks at Candy and makes deliberate eye contact: Candy doesn't react. "Can you help me get her on her feet?"

"Yes, ma'am." Together they close in on the low-slung dog and gently ease their hands under her until they can pick her up.

"Over here—oh. Well." Candy is clearly awake, but as they lower her feet back to the floor she whines, then topples over sideways. "Hind legs are weak." The vet touches the base of Candy's tail, then rubs the pads on her uppermost hind leg. "Note the rounding of the lower back and the lack of touch response. There's no sign of a fracture or torn ligament." She gently lifts Candy's head and peers into her eyes: "Horner syndrome is absent, doesn't look like she's had a stroke, but see the tremors? I need to get her to the surgery. I'm pretty sure she's going to wind up in hospital for an MRI and further tests overnight."

The dog handler nods. "I'll fetch her crate. Her Majesty is not going to be pleased."

Talking Pete down from the window ledge is the highlight of my week—and the one thing I can point to as an unequivocally good deed.

On Tuesday afternoon I get to sit through another interminable LONDON BRIDGE meeting. I'm ordered to waste money better spent on computer games on a *Reservoir Dogs* cosplay suit—all black except for the shirt. (My plea to be allowed to go 100 percent black, complete with a veil and pillbox hat, is harshly rejected.) Worse, I'm tasked with enforcing this mandate on junior staff with smaller pay packets.

On Wednesday I get to drag my sorry ass to Hicksville UK, a giant concrete office block in the middle of Slough, to deliver the now-familiar dog-and-pony show again: magic is real, see Bob, see Bob do magic, Iä, Iä, all cursed now, any questions?

On Thursday I am read into various aspects of the restructuring that we're careening toward like one of the mine carts in that Indiana Jones film where everybody hurtles over a cliff and dies. No, really: Q-Division SOE is set to be dissolved and everyone will be raptured up to Ministerial Heaven as part of DEAT, the Department of Existential Anthropic Threats. We will then be led by an actual Minister with a cabinet seat, namely His Nibs, Fabian Everyman MP, Prime Minister of the United Kingdom. (Yes, the PM can head up a ministry if he wants. Why do you ask?) Yay, bigger budget, more responsibilities; boo, direct oversight by the lidless fiery gaze of Darth Sauron himself.

Finally, in my copious spare time I work on the POISON APPLE investigation, where nothing is the new something. Mo hasn't heard back from the Palace, I'm not allowed to interrogate the Lord Chancellor in person: we're just stuck in limbo waiting for the shoe to drop.

Little do I realize that my treadmill of boredom is about to be disrupted by a sad puppy.

Buckingham Palace doesn't have an on-site veterinary hospital, but there's a private one in Belgravia. Fifteen minutes after the dog handler and the vet load Candy into one of the palace Range Rovers they wheel her into an examination room in the back of the clinic, where Candy is weighed, sedated, whines as blood samples are taken, is told she's a good girl (she isn't: she nips, a bit like her owner), then is prepped for her MRI.

No expenses are spared: the bloods are whisked across London by a motorcycle courier for urgent out-of-hours processing. The MRI sequence is run. It's clear that there are no internal injuries and no hard tissue tumors; no sign of aneurysms or brain hemorrhaging either. Candy hasn't had a stroke or thrown a blood clot. She's not constipated, her kidneys are still functioning, her bowels are perfectly normal for a pampered four-year-old dog, her ECG is normal . . .

But Candy is clearly unwell. She's having difficulty standing and staying upright, seems unusually fatigued, and is showing signs of neuropathy. (The vet can poke her paw pads with a wire without getting a reaction.) She's drooling continuously, and her nictitating membranes are showing. The vet would worry about rabies—except she's been vaccinated. It's not food poisoning: the other dogs, on the same diet, are fine. It's a conundrum.

Then at nine o'clock the bloods come back, and the plot thickens.

Platelet count is up. Leukocyte count is up. These are signs of inflammation, or possibly leukemia. Her liver enzymes are up. Her kidneys are damaged: they're leaking amino acids, glucose, and other small molecules.

The vet phones an off-duty senior colleague to brainstorm possible causes. While she's on the phone Candy has a brief seizure. As fits go it's not serious (the patient's lack of muscle tone reduces the risk of damage), but it's an alarming progression.

"Have you screened for heavy metals?" asks her senior colleague.

"No—" The vet pauses. "It's worth a try, I guess?" She draws more bloods and phones the lab again, just in case.

This time the samples get run through the gas chromatography/mass spectroscopy machine to look for traces of heavy metals, plus radioimmunoassay screening for a handful of diffuse and small organ cancers.

The vet is napping in the staff break room in the early hours of the morning when the report comes in. It takes her a few minutes to make sense of it. But when she does, she's instantly alert. She forces herself to drink a cup of strong coffee and read the email again, making notes before she does anything. Then she goes to the books, specifically the veterinary medical formulary and the poisons handbook, and starts looking up data sheets.

The hospital doesn't routinely keep chelating agents in stock, but she orders Succimer and Unithiol for urgent delivery, then writes up a prescription and a memo for the duty vet who's on at eight.

After she finishes writing, the vet collects her medical kit and drives back to the Palace. It's essential to take samples of the current batch of dog food and test it before the pack get their breakfast. The GC/MS results indicate Candy has high levels of dimethyl mercury in her system, and her symptoms are consistent with Minamata disease—acute organic mercury poisoning. Worse, it's come on frighteningly fast. The vet doesn't hold out much hope that the DMSA/DMPS treatment she's prescribed will save Candy, but it's worth trying. But the next question is, how was it administered? Because dimethyl mercury is a horrific neurotoxin, and if it's deliberate, the entire Palace could be at risk.

Happy joy: The following Tuesday afternoon finds me in Conference Room D7, because it's time for another meeting about the progress of MUGGLE WONDERLAND. Various concerned persons, from Gerry Lockhart down, want to know how it's going. In fact, Gerry seems to take an unholy delight in my gaslighting at the hands of the provincial Flat Earth brigade—until a mobile phone begins to ring. I thump my pocket, then realize it isn't me: it's Gerry this time. He jerks as if he's just been goosed, then pulls out a device that clearly dates to the last ice age. He glares at the screen in disbelief, then snaps, "I have to take this," and double-times it out of the meeting without further ado.

I look around the table and see everyone wondering the same thing: What was *that* about? The Director of External Assets does not simply walk out of a meeting to answer the phone.

Doesn't he have a PA to handle his calls and schedule his every waking minute? I have a bad feeling about this, just an itch between my shoulder blades—

Then *my* phone vibrates with an incoming message, which is an *oh shit* event. "Got to go," I say, standing up from the table. "Urgent call of nature." Which is a rubbish excuse, but nobody calls me on it as I march through the door then book it. One glance is all it takes to get me moving: Gerry has just invited me to Secure Briefing Room 14, FLASH meeting, subject: POISON APPLE.

Scooby 14 is down the road and I have to go out through security, then back in through a different security checkpoint, and it's raining outside and the lifts are either out of operation or loading and unloading Galapagos tortoises, so I take the stairs. By the time I'm four floors up I am feeling every one of my four hundred and sixty-odd months and my knees are sulking. (Unfortunately the ghost roads are blocked and warded in Agency-occupied buildings—it's an elementary security precaution—so there is no shortcut I can take.) So I finally stagger, wheezing, up to the door with the illuminated red light, badge the panel to request admission, and wait for one of the occupants to buzz me in.

"Where's Gerald?" asks Iris, fixing me with a stare about as forgiving as an anti-tank shell.

"I passed"—I gasp—"must have overtaken"—my back hits the wall by the door and I slither down, panting—"were both in"—pant—"MUGGLE WONDERLAND meeting—"

A pudgy hand grabs my upper arm and lifts with unnatural strength. Derek heaves a chair out from the table with his free hand and deposits me in it like a sack of potatoes, just as I notice that the lighting in the room is distinctly reddish. "Thanks," I wheeze, momentarily gobsmacked by his display of anomalous strength.

"You're welcome." The DM sits down again and resumes

looking like a portly fifty-something guy in coke-bottle glasses, while Iris goes back to pacing a hole in the carpet. She looks at her watch every ten seconds and she's ignoring her phone (which is fair do's, the Scoobies are all Faraday cages, the mobile signal is blocked), but she's clearly got withdrawal symptoms.

"What's going—" I begin as the door buzzes again. Derek hits the button to admit Dennis, Emma MacDougal's henchman from HR, who looks flustered: Lockhart is close on his heels.

"One more," warns Iris, holding up a bony digit. "Any moment now . . ."

The door buzzes and Derek admits my wife, wearing a very unhappy expression. "What now?" she demands, yanking out the chair beside me and throwing herself into it without giving Derek a chance to show off.

"It's the Queen." Iris points at Derek. "Take it away."

"Wh-what? M-me?" I haven't heard Derek stutter like that in ages: he looks stricken.

"Who else?" Iris finally forces herself to sit down.

"Oh. Well."

Gerald makes eye contact with me and shakes his head minutely. I manage not to blink.

"W-we got a lock on a, a vision," Derek begins. "Primary source is oneiromantic with haruspex-derived secondary con-confirmation. Adversarial fuzzing makes it h-hard to be sure, but there w-will be a ceremony in Westminster Hall before the end of May and it will be a mass casualty event. W-with mourners."

"A funeral?" Gerald leans forward sharply.

"I—I—I—" Derek jolts to a stop, visibly takes a deep breath, and shakes his head. "I don't know. B—but—" He gives up and looks at Iris imploringly.

Iris takes a deep breath. "We received word from the Palace this morning. One of the royal corgis has been poisoned. We don't know much more yet, but." Another deep breath. "If this is POISON APPLE we may have been thrown a blinder. Or it could be worse than anyone imagined. So I called you here to read you in on FAIREST, otherwise known as POISON APPLE Phase Two: the plan for handling the aftermath of a royal assassination."

PART TWO

PART TWO

TERMINAL PROGNOSIS

The POISON APPLE meeting descends into barely contained panic before Gerry Lockhart wrestles it back into a semblance of brainstorming about strategies for addressing the situation we find ourselves in, viz. Dead Queen Walking.

What we know so far: Candy the Dorgi, aged four years (in human), has been dosed with dimethyl mercury, a compound notorious for killing an eminent toxicology professor and expert in the substance in question, Professor Wetterhahn. She was working in a fume cupboard with all due precautions—wearing two layers of protective gloves, breathing filtered air, generally doing the full Andromeda Strain—when she spilled a drop on the back of one glove. That was enough: she died, paralyzed and blind, some months later. DMM is a thing of horror. It dissolves right through rubber and plastics, not to mention skin, and there's no effective antidote. It's the poor man's polonium: exotic, lethal, and hard to obtain.

We don't know how Candy was poisoned, but it's a fair bet that she wasn't the target. So, who was?

This may surprise you—but the most likely answer is: the Laundry.

Listen, nobody sane would assassinate the Queen. Everybody knows she's a figurehead, a ceremonial head of state whose main job is to make a speech to Parliament once a year setting out the government's coming legislative program. Moreover, if and when she dies she will be replaced instantly by a big-eared homeopathy enthusiast, and if *he* dies it goes to a thirty-something prince: it turns out to be royalty all the way down. (You could drop an asteroid on Westminster Abbey during a royal wedding, and before the rubble stopped bouncing there'd be a very surprised newly minted monarch with absolutely *no* idea how fucked-up their life is about to get.)

The Queen is merely a symbol—the living head that wears the crown. The actual wellspring of legal, constitutional power in the UK is an abstract entity called the Crown. This is not just a piece of expensive headgear, any more than the US Constitution is a piece of sheepskin covered in ink. If you were to melt down the jewellery or burn the paper a lot of people would be very annoyed, but the Crown or the Constitution would still persist: they're ideas, not physical objects. Egregores, in other words.

But there's some confusion between the Crown and the crowned head. Public servants swear an oath of allegiance to the monarch by name. A new monarch means a lot of ceremonial reswearing of the oath of allegiance.

For most people this is a formality. But for those of us bound by the Laundry's Oath of Office, it has a deeper significance. The Oath of Office is a powerful *geas* that commands our obedience, at a very low level. Mostly it's used by the Auditors to compel us to testify truthfully in hearings, and to block other occult agencies from sneakily installing spyware in our brains. But because it's anchored by the Oath of Allegiance to Her Majesty, when the Queen dies, we all get called in to reswear immediately, under Auditor supervision, to the new crowned head. No deferrals can be allowed: a sorcerer with an unanchored Oath of Office is like a computer on the internet with a factory default password.

You might think this is stupid—having a national security agency that can be forced to suddenly drop everything and perform a magic chicken dance whenever an old-age pensioner dies—but remember, Elizabeth II has been Queen for nearly sixty-five years. Nobody now living and working for us was around for the coronation, so we're going to have to go to the archives and blow the dust off some really ancient plans, check them for buried thaumaturgic bugs, and bring them up to date in a hurry.

And that's before we start asking who dunnit . . .

"Dimethyl mercury, Professor. Have you found it yet?"

Mo has returned to the misleadingly signed office in the Palace, and she's on the war path.

Professor Phibes glares at her from his side of the desk; his companion—a nurse or medical receptionist perhaps—remains silent. "We're working on it. The proprieties must be observed—"

"The proprieties can take a back seat. If Her Majesty's been poisoned—"

"I can't just demand a blood sample!" Phibes looks appalled. "She's very upset. Candy is her favorite dog—"

"Candy has been poisoned, Professor. I appreciate your concern for your patient's privacy, but the vet has been more forthcoming. This is an animal that is in frequent contact with Her Majesty and DMM is a contact poison. My agency is concerned that this may have been an assassination attempt. You need to screen the target, then search for delivery vectors. If we're lucky it was *only* the dog—"

Mo is pretty sure it's too late, but she needs a smoking gun—a mass spec report on a sample of royal blood—before she can take this to the next level.

Phibes's face sags lugubriously. "Her Majesty is due"—he looks sideways at his companion—"Vulnavia? If you would explain?" His voice is hoarse, as if his larynx is somehow damaged.

Vulnavia wears the starched uniform of a staff nurse straight out of the 1930s: the Palace makes a fetish of rejecting modernity. She has model-perfect skin and straight black hair yet seems curiously ageless, and this puts Mo's back on edge. But she also knows her stuff: "Her Majesty's diary is booked up six months in advance. She maintains a work routine of over three hundred public appearances a year, and her daily schedule is blocked out the week before, in fifteen-minute periods. So you see, we simply can't schedule a medical examination at short notice without giving a reason. It would be headline news."

"That's not—" begins Mo, but Nurse Vulnavia hasn't finished. "Her Majesty *is* due for a checkup this Friday afternoon." Mo catches her quick glance at Phibes, and his grudging nod. "We can take bloods then, as long as her diary is running to time and she's in a good mood."

"Friday?" Mo shakes her head. "But we need an update *immediately*."

"Mrs. O'Brien," Phibes's expression is patronizing, "with all due respect, if Her Majesty was exposed a week or more ago, then a three-day delay won't materially affect her prognosis. And if she has *not* been poisoned, which seems more likely to me, I see no benefit in unduly troubling her. I will write her up for a full set of bloods on Friday afternoon, and that's final. And I'll request a full heavy metal workup."

Mo fumes, although this is as close to cooperation as she's gotten from the medical household so far: "How soon can we get the results? The veterinary hospital was able to get the lab tests turned around overnight."

"I'll expedite it." Phibes is obviously reluctant but at least it's not a no.

"Well then. I'll see you next Monday morning." Mo stands. "And it's *Doctor* O'Brien."

Despite the vet-prescribed course of chelating drugs, Candy continues to worsen over the course of the week. On Friday morning, a few hours before the Queen is due to give blood,

Candy undergoes a major seizure and is subsequently pronounced dead.

PHANGs don't play well with daylight, which leads to logistical problems when I need to meet with Pete and Derek in a secure briefing room.

Chateau Dracula, as we've nicknamed the PHANG safe house, meets regulation standards for security. But we can't simply take top secret documents out of a secure building and transport them across town to work in a badly insulated 1920s suburban terraced house with internet and possibly nosy neighbors. I am pretty sure if I suggested it to the blue-suiters their reaction would be somewhere between "Hell, no!" and "When did you stop taking your meds, sir?"

So in the end I ask the experts what to do about secure vampire transport. Which means interacting with Mhari Murphy, Dame Karnstein, Chair of the Permanent House of Lords Select Committee on Sanguinary Affairs, and my long-before-I-met-Mo ex. "We use prisoner transports," she tells me over the phone—she's a PHANG, too, and I'm not walking into her nest again during daylight hours. "It's all outsourced: I can give you the name of the bloke at HiveCo Security who subcontracts for us."

"HiveCo?" I stare at my handset. "The outsourcing and management consulting company?"

"They do public sector outsourcing management, yes." Mhari's tone is dry. "Do try to keep up, Bob. They won the metahuman prisoner transport contract from SerCo during the last auction. SerCo still handle normies but HiveCo's people are equipped for handling supervillains, sorcerers, anything above and beyond your run-of-the-mill gangster." She clears her throat. "I'll email you Jared's contact, the rest is up to you—I assume you've got someone in Facilities who can handle it."

"Okay, thanks—" I find myself listening to a dial tone. That's different: I'm usually the one who hangs up on her.

So I ask Dennis, our point man in HR, and Dennis hooks me up with Alice from Facilities, our fixer for general logistics, and she talks to Jared (after confirming with Legal that we don't need to hold a full tendering process because HiveCoSec already hold the portfolio), and I then forward her deal memo to Iris to sign off on and then, *only* then, after two whole days and innumerable emails, do I get to look for a vacant slot in Scooby 14 and invite Derek and Pete to the meeting. Next I email Jared that I need a prisoner transport from Chateau Dracula to Mahogany Row and back again and by the way, they're staff, *not* prisoners (this last bit is *very* important). And then I have to go round up an escort who will get Pete out of bed and into the van on time and who can be read into the program, and there's really only one possible choice, so I end up going back to HR (for approval) and Security (for vetting) and Iris (for budget) and Mhari (for a chewing-out) and then finally a phone call to beg Janice's indulgence (because misery loves company).

Bureaucracy, huh?

The following day finds me lurking beside the loading bay, acting like a smoker who's left his lighter at home. It's cold and gray and threatening to rain when a white armored box van with tiny mirrored glass windows pulls in and parks beside me with its hazard lights blinking. A bloke in uniform hops out of the passenger side door and heads for the door of the prisoner compartment, side-eying me warily.

As he's about to slide a key in the door I realize what he's doing. "Hey! Stop that! You can't do that here!"

"What?" He turns toward me, hand moving toward his holstered taser.

I hold up my warrant card. "You're the transport for the POISON APPLE team, two officers, right? You can't drop them off here. You have to pull inside the loading bay and lower the shutters before they debark."

"Nah, got a schedule to keep to. End of the line, mate." He turns the key so I flex my mental muscles and *squeeze*.

"No," I say very firmly, then relax my grip on his soul just before he squishes. "Try again. Pull indoors and I'll lower the shutters for you, then you can open that door. Unless you want to explain your schedule to a pair of very angry vampires with sunburn."

The driver's mate blanches. "Vampires?"

"Lovely people, they will just be *slightly* irate if you kick them out in the daylight. Tell your mate to repark while I let you in." I smirk at him, then step through the side door and hit the start button on the shutters.

Some minutes later the driver and his mate hunker down in the locked prisoner transport cabin as Janice climbs down the steps. She's clearly annoyed to be up this late, but she's a trouper. "Hey, Pete," she calls inside. "Get your ass out here, time is money."

It takes a few seconds, but Pete finally shows his nose. "Go on inside," I say, waving at the inner door on the loading dock. "I'll meet you in a minute, got to work the shutters first." I should have applied for a PA, I tell myself.

Janice hauls Pete along behind me as I lead them to Scooby 14, where Emma and Morgan, our Security Officer, are waiting with Derek and a stack of paperwork. Pete startles violently when he sees Derek, then shuffles to a seat opposite.

Derek rubs his hands with glee as he sorts his documents alphabetically, then reaches for his pen: Janice frowns irritably as she signs, but Pete just slumps like a badly hungover party survivor.

"Pete." I nudge him verbally. "You need to be read in. Start with the top copy"—the Official Secrets Act, complete with the not-for-public consumption classified schedule—"then work your way down." I wait almost a minute. "*Pete?*"

He finally raises his gaze but declines to make eye contact. "What is the point," he says. It's less a question than it is a smoke-signal of despondency.

Think, Bob. "We need you on this team." I tap the printout of the Act in front of him. Then I wait.

"You don't need me. Nobody needs me." Behind him, Emma and Morgan exchange a significant look. But he reaches for the top page and initials, not bothering to read any of it.

"That's where you're wrong," I tell him. "Keep signing." It's per regulation. Pete's already signed the OSA multiple times but we need him to re-up on this one because he may be dealing with the Palace, there's the potential interaction between the oath of office and the oath of loyalty to the Queen to worry about, and Cthulhu have mercy on us if we fuck up.

"I don't see the point." Pete signs anyway. "I'll just get people hurt . . . or worse." He glances at Derek.

"What?" Derek looks perplexed.

Pete looks at me helplessly. "I killed him."

"He's sitting right there," I point out. "Looks pretty much und—I mean, alive, to me, all right?"

Janice clears her throat. "A word?" She raises an eyebrow at me: "Outside?"

Morgan buzzes us out into the corridor. Janice leans against the wall. "I swear, those two . . ." She shakes her head.

"How long has this been going on?"

"Pete's been avoiding Derek. I mean, *really* avoiding him. He only comes out of his room when Derek's not in the house, working or visiting his girlfriend"—*Derek has a girlfriend?* I want to pinch myself—"I caught Pete emptying a half-gallon milk jug he'd been using as a commode the other day. Living with them under the same roof is like living with a pair of tomcats—I swear, it feels like Pete's afraid Derek's going to murder him in his sleep, meanwhile Derek is oblivious—"

"This is about what happened in D.C., isn't it?"

"Yeah." Janice nods. "Pete got infected, and his puppet-master made him bite Derek. So he thinks he murdered Derek."

Pete, I gather, has not regaled Janice with his take on modern theology, otherwise she wouldn't imagine his sense of guilt to be so puerile.

"Okay, clearer now," I tell her, and hit the buzzer, thinking, *Spare me from this middle management bullshit.* Because what comes next is middle age and responsibility and, *oh noes*, I might be in danger of having to grow up or something.

I go in and sit beside Pete, displacing Janice, who plops into my previously occupied chair and rolls her eyes at me. "Pete," I say, "Derek's right here. Still breathing and everything, you know? So have you finished signing the Act already so I can tell you what this is about?"

Pete shoves the stack of pages toward Morgan and leans back. "I suppose so."

He's not going to make this easy, is he? "I get that you're feeling bad right now, but I want you on this operation"—little white lie, I'd prefer pretty much anyone else—"which is all about *preventing* a murder, and possibly averting a mass casualty attack on the nation." Pete doesn't seem captivated, but at least I've got Janice's attention. "The cover on this file is coded POISON APPLE, and it's classified TOP SECRET because it involves a risk to national security." Pete still isn't showing any interest, so I push harder: "We think the assholes who turned you both in D.C."—my gesture takes in Pete and Derek—"are hot for payback, and to get the point across they're going to assassinate the Queen."

"What the fuck?" Janice looks scandalized.

"Well, we rescued the President right under their noses, didn't we?" Derek sounds just a little bit smug. "It's bound to be a sore point." Especially as his POTUS-ness was very grateful, but that's beside the point when you're dealing with the US government in the wake of an autogolpe—an internal coup—carried out by the Operational Phenomenology Unit, also known as the Nazgûl, our archrivals (and the ultimate worked example of the perils of regulatory capture). "They probably think Brenda is a purely ceremonial cake-topper with no actual power, and it won't matter anyway once they dismantle the moon and use it to build the ultimate summoning hypergrid or whatever the fuck they're really working on."

I lean forward. "The trouble is, Brenda is not without power—it's just that her power can only be used *once*. So, Pete. We are putting together a team to keep the Queen on life support even if it all goes pear-shaped, and we have a very specific role in mind for you.

"Are you on board?"

Getting dragged out of the wankfest last Tuesday to attend the POISON APPLE meeting where Iris announced that the Queen's dog had been poisoned gave me an excuse to bail on the execrable and interminable FLAT EARTH briefings. But instead I got to spend an entire day in one-on-one tutorials about forensic toxicology. So I feel the correct amount of Imposter Syndrome while I'm briefing everyone on the POISON APPLE team.

While we were still waiting for more information about Candy's owner—no thanks to the Palace—we have preparation work to get on with.

Iris put it in perspective in our next team meeting: "POISON APPLE has been set up—on paper—as an exercise exploring the response to an attack on the head of state. That's the cover story. What's not public is that it's not an exercise. It seems almost certain that the Queen has been poisoned. Which means POISON APPLE will be followed in due course by Operation FAIREST.

"POISON APPLE focuses on investigation and response. The investigation team will trace the attacker—DMM is not widely available, it's an exotic neurotoxin. The response team will then go after the attacker." Everybody sat up a bit straighter on hearing that. "If there are threat actors on British soil, you will use any necessary force to neutralize them. Arrests would be ideal: live witnesses, evidence to back it up in case it leads to sanctions or even a shooting war. But if you can't arrest them, kill them. Skulls on spikes, ladies and gentlemen: the PM likes to see skulls on spikes."

Iris stalked around the front of the room, oozing malice. She wasn't the only angry one: the mood around the table was febrile. I didn't vote for her, but Brenda's the national granny figure, a unifying aegis who smiles and waves benignly and doesn't put people's noses out of joint the way politicians do. Even the IRA knew better than to go after her. If someone poisoned *your* government-issued great-grandmother, you'd be pissed off, too.

(To say nothing of the dog.)

Anyway, to cut a long meeting short, read the minutes:

Mo is taking point on Investigation, along with some former colleagues from the Home Office and a senior officer from Royalty and Specialist Protection. I've been given overall responsibility for the Response team. I've got Derek on tap for planning, Gerry Lockhart on speed-dial for external assets, and meetings to come with: the RaSP cops (who are very protective toward Her Maj), our friends from the Artists Rifles (I have an OCCULUS team on standby), a couple of Q-Division support people who come highly recommended by my old mate Brains, and . . . Pete?

What am I going to do with the vampire vicar?

Quite a lot, as it turns out . . .

So. While we're ploughing through the paperwork and onboarding a dozen operatives who've been pre-vetted for Top Secret work, some routine work oozes in to fill the gaps in my schedule. Including my regular monthly session with Dr. Mike Armstrong, who is still the Senior Auditor—but not for much longer.

"What's the plan for, uh, your succession? I mean, with me?" I ask, taking a seat in the visitor's chair by his desk. (It's an all-new office, larger than his old one, with a pair of bland Victorian paintings on the wall that signal his civil service pay grade to those who understand how the Government Art Collection works.) "I mean, obviously Mo can't..."

"Yes, that *could* be seen as a conflict of interest." Mike is amused. "I believe His Majesty is leaning toward commissioning an External Auditor, someone who is both above question themselves and has experience in that area."

"Would that someone happen to be you?"

"Maybe." He tilts his head thoughtfully. "At least at first? I expect to retire in a couple of years, but for now it's still you and me and the priest's confessional."

"Right." Because this is what the Auditors do with us, when they're not sitting as a tribunal. "I'm ready." I lean back in my chair.

Dr. Armstrong leans toward me and enunciates, very clearly: "Ruby. Seminole. Kriegspiel. Hatchet. Execute Sitrep One."

My brain checks out but my lips and larynx move without my involvement. "Subjective integrity is maintained. Subjective continuity of experience is maintained. Subject observes no tampering." It's not me speaking, it's the Oath of Office. It's like secure boot firmware for the brain, it gets to run before my mental operating system. Dr. Armstrong is my authenticator—it's not just about the codewords, it's about the person using them being bound by an Oath of Office with the responsibilities of an Auditor. He gets to sign off once a month on a piece of paper, using a quill pen dipped in his own blood, to the effect that I am not demonically possessed, ideologically compromised, knowingly attempting to circumvent my Oath or otherwise violate the Official Secrets Act, committing acts of gross moral turpitude—

I only made that last one up. But the rest is, as the kids say, totally for realz.

"Exit supervision mode."

I blink woozily while I regain conscious control. I glance at my watch—the old-fashioned clockwork kind you're allowed to wear in a secure area—and see that about fifteen minutes passed while I was outside my own head. "Am I clean?" I ask.

The Senior Auditor makes a noncommittal sound as he pours tea. His hand shakes slightly. We've been doing this dance for years now—and it's a regular part of the ritual.

"You're not under investigation or suspension at this time," Mike finally announces. "You know I'm not allowed to tell you any more." I don't bother rolling my eyes. "I know you're lying to the Reverend Russell: I also know why and, on the record, I think you're entirely justified." I relax slightly. "If I may make so bold, though, you might want to lay off the irreverent humor for a few months, especially with respect to the royal family." His lip wrinkles in mild distaste. "I know, but it's the framework we operate within, and you're in a visible management role now. Got to lead by example, alas, and that means not making fun of, how did you put it, Jug-Ears and the Nonce, when you might be swearing allegiance to one of them before long."

Did I really say that out loud? "It's a fair cop: but I can't help it if every time I see Prince Andrew on TV I want to put salt on his back." The classified Epstein briefing crossed my desk back when we were panicking about cultists getting their claws into the Cabinet. The Cabinet mostly stayed out of Epstein's little black book, but the future King's kid brother left a slug trail through its pages: that came as a nasty wake-up call, let me tell you.

Dr. Armstrong gives me a thin smile. "He's above your pay grade or mine, but there's always a plan on file somewhere; meanwhile he isn't next-in-line anymore unless something happens to the Duke of Cambridge *and* his son."

"Corgi attack. Ravens at the Tower specially trained to drop hand grenades. Rabid ferrets in the cockpit of the royal helicopter. It could happen. Just saying."

"It won't," the Senior Auditor says repressively. "Now, on to other matters—"

"Is my audit complete?" I push.

"Yes, Bob, your audit *is* complete. Sit down and drink your tea, we have other things to discuss."

"Shoes, ships, sealing wax? That kind of thing?"

"And why the sea is boiling hot, and whether pigs have wings; also whether you're hunting a Snark or a Boojum." I see Mike's winding up to make an important point, in his own indirect manner. "The POISON APPLE team is hunting for an apple-poisoner, obviously. And maybe the poisoner is the obvious sort of miscreant—a snark, let us say—but what if it turns out to be a boojum instead, and softly and silently vanishes you away?"

"A trap?" I blink at him stupidly.

"A trap for the Agency." Dr. Armstrong crosses his arms. "Ask yourself if it isn't a little too obvious? The gloves are coming off, we're in an endgame now with the stars come right and CASE NIGHTMARE GREEN as our new normal, an endgame where the power sources we tap into and seek to control overwhelm. Our current Prime Minister is one outcome of that tendency. There are others. Tenochtitlan State in Mexico is building a giant temple to Santa Muerte, human sacrifices have resumed at Çatalhöyük, the Vatican has reinstated the Holy Inquisition . . .

"So, here's the thing. The UK has always been run by a Deep State. It's not a hidden conspiracy: it's the aristocracy, sitting on the bedrock of the monarchy. Its members are out there in full view, *Hello!* and *People* magazines publish their wedding photographs, they send their children to run parliament. We have a democracy in theory, but really about a thousand families own most of the country. And it's our job to keep them in power.

"Now, I invite you to think like a foreign intelligence analyst. Outsiders who think the UK is a democracy don't always recognize that it's actually an autocracy with democratic forms. His takeover was relatively painless because the system evolved to support a monarchy, and He's the Black Pharaoh: He just moved in and used His glamour to displace the existing executive authority. We still follow democratic norms and the PM stood for election. He didn't declare a dictatorship. The Deep State, in the shape of the monarchy and the House of Lords, is still intact. So there was no crisis of legitimacy."

I am stunned and silenced by Dr. Armstrong's constitutional infodump, which is simultaneously breathtakingly cynical and made out of purest organic horseshit. Although if this is how Mahogany Row view the government we serve, it shines a very different light on everything we do. But he hasn't finished yet . . .

"All hierarchical states contain multiple power centers, and the most stable ones are generally those where there's no obvious head you can decapitate to effect a change in policy. So, to an outsider the UK right now probably looks like a democracy with a very small, isolated, putative dictatorship bolted on top. And if you can knock over the dictator, you can make the state change direction. What's not obvious is that this dictator is welded on top of the existing framework. He's not going to go down easily. But anyway: I believe this attack is a false flag operation intended to lay the Queen's poisoning at the feet of the New Management."

He smiles sweetly. "So if you go looking for the poisoner I predict you'll pick up a trail of bread crumbs leading to our own Deep State, because that's how it was set up. And we're in the sights."

Days pass. Friday rolls round, and Mo is in a tizzy, insisting someone checks on Professor Phibes at the Palace every hour. Eventually we gather in one of the medium-security rooms to get an update from a courtier who sounds as if he's been preserved in aspic since the eighteenth century. "Her Majesty is in good health as expected, but at your insistence and the request of Privy Council"—he sounds as if a swarm of wasps is attacking his scrotum with their arse-daggers—"a blood sample has been taken. We will have the results for you no later than next Tuesday—"

"Please hold." Mo hits mute on the speakerphone. "Any inputs?" she asks pointedly.

"Yes." Iris smiles like a megalodon, then makes eye contact. "They're dragging their heels. Allow me."

Mo hits unmute and Iris takes over. "Good afternoon, sir. I am Iris Carpenter, Chief of Staff to the Prime Minister." There's a garbled squawk from the other end, hastily cut off. "Number Ten's understanding is that the royal blood was drawn at a quarter past three this afternoon. Number Ten is *extremely concerned* about Her Majesty's state of health. So your report *will* be on my desk before three p.m. tomorrow. Yes, I know it's Saturday." A pause. "If the report is not delivered before the deadline there will be consequences."

Another voice—somewhat younger—pipes up: "What kind of consequences?"

Iris snarls: "The view from on top of Marble Arch is very scenic these days." On which note she ends the call.

"Bob, Mo. I want you at the Palace by noon tomorrow. Camp on that royal physician's desk and do *not* take no for an answer; I've had enough of their stonewalling. Probably they think the Palace outguns Number Ten. I want you to show them otherwise. If they don't cave *at once* you may make an example of whomever you see fit, *pour encourager les autres*. Is that clear?"

Mo looks at me: I look at her. We nod simultaneously. "Good," Iris says firmly. She stands to leave. "Bring the report to Number Ten in person tomorrow, harvested scalps optional. I'll authorize holiday pay and time off in lieu for the whole weekend—you'll be busy on Sunday, too."

Colonel Lockhart follows her, with a brief backward glance that seems to say, *Rather you than me.*

"Did you notice if there were little skulls pinned to her collar?" I ask faintly.

"Of course there were, Bob! Don't you know a Hugo Boss suit when you see one?"

(Exeunt Bob and Mo, the former muttering *Are we the baddies?* under his breath.)

The next morning Mo badgers me into my new funeral suit and the squeaky leather shoes that go with it, then forcibly adjusts my tie until she's satisfied about something I can't quite work out—I half-expect her to do the mom-thing of wiping something off my face—then drags me to a waiting police BMW. She's in her own funeral suit and heels, and has actually applied makeup, which is something she normally only does for concerts.

"Leave the talking to me," she says, and we ride in silence until we arrive at a discreet door in the wall around the Palace. "Put your sunglasses on," she orders, so I oblige—black Ray-Bans, at her insistence.

She leads me through a warren of corridors to a small medical clinic. Mo knocks once on an office door, then opens it immediately and walks straight into what turns out to be an examination room. "Professor Phibes." She nods at an older fellow sitting behind an excessively large desk. I step sideways and take up a position beside the door, fold my hands in front, and try to look like a brick wall, which would be easier if I'd remembered to hit the gym more than twice in the past fortnight. "I'm here to collect the test results," Mo continues.

Professor Phibes stands up. Half his face has the weird uncreased shininess that comes from reconstructive surgery, there's something subtly wrong with his nose—I think it's a prosthetic?—and his hair appears to be made of polyester. "I didn't say you could enter," he buzzes, his voice coming from a box on the desk. "This is a clinic, you know. Patients could be—"

"*Your report.*" Mo snaps her fingers at him, which is *very* unlike her—I would consider it beyond rude if she hadn't filled me in on his heel-dragging and I wasn't also acutely aware of the countdown to the Prime Minister's ultimatum. "Where is it?"

"The raw data should have been emailed to us this morning, but I haven't reviewed it yet." Phibes's voice box buzzes like a trapped hornet. "It's extremely technical."

"We do not care." Mo leans forward intimidatingly: "Number Ten *does not play games*."

Phibes recoils slightly, then picks up the receiver of a black telephone so ancient Queen Victoria probably used it. "Jensen? I say, Jensen?" He waits a moment: "Please print out the bloods for Her Majesty and bring them to me." He hangs up, then looks at Mo. "Please take a seat."

"You know, I don't believe I will," she says expressionlessly. I feel a secret stab of pride. My wife can be a total hard-ass when the situation requires it—like denying this posturing fool control of our interaction. But she does step sideways, to mirror my pose on the opposite side of the doorway. "You have five minutes—"

The door slams open behind me and a footman in red-and-gold livery barges in, clutching a sheath of paper in front of him. *Something is wrong*, I realize. My ward buzzes and heats up. I look at him and see there's nothing remotely human at home in his head so I shout, "Gun!" I'm already opening my imaginary jaws wide to bite down on whatever has eaten his soul as I move to shove Mo out of the way—

"*Un-be!*" she snaps in Old Enochian. And the abruptly unoccupied body drops like a sack of potatoes, papers flying in all directions.

The dead guy was holding an army-issue Glock with a drop safety, so it doesn't fire when it hits the floor. I turn and slam the door shut and stab an index finger at Phibes: "*Freeze*," I command him, not *quite* ready to kill him: I am absolutely furious, I realize, and a little bit frightened, but we need him alive. "Who is *that*?" I point at the body.

Phibes has half-risen from his chair, mouth open, his posture expressing bafflement. Mo kneels swiftly and gathers up the

THE REGICIDE REPORT 111

papers, then steps over the body and kicks the pistol toward me. "You, you—" Phibes is on the edge of having a seizure.

Mo scrutinizes the papers. "Looks technical to me." She shoves them at Phibes. "Is this what we're here for?" She side-eyes the door so I nod, pick up the pistol, and hold it where anyone opening the door will see it. I can feel human minds moving around on the other side of the wall, juicy and unaware, but so far nobody outside seems to be paying attention to us. "Well?" Mo demands: "Is this the blood workup?"

"I—I—" Phibes's voice box buzzes like a shorting PA system. "Yes." His eyes widen. "That is. Oh dear. Oh no." The report in his hand shakes. "This can't be right." He seems curiously cold-blooded, for a civilian: there's a corpse on the carpet and I'm holding a gun and Phibes still manages to look as if he's mainly afraid the paperwork will bite him.

"Explain it to me like I'm a layperson," Mo orders. I keep the door covered with the pistol. More as theater aimed at Phibes than because I expect intruders: while he knows Mo can drop a man with a single word, he doesn't need to know that I can do worse.

"Her Majesty's liver enzymes are up, kidney function is down, but, but *the heavy metals*—there's mercury here. Yes, yes, methyl mercury, point zero four moles per liter—oh dear. Excuse me." He stands and walks to the bookcase, rummaging through the reference books with shaking hands.

"How bad is it," Mo asks tonelessly.

"Very bad." Phibes frantically leafs through pages. "Very bad indeed. Dimethyl mercury is metabolized to methyl mercury after several days—"

Mo catches my eye. I lower the pistol, eject the magazine, work the slide, and put all the pieces in my pocket.

"Call security," I tell Phibes. He can deal with the mess once we're gone. "After you've identified him, notify us, then box up the head to go. The PM will appreciate it as a token of your loyalty." Then I follow Mo back to the police car to convey the bad news to Number Ten.

We emerge from the grounds of Buckingham Palace and surge along Birdcage Walk, disturbing the ducks on the pond in St. James's Park with sirens and strobes. A few minutes later our driver is presenting his ID to the officers guarding the gates to Downing Street. "We'll walk from here," Mo tells him, and he pops the door for us.

Downing Street is a short cul-de-sac with former town houses on one side, facing the arse of the Foreign and Commonwealth Building on the other. The town houses have been cored out and filled by various government offices, much like a parasitic fungus growing through the body of a hapless caterpillar: however there are still a handful of residents. The Prime Minister occupies the apartments above Number Ten, and the Chancellor of the Exchequer gets the flat over Number Eleven. But really, it's just three office raccoons in a trench coat, government departments pretending to be a posh residential side-street.

I have mixed feelings about this place, and not just because of his Dark Majesty. I'm pushing forty, and although I vote in general elections I have never actually voted for the winning party. I'm out of step with the marching band of British politics this century, I guess. But I wasn't given a choice about joining the Laundry, and I've seen enough crazy shit to know that politicians are generally the lesser evil. Until now . . .

"Dr. O'Brien, Mr. Howard, this way please." A terribly earnest young thing twinkles brightly at us, then leads the way through a warren of dingy corridors and fading wallpaper. We end up in a drawing room full of overstuffed armchairs, with long curtained window bays that don't quite conceal the bulletproof glass. The view overlooks a courtyard and garden terrace at the back of the building. "His Dark Majesty will be with you shortly," gushes our escort; "May I get you anything? Tea or coffee?"

I defer to Mo. "Thank you for offering, but I don't expect we'll be here long," she says, then perches on the edge of an armchair facing the doorway. I take the one beside her, remembering at the last moment not to manspread in the direction of the Prime Minister.

We don't wait long. The door opens and I hastily stand. The PM strides in, continuing a conversation with a tweedy-looking woman and a SPAD or flunky who's following him around clutching a tablet—"Keep me updated on the fabrication process, there's a good chap, now I have a meeting with, ah! The fragrant Dr. O'Brien! And Bob." He beams at us like a black hole sucking all perception inside his event horizon, and for a moment my inner eye catches a glimpse of what lies behind his blank visage. (I really wish I hadn't.) We shake hands. The PM doesn't make us get down on our knees and prostrate ourselves—he's very progressive for an ancient eldritch horror. "I believe you have a report for me?"

Mo hastily proffers Phibes's printout. "There was an incident as we collected this," she begins, but the PM is already nodding.

"So I gather. One of the possessed, not mine, what?" *How the hell does He already know?* I puzzle.

"Dealt with," Mo says repressively.

I nod, trying to ignore how I feel insignificant and edible in His presence.

"Yes indeed, and the loose ends will be taken care of. Think no more of it," He says, and it is a command I can't ignore.

Iris opens the door. "Sir, we have—" She pauses. "O'Brien, Howard. How bad is the news?"

The PM gives every appearance of reading the front page of the report before He hands it to the tweedy lady. "This is Professor Jenny Sadowitz, an expert on organomercury poisoning." He twinkles darkly, an eerie counterpart to the young functionary who led us into His presence. "Please have a seat Professor, Iris."

He leads us over to a small conference table, where a throne-like executive chair obligingly moves to accommodate Him: the rest of us have to take a more hands-on approach to the furnishings. "Perhaps the Professor could explain."

Professor Sadowitz dons a pair of half-moon spectacles and frowns at the paper. "May I ask who the patient is?" she asks.

"You may ask." The PM nods sagely.

Iris picks up the thread: "Naming no names, she's an eighty-eight-year-old great-grandmother, otherwise in good health for her age. Two to three weeks ago she was exposed to dimethyl mercury, presumably administered in her food. Unfortunately it took until yesterday for us to obtain a blood sample. The report is in your hand."

"But the dose—" The Professor stares at the page. "You mean this was *deliberate*?"

Iris nods. "Yes, that appears to be the case. Unfortunately it was not discovered until several days after the event, when a family pet also fell ill. What can you tell us about her likely prognosis?"

The PM watches the Professor avidly, as if her evident horror is a delicacy to be savored.

"I'm sorry, there's no way to sugarcoat this: she's going to die." Professor Sadowitz is ashen. "Treatment will only draw out her suffering. There's no hope of coming back from this. Whoever she is, she needs to be assessed as soon as possible for neurological impairment—reflexes, cognitive functioning, peripheral neuropathy—and also renal and hepatic function. If it was administered orally more than a few hours ago there's no point bothering with absorbents like activated charcoal or chelating agents to partition it out of her lipid circulation." There is a significant pause, as if Professor Sadowitz has just remembered who she's talking to. "Who is the patient?"

The Prime Minister smiles like a dead star rising over the frozen landscape of a murdered planet. "Her Majesty the Queen." His smile slides below an invisible horizon, leaving us in darkness. "Needless to say, this is a matter of national security. You will speak of it to nobody outside this room without My permission."

The Professor slumps. She seems to have aged a decade between breaths. "What do you need from me?"

The PM nods at Iris. Iris has developed an even better poker face over the past year, and right now she looks positively botoxed. Her voice is even and she sounds only mildly concerned, as if discussing an overdue report. "How long will it take for the symptoms to become visible? And what will the progression look like?"

"Ah, I, um. I can't say for sure." Sadowitz is defensive. "She's eighty-eight years old and I don't know her medical history so I can't tell if there are complicating conditions—in geriatric medicine it's rare for there to be only one chronic illness. What I *can* say is that with this blood titer of DMM it will be a miracle if she lives into 2016. Even with heroic measures. Most likely she has three to six months.

"If she was poisoned two weeks ago, she should be showing clinical signs within the next couple of weeks. There will be visible symptoms within another month or so: pins and needles in her hands and feet, dizziness, numbness, muscle weakness. There may be blurred vision, confusion, memory loss, dementia. The symptoms are irreversible, although the progression is highly variable. She may suffer multiple organ failures. By the time she dies she will be too weak to move, probably blind, and most likely unable to talk or understand.

"It's a horrible, horrible way to die."

I shake myself. Mo is wool-gathering, or maybe having a flashback to some private moment of horror she thought she'd buried. I know I am: I've seen deaths, even been responsible for a few, but this is something else again.

"So we may have as little as a month until public awareness becomes unavoidable? Thank you, Professor." The PM manifests another smile: "Julian will walk you out." The SPAD rises from his seat. "Further communications may come from my Chief of Staff." He nods at Iris. "You may also hear from Mr. Howard or Doctor O'Brien." I shiver as His eyeless gaze tracks across us. "Thank you for your time."

We wait in silence while the Professor leaves.

The PM's posture shifts abruptly. "Excellent!" He declares. "I think that went swimmingly! What do you think, Dr. O'Brien?"

Mo looks at Him as if she's wondering how to sic Mental Health Services on a Prime Ministerial horror who has lost the plot. "Come again?" she asks.

"We have a diagnosis! And a prognosis! And even a tentative timeline!" (*Is He* happy? I wonder, boggling.) "Which means you can commence Operation FAIREST." His chair rolls backward as He rises to His feet. "Iris, please read Dr. O'Brien and Mr. Howard into the plan. It's time to get a move on: you should aim to execute within the next four weeks." He nods at us. "Until next time." And then He leaves us looking at each other in perplexity.

DEAD QUEEN WALKING

It turns out that all those LONDON BRIDGE meetings I got roped into had a purpose. Who could have imagined that?

Iris looks old, I think, then I do a double take as she stands up: she looks *tired*. "Bob, Mo. We've got this room for the next"—she glances at her watch—"forty-six minutes and it's warded, so let's make the most of it. You're both fully briefed on POISON APPLE, and you've both been attending training for LONDON BRIDGE, even if"—she skewers me with a gimlet stare—"there have been *reports*."

(Mo elbows me. At least, she'd elbow me if we weren't being hauled over the coals. Being married for over a decade gives you superpowers, like the ability to realize you've stepped on a conjugal garden rake less than fifty milliseconds after the event. Silver anniversary feat: precognitive rake detection.)

"Anyway: FAIREST is our plan for this situation—and you're going to be assigned to it."

Iris proceeds to read us in on the plan, and I wish she hadn't.

Some years ago, a couple of very old PHANGs had an epic pissing match over some perceived slight going back centuries. It ended with about twenty of our people dead and our headquarters building permanently inaccessible. Anyway: one of these PHANGs, a harmless-looking geezer called Basil, had perfected a way of keeping his blood bags fresh.

When a PHANG feeds from a new donor the donor goes downhill rapidly, because the V-symbionts use the law of magical contagion to dive into their gray matter and chew holes in it.

But Basil, who had been embedded in the Laundry for decades, had figured out how to use a containment grid to pause the deterioration. Normally a grid walls off whatever's inside it from the rest of the universe: we sometimes use them for really secure briefings. It's a variation on how we access the ghost roads, a relative of the hotel-space passage I used to get into that bookshop in Brum.

Basil figured out how to stop time inside a grid. He'd stash each victim inside one and while it was energized, the V-symbs couldn't get at their meal. He had to turn it off regularly to feed himself and his parasites, but it stretched out their remaining days across several months.

"We're going to place Her Majesty in a state of suspended animation in a glass coffin in Westminster Abbey," Iris explains. "The medical side will be carried out by a doctor who successfully pioneered a process for maintaining critically ill patients indefinitely, in a state between life and death. We're going to leak the existence of the technique through media channels next week, before we announce the Queen's illness. We're going with motor neuron disease," she adds. "It has similar symptoms to DMM poisoning but doesn't raise any questions about assassination."

Mo blinks. "How are you going to handle the transfer of binding oaths and privy council stuff?"

"With a Regency. Officially we're working on a cure, but it's going to take years. Hence the suspended animation. It's an innovative medical treatment called the Phibes process: only the best for Her Majesty."

The Phibes process? Where have I heard—oh, him. This can't be a coincidence, I tell myself.

Meanwhile, Iris is explaining: "Prince Charles has taken on a lot of Her Majesty's ceremonial duties—she doesn't have the stamina to make four hundred public appearances a year anymore, and he's eventually going to be King anyway. We'll reanimate Her Majesty for the annual State Opening of Parliament and Queen's Speech. Otherwise the Prince Regent can handle the other ceremonial stuff once the Articles of Regency are signed. He gets to wear the crown and act as the royal MC. He'll like that."

Meanwhile, Her Majesty will be taking a long nap in a glass coffin built by Phibes. *Hmm.*

"The protocol will be based on LONDON BRIDGE," Iris continues briskly. "I mean, it's all there: the protocol for changing over to a new monarch—or in this case a regent. There will be minimal changes. Dr. O'Brien will be in direct contact with Her Majesty—not you, Bob. But you'll be running the security operation on the ground for the formal handover of power. Certain rituals will need to be conducted in the basement of Buckingham Palace to ensure an ACID-compliant transfer of bindings. There will be a service in Westminster Abbey led by the Archbishop of Canterbury, then she'll lie down in the coffin. But we're not going to warehouse her with the stiffs in the crypt—at least, not until she's actually dead."

"Are any sacrifices planned to mark the occasion?" Pete asks grimly.

"Not at the Abbey, no—" Iris hesitates. Suspending the Queen is going to be a *mana*-intensive ritual. And you generally extract *mana* from computational transactions *or* from parasympathetic nervous stimulation, either during sex or death. Obviously, Pete wants no part in *that* side of the ritual. "That's not for you to worry about."

"If not, then what purpose does this serve?" Mo asks. "Why are we needed in attendance? Why can't it just be a medical procedure followed by Her Majesty going into seclusion at Balmoral?"

"It needs to be public," Iris stonewalls uncomfortably. "Her Majesty is a powerful *mana* concentrator—she's the focal point for all the belief in Monarchy of a hundred and fifty million citizens across the twelve countries she rules. We have to be very careful about redirecting that stream of belief, or doing anything that might throttle it. The Queen can't simply vanish:

as she has said, 'I have to be seen to be believed.' We need to control the narrative."

I am getting a very uneasy, itchy vibe from all this. "What's the business at Buckingham Palace, then?" I ask. "What needs to take place there to transfer the bindings?"

"It's the Regency problem. We last did this in 1811, so the documentation is very out of date. But we need to ensure the public's faith in the divine rule of the monarchy is undimmed. 1811 was a bad time—Napoleon, war with the American colonies, and so on. This time around we're not picking a fight with the EU and North America at the same time—I mean, His Dread Majesty may be an ancient evil but he's not *stupid*—but Washington, D.C., belongs to the Nazgûl, they're holding human sacrifices to Chernobog in St. Basil's Cathedral, and don't ask about the Vatican. The geopolitical theology is all messed up. Anyway, we have to ensure that the Palace courtiers make the necessary sacrifices to power the ritual, that the eyes of the world are upon Her Majesty, and that there's no *mana* leakage from the monarchy."

"The eyes of the world," Mo says diffidently. "Just how big an event is this going to be?"

"LONDON BRIDGE was planned in the expectation of an audience larger than the last royal wedding, which, if you include internet impressions, had a billion viewers." Iris stands. "*Nothing* can be allowed to go wrong with FAIREST."

Prince Otto Von Bismarck is said to have quipped, "Laws are like sausages. It's better not to see them being made." And as a civil servant, it behooves me to be familiar with the rhythm of the sausage machine.

The sausage machine I work for was first switched on in 1801, has been repeatedly patched and repaired ever since (it's overdue for a full-scale redesign), and it's held together by chewing gum, string, and constitutional wishful thinking. Nobody sane would design a legislative system like this, which is probably why the Crawling Chaos is right at home in it.

It's very simple: Parliament is the supreme legislative body of the United Kingdom, Crown Dependencies, and Overseas Territories. It is a bicameral legislature with three parts:

- the House of Commons (elected by the public, except about 80 percent of the seats in it are owned outright by one party)
- the House of Lords (unelected except for the 92 seats allocated among hereditary peers—they run for election among their own kind)
- and the Sovereign, who is all-powerful, except that the Sovereign normally does whatever the Prime Minister tells her to do. Unless she doesn't feel like it.

Exceptions:

- The House of Lords can poke a stick between the bicycle spokes of the wheel of government and delay any piece of legislation for a year.
- The House of Commons can trigger a general election at pretty much any moment by throwing an epic tantrum that makes the government lose a vote of confidence.
- There are bishops of the Church of England (which the Sovereign leads but doesn't control) in the House of Lords, also a pile of very senior judges and one extremely confused Chief Rabbi.
- Listen, I don't make the rules, right?

Contrary to vile foreign innuendos there *is* in fact a British constitution. Understanding it provides valuable employment opportunities for law professors and civil servants, because it is set out in only about twenty-two different pieces of legislation, and Parliament can modify it whenever it feels the urge. Some constitutional laws are more equal than others—international treaties tend to override random populist nonsense like the Home Secretary attempting to deport refugees to the icy plateau of Leng.

Now it gets complicated.

Parliament creates laws for the United Kingdom, except where it doesn't. The United Kingdom consists of four squabbling countries, not all on the same land mass. Try to visualize three raccoons in a legislative trench coat dragging a fourth, possibly rabid raccoon around by the tail. One of the trench coat raccoons has its own parliament with a separate legal system, another has a regional assembly with slightly less legal autonomy, the third—England—is about the size of a brown bear but *doesn't* have its own parliament, and the fourth raccoon is foaming at the mouth when it's not biting itself because it's Northern Ireland.

I mentioned the overseas stuff, didn't I?

The Monarch is the source of authority for Parliament. She's also the Monarch of Australia, New Zealand, Canada, the British Antarctic Territory, the South Sandwich Islands, and oh god this ought to be an exam question on the Citizenship Test, alright? I mean, the one that stuck in my head was the Pitcairn Islands, population forty-nine, occupied by the descendants of the mutineers from HMS *Bounty*. If anyone ever plants a Union flag on the Moon, we're in trouble.

Oh look, I left out the weirder bits:

- The heir to the Monarch receives the title of Duke of Cornwall. But due to some historical weirdness from the fourteenth century, the Duchy of Cornwall is exempt from certain laws, including the part of the Nuclear Explosions (Prohibition and Inspections) Act of 1998, that would otherwise make it an offense for Jug-Ears to cause a nuclear explosion.
- The Channel Islands are not part of England, nor are they ruled over by Parliament, but the Queen is their head of state in her capacity as the Duke of Normandy. They have

their own mini-parliaments running on weird descendants of medieval Norman law, occasionally tinkered with at the whim of Parliament (who advise the Duke of Normandy—and yes, I know the Queen is female, she's still a Duke, okay?) . . .
- I need a beer. Or six. British constitutional law is obviously the product of strong hallucinogens, or maybe barristers trolling each other on Reddit.

The British government has gone to great lengths over the past century to ensure that the Monarch is never put in a position where they might break the law. If a law needs to be broken on her behalf, she has very scary men with guns to do it. Just to ensure that the law is not broken by the person from which the rule of law emanates. The nation's granny is a walking legal embodiment of Gödel's incompleteness theorem: if she chose to go on a killing spree at the head of a rampaging pack of corgis, then it wouldn't be murder because murder is illegal and whatever the Crown does is by definition legal (unless she declares war on Parliament—and nobody wants a rerun of the civil wars).

Anyway. As noted, the Monarch is kept in a constitutional padded cell and leaves the heavy lifting to Parliament. Her job is to come forth at the start of every year-long parliamentary session and sprinkle magical monarchy dust over their proceedings by reading a speech in which the government announces its legislative program for the year ahead.

It being 2015, this year the State Opening of Parliament is due to take place on May 27th.

And this is a *problem* for us. Because it's currently February, and by the time late May rolls round Her Maj will be dying of acute mercury poisoning . . .

*

Professor Phibes is not the kind of consultant who makes ward rounds or visits patients at home. He's far too elevated, having graduated to a tier where he alternates between teaching other doctors and accepting their praise graciously while reclining on a pile of diplomas and accolades.

However, sometimes he has to treat a less elevated patient. He is in the Palace a couple of days later when the medical receptionist takes an internal call that names a person of interest to him. "Sir? I have a call about a member of staff on your alert list. Should I ask for him to be sent up?"

"Who is it?"

"Harold Huntsman, sir. Second butler in Her Majesty's apartment. His supervisor is concerned."

Mr. Huntsman arrives in the examination room a quarter of an hour later, accompanied by his supervisor (a worried looking woman called Nancy) and two young footmen in red-and-gold palace livery. The footmen are there to provide support, for Harold Huntsman is clearly having difficulty standing upright, much less walking.

"Here, have a seat." Nurse Vulnavia leads Huntsman toward the examination table under Phibes's watchful gaze. The second butler is in his thirties with prematurely salted brown hair, but looks very un-butlerish indeed. He's clearly unshaven and has pulled his tailcoat on over pajamas and a single bedroom slipper—the other is missing. He shuffles painfully and when the footmen lower him to sit on the edge of the padded table and release his arms it's apparent that his right hand is trembling uncontrollably.

"What have we here?" Phibes grates through his voice box, leaning close. Huntsman recoils from his presence, then begins to topple sideways—the nearest footman grabs his shoulders hastily to stabilize him.

"Don' feel so well."

There is no smell of alcohol on his breath and his pupils are normal. "Smile for me?" Phibes says. Huntsman forces a tremulous smile: it's symmetrical and the tremor is showing up in his left arm, too, now that he's seated. Over his shoulder, to Vulnavia, Phibes adds, "Records, please." Back to the patient. "When did you start to feel unwell?"

"Friday."

Phibes looks at him sharply. "This last Friday? Or some earlier Friday?"

Huntsman nods. He swallows convulsively. "This'un. Began feeling dizzier, and pins'n'needles in my hands and feet. So I spent Sunday in bed, hoped I'd get better."

Vulnavia hurries off. When she returns she hands the Professor a battered manilla file full of papers going back many years. While Phibes leafs through it, the nurse checks Huntsman's blood pressure. "Bloods," Phibes murmurs as she puts the machine away. "Full workup, include the extras we ran for last Friday's patient." Vulnavia silently fetches a kidney dish, cannula, tourniquet, and sample tubes.

Phibes questions Huntsman. "When did you notice the pins and needles? Any difficulty picking things up before this morning? Anything else?" It's a formality: he already knows the cause. "I'm going to check your reflexes now," he says, "then I'm going to test how sensitive your feet and hands are." Later he'll need a report on the butler's visual perception and cognitive functioning, but those aren't Phibes's specialties. If it's what he thinks it is, there may already be numbness in Huntsman's extremities.

"Do you think I'll get better soon, Doctor?" There is only a faint tremor in Huntsman's voice.

"I really can't say," Phibes remarks, his gravelly voice the opposite of soothing. "You haven't had a stroke. It might be a passing virus." (This is not quite a lie.) "I'll know more once I see the results of your blood tests."

The patient is eventually placated, and Vulnavia and the sole remaining footman transfer him to a wheelchair. After the door closes behind him, Phibes spares his nurse a lizard-eyed glance.

"Give the bloods the same priority as Her Majesty. Most urgent that I get the results within twenty-four hours." Then he picks up the telephone and dials an internal number.

"Hello, Medical Household, this is Professor Phibes speaking. I have a message for your office. We appear to have a second case, from belowstairs this time. I'm awaiting the result of blood tests, but should know more tomorrow. The signs are consistent with . . . yes, that. I'll keep you posted. The main thing is, if it is the same condition, we have a . . . yes, yes, I know, I was going to say, testing the protocol before we apply it to FAIREST would be useful, wouldn't it?"

A little later on the same morning that Harold Huntsman tries and fails to get out of bed unaided, Mo drops in on me.

My current digs are sparsely furnished and lack a bunch of the equipment I need to do my job—stuff like Angleton's Memex is marooned in the New Annex, just barely accessible without entering the Exclusion Zone—but at least I don't have to hot-desk with anyone. (Indeed, I've leveled up: I can hit up the Government Art Collection for wall-mounted eyeball candy, although my request for the Roger Dean album artwork for *Relayer* was met with a predictably withering knockback by the fine art snobs, who obviously don't appreciate the prog rock classics.) So I'm leaning back in my chair, torture-testing the lumbar support, when Mo sticks her head round the door.

"Are you busy right now?" she asks, with the same gleam in her eye that comes over her when she's about to ask when I last scooped the litter tray: "Because I've got a little problem."

I sigh. "What's come up?"

She plants herself in the number one visitor's chair. "I want an IT forensics boffo to investigate the dimethyl mercury supply chain. That stuff doesn't grow on trees."

"Well, no shit." *I* should have anticipated this. "Who do you need?"

"Someone who can trawl chemical suppliers' databases, fast and quietly. Pinky and Brains are both hors de combat, so I thought you might know who."

I wince. Pinky's officially sight-impaired since the bad business in Leeds and Brains got hit by the Nazgûl PHANGs while engaged in YELLOW OLYMPIC. They were my go-to tech support bros for many years, but it's anybody's guess if they'll ever return to the office. I used to do that kind of shit, too, but I'm years out of practice. (It's like I've pupated and am turning into a manager.)

"I could ask Peter-Fred . . ." I trail off. "Wait. Didn't you have a research assistant on your pull list?"

Usually everything moves at a snail's pace, but when the Bureaucracy Fairy waves her magic wand over you and the stars align sometimes shit happens unbelievably fast. Which is why less than two hours later I find myself in a meeting room with Mo, a plainclothes cop called Denise, and Willard, a shiny new researcher assigned to Operation FAIREST just last week.

Mo takes point. "Willard—" Mo eyes me. "Bob, your requirements."

"Okay." I look at Willard, who shrinks visibly in front of me. He's wearing a suit because this is Mahogany Row but it's a bit baggy and his shirt collar fits so badly that if he shrinks any more I do believe he's going to retract his head like a turtle. "I need you to identify possible sources of the dimethyl mercury implicated in POISON APPLE. It's a regulated poison per the 1972 Poisons Act, so a retail purchaser would have had to provide a valid EPP License to get hold of it. Businesses can also buy the stuff, but there'll be a record on file with the Home Office and the local police. Unfortunately online marketplaces aren't adequately regulated, and our subject might have used a darknet site to import it. Luckily almost nobody has a legitimate use for it these days, outside a handful of analytical labs. Um . . ."

I pause, then make eye contact with the detective, who is looking twitchy. "I must emphasize, this stuff is *absolutely* deadly. You don't need to inhale or swallow it. If you think you've found some in a container, do not put it in an evidence bag, it'll dissolve right through the plastic and kill you. Cordon off the area, call in SO20, and warn Crowd Control it's a nerve gas incident."

Denise looks increasingly sick as I work through the list, but finally she nods. "I'd better get over there and warn them," she says. Her eyes narrow. "You *did* warn SO14 about this stuff, didn't you?"

Mo looks at me. I look at Mo. It's a classic *Who, me?* moment. "Oh shit," I say, as Mo pinches the bridge of her nose.

"Action this day," she says firmly. "Arse-kicking later."

Denise leaves the meeting room at a run.

"What just happened?" Willard asks, glancing between us blankly.

"Bureaucracy just happened," I say, trying not to sound too bitter about it. Bureaucracy means procedures and rules, so that it takes more than one person to fuck up. Unfortunately there aren't any rules for this particular one-legged arse-kicking contest.

"Go build us a list of everyone who has purchased or imported dimethyl mercury in the UK in the past year, or reported losing the stuff," says Mo. "There'll be a lot of duplicates but keep everything for now. Ask HMRC for a list of all declared import shipments. Make a separate note of anything that looks flaky. If you need security authorizations, ask Bob: Bob will get them for you."

"When do you need this by?" he asks hopefully.

"Yesterday. And if not yesterday, as soon as possible."

"I'll authorize expenses for pizza, coke, and a sleeping bag if you have to camp out in the office," I tell him. "Just get it done."

"On it." He pauses. "One thing . . ."

"What?" Mo is ominously quiet.

"I have a fancy rat," Willard confesses. "She's called Olive and I need to feed her by hand at least twice a day. She gets lonely so I—"

"Bob. Schedule a home visit with a rat-sitter for Willard. I'm done here." She stands up. "Got to brief Iris next." And she walks out.

"Iris?" asks Willard, looking slightly stunned: "Who's Iris?"

"Don't ask." I hold the door open. "Just email me your rodent requirements and get to work."

Her Majesty is not feeling quite herself this Monday morning.

She's sitting at the breakfast table in the apartment she shares with Philip, who is reading *The Daily Telegraph* and crunching away at his second slice of slightly charred toast covered with coarse cut marmalade, periodically shedding sticky crumbs on the newspaper.

Elizabeth tries to ignore the mess because she has a red box open and she's trying to focus on her appointments for the week. She's lightly programmed with just four public appearances. All she needs to do is turn up, smile, shake a few hands, and declare the new research institute/army barracks/hospital open. Really, she could do this stuff in her sleep—and she has.

But something's not quite right this morning.

Elizabeth raises her teacup, and that's when she realizes her right hand is shaky. She can see ripples in the surface of the liquid. *Odd.* She takes a sip, then sets her cup down; there's a clatter as she releases the handle, a slop of pale brown liquid over the rim.

"Jack!" The butler on duty this morning is not her regular, Harold.

He steps forward smartly. "Yes, ma'am?"

She gestures at her teacup, her index finger not quite pointing where she aims it. "Please notify the medical household that I'm not feeling quite myself this morning." Not since the previous appointment when they'd drawn blood—filling more sample tubes than normal, *why?*—"I'll see that new doctor after breakfast."

"Yes, ma'am." Jack picks up the teapot to refill her cup, then pauses discreetly. "Will that be all?"

"Yes." Elizabeth turns away and the butler, dismissed, ghosts away to notify the physician.

Elizabeth is not an idiot and she peers at her left hand suspiciously, then attempts a smile, before concluding that she has not in fact suffered a stroke. But this is one of those things that, once noticed, can never be ignored.

When she arrives at the clinic, a full reception is waiting for her—Phibes, his oddly silent nurse-assistant, three orderlies, and a wheelchair.

"Your Majesty," buzzes the Professor. "How may I be of service?"

Elizabeth fixes him with a beady stare. "Something is *wrong*," she says. "'M not quite right this morning." She holds out her right hand. "Tremors." She pauses a few seconds, allowing her displeasure to leak out: "Is it to do with those blood tests?"

Phibes is very good at concealing his disquiet, but not good enough. He tips his head toward the open door of his office. "If you'd like to take a seat, Your Majesty, this may take some time to explain." To her equerry, he asks: "How far out are they?"

Got you, Elizabeth thinks, feeling no satisfaction whatsoever. It's not the first time the medical household have tried to keep bad news from her. She is, she believes, wise to their little tricks—there was no morphine overdose for mummy or daddy, she made sure of that—but she doesn't entirely trust this Phibes cove. It's not the burn scars, the artificial larynx, or even the midnight organ-playing in the Palace basement: he's just plain creepy. *Assessing.* Utterly unimpressed with everyone. Which is probably a good thing when dealing with the boy Andrew, but totally unacceptable disrespect toward one's monarch—

The door clicks shut behind her and she takes her seat in front of the desk. She composes herself as Phibes walks round to the other side. "Tremors, Your Majesty." His tone is measured as the grave. "When did you first notice them?"

"Half an hour ago, at breakfast time."

Phibes nods. "I would like to schedule a full physical examination," he says. "Any pins and needles? Coldness in your fingers and toes? Numb patches?"

What? No. "I can't say," Elizabeth says repressively.

"That is ... good." Phibes nods again.

"What were those blood samples for, Doctor?"

"A request from Number Ten, in response to advice from the Security Services, Your Majesty."

"I beg your pardon!" Elizabeth is furious.

Phibes sighs lugubriously. "I am terribly sorry to be the bearer of bad news, but you recall that your dog, ah, Candy, died last week. And your assistant butler, Mr. Huntsman, is suffering from similar symptoms. I was reluctant to believe it at first, but the Prime Minister personally intervened, and I am afraid he was right to do so.

"The blood samples indicate that you have been poisoned. The tremors are among the first symptoms. An officer from the Security Services—which branch I am not sure of, but they're not the police—is on her way here to brief you."

Elizabeth feels curiously dissociated, not quite present in her own body. "Poison? Is there any treatment?"

Phibes doesn't need to reply: his expression is eloquent. "There is no *orthodox* medical treatment for this toxin, I am afraid. But you have some time in which to make decisions, and I gather the person we are waiting for will discuss certain unorthodox options with you that were recommended by Number Ten."

The Queen swallows. Her mouth is as dry as a tomb, despite all the tea she drank barely half an hour ago. "Magic."

"Not the *bad* kind, Your Majesty." Phibes is clearly trying very hard to walk a line between lying to his liege and being the bearer of unwelcome news. "If you choose this option it must be carried out on consecrated ground, in Westminster Abbey—"

They are interrupted by his phone jangling on its hook. Phibes lifts the earpiece. "Yes? Send her in."

The door opens. "Your Majesty," says her equerry: "Dr. O'Brien is here to brief you."

After Iris gives us our marching orders things begin to move fast.

Mo and I head to the Palace, where I'm issued a permanent identity and access badge. It actually says SOE Q-Division Senior Agent, which makes me feel like I forgot to put my underpants on outside my tights. (The habit of secrecy is deeply ingrained.)

I am introduced by name to the chief inspector in charge of palace security and confirm that my backstage pass allows access to all areas except the royal apartments: I can even visit those by arrangement with the security office.

Next, Mo and I are taken in hand by an excruciatingly correct lady in twinset and pearls from the Palace equivalent of HR, who hauls us into a broom closet and proceeds to lecture us for three hours about the bare minimum of royal etiquette because apparently exposure to Prince Andrew is a very real danger. There is a strict dress code while we're on Palace grounds and I'm patronizingly told to get myself a better suit than the one I bought for the LONDON BRIDGE hijinks. I leave the interview in possession of a business card for a tailor with an address on Savile Row: it's clearly a weapon designed to inflict +3 damage against paychecks. I refrain from eating Etiquette Lady's soul, but it's a near-run thing. ("Expense this one and I'll get Iris to sign off on it," Mo murmurs on our way out the door. "Bloody snobs: I think you're fine as you are." She rubs my arm. *Bless*.)

The cop on desk duty in the security office makes us sign out paper maps of the Palace: not the tourist version but ones that include the private areas. I learn that not only is there a basement but a subbasement and several attics.

Of course there isn't an app, or even a downloadable PDF. Our maps have been scribbled over in red Biro to indicate building work in progress, and they're stamped with PALACE CONFIDENTIAL. We're also given a stern talking-to about the consequences of retaining them at the conclusion of our duties. (I guess nobody in royal security has heard of photocopiers.)

Anyway, after we finish with the police and HR Mo and I visit the staff dining room, where we are ushered to a table set with snowy linens and Wedgwood china because apparently we're management-tier and there's a strict social hierarchy in force here. Then after lunch we split up.

I head back to the POISON APPLE team sandpit, drop in on Willard (who has set up an elaborate multistory rodent Habitrail beside his desk for Vermintrude), then go down to Facilities and check out a high-end field thaumograph. Then I return to the Palace, spend half an hour explaining my equipment to the security bod on the staff entrance, and prepare to walk the grounds. Yes, squeaky dress shoes and all.

With the aid of a red-uniformed footman I start on the stables, then map the perimeter wall around the gardens. That takes me the rest of the afternoon and early evening. I go home with sore feet and a grumpy mood. I resolve to drag a minion or two along when I resume tomorrow, because at this rate the job's going to take days.

You are probably wondering what I'm trying to achieve here, so I'll explain:

Willard is digging down into the data trail in search of poison sources and I am checking on him daily. Mo is grilling the medical household and, I believe, briefing the Queen. The Police can handle the forensics side of the case. Next week I'm going to get stuck into preparation for Operation FAIREST, and my remit includes the Palace and its staff, but right now I don't have a lot to do, so I'm doing my bit by surveying the field in case there are any buried nasties lurking in the bushes.

A *geas*, a magical compulsion, is the most likely explanation for how the poison was delivered to Her Majesty. The palace grounds are warded, but most wards can be undermined if you've got enough people moving in and out every day: the Palace isn't a soft target, but it presents a huge threat surface to a sufficiently determined attacker. So I'm looking for weak spots, entry points.

(His Eldritch Darkness seems to think that there is some kind of occult threat here, and I've learned not to underestimate the Black Pharaoh. He really *is* playing eleven-dimensional chess while the rest of us are losing at Solitaire.)

Taking down the Queen will force us to reset the Laundry's entire cascading hierarchy of binding oaths, a once-in-a-working-lifetime opportunity for mischief on the part of hostile state-level actors. And there may be a more specific target. On a broader level, it will undermine all the nation's magical defenses, including the Palace's wards, and the less-public bindings that protect Her Majesty's privy council and parliament.

Last year, cultists masquerading as the Golden Promise Ministries successfully installed rootkits in the brainstems of half the cabinet—that's why Mahogany Row executed a successful insider coup, installing the Black Pharaoh in their place. But the GPM are strictly amateur hour compared to the Nazgûl. So someone has to tote a glorified *mana* detector around the grounds of the palace, looking for any suspicious hot spots. Next week we move in an entire team to set up the bindings for FAIREST, to prevent the Queen's bottled-up *mana* from flowing back to the Palace when she checks out and being diverted to power who-knows-what mischief.

The problem with magic is that while software scales (you can just throw more processor cores at it), ritual magic is single-threaded, bottlenecked by the need for a sufficiently powerful practitioner. So the person doing the scan needs to be both experienced and powerful enough to survive any reasonable attempt by a top-notch adversary to subvert them.

And that's why I'm doing grunt-level field work, albeit in a very expensive suit and tie.

Fuck my life, right?

You may think I'm being a complete bastard to Willard, expecting him to camp out in the office until he gets results. But we need to get that poison locked down and we need to track down whoever brought it into the Palace: it may be a matter of life or death. So I'll try to remember to make it up to him later.

I hit the sack after 10 p.m., am on my way to the office the next morning at 6 a.m., nail down my usual administrative email within an hour, then go and drag Willard to the canteen for caffeine, bacon rolls, and a daily report.

"I, uh, it turns out there are a lot of chemical suppliers, who knew? But not many who make dimethyl mercury. Most of them are in China and India for some reason?"

I valiantly ignore the way Will talks around a mouthful of dead pig and nod encouragement.

"Anyway, nobody in the UK makes it, at least not officially. Although it's not a complex synthesis? Any secondary school chemistry lab could do it, given some mercury and a death wish." Will pauses to chew for a moment. "I can't audit every secondary school in the UK."

No shit. I nod. "That'd be a last resort," I deadpan, and he turns white. "What else?" I ask before he chokes.

"There are sixty-one wholesalers who import organomercury compounds in the UK, and another two hundred or so in the EU. I contacted HMRC like you said, and they said it'll take two weeks." He catches my expression and hastily clarifies: "They're not dragging their heels! It's just, they store everything on IBM mainframe hardware that purges older records to progressively slower storage. A month after the import licenses are signed the records get dumped to a line printer."

"So there's a printed record?" I ask hopefully.

Will's shoulders sag. "One page of printout per record, several thousand records of listed poisons every day, they load it all onto a wooden pallet once a week and stash it in a hangar with a leaky roof on a disused wartime RAF Bomber Command base in Kent. Where they leave it for the mandatory seven years, then compost it." He shakes his head. "So the records I need are somewhere in several tons of wet paper in an airfield near Thanet, which *technically* meets the ISO 19475:2021 minimum standard for document retention." And he puts down his bread knife.

I pinch the bridge of my nose.

"Okay, moving swiftly on from . . . that." It's not even HMRC being HMRC: this is departmental level, weaponized obfuscation. Either that or malicious compliance, a highly efficient system put in place years ago to bury something embarrassing. I'm tempted to draw it to Iris's attention, but the likely level response when His Darkness hits the roof would be excessive and won't solve anything, aside from adding a few more skulls to the Marble Arch Tzompantli.

"Okay, so let's limit it to last month." I nod to myself. "Whoever did probably imported it recently—you don't keep DMM sitting around if you've got any sense—and that's still online, isn't it? Have you checked under the street light?"

"I've begun. HMRC was notified of thirteen import shipments last month. Three went to commercial analytical instrument vendors—it's used for calibrating mass spectroscopes—four went to university labs, one went to Porton Down"—the army chemical warfare research center—"three went to chemical wholesalers, one to a semiconductor factory, and the last one . . ."

"Will." I smile at him, not entirely nicely. "Don't leave me in suspense."

He licks his lips. "They ordered a five-gram analytical reagent grade ampoule, like the ones for calibrating HPLC-MS installations. Delivery addressed to a box number in the Ziggurat."

"Oh fuck," I say, then lean back, finally at a loss for words.

The Ziggurat at Vauxhall Cross is an office building that opened in 1994, on the site of the old Pleasure Gardens on the south bank of the Thames, next to Vauxhall Bridge. It is currently the headquarters of SIS, the Secret Intelligence Service, also known as MI6, one of our sister agencies.

"Carry on tracing everything you can find about those import shipments," I say, "but I want everything you've got on the SIS shipment on my desk ASAP. Hardcopy only." I stand up. "Then you should forget about it."

I head for my office, not quite at a run, to set up an urgent meeting with Mo so we can figure out what the fuck to do next.

Because I suspect the call is coming from inside the house.

Mo is still rattled from having been introduced to the Queen in the worst possible way—"I'm sorry, ma'am, but you have less than six months to live" is *not* the way to make a good first impression—so she barely registers what's happening until she's alone with Professor Phibes. (His creepy nurse is evidently needed elsewhere, judging by her whispered aside in Phibes's ear. A pat on the shoulder, a hooded glance: Mo wonders whether their relationship is entirely professional.) His behavior toward Mo today is different. Almost solicitous?

"Please, have a seat, my dear Doctor." He gestures at a pair of armchairs beside an ornamental side table, rather than the visitor's chair in front of his desk. His voice is as scratchy and damaged as ever, but lacking the chilly emotionless tone. "We have much to discuss and we are perilously short of time if it is all to be accomplished before the conjunction."

Conjunction? Mo can produce a poker face on demand so

she nods politely and tucks her feet under her chair as she leans forward. "Yes, indeed. What exactly are you proposing to do to the patient?"

Phibes's eyelids droop. "There is currently no cure for Minamata disease—severe organomercury poisoning. Even with aggressive chelation, the patient is likely to experience dementia-like symptoms and will be brain dead before the year is up. But by use of a medical process I have already trialed extensively I believe it will be possible to pause the process of deterioration. Normally this would be my recommendation—who knows? A better treatment might be developed in future—but of course there are complications."

Mo leans forward. *I can see several*, she thinks. "What kind of complications?"

"Come now, Doctor." Phibes's face twists in a lopsided smile, the scars on one cheek pulling it askew. "As a practitioner you must have a better idea of how problematic it would be to isolate the anchor of so many sorcerous bindings than I. All *I* know about is music, medicine, murder, and suspended animation."

"I have some ideas, yes." Mo keeps her face still. "But I still want to know what *you* can foresee."

Is it her imagination or is Phibes looking slightly shifty? "Necromantic impairment is not my field of expertise, my dear Doctor, I deal purely in matters of a medical nature. However, I am led to understand that sufficient accumulations of belief can be tapped for, ahum, magical power. And there are few such accumulations as potent as the Queen. Why, his Dark Majesty says—" He jolts upright and abruptly stops talking, eyes twitching.

This is not Mo's first rodeo and she knows a *geas*—a magical compulsion—when she sees one.

"On my authority as an Auditor, I compel you to speak," Mo intones. "Who has bound you?"

Phibes shudders, but remains silent. Which tells its own story: "I release you!" Mo snaps urgently as a wisp of smoke curls from under his collar. Phibes slumps. Mo opens the door and looks outside. Nurse Vulnavia is waiting, entirely inscrutable. "Come quickly, Professor Phibes is having some sort of episode," she says.

Thirty seconds later Phibes is lying askew on the chaise, collar popped and tie loosened, while Vulnavia hovers over him chafing his wrist (or so it seems: Phibes wears disturbingly flesh-toned leather gloves). Vulnavia turns and gives Mo a murderous glare. "No more questions," she snaps. "The Professor is indisposed."

Mo acknowledges her with a short nod. "Please let me know how he gets on. I'll be back tomorrow." If looks were daggers Mo would be a pin cushion; she picks up her handbag and leaves, heading for the security office.

Mo is not only an Auditor, one of the commission with oversight authority over everyone else in the Laundry—the authority to audit their souls, not just their accounts—she's on track to be the next Senior Auditor, the person who monitors the executives of Mahogany Row. Her power should in principle compel everyone who has sworn an oath to the Crown, not just officers bound by the Laundry's own Oath of Office. She can think of very few people who have the authority to block her: Dr. Armstrong himself, the reigning monarch, the Black Pharaoh, and agents of certain foreign governments. Phibes is clearly not any of these, and his inability to answer when she questioned him is highly suggestive. As is his reference to the Black Pharaoh.

So it's the Prime Minister, Mo concludes dismally. and closes her note file. One does not write His name in a classified document unless one wishes to attract His attention. *FML*. She normally leaves the strong language to Bob, but this circumstance seems to justify it.

The modern offices occupied by Mahogany Row, just off Whitehall, are a short hop across the Thames from the Tudor grandeur of Lambeth Palace. But because the Reverend Peter Russell has lately developed an allergy to sunlight, getting him to his 5 p.m. appointment is problematic.

In the end it takes Janice, an unmarked transhuman prisoner transport, and a furtive arrival through a kitchen backdoor to get Pete into the Palace. Because of the formal nature of the meeting Pete has reluctantly donned a dark suit and dog collar. (With some trepidation he added a small cross to his lapel. It doesn't burn his fingers when he touches it, which somehow leaves him feeling worse.)

Lambeth Palace is the residence of the Archbishop of Canterbury, senior bishop of the Church of England and leader of the worldwide Anglican Communion. It's also a national treasure, several centuries older than Buckingham Palace, and contains the Church of England's archives along with the largest library of religious texts outside the Vatican. Tucked away in one corner is a suite of rooms for the Archbishop and his family. A discreet usher guides Pete to a reception room, where he is invited to take a seat.

When the Archbishop finally arrives, he approaches Pete with a smile, hand extended. "Doctor Russell, I presume. I'm very pleased to meet you at last, although not under the current circumstances." Tall and skinny but slightly stooped, he has a receding hairline and wears rimless spectacles and a suit with clerical collar. He could pass for a headteacher at a particularly exclusive private school, or perhaps a retired oil company executive—the latter being exactly what he was at one time, before he discovered his calling.

Pete stands and shakes his hand. "Likewise," he murmurs, taking a deep breath: "Can I ask why you think I'm here?"

"Well, you requested a meeting . . ." The Archbishop's cheek twitches: he has a very dry sense of humor. "Please take a seat." It's an order, politely phrased. Pete sits. "The dean's office received a memorandum about your affliction last month and it's currently under scrutiny. I gather it was involuntary?"

"Yes, absolutely." Pete nods. "It's a nasty blood-borne disease and I was deliberately infected by very unfriendly people, but to the best of my knowledge I've never died or risen from the grave. You understand I have a part-consulting role with the Security Services, so I'm not at liberty to say how it happened: what I *can* say is that while most of the mythology surrounding my condition is just that, there's a dismaying core of truth."

"Hmm." The Archbishop's gaze strips him to the bone. "Yes, so I can see—we're on consecrated ground, your lapel pin, hmm again. I take it you still have a heartbeat, too." He relaxes slightly. "How do you take your tea?"

"Milk first, no sugar." The door opens again as the usher returns, pushing a tea-trolley. They sit in silence while cups are filled, then the usher withdraws. "Thank you," says Pete, raising his cup and blowing on it.

"Don't thank me yet," says the Archbishop. "It's a diabolical trap you've been pushed into, isn't it?"

Pete nods and sips his tea as he considers his reply. "I feel as if I truly understand damnation now," he says slowly. "I'm not sure I did before, but . . . damned if I do, damned if I don't, you know?" (He's referring to suicide.) "There's no way out, and I'm not comfortable with any kind of utilitarian moral calculus."

The Archbishop stares at his mouth. "So why are you here?"

"On behalf of the Agency." Pete takes another sip of tea. "This is in strictest confidence, but I'm to tell you to expect a call from the Palace in the next few days."

"The—" The Archbishop sits up. "I think you'd better explain."

"Her Majesty is unwell. The details are confidential, but I can tell you now that she's not expected to recover. Normally we could expect a funeral within six to twelve months, but these are not normal times and there are national security implications. So—I'd like to emphasize that I had no involvement in this at any stage—the government intends to use a new and highly experimental technique to place Her Majesty in suspended animation and declare a Regency while researchers attempt to develop a cure."

The Archbishop's teacup rattles on the saucer he holds. Finally he shakes his head. "Good grief."

"That's not the worst of it." Pete continues to speak, rapidly and softly, leaning forward to confide: "There are magical complications that concern the government. Simple suspended animation will not suffice to protect the realm. There are oaths and sacred obligations that must be maintained or transferred to the Prince Regent. Accordingly, I expect Downing Street will ask you to officiate at a ceremony in Westminster Abbey, where prayers will be said for Her Majesty before she is placed in a sorcerously induced coma in a life-support capsule before the altar."

"A sorcerously induced—" The Archbishop finally blinks. "Have you turned her already?" he asks.

"What? No!" Pete is halfway out of his chair before he stops himself. "Absolutely not!" The accusation is shocking, but—on reflection—should have come as no surprise. "I would never." He swallows, gripping the arms of his chair so hard that the wood creaks. "Doing that to anyone, for any reason, would be abhorrent."

"I . . . see." The Archbishop steeples his fingers and nods, very slightly. "What if it becomes necessary, in a higher cause?" he asks.

"I . . ." Pete hesitates. "I wouldn't make that decision," he finally says. "I'd consider doing it if I was ordered to, by a higher authority, who could justify themselves . . . but it's not my call to make."

The Archbishop nods again. "Finish your tea," he says, an oddly flat note in his voice. Pete obeys instinctively, draining his cup and setting it down with a clatter. The Archbishop regards Pete thoughtfully. "The Denizen of Number Ten did that to *you*. He isn't making this easy for those of us who don't want to believe in evil incarnate, is He?"

Pete shudders. "Why would He?" For a moment, he looks haggard. "You've met the f-fellow, I take it."

The Archbishop leans forward confidingly: "While we've been introduced I'm not exactly a confidant of His. Would you care to share your impressions with me?"

"I've more than met Him: He's the reason I'm able to discuss the problem of evil from the inside, rather than being a mindless cannibalistic horror. To cut to the chase: I can't say that He's the God He claims to be, but neither can I say that He isn't. He's definitely an ancient and powerful entity, terrifyingly astute, cruel and malicious, and abominably self-aware. If He told me He was Satan Himself I'd have no trouble believing Him. But so far, His evil is restrained by circumstance—because He rules as a human tyrant, His rule is no worse than a human dictatorship. There are far worse beings out there. I've met a—*thing*—in Washington, D.C., in a secret bunker under the Pentagon. There is a labyrinth around a throne, and on the throne—I'm sorry, I shouldn't have shared this with you. Either you won't believe me or it'll upset you and I'm sorry."

Pete slumps, chest heaving. "Please forgive me." He pauses. "The PM is *definitely* no friend of the Church, but in my opinion He's unlikely to attack us directly. The Queen"—Pete's pupils dilate as realization hits him—"must be part of the reason."

The Archbishop nods slowly. "On another note, then, what is the purpose of the ceremony in the Abbey?"

"I'm not entirely clear," Pete admits. "But the power of faith is undeniable, and a lot of people have faith in the person of the monarch—not just the Crown, but the head that wears it. Apparently it has actual tangible magical power and my—the agency I consult with are extremely concerned about what happens the instant Her Majesty dies. The *mana* she controls as wearer of the crown and head of the Church must be holding Him in check."

"God save the Queen," intones the Archbishop.

After a momentary double take Pete echoes him, then continues: "She's very nearly the longest reigning British monarch ever—only a few months to go to beat Queen Victoria. And she rules more people than almost any of her predecessors. This makes her a ticking magical time bomb and they expect all hell to break loose when she dies. I'm not speaking metaphorically here."

The Archbishop looks increasingly unhappy. He finally nods, then stands up. "Go and find out exactly what's going on," he tells Pete. "I need to know what's truly happening here first, and you're my ears on the inside. We mustn't allow an abomination to seize control of the head of the Church: I need to know if there are any better options! May God be with you." He raises his hand in blessing and Pete bows his head as he rises.

"And the question of my damnation?"

"As you said, most of the folklore about vampires is nonsense. You drank your cuppa, didn't you?" The Archbishop gestures at the empty cup. "It was brewed with consecrated water: I had to be sure. Anyway, I think you'll be fine as long as you do the right thing when the time comes, my son. Keep me posted on developments. I'll be in touch."

A COFFIN BUILT FOR TWO

Dear Reader, do you have any bloody idea how big Buckingham Palace is?

Look, just the site itself, containing the gardens, a helicopter pad, a tennis court, and a lake, is about the size of a farm. (Okay, a small farm—only 17 hectares. Even so, 17 hectares in central London!)

The main palace building has—let me just steal this straight from Wikipedia—775 rooms, including 188 staff bedrooms, 92 offices, 78 bathrooms, 52 principal bedrooms, and 19 state rooms. Stacked up vertically they'd fill a third of the Empire State Building.

But that's not all: that's just the stuff they talk about in public. Needless to say almost all the maps and architectural drawings are out-of-date, bizarrely misleading, hilariously wrong, or feature large blank spots labeled CLASSIFIED. There are electricity substations, at least two of them for such a large site. There are two or more levels of cellars beneath the Palace, with functions including the royal wine cellar, cold storage for the kitchens, coal cellars, a laundry with dry cleaning facilities, a 1930s bomb shelter with bunks for a hundred personnel with a filtered air supply in case of gas attack from zeppelins, an indoor bowling alley they installed just to make JFK feel at home when he visited in 1961, a cinema complete with Wurlitzer and bandstand, and an evacuation tunnel leading to a spur of the Piccadilly Line that was intended for evacuating the King in event of a French invasion. (Because the Palace doesn't trust the entente cordiale to last.)

Anyway, this week it's time for me to haul a field thaumograph all over the site, logging every anomaly and making sure that nothing distorts the *mana* flow on D-day. At first it's just me, but on day three I rope in Janice to tackle the subbasement areas and join me in working above ground after dark. I invited Mo to join the party but she just snarled, *Go play in Phibes's crypt*. I think she's a little stressed.

On day three it's raining so I'm working indoors. Because the public areas of the Palace are off-limits due to tourists, I decide to start right at the top and work my way down, which is why early afternoon finds me in the attic with a footman.

"What 'zackly are we looking for, boss?" asks the footman, a former infantry soldier trapped in a crimson mess dress tailcoat with red braid and white tie, because in this looking-glass world the twentieth century hasn't started yet. (I swear the Palace is so far behind the times that the rats wear knee-breeches and horse-hair wigs.)

I heft my thaumograph. "I'm taking readings," I tell him. "And logging the whole site."

"Which site? The west wing roof spaces?"

"No, the entire palace. What's over there?" I point at an unpromising-looking corner.

We're in the loft of a two-hundred-year-old palace. There are floorboards to walk on—nobody wants to put a boot through the ceiling above a royal bedroom—and at some time in the past few decades someone has suspended fiberglass insulating panels between the overhead joists. But the lights are flickering fluorescent tubes, the floor is covered in a thin scum of dirt, and it's cold. Piles of furniture lurk beneath dust sheets.

"Looks like"—my escort flips dog-eared pages on a clipboard—"says 'ere it's dry storage for"—he frowns—"chamber pots?"

I head for the corner and find a dusty cabinet which, on

examination, is indeed full of thunder mugs. Thankfully they were cleaned before they were put away, and none of them are thaumically active. I take some photographs of the corner, make some notes on what I found, enter the thaumograph reading, and we move on.

The attic space is enormous and drafty—there are no doors up here, just low openings between loft areas and the occasional trapdoor for getting stuff in and out—so I manage to move through it comparatively fast until we reach the southeast end, which is somewhat warmer than the rest of the attic. At which point two things happen. First, the thaumograph starts to click, then buzz, then whine and smoke. I switch it off hastily. (*Oops.*) And secondly—

"What's that doing here?" I ask, raising my voice over the din as I approach a blatant intrusion from the data center dimension. It's a windowless enclosure that someone appears to have boxed in below the ceiling, with a bunch of air conditioning packs roaring away on top.

"Uh, dunno, boss. It's a wall?"

I stifle a sigh. *Minions: they don't make 'em like they used to.* "There must be a . . ." I walk along the edge for a bit: it spans nearly the entire width of the attic, but there's a corner close to the eaves with a flush-fitting door and a security keypad. "Okay, I need you to get me in here. Right now." If it wasn't for the thaumograph going apeshit I'd guess it was the royal cannabis farm.

"How do you want me to do that?" asks number one minion, shrugging his gilt-edged shoulder tabs.

"Any way you like—" I begin, just in time to be brought up short by the footman's inner squaddie asserting himself. "No, wait!"

But I'm too late and his rugby quarter-back shoulder has already made hard contact with the plywood enemy, which crunches open expensively. I wince, and pray that whatever I've discovered has no good reason for being here.

"I thought you wanted it opening?" His expression is simultaneously confused and smug.

"Yeah: not like that."

Inside, I find myself facing a rack of steel shelving units that run from the floor to just below the ceiling. It's about ten meters wide and every square centimeter of shelf space is covered in open PC cases with beefy power supplies and backplanes full of extremely fat expansion cards. Above the racks, fat cables and fatter ventilation ducts descend from the ceiling. It's as hot as a tropical greenhouse—or the aforementioned indoor cannabis farm—and noisy as hell from all the cooling fans.

I toggle the thaumograph on again and hastily twist the attenuator dial. The field wobbles between thirty and forty megaParsons,[1] which is deeply disturbing because a normal background is something like two to three milliParsons—and as I move the thaumograph closer to the rack it starts to whine. So I switch it off again, pull out my penlight, and take a quick look.

There are five fat black cartridge-like cards in each PC backplane, with red go-faster stripes and a fan fighting to keep the silicon from melting. They're Radeon R9 295X2s, high-end GPU cards with six billion transistors a pop, each crunching 700 GFLOPS of floating point numbers per second. So that's about three TFLOPS in this cage alone. Those cards only came out around the end of last year: I take stock and realize I'm looking at two-thirds of a million quid's worth of GPUs drawing almost a hundred kilowatts, which would explain why I'm sweating in an unheated attic on a chilly spring afternoon. The cables are bundled professionally and I see a mains power distribution board with circuit breakers and also a salami-thick cable snaking away toward a hole in the floor.

I could mistake it for a Bitcoin farm if it wasn't for the thaum flux. But that's not what's going on here. Also, this was not done

---

1. A unit of thaum flux named after Jack Parsons, American rocket scientist and noted Thelemite.

on a pocket-money budget, especially the wiring—it's got to be consuming a good chunk of the Palace's electricity draw. I take a deep breath, then catch my minion's eye. "See these boxes?" I point at a server: "I want you to count them. Exact numbers, no guessing, I need a backup before I go find someone in Building Services to tell me who the hell authorized this."

Really, in this day and age stumbling across a homebrew peta-FLOPS supercomputer in the attic is not particularly unusual. There are village cryptocurrency exchanges in China with bijou hydroelectric power stations left over from the Great Leap Forward with more demon-summoning power.

This farm sucks maybe half a megawatt of juice: it's tiny to the point of uselessness, and it'll be obsolete within a year or two anyway—GPUs for sorcery are old school, the new hotness is using custom ASICs to compute the shortest (meaning fastest) Dho-Nha curve.

But I do not linger. Nor do I pull out a fistful of gadgets and go spelunking for an access port so I can Wireshark the hell out of the traffic on the farm's backbone. If I start, appealing as it might be, I'll probably still be scratching my head when they wheel Brenda down the aisle to hook her up to the undead support system they're building for her in Westminster Abbey. Instead I head straight to the security office.

"Got a problem," I tell the bored inspector on duty: "There's an unaccounted server farm in the attic that isn't on the surveyors' drawings and it's sucking a lot of juice. I thought it was a whacky baccy plantation at first, so I got Fred Flintstone here—"

"Hey!"

"—to break down the door. You'll be wanting to secure it ASAP, then find out who authorized it, and why. Do *not*, whatever you do, shut off power to the computers—they're magic crunchers and if you perform a hard shutdown you could release something very nasty indeed. As soon as you find out who put it there I want to know so I can brief my agency head."

And that's basically it until I head back to Mahogany Row, except for a lot of yelling because apparently you are not supposed to open suspicious doors in the Queen's attic without obtaining the services of the Master of the Royal Key Ring or whatever.

Little do I suspect the scale of the hornets' nest I've just whacked with a baseball bat . . .

The next day, while Bob is poking around the Palace in a wild goose hunt for incriminating demonological detritus,[2] Mo intends to return to the medical suite in search of the mad professor.

Phibes clearly knows things about the occult that he can't talk about, and his caginess about his plans for the Queen's suspension is worrying. Mo is worried: Who is Phibes *really* working for?

Her first port of call is not the Palace: it's across the Thames, buried beneath the toxic landfill site that used to be known as Dansey House, the Laundry's postwar headquarters.

A moldering pile of Victorian brickwork that had unfortunately survived the Blitz, Dansey House suffered from groaning radiators, leaky rooftops, and black mold around the window frames. It finally closed for reconstruction over a decade ago: then it was discovered that the laboratories were dangerously contaminated. Crown Immunity meant that fifty years of badly conceived summonings, crude wards, horripilating hauntings, and eldritch emanations had leaked, and the foundations had lost their grip on reality.

The worst of it from Mo's point of view is that the archi-

---

2. This being the UK, a snipe hunt would most likely result in Bob collecting a cage of pissed-off birds.

val stacks in the second-level subbasement are still active—the paper archives were too bulky and sensitive to relocate. The records cover the entire history of the Laundry and its predecessors, all the way to the days of Doctor John Dee and Sir Francis Walsingham, but they mostly haven't been digitized—some of the texts in the stacks give a new and unwelcome meaning to the term data corruption—and now the main building is off-limits. So to check the archives Mo has to visit a former Post Office building, descend to the basement, don full personal protective gear including a noddy suit, respirator, and heavy duty wards, then ride a tiny Mail Rail train along a claustrophobic narrow-bore tube tunnel to the archive lobby area.

Whereupon she is grudgingly admitted to a tiny reading room, where she sits on her own for half an hour while they fetch the files she has requested, and is then scrutinized suspiciously while she reads them.

As she suspected, the Laundry has a history with Anton Phibes, PhD. It's not a happy history, and it goes back a long way. Phibes became a Person of Interest to the Invisible College in 1925, when he evaded Dr. Angleton and Scotland Yard's Finest and deftly executed a fiendish murder spree with an occult angle. At least, it was deft right up until the end, when the final victim survived and Phibes's silent assistant didn't. (She was later identified by Scotland Yard, from her dental records, as Vulnavia Mrożek, a Polish aristocrat's daughter who had fallen under Phibes's spell while he was teaching music in Heidelberg).

Phibes reappeared four years later, along with his very dead but miraculously preserved wife, in the company of a woman inexplicably identified as Vulnavia Mrożek . . . with fingerprints and the likeness of the "Vulnavia" who had previously been dissolved in piranha solution in the basement of Phibes's mansion on Maldene Square. Whereupon the good doctor led Inspector Trout of the Yard on a merry dance all the way to the Valley of the Kings in Egypt, into the long-lost temple of a sleeping god who would arise when a very specific stellar conjunction came around—

"Oh hell no," Mo mutters when she sees a photograph of a pyramid doorway where a triumphant archaeologist poses for the camera: "Trust *Him* to be mixed up in this."

She rapidly skims the rest of the dossier. Phibes's murder spree was motivated by the death of his wife on the operating table, at the hands of a professor of surgery and his students . . . or rather, by her ritual sacrifice by a lodge of Mute Poet cultists disguised as surgeons. Phibes, it seems, was himself an occultist of some standing—there is a reference to his now-lost doctoral thesis on the numerological symbolism of the music of Azathoth. More unusually, he'd stolen his wife's remains and somehow preserved them, then gone to Egypt in search of the gate to the River of Life that opened when the stars were right in the temple of N'yar Lat-Hotep . . .

Mo makes a list of unanswered questions:

- Vulnavia: If she died in 1921, then why was she sighted with Phibes in 1925? And why are they both apparently physically unchanged today, in 2015?
- Phibes: Servant of the Black Pharaoh, or something more sinister? How did he get appointed to the office of the royal physician?
- Victoria Phibes: Dead or alive? If preserved, then how? Is this the technique Phibes intends to apply to the Queen?
- And what is the statute of limitations for serial killers in England, anyway? (Phibes has murdered at least eleven people, and Mo finds the lack of closure upsetting.)

She flips to the next dossier.

Phibes disappeared in Egypt, but came to the attention of the Invisible College again, in Berlin in 1932, when he crossed the path of the thoroughly nefarious Dr. Mabuse. It is unclear who double-crossed who, but one thing is certain: Phibes and Mabuse are not besties.

In 1936, Phibes was sighted in Munich, in the company of a

raven-haired woman identified only as Countess Mrożek. They made at least one visit to Dachau to meet with Sturmhauptführer Zahn, instrument-maker to the SS. They vanished afterward, one jump ahead of a Gestapo arrest warrant for crimes against the Reich.

Countess Mrożek popped up again in 1943 when SOE assigned her the codename RAVEN. She initially trained for infiltration into occupied Europe, but was reassigned to Q-Division, External Assets, then shipped out to Mesopotamia. The rest of her file is missing from the archives.

(There are no files on Phibes after the 1936 Munich incident.)

Mo exits the stacks in a foul mood and makes her way back to HQ, where she writes up her recollection of the Phibes/Mrożek dossiers, then emails it to Gerry Lockhart and the team leads on FAIREST.

It seems clear that there is a deep game in play here, but how deep is unclear. The PM is clearly meddling, the rules of accountability the agency runs on are being broken, even the rules for involving External Assets are being bent. Gerry might be able to shed some light on what Vulnavia does (or did) for EA, and why neither she nor Phibes have aged a day since the 1920s. But for now Mo has hit a dead end, so as it's lunch time she heads to the dining room, looking for Bob.

When I get back to my office I find Willard waiting in the visitor's chair, feet up on the desk, playing with a Google-branded yo-yo that flashes LEDs whenever it hits the end of its string. He's looking unbearably smug and there's a stack of printouts neatly tagged with luminous Post-it notes within accidental kicking distance.

"Is this the DMM stuff?" I ask, plonking my ass behind the desk and trying to burn holes in the soles of his shoes by raw willpower.

Will, evidently feeling empowered by his success, nods. "Yup."

The yo-yo reaches the end of its tether and bounces again. Was I ever that irritating to my managers? *Impossible*. "Summarize," I command, and for a miracle his feet vanish from my worktop.

"I've followed up the other shipments, like you said. The university chemistry department orders are all real, so I got Julie"—our team administrative assistant—"to request a full audit of their DMM stock. It's all accounted for by legitimate research projects. I also asked the instrument vendors and they came back clean, too. One of them nearly had a heart attack over the phone at the suggestion some might be missing, and they'd only ordered a gram of it . . ."

"Okay, who else?" I nudge. "The chemical wholesalers?"

"Same story. I asked our CSO to get the Police to audit their poison registers in person, then watch the warehouse supervisor weighing their stock—that nearly caused a mass casualty incident in Southampton: an idiot cop tried to touch the sample under the fume hood—but it all checked out. Porton Down"— Will sucks in a deep breath between his teeth—"*they* came round here to audit *us*, I mean this time yesterday there was one of those white unmarked trucks with flashing blue lights parked out front."

I bare my teeth. "How *inconvenient*."

"Mrs. Carpenter just happened to be passing." Will cringes. "You could have warned me about her?"

I relax. "She sorted them out, I take it."

"Oh yes." Willard shudders. "Sent them away with a flea in their ear—and a Diplomatic Protection Group escort."

"Well, score one for the good guys," I say, not trying to mask my heavy irony. Again: *Are we the baddies?* I mean, we're part of the MOD, DSTL Porton Down is *also* part of the MOD— their chemical and biological weapons defense institute. "I suppose they have a plausible excuse for keeping dimethyl mercury on hand."

"Yup. So: the analytical labs all came back clean, I'm sure you saw that coming. But I haven't been able to make any headway with SIS. They're not MOD, they're part of the FO." The Foreign Office, in other words.

"Right." I nod. "So did you send them a memo?"

"Yes." He leans forward and riffles through the stack. "Right here. It went in yesterday afternoon, so it's probably working its way up."

"Well, then." I read his memo. It's succinct, but Willard didn't know the right incantations to light a fire under whoever reads it. "Huh, okay—I see what's missing, you needed to flag it TOP SECRET and add the keywords for *assassination*, *hostile government*, and *cabinet office*. Send me the Word doc and I'll resend it via Downing Street."

Will is looking at me with an odd expression, as if I've suddenly grown devil horns and a goatee and started laughing maniacally. "You can do that?" he asks disbelievingly.

I grin and crack my knuckles. "Watch me."

I'm in the directors' dining room, contemplating a spot of mayhem to liven up my afternoon, when Mo walks in. So I wave and of course she comes over and joins me and I realize she's stressed about something. My starter hasn't arrived, so I wave for the waiter and let Mo order before I say anything. "Bad morning?" I eventually ask.

"You could say that!" Her frustration is palpable. "I was in the stacks following up a hunch but didn't get anything but more questions. How about you?"

"Spent a morning in the Palace attic, then had a meeting with Will. And nothing makes sense," I complain.

My wife actually cracks a smile at that. (Misery loves company.) "Try me?"

"Okay, taking it in reverse order: Willard worked a minor miracle tracing the dimethyl mercury. One purchaser sticks out like a sore thumb—can you think of any reasonable explanation why MI6 of all people might order a bottle of the stuff?"

Mo sits up. "Oh dear," she says thoughtfully. "Have you gotten anywhere with them?"

I snort. "Will wrote them a letter. I kicked it up the chain, he didn't know we could use Iris to bypass obstructions. It might be a red herring, but—"

Mo is nodding along. "No, you're exactly right, it's a very fishy coincidence. I assume there was nobody else?"

"Not really, Will's still chasing up the chemical wholesalers but I don't expect him to find anything. The Home Office hazchem tracking system is utter shite, by the way, but fixing it is out of scope."

The waiter reappears with a trolley bearing two steaming bowls of what is hopefully not the polonium special; also a bottle of Zinfandel and a jug of water. Then he leaves before I continue: "And then there's what I found in the attic at Buck House."

"What you—" Mo raises an eyebrow. "Do go on: What was it? Princess Anne's cigarette card collection? George III's marbles?"

"A *mana* farm. Someone has racked up about sixty teraFLOPS of homebrew supercomputer. It nearly melted my thaumograph. So I'm waiting for building services and the cops to figure out who installed it before I start asking pointed questions. It's quite recent, by the way, the GPUs are less than six months old."

Mo eats in silence for a minute. I can tell the gears in her head are spinning furiously, and when that happens it's best to wait until she's finished thinking.

Finally she puts her spoon down. "Let me tell you about my morning," she says, then proceeds to make my head hurt.

"Wait," I say, "so you're telling me Nurse V is an external asset from the 1940s? And Phibes is a serial killer music prof who knows His Nibs from way back? And shows up as the Queen's new royal physician?"

Mo stabs her roast chicken savagely. "We don't *actually* know what he's been doing for the past eighty years, he might have a medical degree or two by now."

"At least he's not partial to cultists," I say consolingly. "I hate those fuckers."

"The thing I like least about it is the connection to Herr Zahn, the instrument-maker. Lecter wasn't the only horror he made. He wasn't even the first luthier to work with living bone."

I push my plate away, appetite entirely spoiled. "Want to go back to the Palace? I need to see if they got anywhere tracking down the server farm, and we both need to pay the doctor a visit."

Mo nods, then pulls out a makeup compact and fixes her lipstick. "Funny how Phibes and Mrożek turn up at the same time as your phantom thaum farm, isn't it? Obviously just a coincidence." She stands.

"Yes, clearly just a coincidence." I get the door. "Let's go."

I pick up the thaumograph, then we head for Buckingham Palace. The security office tells me there is no news yet on who put the mad gaming rig in the attic. So I follow Mo into the warren upstairs that houses the medical household.

"Is Professor Phibes in?" Mo asks the new receptionist.

He eyes her warily: "I really can't say, ma'am. Would you like to leave a mess—"

I'm about to pull my warrant card but Mo doesn't wait, she just *glares* at him. It's like she's flipped a switch, inverting the power of invisibility she picked up three years ago during the business at the Albert Hall. She's mesmerizing: "Tell me where Phibes is," she says icily. "That's an order." Some eldritch resonance freights her words as heavily as if she'd added, *by the power of Greyskull I compel you.*

"B-buh-buh"—he burbles for a few seconds before he spits out—"basement! They're in the basement, renov-ovating the old cinema—" He chokes as if she's digging skeletal fingers into his larynx.

For a moment I blink, lost, at the back of my wife's head, wondering when she turned into Darth Vader—*Are we the baddies?* seems to be a recurring theme—but when she turns on a heel the spell breaks. "Come along, Bob, let's not keep the Professor waiting!" I trail along behind her like a slightly bewildered rubber duck.

The Palace is a maze, and even with maps we get lost a couple of times and end up going in circles until a passing page helpfully points us at a shortcut to a staircase leading down to a basement corridor.

Like a hotel, there are two versions of the Palace: one for the residents and one for the servants. Buckingham Palace is recent enough to have corridors—they arrived in the UK in the eighteenth century—so the service side twists and wraps around the state rooms like a boa constrictor hugging its lunch to death. We pass a staff break room with 1950s fixtures, a mud room, storerooms full of furniture for garden parties, a room labeled PLANS AND RECORDS (to which some wag has added a sign saying BEWARE OF THE LEOPARD), a seemingly abandoned gym with missing tiles, an airlock leading to the international space station's observation cupola, then a spiral staircase down to the subbasement.

Where we emerge into a brightly lit office corridor that instantly gives me a strong sense of déjà vu, because it's an exact copy of the medical household upstairs.

"What the hell?" Mo stops and stares. "Bob, I could swear this was—"

"Yeah, me, too." I unzip the cover of my thaumograph and switch it on. "Weird, isn't it?" The thaumograph clicks, then buzzes steadily, like a somnolent summer bumble bee.

Mo pushes open a door bearing the title DOCTOR THOMP-

SON, where we find ourselves in an exact replica of Phibes's office, right down to the bookcase full of leatherbound compilations of *The British Medical Journal*. I wander over and try to pull one out but it won't move. After a few frustrating seconds I realize it's impaled on a wooden rod that passes through every book on its shelf, like the skulls at Marble Arch. Mo, meanwhile, is at the curtained window. "Over here," she calls me, raising one corner of the curtain.

"That's a—" The window is a glass lightbox bearing an image of the view from the windows upstairs. "Huh. When do you think that photo was taken?"

"Why—oh." Mo thinks for a bit. "The trees. It's summer, isn't it?"

I run my finger across the top of Phibes's desk, disturbing a thin layer of dust. "Looks like they don't clean down here often enough." There's a washbasin in the corner of the room and I try to wash my hands, but the tap doesn't budge. Then I notice the sink is as dusty as the desk. "Is there something wrong with the plumbing down here?"

"Let's find out." Mo opens the connecting door to the examining room, where there's a hospital bed and another sink along with various other fixtures. "Try this one?"

I walk over to the sink and this time the tap works. It's one of those long-arm medical ones designed so you can use your elbow instead of contaminating your surgical gloves. But there's no water, even when I try the other tap. I grab the handle of the undersink cupboard and pull, intending to see if there's any plumbing down there, and the handle comes off in my hand. The cupboard, it seems, is not a cupboard. "Help me here, do *any* of those drawers open?"

Mo rattles a handle. "Apparently not. This is like an IKEA showroom set, isn't it?"

"Yes, but at IKEA they're trying to sell you furniture so they show you an entire range: I don't see the Palace buying a duplicate medical suite that doesn't work . . ."

Mo sniffs irritably: must be all the dust. "This is a distraction! I need to talk to Phibes, you've got readings to take. Follow me." She marches back down the corridor.

"It may be a distraction but it reminds me of something. I just can't quite put my finger on it." Meanwhile the thaumograph's buzzing drops back to a lazy intermittent click. It's a stage set, a version of the Palace medical household facilities above ground—but what purpose does it serve?

"The cinema," Mo says. "That's where reception said Phibes and Vulnavia were. You can ask them what this is."

The next door we try leads to a replica of the security office out front, right down to the gun safe in the back room. There's a bathroom but no actual toilets: not even pipes and waste outlets. Meanwhile Mo hurries onward so briskly that I nearly miss a crackle of activity from the thaumograph.

"Wait up!"

I step back as Mo pauses and looks at me, then take another step back, and—"Fuck me." I hastily twist the sensitivity selector.

"What have you got?"

"Thaum flux," I say grimly. "Very high, very localized."

"Right." She turns in place, carefully scrutinizing the walls for incursions of a tentacular nature. (It's reflexive, she always does this. She has a history.) We're in a stretch of corridor between the fake security office and another pair of doors. "How localized?"

"Let me run this." I start to pace out the corridor. After ten meters there's a sharp kink to the left. The doors are mostly on the right, except for the supply closet, where the thaumograph goes from an intermittent steady clicking to a rising buzz, and then an angry wasp-whine. "Bingo." I pull the door open and turn on the light. From the outside all you can see is a wall of shelves covered in cleaning supplies and a mop and bucket off to one side. But once I'm inside I see that the shelves don't go all the way to the far wall: there's a gap wide enough to walk through, and it's entirely invisible from outside. "There's something in here."

"Okay, I'm right behind you."

I carefully zip up the thaumograph—you don't want to break one of those things, the paperwork is eye-watering—then open my inner eye and *look*, and hastily close it again. "Shit."

"You can say that again!"

Behind the rack of shelving there's a gap of about a meter before the unpainted wall, half filled with fat plastic ducts hanging from the ceiling. They terminate in junction boxes and a 19-inch rack with a bunch of fast ethernet switches sprouting so many patch cables it resembles a cyborg jellyfish. The cables from the bottommost shelf are bundled together in wrist-thick bunches with rat-tail ties, and dive into rough holes in the skirting board.

"I think I found what they used the ductwork for from the nonfunctional plumbing," I tell her.

"This is the other end of that thaum farm you found, isn't it?"

"Can't tell for sure until Facilities trace it, but that's the way to bet."

"Phibes," she swears. "What was it you said, at least he's not partial to cultists?" *I'm never going to hear the end of it now, am I?*

Then I hear something else, a distant rumbling chord echoing up from the holes in the back wall: the strains of organ music.

Speak of the devil . . .

We go back into the corridor and follow the faint sound of silent-era movie music until we come to a set of double doors. They open onto a darkened, carpeted vestibule with steps leading down to a performance space. It's decorated in a mix of styles: it seems to have started out as art nouveaux, but at some point it was redone with art deco paneling and tiles. A dance floor occupies the middle of the room, and at the back there's a stage with curtains and scenery lifts. Circular tables and seating for an audience line the walls around the dance floor. The orchestra pit is occupied by a small jazz ensemble who play rather woodenly—which is less surprising than it might be, for their heads are clearly made of papier-mâché. A Mighty Wurlitzer theater organ looms over everything, and chords swell and fade in waves as the organist plays.

A solitary dancer whirls across the sprung floor in a cloud of silk, before coming to a dead stop before us. It is Countess Mrożek. She steps forward, violin in one hand and fiddle in the other, her eyes blazing as the hooded impresario's right arm rises and falls toward the upper manual of the console, hammering out a final crashing chord. "What are you doing here?" she demands.

The jazz automata grind to a halt behind her, plunging us into an echoing cavernous silence.

"Just the person I was looking for." Mo's smile is icy. "If the Professor has recovered, I intend to continue our little chat from yesterday."

I clear my throat. "I have some questions, too. Starting with, is there a working bathroom down here?"

The cloaked organist rises from the bench, turns, and walks down the steps from the organ platform. Phibes pushes back his hood. My safety ward vibrates: he's wearing a powerful glamour, presumably to maintain his appearance. Underneath the cloak he wears formal court attire, white tie and tails, but it does little to hide his terrible burn scars. He pulls out a portable Bluetooth speaker and speaks through it: "Go out and turn left, the second door along is the gents," he says placidly. "Ladies are next door." He tilts his head toward Mo as he glides down the steps.

Mo crosses her arms. "Are you ready to talk now?"

"Without compulsion, yes, indeed." *Pause.* "But I was assigned this role by His Dark Majesty, and if you force me again you will gain only His ire."

Phibes stalks toward one of the tables while Vulnavia steps in front of Mo, blocking her. Only when the Professor is seated does she step back, her violin half-raised. *Why is she doing that, it's not one of the bone ensemble*, I think, then do a double take and open my inner eye again: *Oh.* No, Countess Mrożek's instrument is not Lecter disguised by a glamour (*and thank fuck for that*), but it has something of the infernal about it, something that warps the mind's eye and whispers horrid inveiglements in the observer's head. *Training wheels.* Which means Phibes's jazz-playing automata are also likely more than they appear—

And speak of the devil: a stiffly marching automaton, Frank Sidebottom in a tuxedo, approaches the table and presents a salver laden with four champagne flutes and a bottle of brut. "Join me in a toast," buzzes Phibes.

Mo takes the seat opposite Phibes, so I sit beside her. The Countess deposits her instrument on the now-empty tray and sits beside the Professor. The automaton jerks back toward its place among the jazz band, and its companions strike up a relaxed rendition of Moloko's "Indigo." *You're mixing with felons, man, pull out the stops*—Is the Professor trying to send us a message?

Mo catches my eye and nods imperceptibly, so I reach for the bottle, uncork it, and fill all four glasses—taking care to rearrange them as I do so.

Phibes takes a glass and raises it without demur. When we follow suit he proposes: "To Her Majesty the Queen, long may she reign." He chucks it back, at which point I take a sip.

"To Her Majesty," Mo and I echo. Vulnavia raises an ironic eyebrow, but nods. I suspect as the last survivor of a noble house older than Saxe-Coburg and Gotha she has a different perspective on monarchy. If our files are accurate, then as a debutante she was presented before Tsar Nicholas the Second and his wife, the Empress Alexandra Feodorovna.

"What *is* this place?" Mo asks, slowly rolling the stem of her glass between her fingers.

"It's a cinema!" The Countess smirks. Behind her the automata play on. (Seen with my inner eye they glow dimly, a sign of bound eaters programmed to repeat the same motions indefinitely.)

"Built for His Majesty King George the Fourth during the First World War," Phibes crackles. "Abandoned for decades when this basement was walled off in 1939. A shame: there are few surviving Hope-Jones Unit Orchestras in existence, and this example took . . . quite some . . . restoration"—bzzt—"as much a creature of its time as am I myself."

"You would know, of course," Mo prompts. I wouldn't—I haven't got a clue what a Hope-Jones Unit is when it's at home—but from the direction of her gaze I infer it's something to do with the insane-looking organ on the stage. (I have visited the flight deck of a Concorde, and this thing looks just as complicated.) "How much work did it take to get it playing again?"

"It was in good condition when it was abandoned, but the leatherwork and all the rubber gaskets had perished and some of the solenoids needed replacing—" And Phibes is off to the races, or perhaps back to his salad days as a music professor with a captive audience.

I zone out while keeping all three eyes on the jazz band, who have moved on from Moloko to Jamiroquai—the exchange of compulsions between the players is fascinating, they're cueing up one another like samples on a music sequencer—and then I notice that the organ is playing, too, just low-key background where a live band would have a keyboardist, and—*Is the mighty Wurlitzer haunted?*—I add it to my list of things to check out. "Just going to the bathroom," I mumble as I stand up.

Phibes is clearly geeking out, Mo is happy to talk instrument restoration and music theory all day, and Vulnavia is nodding along, occasionally chipping in with some pointed detail about the local rodent population's taste for gutta-percha. I don't think they'll try to murder each other for a while, so this is as good a time for a toilet break as any.

I step out of the cinema lobby and turn left into the bland basement service corridor. Which door was it, first or second? *Second*, I think: and yes, there's a discreet GENTS sign on it. I step inside and am instantly hit by the slightly damp, chilly air of a public toilet. It's a period piece: encaustic tiles on the floor, a row of washbasins with separate hot and cold taps, and the urinals are splendid late Victorian floor-standers, shoulder-high and designed to wrap around you lest your neighbor accidentally catch a glimpse of your pee-pee. I check that the plumbing works (it does), wash my hands, and am on my way back to the cinema before I remember the unmarked door between the gents and the musicology lecture in progress.

As my hand approaches the handle my ward stings me sharply. I stop and glare at it. Yup, the doorknob's possessed. But it's not very strong: all I need do is open my imaginary maw and growl at it and the emanation of soul-stealing terror wets itself and flees back to whatever universe it was summoned from. At which point I open the door and peer inside, then hastily grab my thaumograph.

It's a long, narrow room, and the front seems to be occupied by a plumber's nest of pipes and ducts. I realize it's probably part of the organ next door—as I turn the lights on and step further inside, I recognize a long cabinet with a rank of metal organ pipes protruding from the top. There's a table with pipes and workshop tools lying on it, and a rack of dismounted pipes against the other wall. Beyond that, there seems to be something that doesn't look like disemboweled organ gizzards. So I walk deeper inside.

It's a low cabinet about the size of a grand piano's body, but rectangular rather than harp-shaped and sitting directly on the floor instead of standing on legs. Like a grand piano it has a lid, hinged at one end. It's currently raised and propped open with a rod, much like a car's bonnet awaiting an engine inspection.

As I look closer, details come into focus. The lid is a frame around a plate glass window, which is polished until it gleams. The box is lined with white satin, padded like the interior of a coffin. There are two thin pillows at the open end and now I realize that it *is* a coffin—one sized for two bodies. The thaumograph buzzes continuously as I approach and, sure enough, there's a containment grid etched on the floor around the box. I walk round to look at the far end and see half a dozen glass bottles in a rack bolted to the far end of the coffin, with tubes and hoses leading into it. There's one final telling detail: a bunch of cables snake across the floor from the back corner of the room, plugged into a portable equipment box with flying leads coupled up to the grid. Paydirt—or rather, gravedirt. This is the last stop on the line to the *mana* farm in the attic, isn't it?

The Phibes process—the technique FAIREST centers on, our Hail Mary pass at putting the Queen into suspended animation—had to come from somewhere, didn't it? Phibes and the Countess go back almost a century, if what Mo found in the stacks is accurate. Suspended animation could explain the lengthy gaps in the Phibes files. And this weird coffin-built-for-two with a direct line to the *mana* farm upstairs might be a prototype . . . or it could be Phibes's very own one-way time machine.

Of course there are still gaps in my theory. Phibes was obsessed with his murdered wife Victoria, wasn't he? And he went to Egypt where the Black Pharaoh agreed to do something for Phibes involving the River of Life, or vice versa . . . *or something?* There's too much I don't know yet, too many details missing from the files. Vulnavia's clearly not just a minion, and that violin she was carrying—I've met Lecter. Vulnavia's instrument isn't in the same league, but it *does* have some scary necromantic mojo.

"For fuck's sake, why can't anything be simple, just for once?" I complain at the empty coffin. Then I head for the door, and thence to the cinema, where I find Mo nodding along as Dr. Phibes's Clockwork Wizards play "Sgt. Pepper's."

I eventually drag Mo away from her new friends (or, more accurately, frenemies: my wife is not naive enough to mistake a bonding experience over 1920s musical instruments and sparkling white wine for anything deeper) and we revisit the security office, where they have made no progress in tracking down the work order for the server farm. Then I suggest we head home early, and to my non-surprise, Mo agrees.

We reach our front door around 3 p.m., Mo fires up the coffee maker and kicks off her palace-approved heels, and then it's post-mortem time.

"You spent upward of fourteen minutes visiting the bathroom," she opens. "What did you find?"

"Nothing good." I fill her in on the glass coffin with the embalming works.

"Wait. Only *two* pillows?" Her gaze sharpens.

"Yes, I have questions."

"Victoria Phibes was murdered by the cult of the Mute Poet—a ritual sacrifice. And Phibes has a Black Pharaoh connection. Who *was* Victoria Phibes, marriage aside?"

"We're going to have to find—" I snap my fingers. "I know. Going to make a call."

I grab my phone and call Willard. "Will? It's Bob. I've got a request for you, in your spare time—a census records search? I'm looking for a woman, married name Victoria P-H-I-B-E-S. She was probably born no earlier than 1880, more likely in the late 1890s, and died in 1922. Buried in Highgate Cemetery. I need to know her maiden name and birth date, can you find them for me? What? You want a wheel? Yes, okay, I'll do that. You're a champ, thanks, bye."

"A wheel?" Mo raises an eyebrow.

"Vermintrude is bored with her Habitrail, bless her little ratty paws." I put the phone down. "Bribing rodents, how the mighty have fallen."

"I think we're going to discover that Victoria was a priestess of the Black Pharaoh," Mo says pensively. "Phibes is at least an initiate: a man of many parts, not all of them his own. But the Black Pharaoh likes to delegate to women. So Victoria was probably in charge. Men were carefully trained to ignore women—especially a century ago—and His Nibs is always happy to take advantage of human blind spots."

I shudder. "Gotcha. But if Victoria was one of His, Iris will know."

"Whether she's willing to tell *us* is another matter. Let's not show her our hand just yet." The coffee maker wheezes asthmatically and spits a couple of times as she fills two mugs. "So we've got Professor Phibes—an artificer as well as a music professor, serial killer, and surgeon—and we've got Victoria, possible High Priestess of the Black Pharaoh in London around the time of the Great War. Which leaves Vulnavia, Countess Mrożek."

"Who plays an oddly familiar instrument." I wait for Mo to put her coffee mug down: she doesn't spill too much of it. "Did you notice her violin?"

"It's not a Zahn piece," she says tensely. "I'd know." I reach across the table for her hand and wait her out. "I think it's a perfectly normal instrument that's been contaminated by proximity. Either stored in the same cabinet, or played by the same hand."

Well, fuck. I lick my lips, which are suddenly quite parched, and take a sip of too-hot coffee. "Do you think Lecter's found his way back?"

"Gods, I hope not." She shudders violently.

"What do you know about Vulnavia?" I ask, trying to change the subject to something less unnerving.

"Her file's thin, but it's there. She was with Phibes when he first became a person of interest, probably had a Black Pharaoh connection of her own—she was with Phibes when they popped up in Germany during the inter-war period. She did *not* play well with Nazis: rivals for the same occult niche, at a guess. She was recruited by External Assets, then went dark, and a bunch of pages from her file are missing. Obviously nothing suspicious about *that*."

"Right, there's *obviously* nothing suspicious about a violinist in External Assets whose file has been edited with a shredder: nothing to see here, these are not the droids you're looking for . . ."

"Enough, Bob. What does your galaxy brain tell you is going on here?"

"It doesn't tell me any—" I grab control of my runaway mouth before it can do any damage. "Wait up. Is she, in your estimate, someone who would have been a suitable custodian for Lecter, back in the day?"

Mo snorts by way of an answer.

"Right, didn't think so." I pause. "But how many other pale violins are there out there, anyway?"

Mo takes a mouthful of coffee. "Too many. Zahn made at least a dozen—Lecter was by far the most powerful, but the others were pretty deadly too, just less inclined to Renfield their soloist and go on a killing spree. And there were a bunch of test pieces that went into the crematorium at Auschwitz, or were otherwise missing at war's end."

"That piece the Countess was carrying, that she squirrelled away on the drinks tray while Phibes was trying to distract us—"

Mo smiles humorlessly. "So you spotted that, too."

"Could that be . . . ?"

"Maybe a test article? It was mostly wood but it had a sense of petrichor and open graves about it, if you know what I mean."

I shiver. "Yes."

Lecter—which Mo carried for years—is terrifying, and even the weak sauce prototypes are scary as fuck. They're necromantic-vampiric in nature, they can suck the *mana* right out of you. I've grappled with monsters, I've gotten closer than I'm happy to admit to a couple of things we call gods, and Lecter is damned close.

I lick my lips. "Look, there are gaps in the archives, but we've got other avenues, right? We know what we're supposed to be looking for, and now we've narrowed down the field of suspects—"

"Have we?"

"We have, at least enough to ask Derek and Forecasting Ops, right?" Mo nods, reluctantly. "We can ask very specific questions. Such as whether Victoria Phibes is alive again. Or if Vulnavia was behind the poisoning."

"What about Phibes himself?"

"He'll be a tough nut to crack. He animated an entire jazz band of automata, and he took out at least a dozen priests of the Mute Poet: he's a heavyweight. You failed to crack him with your auditor override. The Countess isn't exactly weak sauce, but she's our way in."

"Right, right." Mo is nodding along emphatically. Then her face falls slightly. "I need you to write me a memo setting out the business case. If we're going to blow our quarterly budget for Forecasting Ops, I need a paper trail."

The crystal ball gazers have limited bandwidth and asking too many specific questions can fuzz the future, twisting it away from whatever outcomes you're probing. So we have a notional budget, internally billed in Cassandras, an in-house cryptocurrency for unwelcome questions. (The blockchain is immutable and the questions and oracular answers are pinned to it, which makes it easy to debug temporal paradoxes.)

"I'll work on it." This is going to take at least half a bottle of wine to lubricate the brain-gears. "Three questions now, then reassess?"

"Yes, that's—"

"Mrrrp? Mew! Mrrrrmph!"

I glance at the clock on the wall. Sure enough, it's five minutes to feeding o'clock. Mo sighs. "Bob, would you do the honors?"

"Sure." I stand up. "C'mon, pest, time for din-dins!" The cat brushes past my ankles, tail erect and kinked at the tip, then follows me in advance to the kitchen. Because we humans may have many questions but like every other low-level eldritch horror, Spooky only has one: Where's my food?

There is a protocol for handling royal health announcements. It's about what you'd expect of an incredibly hidebound and crusty institution dating back nearly a thousand years; bearing in mind that when most people think of "a thousand years" they're actually imagining a single century, because we're terrible at dealing with lengths of time greater than a single human lifespan.

The Monarchy, unlike everyone else, really *does* have bits that go back a thousand years. And they're very sensitive to announcements that bear on the monarch's fate—it's less critical these days, but until the nineteenth century rumors of a royal illness could trigger rebellions—it was treason to consult a horoscope for the hour of the monarch's death.

These days we don't hang, draw, and quarter people for treason—His Nibs prefers a simple beheading—but the Palace still likes to keep a tight lid on rumors of Brenda's demise.

So the first thing that happens is His Dark Majesty delicately sounds out Brenda's feelings on the subject of her impending demise, and the FAIREST plan for deferring it. Then the PM chairs a special meeting of the Privy Council which drafts an Order for the Queen to sign, setting up the coming regency—something the UK hasn't seen since 1820. The Order is drafted by the Judicial Committee, a superset of the Supreme Court of the United Kingdom, without parliamentary oversight—

because temporarily replacing the head of state due to terminal illness is a low-key constitutional crisis and nobody wants to give the Awkward Squad an opportunity to demand a debate on the future of the monarchy.

The Order in question is the royal equivalent of a power of attorney, authorizing the regent—who as the next in the royal line of succession is Prince Jug-Ears—to discharge all the privileges and duties of the Crown until such time as he relinquishes the regency or his mum dies (at which point he's suddenly King Jug-Ears, God Save the King).

The actual transfer of power doesn't happen instantly. First the Queen has to sign the paperwork in front of witnesses, thereby arming the ticking constitutional time bomb. Then there will be a ceremony in Westminster Abbey where Her Majesty is installed in her necromantic suspended animation capsule. Then Prince Jug-Ears takes his seat and the Archbishop of Canterbury sticks a fancy hat on his bonce and sprays him with holy oil or whatever it takes to activate the mystical transfer of monarchy, in a ceremony full of the sort of romantic guff that appeals to flag-shaggers. It's an archaic throwback pantomime, full of government ministers in frocks and robes carrying six-hundred-year-old broadswords up the aisle, trumpets, horse-drawn state carriages, beefeaters, and the sort of weird pageantry the Victorians invented out of whole cloth then blamed on Henry VIII.

And all of this will happen in front of a television audience of about a billion people, because the royal family is the world's most popular TV reality show.

Between the issuing of the Order in Council and the Queen doing her Snow White show, a series of carefully timed public announcements will be issued by the Palace, a public holiday for contemplation and prayers for Her Majesty will be declared, the whole LONDON BRIDGE sequence will be triggered—as amended, because Operation FAIREST isn't precisely a royal funeral—and everyone in the Laundry will swear a new oath of allegiance to the Prince-Regent.

(And something horrifying will break through the crack between worlds that is momentarily open in Westminster Abbey. But I don't know that yet . . .)

EVE OF DESTRUCTION

Two weeks later, the news about the Queen's illness is released to the clueless public.

It's a carefully handled exercise in press management, and it's made clear to the newspaper owners and TV networks—and a couple of billionaire social media magnates—that complying with the exercise is not merely polite, it's a good way to ensure one doesn't die by accidentally falling out of a window in a police station subbasement. Ahem.

The first step in the carefully choreographed dance is for the Queen's upcoming public diary to be cleared. A bunch of stuff is shuffled off onto Prince Charles: the crown prince in turn dumps some of his appointments on the Sweatless One, and bottom-tier stuff like cutting the ribbon on a new Chicken Shack takeaway down the high street gets quietly dropped.

Once the appointments are rearranged, Her Majesty checks into the London Clinic—a very exclusive private hospital—for "a day of tests." This is intended to clue the press in that something unusual is happening.

One day becomes two, and then the formal announcement is made, and every newspaper on the planet collectively loses its shit. Hyperbole, I know, but #SickQueen is trending on Twitter (so is #RepublicNow, but under the New Management those people have a death wish). Royal correspondents in black suits and constipated expressions are being interviewed in front of the Palace gates, and I'm stuck in an almost-all-hands FAIREST meeting.

Certain stakeholders are missing. Gerry is elsewhere, on urgent External Assets business. Iris is busy doing very important stuff in Downing Street and the Cabinet Office, but demands the minutes by email. I'm shit out of excuses, and Mo is chairing this fustercluck.

"Willard. Any progress on the poison trail?"

Will has bags under his eyes and unshaven cheeks. "Ish." He wobbles one hand, equivocating.

Mo is very good and merely says, "Iris wants minutes," then waits.

"I heard back via channels from SIS." Willard scans the other seats at the table apprehensively. "Is it okay to disclose here?"

"Everyone here is cleared for FAIREST and POISON APPLE. If you need to disclose other codeword-tagged secrets, ask."

"Well. SIS did in fact order the dimethyl mercury sample, for an unknown project. They won't tell me what, or why, or who ordered it. *We're not cleared*, apparently."

Will looks scandalized, as well he might—this is close to insubordination.

"Tell me you have that in writing?" Mo asks. Will nods. "Then send it to me and I'll take it from there." Will nods, and that's that. Mo doesn't tell him he's just slid a bomb under the conference table in the Pharaoh-bunker: if he can't figure out what "I'll take it from there" means he doesn't belong here.

"Next item." Mo flashes Willard a quick smile, verging on a grimace: "How far did you get tracing the census records for Victoria Phibes?"

Will breaks into a grin: "Job done!" He catches Dennis and Janice staring. "What?"

Mo clears her throat and addresses the peanut gallery. "Bob and I are liaising with the Palace because the Queen appears to have been poisoned. The Queen's Honorary Physician in residence, Professor Anton Phibes, is a person of interest—not as a possible assassin, but he has a record with External Assets." Her eyes drift to Gerry's vacant seat and suddenly I wonder if this meeting never made it into his Outlook calendar for some reason. "In addition to vetting Professor Phibes we are investigating his assistant, Senior Staff Nurse Vulnavia Mrożek, who was formerly known to External Assets as Agent RAVEN. In 1942."

Mo's got everyone's attention now: you could hear a pin drop. And this room's carpeted.

"Phibes was assigned to the Royal Medical Household at the direct request of the Prime Minister. He in turn on-boarded Agent RAVEN after taking up his post. They are clearly qualified, but they both have files in the stacks—and their files have been redacted."

(Forget hearing a pin drop: half the people in the room have forgotten how to breathe.)

"Debrief on Victoria Phibes," Mo asks Will, who exhales abruptly, doubles over wheezing, and finally sits up and nods.

"I found her in the 1921 census, held on Sunday June the 19th," he says. "Occupation, housewife, residence, Maldene Square. A very exclusive neighborhood that was bombed flat during the Blitz. Today it's a bank headquarters. Her maiden name was Barclay, her father was a Baronet from a minor branch of the banking family, and her mother was a McTavish, which is flagged in our records for some reason. I traced her back to the 1891 census but there's no sign of her in the 1881 census. Her death certificate was filed on August 18th of 1921. She died on the operating table aged 32, and she's buried with her husband in Highgate Cemetery." Will raises an eyebrow. "This is the same husband who is the Queen's Honorary Physician, nearly a century later?"

Will's is not the only raised eyebrow. "May I?" I ask Mo.

"Be my guest." She leans back, wearing a sphinxlike expression.

"Your next task," I tell Will, "is to search for everything you can find on Lady Victoria Barclay, also known as Victoria Phibes, between 1900 and 1921, in our archives. I'll arrange the necessary clearances. In particular I want you to report on how

Victoria Phibes came to be ritually sacrificed by Doctor Henri Vesalius, high priest of the Mute Poet, and his coven."

"Wait, what?" Pete is scandalized.

"The followers of Ppilimtec practice anthropomancy or splanchnomancy, forecasting the future from the entrails of dead or dying victims of vivisection. Their high priests disguised the practice of their faith by working as surgeons during and after the Great War. There was an underground war between the Mute Poet's followers and those of the Black Pharaoh back then, and Professor Phibes was recommended to the Palace by the Prime Minister. It's no great leap to deduce that he and his wife were members of the Cult of the Black Pharaoh, and Vesalius's congregation kidnapped and murdered Victoria."

"How is Phibes still alive? He must be well over a hundred!" Pete protests.

Janice side-eyes him. "Who's going to tell him about vampires and longevity?" she snarks.

"But . . . !" Pete is still outraged.

"Phibes has a suspended animation process," I explain. "He used it to preserve Victoria and spent most of the 1920s trying to revive her."

Mo takes over. "According to our records Angleton tried to catch him in the 1920s but failed. He and Vulnavia showed up in Weimar Germany, dealing with the Mabuse ring, then again in the late '30s, where they obtained a violin from Erich Zahn." (*Oh shit*, someone mutters. It might even be me.) "After the war someone edited their personnel records with a razor blade." She leans toward Will. "I didn't go through the stacks looking for the records of Lady Victoria Barclay, but I expect you'll find her before 1921."

She looks around the table.

"*This* aspect of FAIREST does not go in the minutes and will not be minuted to Iris Carpenter until I have made a determination. Am I clear?"

Petrified faces stare back at her as the penny drops that we are now a black op, cut off from supervision by Number Ten, on Mo's authority as incoming Senior Auditor.

"Have a seat." I usher Derek into my office, shut the door, and switch on the DO NOT DISTURB sign.

"Is-is this about FAIREST or something else-else?"

Derek lowers himself into my guest chair and plants his folio on the desk, then subsides in a slightly rumpled heap. Since he turned PHANG he no longer needs to wear coke-bottle glasses, he's lost girth, and he's stopped wheezing, but he still has that faint stutter and the air of apprehensive diffidence.

I shrug. "Yes."

Face blank, Derek reaches inside his folio and pulls out a plastic Blu-ray disk case. "F-fine. Here's the answer to your first question. I assume you'll authorize the expense?"

"*What*—" I boggle at the garish cover. It's a double feature, half-black and half-yellow background: *The Despicable Doctor Phibes* and *Dr. Phibes in the Valley of the Dead*, starring Vincent Price and Peter Cushing. "The *whatting* hell?"

Derek's mask melts away, revealing an unholy self-satisfaction. "Gotcha!"

I *hate* being trolled by Forecasting Ops. And Derek is *clearly* trolling: he obviously knew about this before we sat through the FAIREST meeting, didn't he. "Spill the beans. Everything, Derek, you can gloat later, but I need to action this."

"I know." His smile fades and suddenly I'm sitting in the same room as a fifty-something vampire with a fiendish aptitude for scenario design and powers of astragalomancy—divination through dice rolling. "Believe me, I *know*."

I wait for him to continue. He's clearly gathering his wits because whatever he's seen coming up has disturbed the fuck out of him.

"I-I-I've had a sense of déjà vu about this meeting for weeks now," he finally admits. "But I c-couldn't tell you about it before you were ready."

Oh for fuck's sake, this is some real Forecasting Ops bullshit. I bite my tongue and nod sagely because looking wise and nodding sagely seems to be half my job now I'm a DSS. "Can you tell me about the"—I glance at the Blu-ray packaging—"making of these movies?" (Subtext: *Do we have a leak?*)

"They were both filmed in the 1970s, by American International Productions. The producer d-died about five years ago so y-you can't question him. Black comedies with a c-cult following. Uh, I mean a fan-cult following, not a cult-cult following. Anyway the n-n-names m-made me *itch* until I looked them up and found th-them in the Royal Medical Household of a-all places."

He leans back, looking profoundly tired.

"Have you watched them?" I ask, then add: "How relevant are they?"

"I-I-I've never met Professor Phibes? Or the-the-the Girl Vulnavia, he calls her—his mute, beautiful assistant who murders people and provides violin accompaniment when he plays the organ for his victims?"

Oh God, and by God I might actually mean the Prime Minister for once: *violins*. I facepalm slowly. "Am I going to have to *watch* these?"

That evening I'm waiting in ambush when Mo gets home. It's my turn to cook supper so there's a boringly pedestrian supermarket chicken in the oven along with a tray of roasting potatoes: I'm sautéing carrots in beer on the hob when she opens the front door. "That was *quite* the most annoying day," she kvetches as she hangs her raincoat in the hall and kicks off her heels.

"Meetings ran late?" I ask.

"Oh you have *no* idea. I'm getting the runaround from Whitehall Gardens." The Whitehall Gardens building is where the Ministry of Defense is headquartered, a ten-story-high neoclassical monstrosity with Henry VIII's wine cellars tucked away in the basement. "Nobody knows who in SIS might be responsible for ordering chemwar agents, nobody wants to give me a point of contact, in fact nobody wants to even admit that SOE(Q) exists much less has investigatory jurisdiction—" She snorts. "I think I rattled a few cages, so in a day or so I'll escalate. Keep an eye on your Outlook meetings, I might have an off-site I need you to come along to."

I stir the carrots and check my phone: the spuds should be done in another ten minutes, the bird in another five. "Supper's ready in a quarter of an hour. Do you have any plans for afterward?"

She sighs and shoves her briefcase under the table. "Some light reading before bedtime. Homework, in other words."

"Hmm." I tilt my chin toward the kitchen table. "Well, can I interest you in a movie night instead? Derek passed me a couple of DVDs that look interesting, and I think we ought to watch them together."

"If this is another attempt to get you to join his D&D campaign—" Mo's gaze falls on the first DVD. "Wait, Phibes? As in, *our* Phibes?"

"Looks like it." The carrot glaze is thickening nicely. "They're only three hours between them, and Derek thinks they're relevant. So: Movie night? It even counts as homework for once!"

Which is how we end up on the sofa after dinner with an open bottle of sauvignon blanc and a period piece horror movie on the DVD player which would be funny if it didn't seem to be a lightly fictionalized account of—*well*.

Bob here, breaking the fourth wall in my own workplace journal for a brief period: this is a recap of the plot of the first two Phibes movies, if you've already seen them you can skip ahead:

The Damnable Doctor Phibes takes place in London in 1925.

Our protagonist is a hideously disfigured professor of theology, a talented surgeon and musicologist, and a widower. His wife Victoria died during a botched operation in 1921. Phibes, who was overseas at the time, raced to get to her side but took a hairpin bend in the Swiss Alps too fast, went over a cliff, and was burned to death in the resulting car crash. Years later he returned to London to seek a grisly revenge on the medics he blames for murdering his wife, who are all members of a club of some sort.

Phibes has preserved his wife's body, which he sleeps with in a glass-lidded coffin sized for two. His murders allude to various biblical plagues, and Scotland Yard's finest fail to catch him before he confronts Victoria's nemesis, Dr. Vesalius. At this point Vesalius exposes Phibes as a devotee of an evil god, but Phibes one-ups Vesalius because (*surprise!*) it is not Phibes but the dead and undecaying Mrs. Phibes who was the priestess, and Vesalius murdered her on behalf of his own god.

Phibes, Mrs. Phibes, and Vulnavia descend into an underground time capsule right before the Keystone Kops crash the party and find Vesalius taking a piranha solution shower.

Mo empties the wine bottle into her glass as the end credits roll and kicks off: "That bastard!" She splutters at the screen.

"Who, Phibes? Or Vesalius?"

"The director!" Mo is distinctly unamused. "I'm left speechless! Which I suppose is the point. Did you notice how *neither* of the leading ladies got a spoken line in the whole film? Victoria I can just about understand, although she's your classic woman-in-refrigerator motivational plot point to explain the anguished male lead's subsequent murder-rampage, but *Vulnavia*—" She splutters some more. "That absolute male chauvinist pig!"

Now that Mo mentions it, I realize she's got a point. "It's fifty years old," I say defensively.

"No, Bob." She pushes back. "Even the special effects were

terrible. I thought *everyone* knows that locusts can't deflesh a human body down to skeletal remains in half an hour."

"I suppose they could have been hideous Hammer Horror death locusts?"

Mo stands. "I am going to need something *much stronger* if we're going to get through the sequel tonight." She sorties for the drinks cupboard in the kitchen while I swap disks, and returns with the open bottle of Glenmorangie Quinta Rubin and two tumblers just in time for the opening credits of *Dr. Phibes in the Valley of the Dead*.

Three years after the preposterous murders on Maldene Square, Phibes and Vulnavia emerge from their time capsule. There is a lengthy, not to say deranged, recap narrated by Vincent Price in character as the doctor, giving a good impression of the sort of creepy stalker who won't let a minor issue like his unrequited love interest being dead for eight years discourage him. Phibes takes ship for Egypt, accompanied by Vulnavia and the clockwork band, the glass coffins, his wife's mummified remains, and his Wurlitzer. (Phibes does *not* travel light.) A stellar conjunction is approaching as the stars come right. It is time for the Priesthood of the Black Pharaoh to catch a boat ride on the underground River of Life, enter the tomb of N'yar Lat-Hotep, and summon their Dread Lord back to Earth.

("What the everloving fuck?" Mo hits pause: "Censorship should have been all over this! *How* did it fly under the radar?"

"Maybe it didn't," I reply: "The director died the year after it came out." And I hit play again.)

There is a maggot in the cultist's canopic jar. His Nibs needs to be invoked by an arch-priestess descended from His priesthood. And Victoria is of course dead. This will not do, but Phibes is convinced that the waters of the River of Life can restore the dead. And if the water isn't enough, he is going to bloody well *demand* that the Big Boss does a *Jim'll Fix It* for his wife.

("Can you *believe* this?" Mo fumes, making use of the pause button again: "Why would Vulnavia ever put up with his shit? Why doesn't she"—Mo makes an expansive gesture with her whisky—"just dump him, lady!"

(Mo's got a point. Phibes is patronizing and dismissive, repeatedly calls Vulnavia "the Girl" in his monologues, and treats her like a mindless piece of furniture. "Exactly how many men has Vulnavia murdered[1] using venomous snakes, scorpions, rabid ferrets, and a white violin so far?" I ask.

"I've lost count," Mo admits, then adds, "but definitely one too few.")

Phibes's ship arrives in Egypt. Along the way he gruesomely disposes of a couple of meddling archaeologists. The action promptly moves inland to a camp in the desert, surrounded by cliffs with assorted holes (not *all* of which are occupied by camel spiders, giant centipedes, and the skeletons of unwary grave robbers). Phibes and Vulnavia find an empty pharaonic tomb to which, conveniently, Phibes has a key.

Meanwhile, in the valley below, Phibes's archrival, Aquarius Biederbeck, has set up camp with his assistants and is attempting to locate the Tomb of the Black Pharaoh. Biederbeck is a chancer who is after the Water of Life for his own purposes and is traveling with his "fiancée" Diana. Biederbeck leads a posse of archaeologists, including the Stetson-wearing, bullwhip-wielding Hoosier Jones and his mute gymnast sidekick Lara, who seem to be intruders from another franchise. Also present are Nazis from the Ahnenerbe SS, *which makes no sense at all* as the SS did not exist in the 1920s.

"This is revisionist bullshit," Mo complains bitterly. "Misogynist revisionist bullshit at that! Totally erases Agatha, gives all the credit to a man—one who didn't even exist, at that!"

According to the files Mo found in the archives, Phibes's adversary wasn't Aquarius Biederbeck but *Agatha* Biederbeck.

---

1. All while maintaining a perfect resting Botox face, possibly because, according to IMDb, it's the actor's only recorded appearance on celluloid.

There was no Diana: Agatha was a priestess of the Mute Poet (Vesalius's mob, who whacked Victoria). Yes, the director of *Valley of the Dead* did a blatant misogyny on-screen and got away with it. How else was he going to avoid giving any of the women a speaking role?

More *Rotten Tomatoes*: Hoosier is there to punch Nazis and find the Ark of the Covenant (he's in the wrong movie), and Lara is there to kickbox Nazis and thrust her E-cups at the camera—this is an early '70s script, after all.

I said it was a *cult* movie, not a *good* movie, okay?)

You know what's coming next: it's a Phibes movie so of course there is a series of gruesome killings as Phibes works his way through Biederbeck's minions, spoiled only slightly by the minuscule budget and rudimentary special effects of the day.

There is pathos, there is bathos, and there is Porthos—lurking behind a pillar with dagger in hand. Hoosier is trapped in a ghastly procrustean wine press and compressed horizontally until his head pops off like a cork. Lara is sprayed with some kind of syrup made from distilled Brussels sprouts and forced to sprint naked over a pit full of snapping turtles: her skeletonized remains turn up later, because she's a woman in an American International Phibes movie. Nazi Minion #1, after being punched and drop-kicked by combat archaeologists from the planet Spielberg, is buried alive in an oubliette with only a screaming skeleton for conversation. (Admittedly this is an improvement on the rest of the dialog.) Vulnavia fills Nazi Minion #2's jackboots with live scorpions and makes him dance: in this sequence she wears a Gestapo uniform with a very short skirt, because Hollywood.

Finally the directors run out of money or get bored playing with their food and send Phibes off to the writers' room for an ending. With Vulnavia's assistance he dispatches his enemies, loads Victoria and her crystal sarcophagus into a papyrus boat, and poles off down the River of Life to the strains of *We'll Meet Again*.

Deleted final scenes for which only the script survives, copy discovered misfiled in the Laundry archives with classification TOP SECRET BLACK PHARAOH a few weeks later:

They reach the Land of the Dead, walk across midnight-black sands at the head of a funeral cortege of mummified courtiers, and make obeisance before the Throne of the Black Pharaoh. But His Nibs is still snoring, because the star charts Phibes was working from didn't take into account gravitational frame dragging as predicted by the general theory of relativity.

Fade to black as Phibes plots his return to Europe, only slightly hampered by having murdered everyone in the camp who can drive a truck.

Afterward, Mo drains her tumbler and rubs her forehead. "You owe me three hours of my life," she berates me.

"I'm sorry!" I push my glass away. "Derek said it was important."

"That was *terrible*. I mean, that was only saved from being *Plan 9 from Outer Space* terrible because Vincent Price didn't die halfway through filming and the directors didn't replace him with a stuffed marmoset."

I shrug. "Reviews were mixed?" I try again. "At least they never made the third movie?"

"I know *exactly* why. And not just because Vulnavia put an electric eel in the director's bathtub."

Mo stands, a trifle unsteadily—it took two-thirds of a bottle of wine and about four shots of single malt apiece to get us through that double-bill—and ejects the DVD. "I think you should ask whose interests were served by allowing that travesty to get past the censors?"

"Wait, what." My head is spinning by this point so it takes me a few seconds to cotton on to what she's suggesting. "Are you suggesting . . . ?"

"Disinformation, Bob." She smiles tightly. "That was a *lot*," she tells the whisky bottle as she gingerly picks it up and turns toward the kitchen. "Just ask yourself what agenda a propaganda movie like that contributes to."

And on that note we turn in for the night, and I dream uneasily about a pyramid on a darkling plain, beneath a sky dominated by dying stars, and a robed figure poling a flat-bottomed punt along the river of a million years.

There is a private members club in Knightsbridge that caters largely, but not exclusively, to senior civil servants in the Ministry of Defense. It hides behind a discreet town house facade but boasts a noteworthy dining room with private accommodations, and a wine cellar that predates the Napoleonic wars. Its remit, ever since it was founded with the assistance of an endowment arranged by Samuel Pepys, has been to provide a discreet talking shop as well as a drinking den for sozzled ex–Sea Lords and Admirals.

Dr. Armstrong leads his guest, a tall, dark-haired woman with the grace and presence of a supermodel, to one of the small dining salons. After the waiter takes their order and leaves, Armstrong takes a deep breath and asks, "And how are you enjoying the Palace?"

Vulnavia gives him an unreadable stare. "It's been quite the experience," she says emotionlessly. She's not ready to tell him that it's beyond infuriating to walk such rarefied halls in the guise of a nurse, one step above a common servant.

Vulnavia spent her Galician childhood in the nurseries, gardens, and grounds of her noble father's mansion. She was at home in the palaces and hunting lodges of his peers and made her debut before the Great War, presented to the Archduke Franz Ferdinand and his wife the Duchess of Hohenberg as a teenaged girl, dancing until dawn with a diamond tiara in her hair. Had her life been more normal she would have married, raised a family, and died of old age before 1960. But she'd drawn attention of a different kind, been groomed and seduced and finally sworn her troth before a darker altar. And now she was here, almost a century later, yet to all appearances only a decade older. Doomed to skulk through service corridors and slither between the shadows of history: forever searching for her true love, with an aching void in place of her heart. "Quite the experience," she repeats.

The sommelier interrupts with the wine, presents it for the SA's approval, then pours and leaves. Vulnavia takes a sip, then adds: "The Palace is, how do they put it these days, a blast from the past? Punctilious about hierarchy and decorum, unforgiving of transgressions by those who serve. One is forced to move in tiny steps, oblique, always around the edge of the chess board."

"And your partner?"

"Don't call him that!" she snaps, then knocks back a substantial gulp of the Bordeaux. "I find him—no, I find the role I play—humiliating. But needs must, and I can swallow my pride while that supercilious, patronizing, *odious* chauvinist prances and postures in the limelight."

"Really? I thought—"

"I do not care what you thought: you obviously thought *wrong*."

"What? But your file said—" Dr. Armstrong looks momentarily confused. "It said you were lovers? A love triangle?" Registering her expression he instantly adds: "But you know files are misleading, they only convey what the original author saw, and in this case it appears the author was wrong. Wasn't he?"

Vulnavia's rage is like heat lightning, there and gone in a moment. She takes another mouthful and draws it down slowly, then puts her glass down. "It *was* a triangle," she admits, "but not an equilateral one. There were the three of us, he and I and she in the middle, and I *did* sleep with him, more than once, which he took as license—she had married him, after all, and in those days it was not done for two women to be more than close friends. Victoria and I were allowed some liberties in looser company, but only if I was seen as Anton's mistress, never as hers: in polite society I could only ever be her companion.

"Then during the war I was stranded in England. Cut off from my family's estates, I was penniless. And after the war my country no longer even existed. Luckily Victoria was born into money and Anton was not poor. But Victoria was murdered and Anton was maimed, and it fell upon me to preserve Victoria and nurse Anton through his recovery as we fought the fanatics of the Mute Poet." She shrugs, then throws back the rest of her glass.

"The progress in reconstructive medicine this century has been remarkable, and the new stem cell treatments led Anton to hope that his own restoration may be possible in only another decade or two. Which he intended to sleep away, much as we slept through most of the past century, but the best-laid plans'..."

She is about to take a sip when the door opens and the waiter appears with fresh bread rolls and soup. Vulnavia sets her glass down and for the next few minutes she and the Senior Auditor devote themselves to a passable carabaccia.

Some details Vulnavia will not share with the Senior Auditor, because they are none of his business; also, there is no statute of limitations for most of the crimes she committed in the service of the Black Pharaoh. While it is very unlikely that she will be prosecuted for them while he leads the government, a century of freeze-frame futures has taught her that there is *always* an afterward.

The SA pushes away his empty bowl. "How is Victoria doing?"

Vulnavia tears at her bread roll, fingers whitening, and mops it around her soup bowl. "His Dark Majesty is magnanimous, as ever." Her tone is bitter. "He gives life to His servants: it is no reflection on Him if sometimes we need more. Or in this case, approximately half a million pounds more than Anton and I have in the bank."

There is a common misconception that immortals are all loaded, enriched beyond the dreams of avarice by the magic of compound interest. But it's only true during periods of political and economic stability. Vulnavia's family wealth was alienated and then expropriated by two world wars, a depression, and nearly half a century of Communist rule. Meanwhile, Phibes squandered his wealth in a frantic dash to take revenge upon Victoria's murderers, then to preserve her mortal remains by arcane means—a combination of thaumaturgic containment and thanatocryptic suspension—until he could petition the Black Pharaoh in person for the key to unlock her tomb.

Vulnavia cannot resent Anton's hopelessly optimistic quest to find the headwaters of the River of Life, nor the expedition to the Valley of the Kings—she herself was party to it—but the cost was ruinous. And attempting to recoup the expenditure by taking the Wurlitzer and the Clockwork Band on a world tour in the 1920s had been a trifle unwise. But how should she have known that even a genius like the doctor could fall victim to a silver-tongued confidence trickster like Mr. Trebitsch-Lincoln? The man had impeccable credentials—he'd been a Member of Parliament!—he had connections at the highest level in the Czechoslovakian government!—and yet, and yet. Licking his wounds (and fleeing yet another INTERPOL arrest warrant), Phibes had dragged Vulnavia to Vienna where the polite society she had made her debut in no longer even existed, and then to Berlin, in search of Mabuse the Gambler, who Anton thought might be a like-minded fellow. Well, he'd been entirely right, if by "like-minded" one meant "another murderous criminal genius with aspirations toward necromantic full-spectrum dominance."

The 1920s had been a wasted decade except for the glass coffins and the precious test tubes filled from the headwaters in the Duat, the land of the dead, with which he had reinfused Victoria. So Phibes had invested his remaining funds wisely, choosing only good stocks listed on Wall Street. He'd then settled down to a five-year dirt nap, with Victoria at his side and Vulnavia in a crystal casket of her own on the other side of the crypt.

They'd awakened right on schedule—four months after the Wall Street Crash that ushered in the Great Depression. And that had set the pattern for the rest of the twentieth century.

Vulnavia is quiet but vehement: "Victoria is not dead, thanks to His Majesty. Yet it was best for her to sleep until now." In order to prevent decomposition Phibes had subjected her mortal remains to a very high dose of ionizing radiation using a radium-enriched embalming fluid, sufficient to destroy all the bacteria and fungi living in and on her body. The Water of Life and the Black Pharaoh's blessing had mostly reversed the damage, and she had returned to life in 1926—but only briefly. Severe radiation sickness and the complete destruction of her bone marrow were unknown to medical science at the time, but the downward spiral was so obvious that when Vulnavia frantically implored Phibes to put her back in stasis he agreed immediately. Together they'd skipped forward in time in five-year then ten-year hops, surfacing for six months in between to monitor his remaining investments and scour the medical literature for signs of a breakthrough.

"She needs a bone marrow transplant," Vulnavia explains. "Then intensive nursing in a germ-free environment while her immune system regrows. Anton refused to settle for anything less than a 90 percent probability of success. And then he needs more time, until stem-cell-derived skin and muscle tissue can be developed to repair himself. He suffered third-degree burns to half his body, including his face and head: he is in dreadful pain much of the time, and he cannot bear to inflict himself on her in his present condition."

She picks up her wine glass. "It's possible his Dark Majesty may be able to help. But only if given sufficient reason."

Dr. Armstrong nods. "Have you established a treatment plan for Victoria?"

"Oh yes. This time around Anton and I have been awake since 2005. There is a consultant oncologist in private practice who is willing to handle her case—again, for a consideration."

Phibes and Victoria have legal identities in the twenty-first century, but they're tenuous and they lack any records in the NHS Spine, the national-scale database of medical records. And in any case there's no medical code for *Patient requires whole bone marrow transplant due to embalming with radium solution in 1926.* Eyebrows would be raised, and ancient INTERPOL Red Notices might be dusted off. (Vulnavia is ironically more secure, for her cover was updated by External Assets back in the 1990s.)

"Which brings me to our arrangement." She pauses. Talking about money—vile commerce—doesn't come easily to one of her breeding, but of necessity she's reconciled to the need to shake the performer's upturned hat.

They are interrupted by the waiter again, this time delivering their main courses—fillet of plaice in a white sauce for the Senior Auditor, duck à l'orange on rice for Vulnavia—accompanied by a white wine. Further discussion of money waits out of respect for the chef's art.

"I need your consultant's office details, and Victoria's current identity of record, in writing, on paper. No email, no computers," the SA says. "I also need to know what you've told this consultant about her history. If they want to know why she's immunocompromised, it can be due to a radiological accident at a classified government installation. I also need a passport-grade photograph and a full set of fingerprints from her. I'll have External Assets request a blind cover from SIS"—a cover identity good enough for a spy, SIS has authority to cover stuff like birth certificates and an authentic passport—"and a new name. The agency has a billing code via the NHS: I'll impress upon your consultant that this is a high priority job and we'll pay for extras like a private room and any necessary contract practitioners they need. I think we can also bump her to the top of the transplant waiting list once they've established her donor compatibility."

He pauses. "I believe we can also provide access to the Scabbard to increase the probability of success." The scabbard of Excalibur, long believed to have healing properties, is a potent *mana* source, dispensing the *mana* accumulated by the sword during the pomp and ritual of a state-sanctioned execution.

Vulnavia blinks at the unexpected largesse. "I was expecting cash."

Dr. Armstrong leans back and drops his napkin on his plate. "This way is better: the government pays, she gets the red carpet treatment, everything is kept secret, and you don't have to fill out any tax returns. Is that acceptable?"

She thinks for only a few seconds: "Yes, I should say so."

The Senior Auditor nods. "Then I'll set the wheels in motion as soon as you get me those details. And in return"—he passes her a sealed manilla envelope—"here's the score for the funeral service." He drains his wine glass. "And may the devil have mercy on our souls."

SIS is headquartered in a shiny ziggurat of marble-clad concrete and glass on the south bank of the Thames, built during a brief spasm of optimism about the future in the late 1990s.

Two days later I find myself accompanying Mo to a meeting in spook country. Clearing security is a chore because SIS doesn't hold with new-fangled notions like binding *geases* or Harries on door duty: it's all metal detectors and lockers for your personal electronics and wrist watch, and rentabody security guards from G4S or HiveCo or some other body shop because it's all outsourced to the private sector these days.

"Who are we expecting, again?" I quietly ask as Mo collects

the transparent document wallet full of paperwork that she's selected for this meeting.

"Dr. Dina Abdul and whoever she brings along to stonewall us," she tells me as we cross the lobby toward the lifts. It's one of those polished glass and chrome office atria that led to the law against upskirting pics.

"Dina is from . . . ?"

Mo side-eyes me. "You didn't read your calendar invite, did you?"

I wince. "Guilty." I was up late trying to generate a map of the thaum flux around Buck House and figure out if it had anything to do with the crazy server farm in the attic. Little stuff like tomorrow morning's meeting got overlooked until, er, tomorrow morning. "So. Spill?"

"Research and Development, which shows up as a box on the org chart for Facilities." Our lift arrives and we badge in under the vigilant gaze of the cameras.

"Correct me if I'm wrong, but I'm guessing Dr. Abdul isn't a member of the medical fraternity?"

"Very good, Bob, I'm sure we'll make an intelligence officer out of you one of these days."

I follow Mo to the office doors, she badges us in again—we're only able to enter zones we're authorized for—then we sign in, in front of the gleaming receptionist, who directs us to our designated conference room where we badge in again.

Dr. Abdul is a middle-aged lady of Nigerian descent and very determined mien, who is nevertheless charming and friendly. She's brought a couple minions along to do the other side of the bad-cop routine, one female and assistant-ish, one male and what the RAF would call a "Rupert." (Junior officer, public school posh-boy background, I hate him instinctively.)

"What can I help you with today?" Dina asks, after the niceties have been fulfilled.

"Dimethyl mercury." Mo shoves half her papers across the

table. "We have an audit trail indicating a purchase was made by someone in this building two months ago. We want to know who, and why."

Mo's taking point so I smile diffidently, doing my best hangdog who-me-aw-shucks expression. Dr. Dina looks politely unimpressed.

"I'm afraid I can't help you, not without a bit more justification and authorization from Oversight," she says. The Rupert nods gravely while on her other side, the blonde assistant gives me a puzzled look, as if she can't quite remember where she's seen me before.

I pick up Mo's cue. "We're investigating a murder." I smile. "DMM was the poison in question, target was a protected person, and *very few* people in the UK have access to it, yourselves included. We've investigated everyone else, inconclusively. Now it's your turn."

"An *assassination*?" She's either the world's best liar or Dina is shocked, and scandalized by the suggestion that this house might ever have bumped anyone off on the QT (which is a bit rich seeing we're meeting in the Daphne Park room). "I'm sorry, I *still* can't help you—"

Mo smiles tightly and reaches for her folder of ammunition. This next piece of paper she slides in front of Dr. Abdul, close enough that I can recognize the Cabinet Office letterhead. "This is my higher authority: the Prime Minister's chief of staff, signing on behalf of Number Ten. If you want I can go back for a *direct* authorization, but there might be consequences."

Dr. Abdul has a good game face but the Rupert takes one look at the poison pen of Iris Carpenter and turns white as a sheet: Ms. Assistant-ish looks as if she wants to throw up.

"Who was the victim?" Dina asks.

"We can't tell you," I say bluntly. "It's classified, and besides, they haven't died yet. Even if it wasn't classified, we'd have a duty of confidentiality."

"But then it's not a mur—"

"DMM typically takes three to nine months to kill," I interrupt him. "And there is no antidote."

Ms. Assistant-ish side-eyes me oddly. "I'm *sure* I know you from somewhere," she says out of nowhere.

Dr. Abdul doesn't quite elbow her in the ribs to shut her up but gives me a tight smile. "A murder with a victim who isn't dead yet and who you're not at liberty to name, how convenient—"

"It's *not* convenient!" Mo interjects. "We—"

The Rupert sits up and grins at me. "I know! I know where I've seen you before! You were on *Newsnight* last year, weren't you? Being grilled by Jeremy Paxman about *elves*. You're the Ministry of Magic man, right? Where's your magic wand, man?"

I swear if my looks could kill he'd be a toad right now. Mo doesn't quite facepalm, but I know she's valiantly suppressing the urge, and also visualizing the Rupert's flayed hide as a target at the far end of the subbasement Test Suite.

"There is no Ministry of Magic," I say tightly. *Yet.* "Also, what we refer to as magic has nothing to do with stage magic and everything to do with keeping extraterrestrial entities from eating your brain. Moving swiftly back to the topic at hand, this proximate murder investigation is above your need-to-know level as it affects national security—which is why we, and not the police, are handling it—"

But I've completely lost the Rupert. He's giggling and pointing at me: "Eater of soles! Eater of soles! I knew I could place you somewhere! Come on, give us another fishy story!"

The meeting goes downhill from there.

As evil genius bases go, a shabby industrial estate in Sunbury-on-Thames lacks a certain je ne sais quoi. Had Phibes's fortune kept pace with expectations, Vulnavia is in no doubt that she'd be walking into a spotless chrome-and-steel vault in the caverns beneath an extinct volcanic island in the Pacific. But con men,[2] stock market crashes, and wars have left them in sorely reduced circumstances, and these days Phibes can't even afford the upkeep on the family crypt on Egyptian Avenue in Highgate Cemetery, never mind a legion of boiler-suited minions.

The windowless industrial unit is part of an anonymous complex within earshot of the M3 motorway. It's fronted by a roller door behind which are parked two vehicles: an anonymous white Transit van, and the Doctor's most valuable possession—his 1921 Rolls-Royce Silver Ghost.[3] (Vulnavia's Nissan Qashqai sits out front.) The back of the unit is walled off and partitioned into a cramped office-and-toilet block, a practice room with a brace of MIDI keyboards configured to imitate the Wurlitzer, storage space for the Clockwork Band, and a reconstruction of the Phibes family crypt in Highgate Cemetery.

The crypt is kept clean by one of the bandsmen, who Phibes has lately equipped with a second-hand Dyson in place of his right forearm. The larger of the glass coffins has been moved to the Buckingham Palace basement, but the single-occupant casket sits gleaming and spotless atop its stone plinth. Vulnavia leans over it, and her breath catches in her throat as she stares at Victoria, who lies within.

The passage of nearly a century hasn't touched Victoria's appearance: she's a lapidary blonde goddess captured like a butterfly within a collector's glass-lidded case, still in her white satin presentation gown. She looks much as she did on the sacrificial altar, aside from the leather straps and the fading echo of

---

2. Vulnavia settled Ignaz Trebitsch-Lincoln's account in Shanghai in '43—his poisoning is widely believed to have been carried out by the Japanese Secret Police at Hitler's request, but Vulnavia knows better—alas, Brother Zhào Kōng's safe was already empty by the time she picked its lock.

3. Vulnavia has argued in favor of selling it many times, for it is worth some single-digit millions of pounds and would go a long way toward restoring Phibes's fortune, but to no avail.

her screams. Vesalius and his congregation hadn't quite gotten around to removing her liver when Vulnavia erupted into their operating theater like an avenging fury at the head of Phibes's automata. She'd fled with Victoria's unbreathing body, then followed Anton's instructions to prepare her for suspended animation. Vulnavia's hands had been steady as she worked even though her soul was cold as ice. It had barely warmed up in all the decades since that horrible evening, not even in the sun-baked sands of Egypt or the humidity of Shanghai. Vulnavia took the chill of the grave into her heart that day and held it tight: until now.

Now she works at the foot of the casket, examining the hoses and refilling the fluid reservoirs. There is a checklist and she reads through it twice, ticking off each step, then checking her work an extra time. Once the plumbing is sound, she checks the wards and the containment grid on the floor of the crypt for discontinuities. No alien eaters will be permitted to worm their way into Victoria's vacant head during the revival process. Failure is unimaginable. Finally, satisfied that everything was in order, she twists a valve and starts a clockwork timer counting down. Then she ties on a surgical mask, walks over to the ratty, threadbare office chair in the corner, and settles down to wait.

She's done this before, but the last time—she has to think about it—was five subjective years ago, in the early 1950s. In theory the coffin can revive its occupant unaided to the point of restarting respiration and raising its lid. Nor is this Victoria's first awakening. But she is always disoriented and somewhat delirious at first, and besides, the world outside will be passing strange to her. (Even the electrical sockets have changed this time.) It would be cruel to make her confront the corrosive winds of time without love and support, and Vulnavia won't have it.

Hours pass. Occasionally the coffin clicks, or gurgles softly: forty minutes into the process a gas burner ignites with a soft whoosh to warm the perfusion fluids to body temperature. Somewhat later, there's a rattling splashing confusion as used embalming liquor, no longer even slightly radioactive, drains into the sluice beneath the coffin. Periodically Vulnavia puts down her book—she is rereading the first volume of Fantômas, drawing inspiration for the fanfic she is posting on AO3 for her own amusement—and checks the state of the mechanism. Despite its age it still works flawlessly, and shortly after sunset a motor buzzes softly and the lid opens.

Vulnavia approaches the open coffin. Victoria lies so still that for a panicky moment Vulnavia wonders if she is truly dead this time. But then she notices the faint rise and fall of her chest, the tiny flicker of movement behind a closed eyelid. "Victoria," she says softly, "it is I, Vulnavia. Can you hear me? Are you awake?"

Eyelids flutter. Victoria's voice is barely more than a croak: "Am I?"

"I should say so." Vulnavia smiles tenderly. "I'll fetch you a glass of water."

Half an hour later Victoria is sitting in a threadbare armchair, fleece-slippered toes peeping out from under her gown as she sips a cup of weak tea. Her expression is slightly stunned. Vulnavia has propped a flat-screen television on top of the coffin and it is running a video she has compiled, titled *Welcome to the world of the New Management*. It might equally well be titled *Welcome, Time Traveler, to the Future*.

Victoria has spent a grand total of two weeks out of her coffin since her first incomplete revival in 1925: most recently, a confusing day in East Berlin in 1955 (when her coffin was stolen by devotees of the Smoking Mirror as bait in a fiendish trap for Anton). Victoria is a socialite of the silent movie era, at home with biplanes and Ford Model Ts. Nuclear power, Concorde, and computers are not in her wheelhouse. "These fashions..." She clicks her tongue. "This film, it's not a joke? Please tell me it's not a joke?"

Vulnavia tilts her chin toward a wheeled aluminum suitcase.

"I bought you a selection of suitable outfits, dear. Luckily this century is very tolerant of eccentricity—in dress, at least. Casual attire is perfectly acceptable for the next week, because you need further medical treatment—" She catches Victoria's involuntary flinch. "You needn't fear the followers of rival rulers, though." She smiles triumphantly: "The Black Pharaoh returned to us two years ago, and now He lives in Downing Street! The Mute Poet and the Red Skull have been purged, their followers' heads are displayed on spikes in public, and His supremacy will be absolute in just a few more weeks! Anton and I have arranged for you to be treated in a clinic run by one of our congregation, guarded by the very government agency that once hunted us! It's quite the most extraordinary turn-around."

There are secrets Vulnavia will keep from her love for the time being. A few awakenings ago she learned the term Future Shock, and it explained so much that had confused and frightened her during her stop-frame fast-forward progress through the twentieth century. Vulnavia has been awake for almost a decade since 1925: a year every ten years was barely enough to keep her bearings intact. But the archpriestess has slept for so long, most recently for sixty years, that she has been awake for barely two weeks out of the past nine decades. The shock of the new will hit her like a collapsing New York skyscraper if Vulnavia doesn't ease her in. So she has resolved to spare Victoria the worst of her own disorientation by carefully staging her rehabilitation.

"Once you are awake and suitably dressed I shall drive you to the hospital and we can get you checked in. There will be a battery of tests and examinations, but the actual surgery is quite minor, more like a spinal tap than actual"—she waves her hand in instinctive aversion—"*cutting*. There will be an additional ritual to improve the probability of success. You will be in an isolation room during your recovery, to reduce the risk of infection. But that's good. There are books and educational television, and a thing called the web that I'll have to show you."

Victoria looks guardedly hopeful. "When can I see His Dark Majesty?" she asks. "I have waited so long . . ."

Vulnavia slowly smiles. "As it happens, there will be an opportunity shortly after your treatment is complete—at least, complete enough to leave isolation. A ceremony at Westminster Abbey, after which He shall reign uncontested!"

Victoria's gaze sharpens. "You say that as if it is in question! There is no other god in play—what are you withholding from me?"

"His Majesty rules Downing Street as Prime Minister, head of the secular government, but England remains a monarchy for the time being."

"Oh." Victoria nods, understanding dawning.

"Arrangements have been made. In three weeks' time, the Queen will take your place inside that box." Vulnavia indicates the coffin, ignoring Victoria's raised eyebrow. "There will be a ceremony at Westminster Abbey and the Prince of Wales will be appointed Regent while she sleeps."

"And the King?"

Vulnavia sniffs dismissively. "There hasn't been a King in England for more than sixty years."

"Good. I approve." Victoria smiles. "Please continue."

"The problem is that the current Queen has been in power for far too long to simply depose: she's almost outlasted Queen Victoria! The *mana*, the intricate web of oaths of fealty . . . the transition needs to be handled delicately. But once she is safely isolated from her worshippers His Majesty will assume complete control. The crown prince is elderly, and when he dies the traditional monarchy will be deprecated in favor of our Lord. And you are still his anointed archpriestess."

"Hmm." Victoria puts her teacup down. "But surely there must be an archpriestess in London already?"

"There is *nominally* a high priestess but you outrank her, my dear. The actual position of archpriestess has been vacant since you were murdered—the current high priestess is not of the prophet's bloodline. So as soon as you are cured"—*the sooner you have a working immune system again*—"you will take your rightful place."

Victoria's smile sharpens. "And the world will bow down in fear before us . . ."

GLASS COFFIN

After lunching at his club, Michael Armstrong returns to his office and sends a memo to HR about setting up a cover identity and private medical billing for Victoria Phibes. With the documentation he is expecting from Vulnavia it should be routine. Then he succumbs to an introspective stupor. It's his own fault for trying to work after a heavy meal and most of a bottle of wine: he's of an age when afternoon or early evening naps are a dismayingly frequent necessity. (To be fair, he's not so oblivious that he didn't clear his afternoon schedule of meetings first.) But it's also partly the consequence of the black dog of depression that trails him everywhere these days.

Dr. Armstrong has spent his adult life—almost forty years—in service to his country, quietly working to fix it wherever it is broken. He used to quote an American senator, Carl Schurz, if anybody asked why he did it: *My country, right or wrong; if right, to be kept right; and if wrong, to be set right.* When he was in his early fifties he'd considered getting a sign made for his desk. But motivational rhetoric was frowned upon back then—not because it was against policy, but because it looked like trying too hard—and it seemed prudent to lead by example.

Anyway, today honesty would necessitate a different sign, one more darkly resonant with the times:

Treason doth never prosper: what's the reason?
Why, if it prosper, none dare call it treason.

Sitting on his office sofa with his eyes closed, he daydreamed about explaining himself to an old friend and co-worker who had been killed in action four—*or was it five?*—years ago. "You made a mess, son." Angleton's avuncular icy gaze always made him feel like a guilty schoolboy. "You had a choice and you made an unforced error and now you need to correct it, but are you sure you're not making things worse?"

Angleton—the previous host of the hungry ghost known as the Eater of Souls, before Bob Howard inherited that dubious role—would definitely make that point if he was still around, Armstrong realizes. Come to think of it, so would Jenny, his late wife. But she isn't around anymore—*fuck cancer*—and it seems to Michael that there are fewer and fewer people on his side who he trusts unreservedly these days. Of course he reserves a different kind of trust for adversaries—the Prime Minister, his priestess and chief of staff Iris Carpenter, the despicable Phibes, his not-entirely-sane muse Vulnavia, and a host of other specters—but the certain knowledge of an enemy's malice is grounding and reliable, if not comforting.

Dr. Armstrong feels every day of his sixty years right now. There's no respite in sight: he feels as if he's been in survival mode for decades. He has so much accumulated leave that he can bring his retirement date forward six months if he makes it through the next few years, unlikely as that seems right now. But he has the certain knowledge that if he takes his eye off the ball everything will fall apart. *Let us just get through the next month*, he tells himself, *and things can only get better.* It's his mantra, and if repeating it can make it true, that will be fine. (It isn't fine, though. And he's pretty sure he won't get through the next month unscathed. Or at all.)

Operation FAIREST is the moment of maximum crisis, a crisis that has been snowballing for decades; first came CASE NIGHTMARE GREEN, and then the gods-damned *alfär* invasion triggered CASE NIGHTMARE RED. But the blithering idiots who'd been the government of the day had exceeded expectations *entirely* when they invited the worshippers of the Sleeper in the Pyramid to help them out! He'd been left with no choice but to make a pact with the avatar of a god in order to prevent a greater evil from taking root. But then the lesser evil had proven to be alarmingly competent (*What did you expect? He was a Pharaoh back in the day, he ran an empire of darkness for centuries*), and now . . .

"Three more weeks. Or four. Then it's not my job anymore." He's set things up so that Dr. O'Brien will be ready for the aftermath. He'll be out of the game afterward, but she is competent to take over the reins. Come to think of it, she is about the age he was when he had to step up without notice to take over as Senior Auditor in the wake of events in the South Atlantic. (It was an unexpected promotion, and not the kind anyone ever desired: he still misses Sam's advice and quiet, steady wisdom.) Dead men's shoes.

Fifteen minutes of postprandial shut-eye is all Dr. Armstrong can allow himself. Time, he reckons, is almost up: the reckoning is at hand. It's at times like this that he takes comfort from the sure and certain knowledge that Hell is a figment of the human imagination. He opens his eyes and blinks blearily at his watch, seeing that he's had almost seventeen minutes—unacceptable slothfulness. He stands and walks to his desk, perches on the edge of the chair he still doesn't entirely feel he deserves, then picks up the phone.

"Dominique, how are you? Yes? Good, very good. Can you spare me a few minutes this afternoon? Yes, when? Yes, very good. I'll see you then."

Click.

And the game is afoot.

For a miracle, both Mo and I get through the remainder of the day with no further humiliating meetings, incursions of extradimensional tentacle monsters, or other undesirable trauma: it is, in short, one of those rare afternoons when we both escape the office on time.

Mo looks at me. I look at her. "Movie night," we chorus, then I add, "after a takeaway." Anything to forget the debacle with SIS this morning.

(Reader, we do not get to do this *anything* like often enough these days: this is the first time since the Phibes movie double bill of a week ago.)

I phone in an order and grab a quick shower while Mo fiddles with the TiVo box and queues up a film without telling me what—it's her turn to surprise me—and then it's time for me to go and pick up my goat biryani and her bhindi gosht. I plate it up and we eat at the kitchen table, then I grab a bottle of Big Chouffe and two glasses and head for the living room. "What's on?" I ask.

"It's a surprise!" She gives me a saucy wink, which is a highly ambiguous sign in the context of a movie marathon, as opposed to, say, lacy underwear and an open box of condoms, but then moves over on the sofa and we settle down thigh-to-thigh and she raises the remote.

"Augh!" I shriek, sitting bolt upright. "*What? They made more?*"

"Ssh." Mo puts a hand on my arm (meanwhile holding the remote well outside of my reach with her other arm—she's not stupid). "I did some digging and, well, I thought we could combine some oppo research with entertainment?"

"But I thought they canceled the third movie! Right after Phibes turned up and mummified the director with several reels of Super 35?"

"Yes." She smirks at me mysteriously: "But this is the *other* third movie, the one that eventually got filmed."

The title sequence scrolls, over a backdrop of bloodily illuminated curtains around a cinema organ pit where a sinister black-robed figure is hammering away at the keyboards like a masked maniac: *The Revenge of Doctor Phibes*, starring Vincent Price, Charlotte Rampling as Victoria Phibes, and Diana Rigg as Vulnavia Mrożek. *What?* I boggle slightly. "When was this—*ah*." The credits scroll and I see it was released in 1978. "Okay, that's different." They must have upgraded the female leads to speaking roles in this one: how enlightened.

Mo hushes me. "It's really obscure, it's not fully downloaded to the TiVo, and the rewind is crap, so don't make me hit pause."

I make a grab for the remote and hit pause just after Phibes (for it is he) rises from the organ pit, throws back his hood dramatically, and blats, "Come, Vulnavia, let us descend to the crypt and awaken the sleeping beauty," in his expressionless Dalek voice. (I see they upgraded his vocoder as well.)

"Was this the same script?" I ask. "What changed his mind about it?"

"The one they canceled was *Dr. Phibes Meets Mabuse the Gambler*, in 1973. But *Revenge* got made, followed by *The Brides of Doctor Phibes*, which is coming up next. Either the doctor didn't hate the new script or they paid him off." (I have some sympathy for his position: being the subject of a movie franchise is all well and good, but if it's a horror franchise and you're the monster, that's got to suck.)

"Brides plural?" I ask.

"Remember Victoria was dead for a few years. Now shush," she says, and hits play again.

We are launched into the third Phibes movie without further ado. There is an opening montage. On returning from the River of Life in Egypt, Phibes and Vulnavia established a lair in a bomb shelter below the Kit Kat Klub in Berlin. Phibes (who has lost his fortune) has murdered and replaced Max, the impresario and owner, who he impersonates from behind a curtain. The Clockwork Band plays jazz in the art deco surroundings of the club while Vulnavia performs as the Master of Ceremonies, dapper in white tie and tails. Victoria is alive, or at the very least undead, thanks to the blessing of the Black Pharaoh: but she is frail, her immune system devastated by Phibes's embalming treatment, so she sleeps away the years in a crystal coffin beneath the club.

Outside the jazz club, the atmosphere of impending doom is palpable on the streets of Berlin. Every day the swastika flies from more buildings: brownshirts stomp in jackbooted processions through the streets, fighting running battles with the communists and beating up Jews, foreigners, homosexuals, and anyone denounced as an enemy by their Führer.

Phibes is here to exact a terrible revenge on his rival, the gambler and criminal mastermind Mabuse, who has stolen Vulnavia's bone-white violin—a gift from Victoria's liege lord and one of the band's instruments. Vulnavia also seeks to replace the violin with a new one commissioned from the infamous Erich Zahn. To this end Phibes manipulates the young American writer Clifford Bradshaw using Victoria as bait. She presents herself as a young English chanteuse, Sally Bowles. Cliff has an underworld contact, Ernst the smuggler, and once Victoria is installed in his boarding house a complex sting is set in motion.

Cliff is in debt to the infamous Mabuse, master of crime: Mabuse has a little job for him that requires nothing more than travel to a distant city to collect a violin case from a crazed luthier. *So undemanding!* Cliff thinks, even though his boyfriend begs him to think twice and flee back to Boston rather than fall into the clutches of the man without a face. He means Phibes, but Clifford thinks he's talking about Mabuse—and before he can be corrected on the matter, Vulnavia arranges for the bar to serve his boyfriend a cocktail spiked with manchineel juice, whereupon he dies horribly. (The special effects budget has leveled up considerably since the earlier films in the series.)

Cliff takes the train to Munich, collects the violin case from Zahn, and returns. Along the way he is oblivious to a comically excessive series of deaths as Phibes's minions and Mabuse's men battle it out aboard the train.

(The ticket inspector, an ardent Nazi, is hog-tied and dangled in the path of a passing high-speed Schienenzeppelin's whirling propeller blades; Hermann Göring's aide-de-camp is paralyzed by a blowdart, then skeletonized in his bunk by hungry ferrets; Mabuse's assassin is bisected by a surprise guillotine as he makes his way between carriages to murder the sleeping American; and so on.) While this is happening, the Master of Ceremonies takes to the stage back in the Kit Kat Klub to sing an ominous cover of Abba's "Money, Money, Money," accompanied by Anton on the Wurlitzer. Unwanted guests have entered the jazz club, and the Nazi infiltrators jeer. The atmosphere becomes tense: other audience members leave and are replaced by silent figures in evening dress and jewelled masks.

Clifford's train pulls into Berlin Hauptbahnhof. Victoria (disguised as the ingenue Sally) is there to meet him on the platform: she kisses him and takes his breath away—her lipstick is loaded with curare and he suffocates to death. She takes the violin, and returns to the club.

As the audience applauds, "Sally" walks on stage and presents the open violin case to the Master of Ceremonies. Vulnavia retrieves a bone-white instrument and strikes up a chilling duet with Phibes, as Victoria sings "The Future Belongs to Me." This is the signal for Phibes's papier-mâché automata—who have replaced the regular audience—to turn on the Nazis and garrote them. (From their curious lack of resistance it is not clear whether they are even alive at this point, for Vulnavia's violin is clearly of the same ilk as Lecter.)

As the closing credits roll there is a montage of Phibes and Vulnavia boarding a sealed carriage to Vienna as storm clouds loom. The Clockwork Band loads a pair of glass coffins (one of which holds the sleeping Victoria) aboard the guard's wagon: the steam locomotive chuffs slowly away from Berlin on the very eve of Hitler's rise to power.

Mo hits pause at the end of the film just as I explode, "This is bullshit!" I empty my beer glass. "Good use of Nazis, though. You can see where Spielberg got it from."

Mo's reaction is more philosophical. "I quite liked it! I could totally ship Charlotte Rampling and Diana Rigg in a threesome with Vincent Price, you know? But it's a shame Doctor Mabuse was just a silhouette the whole time, they could have done so much more with his character—"

"What if it wasn't Phibes who bumped off the director of that third movie, the one they didn't make?" I ask. "I mean, what if Mabuse—"

Mo shudders. "Don't invite trouble like that, one tormented mad scientist and serial killer is enough, don't you think?"

I consider for a few seconds. "Yeah," I concede. Do not multiply fiendish serial killers needlessly, right? "But this stuff in Berlin, does it track what you read in their files?"

"Not entirely," she says slowly, "but it's not totally at odds with it either."

"I suppose Phibes wouldn't be keen to allow anyone to make a movie in which he looks too bad, would he? I mean, in this one he's trying to do the best for his family, right? And fighting Nazis. That's never wrong."

She elbows me. "Says the man who now works for The Man."

I roll my eyes. "Is this another 'are we the baddies' moment?"

"Grab another bottle and I'll start the next movie, they're only ninety minutes each."

"What's coming up?"

I already know the answer before she tells me: "*The Brides of Doctor Phibes*." And, yup, the Phibes throuple got an 18 certificate in 1981. Obviously the good doctor was back in his coffin by then and the studio could take liberties without fear of sudden death.

It takes a while for Vulnavia to get Victoria up and ready for travel. (Luckily the twinset and heels Vulnavia has picked out for her are acceptable to Victoria's 1921 sensibilities, although

Vulnavia takes some time to persuade her that going hatless is normal these days.) It takes slightly longer to get Victoria used to the tight-fitting FFP3 face mask she will need for the next few days, but she doesn't really balk until she sees the Qashqai: "What's *that*?" she demands.

"It's a car." Vulnavia uses the key fob to unlock the doors and flash the indicators.

"But where does the chauffeur sit?"

Explanations ensue. Victoria's doubts seem to be allayed right up until the point where Vulnavia guns the engine as she takes the slip road to merge onto the M25. As the Countess slithers into a gap between an articulated tanker and a BMW the size of a Second World War tank, all of them moving at about sixty miles per hour, Victoria's knuckles whiten where she grips the panic bar. "Can't you drive a little more sedately?" she asks.

"There's a minimum speed limit on the motorways," Vulnavia says defensively as they pass a smart motorway gantry bearing a row of defleshed drunk-driver skulls. "But we're perfectly safe, cars hardly ever crash and explode these days. Toot toot!"

"Less Mr. Toad, more Badger, dear," Victoria requests.

They exit onto the M4, then slow right down as they hit the traffic between Shepherd's Bush and Knightsbridge. The skyscrapers on the banks of the Thames loom overhead, and Victoria falls silent. "I see there have been quite the changes," she finally says, then flinches as a jumbo jet bound for Heathrow Airport rumbles overhead.

Vulnavia is in an unaccountably cheerful mood, and can't resist tweaking her nose: "Don't worry, *those* hardly ever crash and burn either!"

"What? We're going to—" Victoria sees her expression. "Why, you . . . you deceiver!"

Vulnavia sniggers, then checks her satnav and begins to keep an eye open for parking spots. "Nearly there."

Vulnavia ends up paying through the nose for a parking spot

a couple side-streets away from the London Clinic. The clinic is a bland brick-faced cuboid with a fake Georgian front that dates to the 1930s: Victoria doesn't blink at it. But once inside, the twenty-first-century hospital interior clearly sets her back, from the automatic sliding doors to the omnipresent TV screens.

"You're already checked in," Vulnavia says quietly. "I'm a registered nurse and I have ID so I can take you straight to your room." To prove her point she badges her way into one of the staff elevators and holds the door open for Victoria.

"Where's the lift attendant?"

"Gone the way of the buggy whip manufacturer." Vulnavia leads her to the ward reception desk and introduces Victoria to the duty nurse. "Let's get you settled in." She glances at her phone. "Anton will be along in half an hour."

Victoria waits until the door to her private room clicks shut before she whirls on Vulnavia. "Where has he been? Is he angry with me for, for some reason? Does he not trust me? Is it about us?" She wrings her hands. "I expected him to be there when I awakened! Is something wrong?"

"Nothing is wrong with you, except for the damage to your immune system," Vulnavia reassures her as she squirts disinfectant gel on her hands. "And that is repairable. But Anton has a very important patient to attend to, one who can't be neglected."

"How important?" Victoria looks skeptical. "One would think his own wife returned from the dead might be a priority."

"Normally you would be entirely correct, but His Dark Majesty assigned Anton the rank of chief royal physician to the Queen, and the security at Buckingham Palace is very strict these days."

Victoria's mouth forms a perfect O. "I see." A pause. "Or rather, I *don't* see."

Vulnavia sits beside her on the bed and takes her hand. "It's very simple, my dear. You need to remain here in isolation while the immunologists replace your bone marrow, which was damaged by the embalming process. You can't go about in public yet, the slightest cold could hospitalize you. But the Queen is getting sicker by the day. We have an appointment at 10 Downing Street next week for His Majesty to take your oath of allegiance—in His capacity as Prime Minister—and anoint you as His high priestess. Then He will explain your role in the coming Regency.

"After which," Vulnavia leans close to her ear and whispers, "we won't need Anton anymore."

Catastrophes always seem to happen slowly at first, then faster than anyone in their path anticipates.

Over the next couple of weeks, Mo and I visit the Palace regularly.

I finish my survey and search for hidden occult power sources: it's a two-hundred-year-old palace so of course I find stuff, but nothing as weird as the thaum farm in the attic or Phibes's glass coffins. Certainly there are no demons in skin-suits masquerading as members of the royal family (not even Prince Andrew, and I checked twice). Maybe this is the wrong royal site to go magic hunting—the Tower of London and Windsor Castle are the obvious standouts, but anywhere a bunch of monarchs have been buried is a good bet, even that car park in Leicester where they dug up Richard III—but I can't help wondering if I'm simply searching under the metaphorical street light.

The GPU-powered thaum farm in the Palace attic remains a sore point.

It turns out that its installation was approved by the head of site security at the express request of Professor Phibes. Phibes insists it's a necessary tool to power the wards on the glass coffin, unless I want to stand in the aisle of Westminster Abbey and sacrifice a goat live on TV. (The press office is understandably unenthusiastic about this option.) Phibes maintains that his glass coffins require a low-level necromantic jump-start, and it would take *at least* a goat, with the strong implication that in times gone by, a Mute Poet cultist was a perfectly good caprine substitute. (The press office is *even more* negative about that contingency.)

I still have Questions.

That server farm contains upward of a million quid's worth of high performance GPUs and assorted supporting machinery. Someone had to pay for it, and someone had to put it together, and I'm pretty certain that the well-funded Dilbert in question was *not* a certain musician and surgeon who trained before the First World War. (Phibes being on his uppers since he lost his shirt during the Great Depression is just another datum in the evidence trail.) The Professor must have an accomplice with deep pockets and occult devops chops. If he was inflicted on the Palace by Number Ten that suggests a name to me, but if you shoot for The Man's chief of staff you'd better shoot first because Iris will *not* give you a second opportunity. And I still can't be sure why it's there, because if Phibes told me that water was wet I'd go to the bathroom to check.

As for the weird offices in the basement, they're supposedly there for some sort of 3D augmented reality documentary the aforementioned PR people are working on. But I have no idea why they just don't do it all in CGI. It's all very hush-hush and absolutely nothing to do with the current clusterfuck, and it stinks like a week-dead skunk.

Finally, there's the SIS fiasco. I still cringe whenever I recall that fatal meeting. Mo *says* she doesn't blame me, but I can't help thinking if she'd gone alone or taken someone else— Willard, maybe? Even his pet rat?—there might have been a different outcome.

For better or worse I am personally associated with the Leeds fiasco in the public eye, or at least enough of the public eye to occasionally count for something. And there's the reason we need the MUGGLE WONDERLAND training in a nutshell:

too damn many civil servants don't believe in magic, so they react to us as if we're wild-eyed loons.

You might think the Civil Service would respond correctly to the right forms and incantations and invocations of the authority of the Cabinet Office, but you'd be wrong. Response (a) is "humor him" and response (b) is "delay, deny, and kick the can down the road." Once she decided we were cranks, Dr. Abdul stopped responding to us—and so did everyone else. And while it's possible to make an administrative end run around human road blocks, it's messy and gets ugly fast. Especially when instead of the municipal parking department in Wolverhampton you're dealing with James Bond (lethal neurotoxin purchase orders optional).

Meanwhile we screen everyone with access to the Palace but it's a tight ship, with a high proportion of ex-military and members of families who've served the royals for more generations than I have fingers.

There's one tentative breakthrough. *Someone* at MI6 finally actioned the red note Mo got Iris to send demanding to know who ordered the bottle of DMM. They don't know or they couldn't tell me, but they *did* confirm it was checked out for an unspecified secret project. That was four days before Candy the dorgi was taken ill. In that period the Queen made three public appearances, had a regular weekly meeting with the PM, attended church once (in the Palace chapel), and had an afternoon off for her regular hair styling and manicure session. She walked with the dogs twice (check), Huntsman was on duty both times (check), and Willard confirmed Huntsman was working on every one of those days.

We narrow down the question of how the Queen was poisoned to two options: Was it through skin contact, or in her food? There's no sign of mercury contamination in the building, so food seems likely. And apparently there was an incident in which Candy got loose and interrupted the Queen during a meeting with the PM where she was served tea and biscuits by Huntsman.

I'm waiting for the police to determine who spiked the snacks when Iris carpets us in Scooby 14 one morning for an unscheduled meeting. Her smile is tight-lipped and unhappy. "I need you to lay off the SIS inquiry," she says.

"Why?" Mo asks bluntly. "We know they're screening for someone—"

"Yes, they *are*."

"But—"

"You need to stop asking questions about dimethyl mercury. You're attracting attention—the wrong kind. This is now above your pay grade, and mine. The privy council is unhappy about the direction your inquiry is taking, so here's a direct order: drop it and walk away. You've got enough on your hands with FAIREST and GLASS COFFIN coming up anyway."

What?

After a week of being prodded and poked with needles (and one mildly inconvenient operation which she drowsed through and retained no lasting impression of) Victoria decides that twenty-first-century medicine is very strange. There are machines everywhere, a superfluity of machines that beep and chirp and display cartoonish diagrams. And there is a strange box on a gimbaled mount behind a door bearing skull-and-radiation symbols that made her fine hairs stand on end while she lay beneath its cone-shaped business end. "It's the Scabbard of Excalibur," Vulnavia explained, "healing magic powered by the souls of executed felons paying their debt to society. Isn't modern medicine wonderful?" (Victoria agreed wholeheartedly.)

The nurses wore pajama-like uniforms instead of proper dresses, some of the doctors were ladies, and her bed had electric motors. But the central experience was essentially unchanged from a century ago: it was a sanatorium for the unwell and the infirm, she'd been admitted for treatment—a passive body to be adjusted rather than an active participant—and she must needs relinquish her dignity for the duration.

Victoria adapted to rest and recovery, poked inconclusively at the thing called the internet, and drowned herself in television, where there were decades of changes to catch up on.

After two weeks, during one of Anton's visits, he looked up from her charts to explain, "Your latest white cell counts are very promising, my dear. And His Majesty is expecting you. Do you feel well enough for a brief outing tomorrow?"

The next morning Victoria is dressed and waiting when Anton and Vulnavia arrive to collect her. It's this century's version of formalwear, which is casual: Anton isn't even wearing a hat. But she takes his arm anyway, and they ride the lift down to a big police car that drives them to a set of high steel gates in a windowless brick wall. It's one of the side entrances to Buckingham Palace, and as Anton and Vulnavia escort her through security (where she is presented with a photographic identity badge) she begins to smell a rat.

"I thought we were here for an audience with His Majesty?" she asks, once they're out of earshot.

"We are, my dear," Phibes assures her. "We can't take you to Downing Street, there are television cameras. But He has a weekly audience with Her Royal Highness and has made time for us in His schedule."

They arrive in the underground theater to find the Clockwork Band busily dismantling Anton's Wurlitzer. "We are relocating to the Abbey tonight, in readiness for tomorrow's ceremony," he croaks. Victoria inspects the bindings on the bandsmen, confirms that their animating demons are correctly enslaved, then catches Vulnavia's eye and inclines her head. The Countess's work is characteristically meticulous: she feels a warm glow of satisfaction at her protégé's excellence. While none of the

Clockwork Band are exactly the originals she animated after the Great War, they follow her design precisely and some of the armatures and limbs have clearly been restored. "Beautiful," she says, glancing at Vulnavia again.

"Come, my dear, and witness our revenge in preparation," Anton intones, beckoning her toward the door.

The crystal coffin she awakened in is waiting in the next room, its embalming tanks and containment grids exposed for maintenance. Fresh silk sheets and pillows sit beside it in an open trunk. "This is for the Queen, I take it?" She touches the side of the coffin.

Prior to awakening in it she had no idea of the depth of Anton's interest in mummification and suchlike preservation processes. Not that mummies are *preserved*, exactly, but Anton tracked and questioned an ancient vampire about pocket universes and temporal suspension, and Basil's arcane research clearly came in handy.

"We slept together in the other coffin, my love. A time machine built for two." Anton's shoulders rise and fall in a chuckle. "This was yours for the journey down the River of Life to Thebes of the Night, where the Jackal-Headed One weighs the souls of the dead before the crocodile and the river-horse, and the Dark Sun sits in judgment."

Victoria doesn't trust herself to speak. It is galling to think that she has been blessed by the presence of her god—His true presence, not just the fragmentary avatar at large in the world today—yet has no memory of the encounter. "I can't wait to meet Him," she says.

"You have been asleep for a very long time, my love. In that time, there have been other high priestesses, but none live in his heart as you do." The Professor pauses. "There is another high priestess, in name only, today."

Victoria nods. "Tell me of her," she says, her words clipped and her throat tight.

The Countess picks up the story. "Mrs. Carpenter is no

usurper," Vulnavia says carefully. "She is a true servant of our Lord and stayed faithful to Him through years in prison. On His return He elevated her to a public position as His Chief of Staff in government. But she is not of the bloodline of the prophets—she is not, nor can she ever be, His true Archpriestess on Earth."

Victoria nods again, the tension leaving her jaw.

Anton's vocoder buzzes. "Come, my love, and let us greet our Lord."

When they return to the theater the band is playing a light jazz composition unfamiliar to Victoria. A tall figure stands in the center of the dance floor, back turned to the doorway, one toe tapping along in time to the rhythm. Anton and Vulnavia both stiffen, then take a knee. The man whose face is a blind spot turns to face them, and Victoria feels His smile upon her back like the opposite of sunlight as she prostrates herself.

"My anointed."

"Your Majesty, I am beyond grateful, I—I owe you so much—"

Victoria is babbling, and Victoria does not *ever* babble, but the attention of her God's avatar has quite undone her. She screws her eyes shut and turns her face to the floor in an attempt to force herself to stop lest she dies of embarrassment. She is entirely clear that this faceless figure is the vessel of her God. She is His creature entirely and without reservation, a screaming fangirl from the century before the cultural phenomenon received a name. Generations of her foremothers worshipped the elder gods in secret, keeping the faith alive in their highland fiefdoms. Her own mother, a dedicatee of the Black Pharaoh, was sent south to marry and establish a congregation in London. And now He is here to see her!

"Rise, daughter," says the Black Pharaoh, and she feels His hand upon the back of her head. "We wish to look upon you and see what Our greater part has wrought." He sounds oddly pleased: Could it be that she is of merit in His gaze? She rises slowly, keeping her eyes downcast, as the god wearing a meat-sack inspects her from all angles. "Very good." He asks Anton: "What of the cytological damage?"

Anton buzzes something about T-cells and lymphocyte counts, recovery time and ongoing treatment. It barely registers with Victoria, who has eyes only for her Lord.

Vulnavia watches her with dark, still eyes. She can feel the Black Pharaoh's interest as a tangible presence in her own mind, as if her skull has turned to glass. It feels good, not pleasurable-good but the good that comes of necessary correctness, of being an instrument found fit for purpose by the engineer of human souls.

He returns his attention to Victoria: "We have a purpose for you, My chosen one. Our reign is not yet secure: while We are merely the Prime Minister, the masses' belief in the sovereign rule of Elizabeth Windsor can be stolen and used against Us. We have therefore arranged for a Regency to contain the monarchy. In two weeks, in Westminster Abbey, Her Majesty will lie down in the containment grid that shielded your body from corruption for ninety years. It will sever her power from this universe for as long as she sleeps, awaiting a cure." He gives a curious chuckle.

"I understand." Victoria's brow furrows as she tries to follow His reasoning, which is characteristically elliptical. "What is my role?"

"Your role?" The Dark Sun smiles upon her: "Your calling is to ensure that affairs at the Palace are handled satisfactorily during the ceremony. And then," He pauses for a moment, "tomorrow belongs to Me."

Iris's jaw-dropping edict leaves me with no alternative and no reasonable route of appeal, but arguing would be unwise: the privy council sits somewhere at a constitution level above Parliament itself, and is chaired by the Prime Minister. Which means His Dark Majesty is *personally* telling us to lay off on SIS and the poison. Which implies very strongly that He knows something, and there's a cover-up in progress—our notional descendants might get to read about it when the archives are declassified in a century or so.

Mo and I go home in a state of shock that day and discuss our options. But we don't really have any. Going to the press is unthinkable, appealing direct to the PM isn't going to work—I know from experience that He has a whim of iron—and the Eater of Souls isn't allowed to resign to make a point. (Neither is the incoming Senior Auditor.)

We've both got jobs to do, whether we're here to serve the Crown or protect the public, and that means we're stuck.

Don't have to like it, though.

Meanwhile, Iris was right about one thing: with FAIREST/GLASS COFFIN looming in the near future, we've got our hands full. Finding out precisely who administered the very slow poison is a lower priority than handling the resulting disaster. So Mo handles liaison with the medical household, the court, and Her Majesty, and I take care of the backstage stuff at the Palace.

The news is grim. Mr. Huntsman, the butler, takes a turn for the worse. According to the experts he took a much higher dose of DMM than the Queen. Within two weeks of his diagnosis he has a palsy, peripheral neuropathy—nerve damage leading to tingling and creeping numbness in the hands and feet—dizziness, hair loss, and signs of confusion. He's so ill that—not to mince words—he's sent home to die.

Which he does after only three days, and for the most unexpected reason: he is bitten to death by a specimen of *Vipera berus berus* that he apparently found in his bedroom.

The common European adder is the only venomous reptile native to the British Isles. It's not a terribly aggressive snake but it *can* be provoked into biting if you pester it. People occasionally die of it—there were two fatalities in the twentieth century—and it's not *entirely* impossible that it wandered into his underpants drawer by mistake. But it's about as likely as him being killed by a falling meteorite. Also his house landline was disconnected in error by the phone company and his cellphone was loaded with a piece of malware that forwarded all attempts to call the emergency services to the speaking clock in New Zealand. Fancy that.

That business has Phibes's fingerprints all over it—it's absolutely his style—and because Iris told us to lay off on SIS and the who-killed-the-queen question but *didn't* mention Huntsman, we're still free to ask questions. But the deadly duo have castiron alibis: Phibes spent the day teaching medical students and Vulnavia was practicing with the string section of the BBC Philharmonic Orchestra. It could be someone else who wants him gone and knows Phibes's history: Palace politics can be brutal even before you drop an elder god in the mix.

Phibes is bound by oath to the PM and Vulnavia is one of ours, so the best I can do is badger Gerry Lockhart to look into her. But I'm not in Gerry's best books these days. So there the matter rests until Mo has time to hold a full-dress audit—but then Mike Armstrong insists he needs to be present after what happened the last time she grilled Anton, and I can't really object.

So it gets kicked down the road, and I *still* have unanswered questions.

Outside the magic circle, a well-oiled public relations operation rolls into action. The news that the Queen has a degenerative neurological condition and can no longer perform most of her public duties dominates the news cycle for several days. Public speculation about her illness rises to a fever pitch, and a couple of carefully planned red herrings are released to deflect attention from the truth. The next step, a week later, comes the announcement that we can slow but not stop her decline; then a few days after that they announce the Snow White–style suspended animation capsule. Finally, two weeks into the process of staged disclosures, the Palace uses Prince Edward's exclusive interview with BBC royal correspondent Philomena Cunk to announce that there will be a formal Regency for the duration of the Queen's hopefully reversible dirt nap.

Then Her Maj's condition takes a turn for the worse and we're out of time: FAIREST and the associated GLASS COFFIN ritual are scheduled for next Tuesday at 11 a.m., and we're on a countdown to the first rebasing of the Laundry's root oath of allegiance in the lifetime of anyone currently working for the agency.

PART THREE

AN ELDER GOD DID IT AND RAN AWAY

On the Tuesday of FAIREST/GLASS COFFIN Mo and I awaken before dawn, eat a hasty but hearty breakfast (I don't expect to get to eat again before tomorrow), then dress in our funeral outfits, still crisp from the dry cleaner last week. We both have go-bags with stuff we'll likely need: emergency protein, cans of Red Bull, and more recondite stuff—Hands of Glory (the pigeon variety: I know Mhari swears by the execution-surplus ones but I am not down with shaking hands with a dead man when I reach for an energy bar), a stereo digicam hacked to run SCORPION STARE firmware, an Airwave police radio and headset . . . you get the idea.

By mutual consent we ignore the news, whether by radio or internet. The British media are very predictable during any kind of royal flap, and right now it's going to be wall-to-wall Very Serious Royal Correspondents in black armbands and ties who don't have a clue whether to treat GLASS COFFIN like a funeral or a celebration as Brenda dodges inevitable death with an octogenarian backflip. So they'll waffle for approximately sixteen hours on all channels while those of us with jobs to do get on with things.

At 7 a.m. we're on the pavement outside our front door when our ride screeches to a stop, and a very big guy with a scary gun leaps out and holds the door for us. As part of the core team we rate a taxi with flashing red and blue lights and zero fucks given for speed limits, which is essential because even this early there's a two-mile-long queue of rubberneckers shuffling toward the front gates of Buck House. The queue for Westminster Abbey is barely shorter.

Central London is on traffic lockdown and all Police leave is canceled because it's a tradition or an old charter that royal succession anomalies are accompanied by the kind of cheerless public holiday that makes paperwork pile up and diverts all the buses. Apparently they've got nine thousand cops on crowd control and various supporting duties today, along with a few thousand armed services and an entire battalion of field ambulances for the inevitable medical emergencies among the million-plus spectators. Our driver and co-driver are notably not cheery about events, but at least the traffic barriers open for us without any bother. They swing by the Abbey first for Mo, then it's just me.

"Where do you want dropping off, guv?" asks the driver.

"Side entrance by the stables, if you can get me there." I sigh. "Big day today."

"Yeah. You got the goss on what's going on?"

"Sadly, no." I smile tightly. I could tell you but then I'd have to kill you and then who'd drive the BMW?

"Shame, she's a lovely old girl, can't imagine what it's going to be like without her just being there the whole time. It's going to be really weird, isn't it?"

"Oh, I'm sure we'll see her again," I reassure him. (Hauled out of a crystal coffin smelling of mothballs to deliver the Queen's Speech at the State Opening of Parliament. Not forgetting her regular Christmas fireside chat to the nation. If they keep to that schedule she could still be going in twenty, thirty years? And who knows, maybe they'll find a cure.) "Never say never."

They drop me inside the compound and I badge in through the security checkpoint, which is heaving with heavily armed bodies in dress uniform today. Signs warn me of DANGER OF DEATH, because the Ring of Steel camera network is up and ready to explosively petrify at the push of a button. (They swear they fixed the bugs in the firmware that caused the disaster in Leeds the other year.) Some of the cops wear fluted gothic plate armor: they carry carbines with multiple cameras locked on them. SCORPION STARE weapons and body armor that kinda-sorta sometimes works against the basilisk effect. The household cavalry are out there in their cuirasses and horsehair-plumed helmets, horses high-stepping nervously around the stable yard. Their brutally functional L85 rifles suggest this isn't a routine ceremonial parade. There are no Harries on display, but a windowless army horse box is waiting across the yard and when I point my inner eye at it I see a jumble of raw head and bloody bones driven by malice and hunger, enchained by powerful bindings. *Good.*

I have no ceremonial role in today's proceedings. My job is simply to be available to assist with security at the Palace. *Available for what* is unclear: we aren't expecting any trouble here, but we weren't expecting Her Maj to be poisoned either.

Buck House is, as noted, swarming with security. Right now the Queen is in her private apartments, eating her last meal—a light breakfast—while her attendants lay out her formal gown and a security team waits to escort her to the private courtyard and a waiting limousine. (The State Carriage isn't getting an outing today—it's not wheelchair-accessible.) Speaker-to-Plants is traveling separately from Clarence House, just across the park, in a separate vehicle. (Just in case.) Miscellaneous other royals, foreign heads of state, and every living Prime Minister will be in attendance: it's a full-dress security nightmare.

I make my way through the rabbit warren until I get to the ops room, which is a windowless bunker with ornate plaster crown moldings and flat panel displays hanging from the picture rails. A bunch of cops in headsets monitor the CCTV feeds from the palace, but I'm not here for them, I'm here for their boss.

"*You* again," snaps Superintendent Sullivan, turned out in her dress uniform and white gloves for the occasion: "I should have bloody known."

"Nice to see you, too, Jo." She's probably still sore about that time I got us trapped in a broom closet surrounded by zombies... is it *really* twelve years ago? "Looking good."

"Never thought I'd see you in a monkey suit." She raises an eyebrow. "Are you here to waste my time or do you have a job to do?"

I shrug. "Your guess is as good as mine, but Number Ten is very twitchy about the sort of thing I deal with. I've surveyed the Palace already—"

"Go, go." She makes shooing gestures at me. "I don't need you cluttering up my ops room today, go secure the Palace against tentacle monster invasions or whatever it is you do. Mike, give this man a headset and"—I pull out my Airwave receiver and wiggle it at her—"good, Mike will hook you up." And she turns away.

Mike the tech support bloke plugs my radio into a headset and logs me onto the channels they're using around the Palace. "Okay, I've got a to-do list, back in half an hour," I tell him—it's not even a little white lie—and off I go to double-check my areas of concern one last time.

My first stop is the attic. This time I've actually got the keycode to the server farm, I let myself in and check for signs of tampering since I was here last. I don't have the official issue thaumograph with me, but if I listen really hard with my not-entirely-human senses I can hear the buzz and chitter of mindless eaters in the void, attracted by the GPUs' endlessly looping *mana* accumulators. They sound normal for Norfolk, which is to say, entirely eldritch.

As I look around I spot a new addition under the eaves. Someone has set up a high-bandwidth switch connected to a really fat pipe going down toward the basement. It's surrounded by black-and-yellow warning tape and there's a sign hanging from it that says DO NOT ADJUST (THIS MEANS YOU BOB). There's an odd harmonic that I can feel in my long bones rather than my ears coming from the pipe, like the rumble of *mana* draining away into a sinkhole under the foundations of the universe.

It's in a locked room in a top security area in the Palace and it's got my name on it. I grumble a bit and make a note to quiz Phibes about this latest addition when there's time, then I move on.

(In hindsight, that was my one pivotal mistake of the day. But I mean, it wasn't a bomb, right? Or a summoning grid configured to teleport tentacle monsters into Prince Philip's smut stash. It was just some kind of *mana* concentrator, obviously installed in the past week or so, on the side of a server farm I've already uncovered and queried. And I was running on a tight schedule, otherwise I'd have gone and hunted down the Professor *immediately*. But it was an anomaly rather than a clear threat, and I had a hard deadline, and besides, I didn't have time to deal with Phibes's bullshit. Especially as he'd just point his finger at the Prime Minister and croak, "An elder god did it and ran away.")

From the thankfully bomb-free attic spaces I move down to the residential workers' rooms, the service areas, and then the various supporting households—heraldry, dentistry, the hairdresser and manicure studio, the live-in tailor (bespoke repairs and adjustments are an ongoing requirement for the Firm, whose members have to appear immaculate at all times in public), and the medical household. It seems to take forever, and indeed it does: for Buckingham Palace is huge and even though I know what I'm doing now, you can't rush an inspection.

"Is Professor Phibes in?" I ask at medical reception, only to get a headshake. "Nurse Mrożek?" Another headshake. "Where are they, then?" I say, a trifle waspishly.

"They're attending to Her Majesty and won't be back today," the receptionist stonewalls. *Of course*. I mentally facepalm.

"I'll catch up with them later," I promise. When I get to the Abbey. But first . . .

I do not actually enter the royal apartments, but I do stare at the doorways with my inner eye. I see no lurking horrors, and precious little sign of anybody human—I can kinda-sorta see souls through walls, a sense that freaks me out when I think too hard about it—and the only people in Her Maj's suite are the maids pushing a vacuum cleaner back and forth and stripping the bedding. By normal day-to-day standards there aren't enough footmen and women about. They're all out front on public display, paying their hopefully not-final respects.

I continue my rounds, periodically reporting a reassuring lack of threats back to the ops room. The ground floor is just as it should be, swarming with cops and soldiers to keep the public out. The royal cortège has just driven out the front gate behind a mob of police motorcycle outriders and armed response cars. So I report, yet again, that all's well. Then I head for the back staircase down to the basement. I have to make a last sweep of Phibes's art deco lair and the weird maze of nonfunctional offices. Then I'll be done with the Palace, hopefully for good, and can head over to the Abbey to watch the main event.

At least that's the theory. Instead I find all the missing courtiers, and the screaming starts.

Westminster Abbey, traditional burial church of English monarchs from the days of Edward the Confessor until the end of the Tudor period, and traditional coronation church of English kings from William the Conqueror onward, defies easy description. While today it looks like many other medieval Gothic cathedrals, that's a late addition from the thirteenth century—the Abbey itself was founded in the tenth century. Since the gothic nave and towers were finished in the fourteenth century it has been under periodic reconstruction and expansion, most recently to repair the bomb damage inflicted by the Luftwaffe in 1941, and to clean the Cosmati pavement, a mosaic floor dating to 1268. It's just round the corner from the Palace of Westminster, now the Houses of Parliament, and roughly a mile from Buckingham Palace.

Look, it's a medieval gothic church. Nave, transepts, a main chapel with the coronation chair and altar, and a bunch of small chapels containing the tombs of kings and queens clustered around it. There's other churchy stuff like cloisters and a chapter house, but the main thing is tombs, so *many* tombs: tombs in the walls, tombs in the floor, tombs in the crypt, probably tombs in the ceiling and concealed in the Dean's beard. They've been planting people here for more than a thousand years. To enter the doors is to tread upon the bones of empire.

Mo arrives at the Abbey really early, but the doors are already open and the place is bustling. The politicians, royals, and assorted other VIPs won't arrive until later. The ceremony proper doesn't get under way until 11 a.m.: there's a lot of backstage setup to be done if everything is to run smoothly in front of the TV cameras.

Mo walks in past the temporary weatherproof awning outside the main entrance. The nave of the Abbey is already full of temporary seats, five rows deep on either side of the polished stone floor, each bearing a printed order of service. Further inside, both transepts are packed with wooden chairs upholstered in blue velvet. These are reserved for MPs, peers, press barons, billionaires, and racehorse owners: seating for people who deserve to lay eggs in each other. There's only standing room for the military, police, and working stiffs like Mo. She's wearing the lowest heels she can get away with: she already knows her feet will be killing her tomorrow.

Today's ceremony is a bizarre mashup of funeral and coronation. Accordingly, the dress code has a split personality: black formal suits for working staff, but also church hats for ladies, medals and decorations on display for anyone who's got them, morning suits and long-sleeved frocks for guests. Mo, who does not generally wear hats, has a black pillbox with tiny net veil for the occasion: it partially conceals her Airband headset, but she feels uncomfortable and conspicuous even though everyone else is dressed up, too.

Speaking of the Airband: her earpiece crackles as she reaches the start of the nave (which is swarming with police officers in white gloves, pushing the chairs around and trying to look conspicuously useful). "Doctor O'Brien?"

"Here." She taps her ear. "Is that you, Pete?"

"Absolutely it's me! I have you in sight, I'm in the south transept by Poet's Corner. Sorry I can't come any closer, too much daylight."

"Got it. With you in five." Mo walks toward the columns where the choir will stand in a couple of hours' time. "Isn't it too bright for you in here anyway?" Many of the stained glass windows bombed out during the Blitz were replaced with clear panes.

"I have sunblock and it's overcast. As long as I don't go outside I should be okay." There are a group of clergy in gold-embroidered white vestments standing in the transept, and as she spots them one breaks away and walks toward her. It's Pete.

"Right." She pulls her earpiece out. "Let's talk offline."

"As you wish." His gown and surplice lend him an unfamiliar air of clerical dignity. It makes her do a double take: this is her old university pal Pete the biker, only suddenly he's a priest. "Gosh, I don't often see you dressed like that!" he exclaims, slightly spoiling the effect.

"Same back at you." She pauses. "I take it you're confined to the Abbey proper? Not the Cloisters."

"Absolutely. I've walked the chancel and checked the radiating chapels already. Also had a sniff around the Dean and the other officiants: there are no ringers as far as I can tell, but I can't speak for those I haven't met before."

"You don't know them all . . ."

"No. My diocese is a little bit provincial. On the other hand, I've met the Archbishop of Canterbury and this is his show and he knows *everyone*, so if he vouches for them . . . he's sharper than he plays on the *Nine O'clock News*, you know?" His smile is strained.

"Well." Mo makes a snap decision. "We've got plenty of time

in hand—how about you give me an orientation tour while we're here? Then if anything goes adrift I'll know where I'm needed."

"You should have been briefed on the Arch—" Pete pauses. "You know what, forget I even began to say that." He shakes his head. "Let's start with a backstage tour of the church arrangements. This way." He leads her toward the screen separating the choir from the nave.

For the next hour (by the end of which Mo is beginning to get a bit worried about the time) Pete gives her an exhaustive tour of the building. They've crammed seats in everywhere with a direct view of the nave and the coronation chair. There's a high altar and screen, of course, and in front of the altar there is a catafalque surmounted by a glass and silver-chased coffin, its top hinged open, with steps to allow an occupant to climb in. Below the stand, Pete explains, there is an electric lift that serves to lower caskets into the royal crypt. "Can I inspect her crypt?" Mo asks.

"Yes. This way."

There are multiple crypts under Westminster Abbey: the oldest surviving is a small one under the Chapter House that used to store the King's treasury until it was burgled in 1303. The one Pete takes Mo to dates to the nineteenth century, and it holds the coffins and reliquaries of many, but not all, of the kings and queens of England. In previous centuries souvenir hunters sometimes pilfered bones from royal skeletons whose coffins had rotted in the less well-preserved tombs. (Moving them underground behind a locked door was a not-unreasonable response.)

Pete leads Mo through a side door and down a tightly spiraling stone staircase, to a brick-walled basement with a vaulted, low ceiling. There are stone shelves up all the walls, and each shelf is occupied by an only slightly dusty coffin. The air is musty, cold, and dry: a portable dehumidifier sits humming away in one corner. In the center of the floor, a lift shaft surrounded by old-fashioned concertina railings ascends through the roof. It's shaped for a single horizontal passenger, and the gate that opens at waist height is barely a meter high. "The coffin lift," Pete whispers in a low voice. "And through here—the dead but unforgotten."

He leads her through an archway into another room, dimly illuminated by a fluorescent tube bolted to the ceiling. There are more stone shelves here, bearing a mix of very old, badly decaying coffins and sealed lead-lined caskets of more recent vintage. (Mo is bemused to discover that Lady Diana Spencer is not, in fact, interred in the temple in the middle of the lake at Althorp: at least, not anymore.) A number of other shelves support plain metal boxes.

"The New Management has been collecting the bones of monarchy for the past year, bringing them home from wherever they fell. That's Richard III, died in the Battle of Bosworth Field in 1485. They found him under a supermarket car park in Leicester. He was due to be reburied in Leicester Cathedral this year, but the PM wanted him here." He points at another tin box: "The Princes in the Tower." And a third: "I'm not certain who he is, pretty much everything before Harold II is a bit vague and DNA profiling is useless at that remove—but the PM *insists* the bones belong to Arthur Pendragon, so he's in the collection."

Mo ducks beneath a loop of cable tacked to the ceiling. It terminates in some sort of electrical rack: the other end trails away toward the lift shaft. "King Arthur is a myth."

"Yes, but a very powerful one. I mean, it's the heart of the Matter of Britain, isn't it? The patriotic foundational myth. If the Black Pharaoh is right, Arthur belongs in this vault."

"Still." Mo closes her eyes and turns slowly in place. Everything here is at peace, more or less, all soul-stuff long since fled—except for the equipment rack which is a new addition, muttering and mumbling to itself restlessly. But it's got Phibes's metaphysical fingerprints all over it, so it's probably something essential to maintaining the Queen's stasis ward. "Okay, I think I've seen enough. Let's go."

"Not going to ask to meet the Archbishop?" Pete asks, glancing askance at the equipment rack. "I've got to talk to him next. Final briefing on my checklist."

"I'm sure you've got him well in hand. We're both going to be needed up top so let's go back."

Preparations have been moving inexorably forward during Mo's inspection sweep. When she surfaces, her earpiece crackles briefly. "Dr. O'Brien to site security HQ, please acknowledge."

"Mo here. Where are you set up?"

"Back of the south transept, in the passageway to the Chapter House. Dr. Armstrong is waiting for you."

Mo makes her way past the rows of posh seats, where a handful of dignitaries are already taking their places. Her feet already hurt and it's not ten o'clock yet: Why is there never a pair of gel insoles available when you really need them? Soft organ music ebbs and swells from the vicinity of the choir, drowning out the footsteps and audience conversations. A uniformed constable checks her badge, then leads her through a discreet side door that is only slightly older than the New England colonies. Behind it she finds a corridor that's been turned into a temporary site office. Tables support CCTV monitors and portable computers crewed by a squad of police dispatchers. "Ah, Dominique!" It's Dr. Armstrong, in black tailcoat and tie, looking like a very distinguished undertaker.

"Is everyone in place?" Mo asks.

"Indeed. At least those we can use—having so many of the core support team go PHANG last year has caused a bit of a personnel problem, to say the least."

Mo nods. Mhari—Baroness Karnstein—won't be attending. Neither will Officer Friendly, or Pinky and Brains (for different reasons), or . . . she does a double take. "We have remarkably few humans left on active ops or in senior positions these days."

"Yes, I *had* noticed. It's almost as if they're an endangered species." The Senior Auditor gives her a sharp glance, then takes her by the elbow and leads her away from eavesdroppers. "A word, if you please," he says quietly. "You should be aware that Forecasting Ops are having a bit of a moment."

"Oh dear." They walk along the passage, away from the police, heading toward a temporary table covered in supplies for the army paramedics waiting offstage in case members of the audience (of whom there are a couple of thousand, and they trend old) are taken ill during the service. "How bad is it? Did Derek flag anything up?"

"I told Derek to focus on the Queen and the Prince of Wales for now, strictly short range. No, this is something more general. Back office Desk Four is sending up smoke signals about an impending Severity Level Three national security failure with a probability weighting over 50 percent, located in the City of Westminster, in the next six hours. This is all very recent, it only started this morning."

"Oh fiddlesticks." Mo's stomach sinks. Severity Three is the same level as the Yorkshire Incursion—a nightmare scenario, the absolute worst. The Yorkshire Incursion cost more than ten thousand lives and led directly to the New Management: right here, right now, she does *not* need this. "Do they have any idea what?"

"Alas, that would be helpful." The SA's tone is one of resignation. "Some phrases keep recurring in the oracle dump—things like 'hour of greatest need,' 'for I am the resurrection and the life,' 'and he shall rise again.' But none of it is very helpful, is it?"

"Something is going to go wrong with GLASS COFFIN," she says grimly. She doesn't give voice to her worst fear: that the assassin is going to make another attempt on the Queen—or worse, His Eldritch Darkness, the Prime Minister. "Can we cancel it? Right now?"

"No. We *should*, but the PM will be irate and you know what *that* means. There's still a chance to avert it—forewarned is forearmed, and all that, so we press on. *Theirs not to reason why, Theirs but to do and die, Into the valley of Death Rode the six hundred,* etcetera." Dr. Armstrong pauses. "Your, ah, special ability—your Albert Hall talent—I trust you can still evade attention?"

Mo nods. Middle-aged female invisibility was a superpower: it sucked when it happened by accident in meetings or the supermarket checkout queue, but when you needed to sneak up on a subordinate who is persistently goofing off or a bad guy it was indispensable. "You bet."

"Well then. I feel it would be useful to have eyes on the altar during the ceremony itself? I reserved an aisle seat for you as close as I could get: if you have to move you'll be in position, and you can assume command of SOE assets once I leave."

"Wait, where are you going?"

"Number Ten." The SA sounds grim. "Iris says *He* wants me there to cover Downing Street and Parliament while you handle the ceremony and Bob holds down the Palace. So, at the very last possible minute, tear up the playbook and run it all by the seat of our pants, eh?"

Mo's left eyelid twitches uncontrollably. "Anything I should keep an eye peeled for *in particular?*"

"Well." The SA thinks for a moment. "Phibes is here to ensure the time capsule works and make any last minute tweaks. He's playing the organ—that Wurlitzer of his, apparently it operates the control logic for the glass coffins. Nurse Mrożek—or should I say, Asset RAVEN?—is Phibes's handler and technical assistant, she's with the orchestra as cover and has something to do with energizing the containment grid on the coffin. Your vicar chappie, Russell, is assigned to the Archbishop of Canterbury in the Verger's Party. The Archbish asked for him personally, he seems quite taken with Pete for some reason. There are two OCCULUS teams deployed, one parked on Parliament Square with line of sight on Her Majesty and one behind the Cloisters to cover the Abbey, police choppers overhead, the entire Royalty Protection Command and Specialist Protection Command are on-shift, and in addition to all the soldiers you can see the

Army has a couple of Apaches in Regents Park ready to dust off if anyone needs them. And of course Derek's in the OCCULUS truck on the square."

The amount of firepower on site or within shouting distance is quite terrifying, and it ought to be reassuring to Mo except none of it answers her key question. So she has the usual mix of dread and nausea when she realizes that not only is she supposed to wing it from here on out, but that everybody else in the chain of command above her is *also* winging it. "So. Who's in charge of this circus?"

"Assistant Commissioner Middleton, gold commander for FAIREST. Let me introduce you to him. Then you can take over from me . . ."

By eleven o'clock the ceremony is under way. Mo watches the enormous and interminable procession from the South Transept, near the corner with the Cloisters. It gives her a view of the orchestra and choir, and in the opposite direction toward the coronation chair in Edward the Confessor's Chapel. She has staked out a position at one side of the front row, in a bank of seats occupied by Very Important People. She's two seats away from the French President, but nobody notices her presence—not even the bodyguards. Which is just as she intends, for Dr. O'Brien has the gift (or sometimes curse) of magically enhanced invisibility.

It's not true optical invisibility—cameras can see her just fine—but human attention slides right past her. She's had a few years to get used to it. Her power very rarely cuts in accidentally these days, when she's shopping or trying to get somebody's attention, but it's not something she has a lot of use for normally. Today is the big exception, and it gives her the best available opportunity to watch the procession while Her Majesty is escorted down the aisle at a slow march, accompanied by her husband,

Prince Philip, and surrounded by close family members and archbishops. Prince Jug-Ears is pushing the state wheelchair.

The royals are stuck behind about a million people in fancy costumes: they range from the college of heraldry to army uniforms harking back centuries. Officers carry royal standards, so many banners. A football side of clergy trail behind ancient crosses like imprinted ducklings following an animal behaviorist's boots. Soldiers and Lords bear rods and scepters and the various regalia of the crown jewels. It's quaint and dusty stuff that ranges from an eight-century-old spoon (for anointing the monarch) and a ten pound gold saltshaker, not to mention a bunch of swords with names from a D&D campaign (although the Sword of Justice has been replaced in the procession by Excalibur Reforged, a grimly functional execution device made from scrap incorporating the rusted remains of the original sword).

The orchestra plays Elgar's *Pomp and Circumstance March No. 1 in D* while the Queen arrives and the royal family take their places. Professor Phibes is at the organ—Mo saw him when she slipped behind the screen during her last inspection. The orchestra—she blinks. *What's she* doing? Mo wonders, with a double take. Presumably, as a protégé of Phibes, Nurse Vulnavia—or rather, Countess Mrożek, codename RAVEN—was picked for her musical proficiency. Something about her violin sets Mo's teeth on edge. It looks like a mundane instrument with nothing of the uncanny to it, but she has a nagging, horrible sense of familiarity. It's as if Lecter is present in spirit if not in body. She's had nightmares that felt less real than this apprehension of his return, and it makes her skin crawl. Almost involuntarily she taps her headset, and announces to the circuit reserved for the Laundry team: "O'Brien here: gut feeling, something is *wrong*."

The Archbishop of Canterbury is at the lectern, speaking in dignified, measured tones of hope and glory, offering prayers for the Queen's safe delivery and for the success of this totally normal medical procedure. Pete is in the row behind the Archbishop, looking nervous. The organ is still playing, but much more softly, a sustained background note that calms and reassures. Mo's attention moves elsewhere as she scans the crowd with what Bob would call his third eye—the finely developed sense of a ritual practitioner for the presence of a thaum flux. It's not as efficient as a thaumograph but it's right here, right now, and that's what gives Mo a definite shock of recognition.

She carried Lecter longer than all but one other custodian of the pale violin. And she knows what its presence feels like. This is not that, but it's very close—too close for comfort. Vulnavia is in the orchestra, inconspicuous among a sea of black dresses and formal suits, and Mo now sees that she's holding a white violin disguised by a glamour. It's an instrument of the same ilk as Lecter, weaker but similarly cursed. A moment after Mo realizes what she's looking at Vulnavia lowers her instrument and slides it under her chair: and when the Countess straightens up she's holding a different bone violin, connected to a cable trailing beneath the seats.

Mo taps her headset again. "Code Red, Code Red, location orchestra string ensemble row three seat two, Code Red, she's got a Zahn string, no, *two* of them—" She stops talking: her headset has gone dead. And as she steps out from behind a row of guards she realizes that the glamour Vulnavia is wearing lends her Mo's face.

Pete stands as deep in the shadows as he can reasonably get—which is not very deep—squinting against the light. He needs to stand close by the officiating clergy, because the Archbishop has tapped him for a very important role in the ceremony to come. And the clergy are front and center in this circus because it's the Church of England at work, conferring its blessing on the head of the church as she lies down for a most irregular nap.

It's not a particularly bright day, and the light in the Abbey is filtered through the high windows, but it's still painfully bright for a PHANG. He's been here since before dawn and is wearing ridiculously high-SPF sun block, and it feels as if he's developing a bad case of sunburn. But needs must: there's a job to be done, the kind of job where you only get one chance to get it right. And Pete is up for that and damn the torpedoes.

There's an order to any church service. Normally he can take comfort in the familiarity of ritual, even if the high church pomp and ceremony isn't quite his thing. But this service is more than slightly unsettling, because it's a one-off scripted for the occasion and certain elements of the process are, if not exactly satanic, then at least touched by the darkness over Downing Street. He finds it mildly ironic that his job, as a creature of the night, is to fight back against that darkness. He's somewhat put out about the way he was diplomatically disinvited from the procession, but: "The optics would be terrible if the tabloids found out and decided to make mileage from it," the Archbishop's press secretary said. "His Excellency thinks it best to keep you out of the public eye." Which was some high-quality bullshit. Translation: *We have a critically important job for you to do but even though you can gargle holy water until you turn blue and sprout angel wings, the Archbishop is worried about the public relations optics.*

On the other hand, here in the cheap seats Pete can scratch his nose unobtrusively behind his copy of the order of service, and meanwhile wait for his call to action once Her Maj is bedded down in the crypt. So there's that.

There is orchestral and choral music, there are a couple of psalms, the Archbishop speaks, more choir music, then the Archbishop speaks again (gravely, consolingly). The Queen remains seated throughout, although she has been assisted from her wheelchair to an armchair alongside the steps to the catafalque. Her expression is calm but she looks small and frail, and a little lost, as if she's having difficulty keeping track of everything. Of an instant the pity and sorrow of the whole affair lands on Pete. There she sits alone, the head of state, head of his own church, one of the longest reigning British monarchs ever, ruler of what was until recently the largest empire in the world: yet she's still human, an eighty-something great-grandmother with numbness and tingling in her hands and legs and a blurring in her vision and a dulling of the mind because she's been poisoned like a dog. *Well, I'll do something about that*, Pete thinks and checks his watch: there's about an hour to go. Then it's his turn to join the Archbishop and other high-ranking clergy downstairs to briefly awaken the Queen and turn her into a PHANG before she sleeps again, as a final Fuck You from the Church of England to the Black Pharaoh.

But then Pete notices a significant omission. Where *is* the PM? He should be here, shouldn't he? Almost all the cabinet are present, along with a number of foreign heads of state. (Not to mention princes and princesses, dukes and duchesses.) But the PM is the first of her ministers, the leader of her government, and for Him to skip this interment is unthinkable. Let alone to absent Himself from the oath of allegiance to the newly sworn-in Prince Regent. Pete taps his earpiece. "Do we have an ETA on the Prime Minister?" he asks quietly. "He should be here already."

"Please hold." It's an unfamiliar voice, and Pete waits for his reply, then a familiar voice speaks in his ear, "O'Brien here: gut feeling, something is *wrong*."

Appalled, Pete glances round. The Archbishop is delivering a short, uplifting homily, underscored by a soft musical accompaniment. A pair of officers lift the Queen from her chair and help her up the steps to the open-lidded stasis capsule, clearly taking most of her weight—it seems she can't walk unaided anymore. Then Mo speaks again, extreme urgency in her voice: "Code Red, Code Red, location orchestra string ensemble row three seat two, Code Red, she's got a Zahn string—"

Pete's headset cuts out. He glances round sharply, then looks back at the catafalque. Her Majesty is half-seated in the crystal coffin, surrounded by a nimbus of purple light, her skin slackening over shriveling flesh as she slumps inward, as if being drained—

And then he sees the bone violin playing in hands that can't possibly belong to Mo, and realizes they've been had and there won't be an opportunity to raise her from the grave—the poisoning was just the prelude, and the actual assassination is taking place *right now*.

If you've ever witnessed a sacrificial ritual conducted by the Cult of the Black Pharaoh you won't soon forget it, especially if you've been picked for the starring role. This time I'm an accidental bystander rather than the victim: but the scene that greets me as I enter the Palace subbasement leaves me at a loss for words.

"Control, this is Bob," I whisper as I crouch in the gents' toilet two doors along from the storeroom, "I'm in the basement, we've got a Code Red! Repeat, Code Red, mass casualty situation in progress."

The mannequin band is playing and the jazz-age club lights are turned down low, but to my inner eye the space is blazing with thaumic energy. It's centered on an altar that someone's dragged in from one of the Palace chapels. It's draped in a blue tarp, now stained with spilled fluids from the pile of bodies opposite the bandstand. A crackling gramophone trumpet sings ominous lyrics—*the twilight will fall, once the world is mine: tomorrow belongs to me*—as another morning-suited figure trapped in a web of luminous compulsion stumbles toward the altar.

Two clockwork automata grasp him with white-gloved hands and push him over the tarp: a white-robed woman steps forward from behind the altar, and when she raises the athame again her gloves drip blackness in the crimson lighting. The *mana* pipe snaking across the floor pulses, carrying his fleeing life away to an equipment rack at the far side of the room.

Fuck. I see what's going on here. It's about the ley line. The server farm was supposedly up in the attic to energize it, but now it's being used to funnel all the necromantically harvested energy from the altar to a receiver somewhere nearby. Somewhere like Westminster Abbey, perhaps.

The bloody-handed automata march stiffly toward the door to fetch another sacrificial courtier. Of course, the basement rooms are done up to reflect the surroundings of the monarch now passing from life into the underworld. It's an ancient Babylonian rite—maybe Assyrian, or even older—whereby the nobles and courtiers of a dead king would be sacrificed inside a tomb built to resemble their throne room. The Black Pharaoh is nothing if not a traditionalist. I remember Mike Armstrong warning me, and I'm having a weak-kneed shuddery flashback to my own time facing such an altar in the crypt under Brookwood Cemetery. But then I realize the woman behind this particular altar is not Iris Carpenter, and I'm older and much tougher than I was then, and—hey, why hasn't Control acknowledged my call?

I step back into the shadows as the two automata rustle past me, and I wish I'd thought to bring along a Hand of Glory. Even one of the half-assed pigeon-derived ones that are only good for about two minutes' invisibility would come in handy right now. But then the music stops and the lights come up, and I realize the blonde woman in the fancy white gown—now somewhat bloody about the hem—has spotted me. "You there, in the doorway! Who are you and what are you doing here?" Her voice rings with confidence and her accent is cut-glass sharp.

"You're Victoria Phibes, aren't you?" I put the picture together in a hurry: "Archpriestess of the Black Pharaoh, I presume? Is this ceremony sanctioned?" I gesture at the bijou pile of bodies stacked to one side of the altar. Even though my stomach churns I can't quite justify randomly interrupting a sacrificial rite that He has ordered without first checking that the officiant has filed the right paperwork.

"Come here." She beckons and I walk toward her slowly, trying to project confidence. I tap my earpiece again and it stays resolutely dead, because *of course* I'm two levels below ground in a structure that was rebuilt after surviving Luftwaffe bombing. "Don't make me repeat myself." I'm not the only one who can project confidence: "Who are you?"

I hold up my warrant card: "I'm the Eater of Souls. Don't make me repeat myself: Are you Victoria Phibes, and who told you to do this? Do you realize you're not allowed to carry out human sacrifices without an execution warrant from the Home Office? Or on premises that don't have planning permission for operation as a red meat slaughterhouse in accordance with DEFRA regulations." I am becoming quite irate as I demand, "*Where is your paperwork?*"

Mrs. Phibes draws herself up and sneers in a manner that tells me she knows exactly what my warrant card is: "I'm here by order of the Black Pharaoh, N'yar Lat-Hotep! Who happens to be your Prime Minister. Don't try to trip me up with paperwork, little man, my work is essential to the rite of suspension in progress at the Abbey! How do you think the crystal caskets are powered?"

I glance at the body pile and try to get a rough grasp of the numbers. "You've already gone through a dozen or more—how many do you need?"

The doors open again as the automata frog-march another equerry to the altar. He doesn't struggle: the glowing green worms in his eye sockets tell their own story. There's nothing at home in that head but an eater: he's not really alive in any meaningful sense of the word.

"I'll use as many as it takes," Victoria says tightly. "They're all volunteers and this isn't a normal suspension: it's important to isolate the Queen from the power of her true believers or the rite will fail. That requires an alternative high-tension *mana* supply. The machinery in the attic isn't nearly powerful enough to keep her wards energized, which means sacrifices must be made. Now are you going to get in the way of saving the Queen's life, or are you here to lend a hand?" She sniffs. "Assuming you know what you're doing."

"For fuck's sake, this isn't my first human sacrifice!" I burst out. Victoria looks scandalized at my language, but then I step forward and grab the equerry. "We don't have time to half-ass this." I glance at her knife: "Get out there and send me the rest of the sacrifices and I'll take over this end." I roll my shoulders and open my imaginary maw wide and pretty much inhale the hapless revenant's soul, or what's left of it—then I spit it right back out, hitting the sacrifice ward dead center so that it flashes green briefly and the *mana* feed crackles. "Next, please."

Listen, *I* am the Eater of Souls. While Victoria is just an Archpriestess of the Black Pharaoh, descended from the same sacred bloodline as Johnny McTavish, BASHFUL INCENDIARY's sorcerous hench-thug. She's wasting time with the amateur hour throat-cutting nonsense. It just squirts blood everywhere and wastes *mana* like a human sorcerer, almost as if she's unaware of the talents her ancestry bequeathed her. I guess practice really does make perfect. Also—I check my watch—it's ten to eleven and the ritual will be underway any minute now. If there isn't enough *mana* in the accumulator at the Abbey the isolation ward *will* fail and the Queen will be killed by the backwash. Then there'll be an *epic* shitstorm.

I mean obviously Jug-Ears becomes King right then and there, but he's not popular the way Brenda is. And that's without taking into account the godawful ungrounded necromantic summoning circle in Westminster Abbey, right on top of the crypt where they stash the spare royal bones. There's no telling what could happen with all that unbound faith in monarchy flapping around everywhere, is there?

This whole scheme is fucking stupid, and I absolutely intend to give the Prime Minister a piece of my mind as soon as I finish saving the day. Also Victoria Phibes is an arrogant, snobbish, probably psychotic (it helps in this line of work) twit, but she's here on official government business. If He'd asked *my* advice she wouldn't be up to her arms in gore, but needs must. And so I let my mask slip, put aside emotional engagement and the veneer of humanity, dismiss the self-protecting delusion that I'm not actually one of the monsters. And I find myself facing an altar not so different from the one on which I left my humanity behind several years ago . . . and now I'm the monster, ripping souls from bodies and squirting them into the ley line connecting palace and church, and at least my way of doing this is bloodless and more effective than Victoria's, and back when I remember to be human again I'll tie myself in knots about it, isn't that sweet?

Just as I've drained the last Assistant Private Secretary, my earpiece crackles. "Code Red! Code Red! Westminster Abbey—" Then the Airwave receiver goes dead, and the router for the *mana* discharge crackles and emits a wisp of smoke.

"Shit." I stare across the pile of sacrifices at the bloody-handed archpriestess, who has raised an eyebrow. "Emergency at the Abbey, I'm afraid. I have to go."

"What kind of emergency?" she demands: "Anton and Vulnavia are there!"

"It's some kind of major incident—that's usually an incursion. They're under attack." I dig my earpiece out and her eyes widen even further. "Are we done here?"

"We'll have to be," she says, wiping her knife on a dead man's shirt.

"Okay, I'm off. Want to tag along?"

SWORD AND SPECTER

Vulnavia—assuming it is she who has stolen Mo's face—is playing the white violin like a woman possessed. Or perhaps the instrument is playing its puppet? Her fingertips leak vermilion stains across the strings and her face is slack. It's not loud, exactly, but every note feels like an ice pick hammering into Mo's head. Agent RAVEN is a better-than-average player and a priestess of the Black Pharaoh besides, but she's outclassed by Lecter: whoever fooled her into taking up the bonestealer's fiddle did so with reckless disregard for her survival.

And now Mo can sense a storm of *mana* spewing out of the fiddle like a firehose of magic. It's mostly directed at the glass coffin but the flow is turbulent, eddying and swirling. The cable leading to the violin burns like a magnesium flare to anyone with the ability to see sorcery, pumping gouts of power into the instrument that overflow into the ward around the catafalque—until it stops suddenly, going dark. Whoever is at the other end of the cable has severed the link. The Queen is half inside the glass coffin, but something has gone wrong: the power feeding the coffin has died, but she glows ever brighter. Her skin shrinks and withers as the unrestrained *mana* of monarchy burns a hole in reality, tearing open a rift in the stone floor below her bier.

The ward energized by the pale violin—itself the head of the firehose fed from Buckingham Palace—served to seal the Queen off from her worshippers. But then the feed was cut, and Lecter overpowered his wielder. Now he's trying to drain the monarch. But Lecter is a messy eater: *mana* is flowing back along the link but also spraying everywhere in great gouts and foaming rivulets, or being sucked away to whatever lies below the coffin.

The crypt, Mo realizes, scrambling from her front row seat. The *mana* release is flooding the bones and relics of medieval kings and queens, and her skin crawls as she realizes the implications. It's a giant thaumaturgic meltdown, a prompt criticality excursion powered by two-thirds of a century of a world empire's accumulated belief. Now it's dripping into an Elephant's Foot of sorcerous corium, mixing with the bones of Richard III, Arthur Pendragon, Mary Queen of Scots, and the Princes in the Tower—among others.

Her Airwave headset went tech just as the *mana* feed to the crystal coffin was cut off: that's no coincidence. "Mike, you *asshole*," Mo snarls as she dashes behind the wooden screen fronting the orchestra. She doesn't know why he did it. All she knows is that Mike Armstrong, outgoing Senior Auditor, is the only person in a position to do both those things. And she isn't in the restrained, procedural headspace of Dr. Dominique O'Brien anymore: she's back in the eyeblink of suspended time during the confrontation at Nether Stowe House, all humanity frozen out as she recognizes a non-survivable event, shrugs, and gets down to business.

Mana swirls around her as Vulnavia saws robotically on Lecter's strings. Mo can feel his monstrous hunger, his satisfaction as every unshielded soul in the church is sucked toward the giant vortex of belief that he munches on. She is shielded. Her team—wherever they are—are shielded. Vulnavia is shielded, too, but she's too close to ground zero and incapable of resisting Lecter: she's not in his weight class and when the ordinary humans have all been eaten she'll be the violin's dessert.

Mo dashes toward the string section, her invisibility shield still in place. She dodges around standing choirboys and lurching clergy who can't see her—the invisibility is an intermittent impediment at this point. Something behind her is clattering and rattling like a badly stacked rack of dishes atop a washing machine that has started its spin cycle, but she doesn't have time to look. She circles in front of the violinists. All but Vulnavia have collapsed, blood trickling from nostrils and ears. (And what of the royal family? What indeed: but Mo has no time to pay attention to trivia right now.)

*** *Give me that,* *** she snarls at Lecter, using an inner voice she knows he can hear.

*** *Make me.* *** The violin is smug. Typical, Lecter still holds a grudge. (Which is fair: if Mo could break the fiddle over her knee she'd do so in an eyeblink.)

Mo grabs Vulnavia's left forearm—the hand still holding her bow—and tugs. The *mana* flowing through the Countess's arm should by rights have fried her already: it should be sufficient to fry Mo, too. But neither of them is exactly normal, and while her follicles try to climb right out of her skin the *mana* flow doesn't really hit her until she grabs the fiddle itself, which is throwing off blue streamers of decaying soul-stuff and tearing a hole in reality. Then she leans over Vulnavia and grabs Lecter by the neck, closing the circuit.

Vulnavia jackknifes backward in her seat and head-butts Mo. Blinded by sudden hot agony in her face, it's all Mo can do to hang on. Vulnavia goes limp and slumps, releasing the instrument, and Lecter slithers back into Mo's grasp like a rejected and vengeful lover.

Mo has just enough time to think *Oh shit* and then she's fighting to push back against an implacable alien will that wants to overpower her and drain—

—Everyone—

—Everywhere—

—Starting with the congregation in the church but then taking in the entire worldwide audience watching the royal transfer of power being broadcast live on TV—

*** *I do not allow this,* *** Mo thinks, loudly enough to echo through every still-living mind in the nave: and some that are not living for that matter, as she stands (nose streaming blood that dribbles across Lecter's chinrest, from whence it vanishes straight into the bone without leaving a stain). She turns, Lecter squirming in her grasp, and sees—

Oh, right.

Behind the screened off entrance to the royal chapels in the east, stone lids are scraping across the tops of mausoleums. Dead monarchs emerge into the twilight. The door to the staircase leading down to the crypt where the skeletons are stored stands open. Something rustles and clatters as the ancient royal bones, marinated in the *mana* released by the Queen's assassin and animated by whatever feeders it attracts, rise to join the dead and dying upstairs. And outside, everywhere outside, Mo feels the bones of the restless dead rearranging themselves beneath the skin of Westminster.

Pete shouldn't be able to see Mo—she has the curse of middle-aged feminine invisibility, upgraded and boosted by sorcerous intent—but he's known her for decades and he *can* see her, or at least he can see where she is not. And it is not her hand on the fiddle or her chin on the chinrest of the bone violin that is glowing and making him so hungry that he unconsciously drops his fangs. He stands and steps forward, shouldering aside neighbors who don't seem to notice him: then he realizes they don't notice anything at all, for their eyes are glowing visibly even in the blinding daylight of the church. The violin saws at his attention and Pete sees a Mo-shaped absence, a void empty of Dr. O'Brien that pushes its way through the orchestra and touches the seated figure who is not Mo. They jerk and suddenly resolve into two distinct women, one of whom *is* Mo. His hunger is replaced by an unpleasant and unwelcome indigestion, as if he's drowning in a swimming pool of sugar syrup and in trying to swim to the edge he has inadvertently over-ingested.

He perceives the white violin as a thing of horror but he already knew what to expect, Mo ensured he'd been briefed on the events at the Albert Hall the other year: what he doesn't understand is why the other instrumentalists have stopped playing except for the organist. Pete squints at them and observes that they're all drooping, and the choir are slumping in their pews. But then the organ music swells and a new bank of voices joins in a thunderous multi-octave chord that almost covers the dissonant arrhythmic clatter of bones rising from the grave.

Pete taps his headset again. It's still dead. So he turns in place, taking stock of the carnage.

Nearly two thousand of the great and the good variously stand, sit, and slump unmoving. Blood trickles from eyes and noses and ears—and bleeding from the vicinity of the cranial nerves is always a very bad sign. Stunned, dying, or possessed by eaters? Pete can't be sure but he fears the worst.

The Queen has collapsed in the glass coffin, shriveled and shrunk in on herself like a body caught in an intense fire. She is desiccated but unburned, mummified in her formal gown.

This is very bad, he thinks faintly: it's a scene out of somebody else's apocalypse. Who isn't dead? Mo holds the violin, and the woman collapsed beneath her, the concealing glamour comprehensively shredded, is now visible as Countess Mrożek. Who was inserted into the Royal Medical Household by no less an eminence than the Prime Minister. *What has He gotten us into? Where is He? Why isn't He here yet? He could stop this in its tracks—*

Then Pete abruptly realizes, horrified, that the PM is responsible for whatever this is. He had access to the Queen. He could have requisitioned the poison and delivered it on a bone china plate, soaked into her favorite shortbread. His clergy are playing in the orchestra: one of them even has a pale violin. *We serve Him, and when our oath is rebased He'll be our source of authority, not the new King—*

The call is coming from inside the house, as the slasher movies put it, and Mo is wrestling with Lecter. The devil's fiddle went down to Georgia, clearly looking for several million souls to steal, and a discordant clattering lends an arrhythmic percussion to the organ music as bare bones climb out of their graves and prepare to dance with the living while the Queen lies as if dead.

Human remains primed by the belief-in-monarchy of a worshipful population can soak up sufficient *mana* in a flood like this to attract eaters, which animate their hosts and use them to hunt and gorge on those still living—

Pete stands frozen in horror, a mute spectator at the end of the world, wondering what on earth he can do—what anyone can do—to stop this.

"Jolly bad form, wouldn't you agree?" The Prime Minister speaks in Pete's ear, nearly scaring him out of his cassock. His tone is much less agreeable than usual, a monster affronted by events spinning out of control. "This is not what We ordered."

Pete tries to look round but his neck muscles refuse to obey him. It is probably for the best, because even the irrevocably damned may be eligible for a greater damnation if they make eye contact with this particular void—he is suddenly confronted with the realization that there is a transfinite hierarchy of damnations, that hell has more than $\aleph_0$ circles, and that the morning-suited and top-hatted horror who stands at his shoulder is merely the four-dimensional projection of a transdimensional nightmare, a flattened vision of N'yar Lat-Hotep squeezed into our reality through the narrowest of slits.

And the nightmare is displeased.

Pete begins to shake.

"This was not supposed to happen," says the Black Pharaoh, His attention is entirely focused on the crystal coffin, where the desiccated mummy of the Queen twitches and flails as the eaters latch on to whatever *mana* is still attached to her body. "You were supposed to turn her, boy!"

"I can't, I can't—" Pete shudders convulsively. "I've never done that before," he admits. It feels like blasphemy to try to raise Her Majesty as a fucking *vampire*, and yet the alternatives are all just as bad. (*And*, a corner of his mind gibbers, *how the hell did He know?*)

"Better late than never, what," says the PM. A moment later He adds, with some asperity: "Why are you still standing here? Do you need an instruction manual or something?"

Pete finds his feet carrying him forward toward the glass and crystal coffin and the shriveled relic within.

As he bends over the purple-glowing Queen, Pete's mind clears briefly. He's standing in a massive spill of *mana*, much of it squirting through the ancient pores of the monarch, and it makes his teeth itch and his stomach rumble—somatic echoes of his metaphysical hunger. A man without a face hands him a scalpel and he pushes his left sleeve up before slashing a line up his forearm. His blood begins to drip out as he leans toward her, rolls her head gently aside, and kisses the base of her throat. She smells overwhelmingly of baby powder and violets and her octogenarian skin is papery and slack as his fangs drop down further and he tears a hole over her carotid artery and begins to drink. Meanwhile he thrusts the fingers of his left hand between her slackened lips to dribble his blood into her mouth. The mindless chittering of the eaters, an omnipresent white noise at the back of his head, pauses: the new host that he is priming has their undivided attention.

There hasn't been a significant royal death in the UK since the onset of CASE NIGHTMARE GREEN eight years ago, and the precise consequences of uncorking approximately twelve billion royalist-years of belief in Her Semidivine Majesty in the space of a few seconds are only now becoming clear. As Pete becomes dizzy, feeling the majority of his V-parasites latch on to Her Majesty, he understands why.

"Your Majesty." It's Iris Carpenter, her voice pitched low and urgent: "We need to leave now." Pete can just see her in the periphery of his vision. Iris, in black funereal garb with veil, looks anxious-verging-on-terrified: her fingers open and close in the direction of the PM's arm, reluctant to touch but desperate to grasp and drag.

"Explain." If a glacier could speak it would sound like this.

"The police radio system is down, and Forecasting Ops said to expect—"

Pete straightens up: the Queen is breathing again. The tip of her tongue extends between her bloodied lips, licking. It's very pink and plump, like that of the about-to-be crowned twenty-seven-year-old princess she once was.

"It's the Senior Auditor," Pete hears someone say, and he realizes after a moment that it's him. "He got inside your, your"—*what would Bob call it*—"your decision loop."

"Ah." The PM inclines His head. "Thank you, Doctor Russell. Confirmation is welcome." He takes in the coffin, the old-young monarch cringing from the daylight within it, and finally Pete. "Seal the sarcophagus, for her safety." He reaches out and very deliberately attaches Mrs. Carpenter's hand to his opposite forearm. "Shall we be going?"

It's a, a— "You offered him an opportunity," Pete speculates. "To see if he'd take it."

Iris tugs impotently at the PM's arm, mute entreaty clear in her posture. "In a moment, my dear." The void inspects Pete closely. "*We* shall beat a strategic retreat to Downing Street. *You* should lower the lid, then you may stay and assist your playmates, or flee: no blame attaches for your part in the Archbishop's little ruse." The void smiles as the rapidly articulating skeletons in the nave clatter and scrape together into a thing of horror. "It won't be long now: the Eater of Souls is coming."

The ghost roads don't just connect hotels and corridors: they connect crypts and ossuaries and cellars. As I drop my earpiece in my suit pocket and look at the archpriestess I realize we've got more than enough *mana* to break open a path to the crypts beneath Westminster Abbey. It's only a kilometer and a half away but it beats running (especially as my leather-soled shoes are soaked in blood).

"Okay, I'm heading out. Want to tag along?" I ask.

"How—"

I utter a set of parameters in a language that makes my throat feel raw, reach into the void beneath us and grab hold, then tear a hole as I declaim a set of constraints on the tunnel. It's hard work. Catching a ride in a police car would definitely be easier: shame it'd take too long.

I take Victoria's hand and pull her into the tunnel, and as the moment snaps in half we step through into a coldly burning blue hellscape. It's an ossuary or a charnel house and it's full of *mana*, full to overflowing. The overhead lights have blown but there's enough illumination to see, albeit dimly, that the bones are shuddering and trying to attach themselves. My skin crawls with proximity to power. Victoria whimpers, then tugs me toward a door. "This way."

How does she even know—you know what, forget I asked. There's a tight spiral staircase corkscrewing up toward daylight and she dashes up it like a squirrel on an oak tree, a bloody trail splattering from the hem of her robe. I follow, at a slightly more sedate pace—she's a century older than I am, but she's spent most of it dead and my knees haven't—and then I'm in daylight again, in a packed church with organ and violin playing as a disaster unfolds all around.

We've come out behind the orchestra, who are hidden from the congregation by a decorative wooden screen. String and wind instrument players are slumped in their chairs or lying in piles on the floor. There's a heap of fallen choirboys and -girls at one side. In the string section I see something that makes my blood run cold. Mo—I'm behind her, but I'd recognize her anywhere—is engaged with a horribly familiar presence. I can't see it from this angle but I can feel Lecter: the malign, spiteful personality, the whisper of deathly intent in the back of my head. Mo is standing over a fallen woman, and when Victoria sees them she cries "Vulnavia!" and rushes forward. I stick close to her heels because I know that damned violin—it tried to murder me a few years ago. I need to keep the archpriestess and her partner alive, if only for someone to throw under the bus during the after-action inquiry into this clusterfuck.

(Yes I'm ill-disposed toward Phibes and his paramours right now: being press-ganged into officiating at a mass human sacrifice does not fill me with joy. If you know what you're doing there's usually a way to optimize the rite and achieve the same results, the same *mana* release, using five drops of blood and a giant prawn or something. But the time for optimization is before the rite to inter the reigning monarch is underway. Once *that* starts you just have to hold on tight and keep going. Bloodthirsty idiots.)

Victoria gets down on her knees and tries to tug the Countess out from underfoot, which is easier said than done. Mo is wrestling with the bone violin and coming off worse. As I sidle around the orchestra I see blood trickling from her nose and a rich pink tint staining the instrument, which is no longer white but a horrible pale fleshy color, turgid and pulsing with life stolen from the musicians and congregation around us. Anyone who's not wearing a ward is likely having their soul chewed on right now. But Mo is up and fighting, which is the main thing. She carried Lecter for years before he turned on her, and she's stronger now: I'm not sure even she knows how powerful she is.

Which is why I take ten (seconds, not minutes), because the first rule of being a first responder at any kind of major incident is: don't let yourself become one of the victims, too. If you're dead you can't help anyone. I very deliberately stop, turn, and force myself to take in everything around me.

The nave is lined with victims. They're bleeding from the eyes and ears, four rows deep on either side of the red carpet. The transepts and choir are pretty grody, too, the body count racking up in all directions. Those who don't have brain bleeds may be worse—eyes are glowing pale green, wormy filaments twirling slowly as the eaters take over, especially among the ceremonial procession that has stalled on the fancy rug. It's like an organ recital for an audience of very fresh zombies in morning suits, posh designer frocks, and dress uniforms.

Not everyone is gone, though. I spot Pete, in cassock and surplice. He's just lowered the lid on the royal sarcophagus, and now he's looking at me, frantically gesticulating toward the back of one transept. Nearby I spot Iris and a tall, instantly recognizable faceless eminence—*it figures*—beating a hasty retreat in the middle of a meat shield of men and women in black suits. I tap my earpiece again but it stubbornly refuses to work. Which is probably why we haven't been swarmed by armed police and an OCCULUS team or two.

And then Royal Harry comes out to play.

Now, I'm used to dealing with Residual Human Resources, and the newer Harry variants (with motors attached to keep things moving and an eater on board to drive the thing around), but this is something qualitatively different. Most of the skeletons emerging from the royal chapels in the east arm of the church are very old and quite small by modern standards—not surprising, in the case of Mary, Queen of Scots, and Queen Elizabeth the First—but they're animated by a power that makes my hair stand on end. There's no need for stepper motors and staples to hold these bonewalkers together. They swim in a sea of numinous power, dressed in what's left of the finery they were buried in. (Most cloth disintegrates over centuries, and not one of these royal stiffs is less than four hundred years dead.)

More bones are rising. A clattering and creaking echoes from the corridor to the Chapter House, and chairs are being pushed aside as the stony floor rucks up unevenly and breaks apart. The burial vaults beneath appear to have indigestion. I can hear the chitter and hiss of eaters all around, converging on the choir and orchestra. They're embodied and there are dozens, maybe hundreds of them: and it feels like Lecter is calling them. I'll have to work fast.

That's when I spot the drooling cabinet minister (blonde, female, had been tapped as Most Likely To Be The Next Leader before His Nibs came out of left field and scooped the trophy) standing in the middle of the carpet. Her eyes are blue and empty because the eaters have had their fill and moved on, but she's still holding a broadsword that's at least three sizes too big for her. Something about it claws ominously at my senses. In a normal royal ceremony it would have been one of the swords from the crown jewels collection, the Sword of Mercy or the Sword of Spiritual Justice—but this one is the Sword of Temporal Justice. And *that will do*, I think as I make a grab for it. "Sorry, Penny," I say to her as I remove Excalibur from her nerveless fingers and take an experimental swing at the first skeleton to make it out of the corridor.

I have no real idea how to use a sword, other than a general understanding that you can't trust what you see in the movies or on stage. Excalibur feels really weird, too: heavier than I'd expected, with a center of gravity toward the tip, which is blunt and squared-off. It's designed for the same job as a headsman's axe, not fencing. But that's not the weirdest thing about it. As I grasp its hilt, I sense that Excalibur feels disgruntled. As well it might: I'm holding it like a cricket bat, and that's *obviously* wrong. I had no idea a sword could feel affronted, but if Excalibur was a cat his back would be arched and his tail bristling like a bog-brush at the indignity of it all, of being grabbed and held the wrong way by an ill-bred commoner oik like myself.

Nevertheless the blade slices nicely through the spongy half-decomposed cervical vertebrae of whichever lord or lady is first out of the crypt, sending their skull and disarticulated mandible clattering across the floor. The light in the revenant's eye sockets goes dark, the rest of the rattling bones drop, and I get a tiny little jolt of *mana* which goes down nicely. *Good.*

You may well ask why I'm not simply opening my imaginary jaws and ploughing through the battalion of Harries like a blue whale through a sea full of krill. Well, here's the thing: not everyone in the church is dead. Penny, the Lord President of the Privy Council who I took the sword from, is staggering and out of her head but not dead yet. I think she was protected from the Queen's *mana* blowout by her very big chopper. The PM is still in the house because He and His entourage are having trouble pushing through the mob of panicking survivors clogging up the main entrance. Mo and Victoria and the Countess are still alive, and so is the Abominable Organist. Phibes is still hammering the organ like he thinks he's Jean-Michel Jarre. So I'm not about to turn this into any more of a mass casualty event than it already is by going full Eater of Souls on the venue.

Which is probably why it all goes wrong.

I back toward the string section, intending to put myself and my sword between Mo and the Harries that are drifting toward the nave (pausing every now and then to touch and infect another human victim) because I'm outnumbered, and forcing the skeletons to come at me in single file is my best bet. Behind me Mo saws frantically at Lecter's neck, and I feel more than see the flood of *mana* slowing: now that the Queen's in the coffin, her accumulated power is in short supply, and Lecter has sprayed so much of it away that—

Oh. That's not good. That's bad.

Victoria is on her feet. She has one of the Countess's arms slung over her shoulder, and Mo is trying to shield them from something. Harries are trying to come at me around the sides and back of the choir, tapping the musicians and singers with bony eater-infested fingers, *tag you're it*, and as their eyes light up they tag the next swooning figure in turn, a wave of possession converging on me. They're all in thrall to *something*, some ancient malign intention unleashed from the royal ossuary. No, not *something*, it's a *someone*, one of the oldest royals interred here: and he wants his sword back.

So that's when the eater-stricken bodies of the Westminster Abbey Choir rise up and swarm me. They drag me down by sheer weight of numbers, uncaring who lives or dies, reaching to seize Excalibur's blade with half-severed digits and arterially gouting limbs. The survivors present its stolen hilt to the bony hand of Arthur Pendragon, king of the Britons. And he has soaked up so much royal *mana* that the royal zap when he is reunited with his sword drops me straight into the black depths of unconsciousness.

Pete watches as a chaotic fight breaks out in the nave: the PM and His entourage hurry toward the exit; a crush develops at the main entrance; a mob of skeletons and eater-possessed bodies swarms into the church and sweeps over the audience; Mo grabs a white violin while the brides of Phibes struggle to stand; the organ music swells; and Bob is dragged down beneath a wave of possessed bodies.

Pete knows he should help but this is so far outside his experience that he doesn't know what he can do other than try to survive and bear witness. He's already done his bit—delivered the Archbishop's plan of last resort to protect the Queen from the PM—only to discover that the PM was one jump ahead of them all along. With PHANG-enhanced vision he can follow the *mana* as easily as a forensic accountant can follow a money trail: a cable feeding the white violin enabled Lecter to latch onto the Queen at the moment of transition, sinking metaphysical fangs into her royalty and draining her power before it could be transferred to her heir. Now she's a PHANG suspended in the crystalline sleep enforced by Phibes's coffin, she's neither dead nor alive, no longer a threat to the New Management.

But after doing his bit Lecter engaged in a gluttonous feeding frenzy, and his messy eating habits have drenched the crypt in surplus *mana*. It trickles down to the dusty bones below and now they're rising, not just the Lancastrian and Yorkist factions or the heirs of William the Bastard, but the revenants of ancient, pre-Norman kings.

Here's the thing: before the tenth century, England didn't exist (never mind the United Kingdom). To the likes of Pendragon, the House of Windsor are the incomprehensibly alien rulers of a foreign empire, heirs to Viking invaders who arrived centuries after his death and massacred the Saxons and Angles who had in turn murdered, enslaved, and supplanted his Britons. They don't speak the same language, observe the same laws, eat the same foods, or worship the same gods. And that's why Dr. Armstrong, the Senior Auditor, arranged for Vulnavia Mrożek to receive Lecter: Armstrong serves the Crown, not any particular monarch or dynasty, and he wants to dump a sufficiency of power into the oldest bones to raise the most ancient ruler with a legitimate claim to the fallen throne of Wintancaester.

It's not clear to Pete why Dr. Armstrong would do this, or why Vulnavia went along with his plan: what is clear is that Dr. Armstrong did so with intent to derail the Black Pharaoh's claim to the throne once the perfidious Windsors were brought to heel. He probably obtained Vulnavia's cooperation by means of bribery, lies, blackmail, or all three. It is also clear that the Black Pharaoh anticipated some sort of betrayal: but the PM gave Pete a choice, didn't He, which suggests He's not *too* upset about the Church's attempt to save the Queen's life. And now Pete is supposed to bear witness to whatever happens next.

Well, thinks Pete, finally shaking free of his horrified bystander syndrome, *fuck that*: he dives into the haunted mosh pit behind the orchestra screen and starts flailing around in search of people to rescue.

Pete is a PHANG: his brain is already thoroughly squatted by V-symbionts, leaving precious little room for eaters to get their metaphysical fangs into him. Which is a really good thing right now because most of the bodies in the choir are thoroughly possessed, eyes glowing, limbs twitching in tetanic spasms as they reach for him. He is also vampirically strong, though he feels the guilt-fires of hell every time he yanks a body off the heap and throws it over his shoulder because he knows someone else will pay for it later when he indents for an extra blood meal. Nevertheless he ploughs into the pile and in a matter of minutes digs down to find Bob Howard, lying unconscious under the woodwind section, who are all beyond saving.

Pete picks Bob up carefully, trying not to damage him—PHANG-assisted strength is dangerous—then looks round. Mo is still wrestling with her violin, which is screeching atonal imprecations at the royal family. Victoria and the Countess have somehow staggered clear of the mob of zombies and are stumbling toward the organ bench. Victoria is screaming something at her husband, possibly along the lines of "You idiot, this is all your fault!" or "Can't I even trust you to assassinate the Queen without me holding your hand?" Everywhere he looks the wheels are coming off the ceremony and bouncing across the landscape shedding chunks of burning rubber, and it's all going out live on TV and streaming on the internet.

Welp. He looks down, and that's when Bob moans, shudders, and begins to wake up.

*** *Too late! Too late!* *** The violin cackles with discordant glee in the back of Mo's head.

Mo feels as if she's living through a bad dream. Not the kind where she's turned up to sit an exam for a subject she hasn't studied, then realized she's naked and doesn't have a pen: that kind of dream doesn't leave you with PTSD. *This* dream puts her right back in the Albert Hall for that fateful Last Night of the Proms four years ago, trying to keep a grip on Lecter and losing. Trying to keep him from dementedly fiddling with the bindings on reality in an attempt to place a trunk call to the King in Yellow.

Only that's not the monarch he's calling this time.

*** *What are you doing?* *** she demands, forcing her mind to confront the squirming inhuman mass of hate that she holds onto with bleeding fingertips. Lecter doesn't feel like a stringed instrument, he's more like the mantle of an octopus that restlessly grasps human bystanders in the coils of its feeding tentacles, draining and discarding their husks, then moving on in search of more. She struggles to let go of the bow, but her fingers are clamped so tightly that they threaten to cramp. Her hands continue to move the fiddle and finger the board in spite of her willing them to stop.

*** *You know what I'm doing!* *** Lecter giggles horribly. *** *I'm feeding!* ***

*** Who *are you feeding?* ***

*** *The unclothed bones!* *** Lecter gloats: *** *They answer to one of their own! Come to me, my children!* ***

Mo squeaks aloud involuntarily. *** *Stop it!* ***

The violin is already bloated with death but he just won't stop: like a fox in a henhouse, he's already sufficiently fed but continues killing for the sheer joy of murder, frolicking over an open grave. And the tenuous stream of *mana* isn't directionless anymore: Lecter is discharging it with precisely targeted malice.

*** *I'm doing what Mike asked me to do! What he convinced the idiot* *** —Lecter is archly contemptuous of Countess Mrożek— *** *to do for him! I'm raising the King of the Britons! Isn't it* fun? ***

Mo wrestles to control her treacherous limbs, but either she has grown weaker or—more likely—Lecter is much more powerful now he's been fed. Either way, it's a very uneven struggle. Meanwhile someone kneeling nearby struggles to lift Vulnavia (*Is she even alive?* a corner of Mo's mind wonders), and a charnel house erupts like a bone volcano around her. It blocks her view of the madly gesticulating organist, who wears a black hood like a judge preparing to hand down a death sentence.

*** *Why?* *** she demands of Lecter.

*** Michael promised me the Black Pharaoh! *** gibbers the cursed instrument, and in a burst of liminal horror, Mo realizes who her actions really serve.

The danse macabre is fearsomely frolicsome, even though the revenants are largely incomplete—none of them are remotely as well put together as the late Harry 61. They're everywhere, but none of them intrudes on Mo's personal space yet: they're leaving Lecter room to play. (And they don't reek, which is a small mercy.) She hears distant shouting and then a crashing and clattering as of skittles being knocked flying. It reminds her of the time she and Bob were invited to an after-work bowling session. (Their team won but lost four sick days due to a rotator cuff injury and various sprains, leading HR to add bowling to the "banned team-building tasks for over-40s" list, along with BASE jumping, five-a-side rugby, and chimp wrestling.)

Lecter screeches angrily, distracted by something happening in the nave. While he's distracted Mo manages to rip the bow away from his fingerboard and throw it across the orchestra pit. Then a sea of skeletons buffets her on all sides. She ducks and covers, and finds Victoria—wholly different now she's alive—hauling Vulnavia's limp body toward the organ, where Phibes is still playing like a madman possessed.

Human skeletons are not particularly heavy: a complete, fully articulated adult weighs only 10 to 12 kilograms, and most of the necromantic mosh pit surrounding Mo are incomplete. They may be animated and energized by eaters—their touch is deadly to the unwarded—but Mo is far beyond their power. They carry other, indirect, dangers. One of them scoops up the discarded bow and three others latch onto her left hand, dragging it down while their companion forces the instrument into her bleeding fingers. The fiddle is passed hand-to-hand until it returns to her unwilling grip. Then Lecter takes charge of her arms once more, playing her as if she is the instrument and he the musician. *No*, she tries to scream, but words don't serve her, and the dance of death resumes.

Lecter's will reaches out, the ghost-octopus expanding in five or six dimensions to pack the church with coils of rubbery inevitability. He resumes sucking the souls out of baronesses and bishops and marquesses and ministers, squirting an efflux of *mana* at *something* that is pulling itself laboriously together in the underground crypt. That *something* is trying very hard to push its way through the veil of years separating it from the present day, to make itself real in an age that has no need for its kind anymore.

Horrified, Mo tries to make it all stop. But there's a gang of skeletons piling up between her and Lecter's victims, her fingers refuse to obey her, and then a body crashes into the woodwind section and a pile of bones descends on whoever it is. Another gang of skeletons reaches for her, and finally Lecter lets go of her bleeding hands and drops. Whereupon he's borne away on an ossuary tide. Pete arrives, casting bones aside like a dog that is off the leash in canine heaven—there is something deeply *wrong* about this, vicars are supposed to treat the deceased with dignity and solemn respect on behalf of the bereaved—then he stoops and rises again, holding an unconscious body in his arms.

It's her husband.

I discovered afterward that I wasn't unconscious for very long—a few seconds, followed by perhaps a minute of utter confusion while the deafening chaos in my head clears up and my vision comes back and I realize the deafening chaos *outside* my head is still very much ongoing. A vampire in clerical drag is leaning over me with an alarmed expression as the organ recital rises to a frenzied crescendo, then shifts into a throbbing techno beat that belongs on a stage at Glastonbury. A line of mildewed skeletons led by a dead prince playing a haunted violin dances the can-can in the aisle, supported by the rapidly but rhythmically lurching possessed choristers of Westminster Abbey. The screams and wails of the not-yet-deceased reverberate around me as Pete mouths something inaudible which, after a moment's confusion, I recognize as *Are you all right?*

"Help me up." Pete grabs my hand and lifts effortlessly until I'm on my feet again.

"Where's—"

(The angry violin is receding: I distantly notice another violin banging inside its case on the floor. Victoria kicked it under a chair but she's not here anymore. I cast around and spot the Countess frog-marching her toward the organist's bench, where Phibes hammers the manuals like a man possessed. He's pulled out all the stops and the thunder of the pipes washes over me in a deafening cascade.)

"—Mo?"

Pete gestures down the aisle and I see her hand waving and then I feel her in my head, incanting something terrible in a voice like thunder. She issues orders to the undead, an injunction to cease and desist, or maybe decease: this is an Auditor in the fullness of her power, tapping into the wellspring of *mana* under Mahogany Row. The entire front rank of the undead lies down and stops moving with terrible finality, but that doesn't even put a dent in their numbers. There must be two thousand people in the audience this morning, a smaller body count than the catastrophe at the Albert Hall: but this one is fueled by almost all the accumulated *mana* of the past sixty years of monarchy. If I leave Mo to handle this on her own she'll be overwhelmed sooner or later. And in the meantime, a dead king stole Excalibur.

I roll up my mental sleeves and get to work, thinning the swarm of eaters gathered to celebrate the passing of the monarchy with an alfresco buffet of Burke's Peerage. I'm the Eater of Souls, the skin-suit of the Hungry Ghost from Dansey House, and individual eaters are like deep-fried scampi to me these days: tasty but not very filling. You can't swallow just one of them, and I don't pause between morsels as their dying wails dwindle down my throat. But something huge and ugly is waking underground, groaning and rolling over in the darkness, and I'm pretty sure it's too big to swallow at a single bite. It may be too big for the likes of me full stop, something even the avatar of the Black Pharaoh might find troublesome.

Mo is still tackling possessed bodies piecemeal, touching foreheads or faces or exposed hands so that the green glow vanishes from their eyes and they fall to the floor. It's the normal outcome when an unshielded member of the public is possessed and then banished: forget *The Exorcist*, this stuff is invariably fatal. But there are more zombies crowding her from behind—and then there's me. I push toward her, leaving a wake of corpses. (Don't look at me like that: they were already dead before I got here.)

I finally catch up with her. "We've got to go!" I shout: "Follow Lecter—"

"I know what I'm doing!" Mo is angry and uptight. She turns her back, but then she adds, "Cover my six?" And this is no time for a domestic argument. So I go back-to-back with her and together we work to put down the undead. They gravitate toward us like lemmings performing for a particularly ruthless wildlife documentary faker. There's no point feeling sorry for them— they're not even alive, strictly speaking—but it's as unsporting as shooting grouse on the 12th of August with a machine gun, and the outcome is just as predictable. Eventually the flood begins to recede, and Mo and I stumble toward the crystal coffin.

The lid is down and the containment grid is powered up. An infinite darkness fills the coffin, shrouding the Queen in robes of midnight. Pete stands beside it, looking unaccountably guilty for someone who just saved the monarchy. "She'll keep for the time being," I tell him, trying for a reassuring tone. (The truth is less palatable. She's suspended between death and dying as long as the coffin is sealed, but there's no coming back from PHANG syndrome. She's not dying anymore, but her sunbathing days are over. Pretty soon someone's going to have to wake her up and explain the facts of vampirism to her, and I do *not* expect her to be amused. Worse: her descendants have been hit hard, like everyone else in the church—the lesser royals lie unmoving between their seats. Although a quick count suggests several of Lizzie's brood escaped before the situation became non-survivable, or weren't here in the first place—it's not a toddler-friendly ceremony.) "What does this do to the binding oath . . ." I shake my head.

"Nothing good," Mo mutters. She leans on me unsteadily. Unlike me she can't extract any *mana* from the eaters she's put down: she must be exhausted.

"Who set this up?" I ask, looking at the organ. The bench is empty, the Phibes ménage having disappeared. Knowing his predilection for underground escape routes they're probably fleeing via the sewers to the buried River Tyburn which flows under Regents Park. He'll have a punt or rowing boat moored there, waiting. It's the fastest way out of the church: there's still a crush near the exits, as the panicked survivors try to escape.

"Mike." Mo's voice is rough, her throat sore from chanting words of banishment in Old Enochian. "He set this up. He'd know exactly how to summon Lecter. How to trick Vulnavia into trying to play him. How to corrupt your oath of office." Her anger is incendiary, building toward a thermite-flare of rage.

"Fuck." It's shorthand for *Quis custodiet ipsos custodes?* Who will watch the watchmen? Very much fuck indeed: Mike was the backstop, the Senior Auditor, but he has form—after all, he's the one who ran Iris as a double agent for a decade, then made a deal with the devil to install the Black Pharaoh in Number Ten. The worm turns, and turns again, and it looks like Mike engineered most of this mess specifically to free all of us in the Laundry from our oath of office while he cheerfully backstabs the New Management. "Where is he?"

"It's a double fake-out. Mike was in the passage to the Chapter House." Pete gestures from behind a pile of bishops: "But the PM was also here, he *knew* the Archbishop wanted me to raise Her Majesty as a last resort, he told me to go right ahead. He's been one jump ahead of the rest of us all along. Let me just lower her into the crypt and we can get out of here." He turns toward the glass coffin again, leaning over a hip-deep pile of dead choirboys.

"Are you with—" I pause: Mo has picked up the violin case that the Countess shoved her other violin in. I can hear it keening in the back of my head, *** *Let me out, let me out.* *** "Never mind, I'm with Mo. Love, are you going to unleash—"

"Yes. This isn't Lecter." She doesn't look at me as she unlatches the case and yanks out a carved bone instrument with glowing blue strings. I swear the thing is quivering in fear. "Right. *You*," she glares at the lesser instrument, "will do *exactly* what I say, or it's the log chipper for you."

*** *Put me back,* *** whines the fiddle, but she ignores it and picks up its bow instead. She plays an experimental note, then adjusts a peg minutely. "Let's go," she says, and leads us past a windrow of dead ambassadors and emissaries.

Priorities, we have them: the thing in the crypt is still slurping up the spilled *mana* in the chapels around us, and it will rise sooner or later. Meanwhile Dr. Armstrong may be escaping and if we can arrest him there's still some hope of regaining control of the situation. My earpiece is still dead, so I can't check in with our support units and confirm that the Black Pharaoh has escaped. If he hasn't, and the flood of eaters gets loose in Central London, there's going to be carnage on an unimaginable scale. But the first law of any summoning is don't raise what you can't put down, and Mike's not stupid: he'll have set up a kill switch this time, even if he fucked up when he invited N'yar Lat-Hotep into the tent in the first place.

"Cover me again," Mo tells me, as she hangs a left toward the imposing doors at the back of ambassador alley. The doors are blocked by a handful of shamblers—cops in dress uniform, their eyes glowing and their protective wards burned out— which for some reason don't want to let us past. Sucks to be them: while Mo is busy intimidating her borrowed instrument I open my imaginary maw and go snicker-snack. The eaters in vacant possession of their bodies are thin and flimsy eating, but they're out of the way.

When Mo glances over her shoulder I shrug: "After you."

Beyond the doors we find the abandoned temporary command post. A handful of bodies are sprawled on the floor and slumped at their stations, some of them still twitching. At the far end of the corridor the doors to the Chapter House stand ajar. Mo makes straight for them, a flat note of horror movie menace rising from her fiddle. It makes my hackles rise. She's the final girl stalking the monster in the horror movie, only it's all wrong: the monster is her mentor and department head, we're doing this to protect an ancient evil that has successfully usurped the Crown (or at least taken it in check), the dead Kings of England are coming out to play and they don't like modernity, and—

My earpiece crackles just as I see Mike Armstrong step into view between the doors. "Hello, Bob," he says through my earpiece, his tone apologetic. "Ruby—Seminole—Kriegspiel—Hatchet—execute Untergang."

Time stops. And when it restarts, Mo and Dr. Armstrong aren't there.

"Something's dashed wrong with our monarchy today, don't you agree?" The Prime Minister is chillingly avuncular as a phalanx of police officers in gothic plate armor with raised basilisk guns screen his escape from Westminster Abbey.

"Not my place to comment, sir." Iris Carpenter speed-walks at his side, wincing slightly as her very expensive shoes pinch her toes. She's desperate not to fall behind. A bolus of icy terror rises in her stomach, threatening to strangle what's left of her sanity like a python. "What *is* that thing?"

As a priestess of the Black Pharaoh, Iris has both the aptitude and training to feel the giant stack of bones watching them hungrily as it tries to claw its scattered body back together. It's a self-assembling sculpture of charnel house matchsticks, nightmarish and ravenous from the passage of time.

"The House of Windsor has been storing up *mana* for decades, and it's finally overflowed its mortal container." The PM sounds mildly irritated. "One possible low probability outcome, albeit regrettably damaging. Omelettes, cracked eggs, you know the proverb. Come along now."

He takes control of Iris's peripheral nervous system and she finds herself a passenger in her own body, reaching out and involuntarily taking hold of his hand. Their police escort barely notices the curiously intimate gesture—He can block their perceptions at whim—but suddenly all the pains of middle age fall away and Iris can prance like an Olympic gymnast. (She'll suffer in hospital afterward, might even end up in a wheelchair for life, but that's better than being eaten by the nightmare clattering at their heels.)

Her earpiece buzzes. She taps it with her free hand. "Yes?" She listens to a scared subordinate: "No, I'm with him right now, we're on our way to Number Ten." A red police SUV with PTU markings pulls up ahead and a guard holds the door open for them. Iris climbs in beside the PM and they move off with lights but no sirens. Whitehall, the main thoroughfare from Westminster Palace to Trafalgar Square, is empty of all traffic. It's like a scene from a disaster movie, in the minutes before the bomb drops or the hours after the Z-virus escapes. There were crowds behind the barriers just two hours ago. They're still here but they're lying down motionless. Luminous green lights spiral hypnotically in their eyes like the colorful broodsacs of worm-parasitized snails. "Activate defense contingency red. Carpenter out." She taps out of the call and sighs. "I hope that's enough."

"SCORPION STARE won't work against Arthur Pendragon, you know."

She looks at the PM, wide-eyed. He seems—she feels it in the angle of His head, the shape of the sucking void He wears in place of a face—almost *amused*. "Why ever not?" she demands, only slightly panicky.

"The basilisk observer-effect transmutes carbon nuclei into silicon. It only affects a tiny fraction of them, and it plays fast and loose with the conservation of mass/energy—shortens the lifespan of this particular universe every time it happens, risking collapse of the false vacuum—but you see, there's precious little carbon on the surface of a moldy old bone." The void in the seat beside her grins like a skull. "Skeletons don't burn." The effect of transmuting a fraction of a percent of the carbon in a body to silicon is more like a bomb going off than fast fossilization. "It'll clear the roadkill quite effectively, though."

This morning there were a third of a million spectators waiting alongside Whitehall for a last glimpse of their Queen. Then the eaters, attracted by the massive *mana* blowout when Lecter attacked her, moved in, looking for something to eat.

The PM smacks His invisible lips, as if He, too, is hungry.

"Isn't that a rather extreme solution?"

"Nonsense, you can never have too many human sacrifices." The PM corrects Himself a moment later: "As long as one refrains from rendering the nutritive species extinct, of course." The BMW pulls up outside the gates of Downing Street and the officers on duty leap to open the doors. "After you, my dear."

Iris stalks inside, the PM on her heels. "Where to?" she asks.

"The back patio, I think." His imaginary grin is toothy. "And thence to the Pyramid of the Sleeper."

Ten Downing Street shares a garden with the Chancellor's residence at Number 12, sheltered and concealed from public view by high walls and security fences. There is an incongruous patio at the rear of the building, and Iris leads the PM out onto the flagstones overlooking the lawn, where the staff have placed the furniture from the chapel He established in the former Admiralty Wine Cellar.

The PM snaps His fingers. "Robe up." Iris dons her black silk surplice, then holds the PM's own robes for Him as he slides his arms through the sleeves of his cassock, like an eminent surgeon preparing for the operating theater.

"May I ask," she begins, then falls silent, her lips painfully dry.

"You may." His grin is cadaverous.

"Wh-what just happened?"

"Never interrupt your enemy when he is making a mistake." The faceless eminence adjusts His surplice. "Which in this case is attempting to back out of a done deal, which would be My assumption of office."

"Who—" Iris's mind snaps to a conclusion with leg-breaking force. "Dr. Armstrong."

"Indeed." The Black Pharaoh nods with terrible gravity.

"That's treason." She pauses. "I assume you planned for it."

"Of course." The head without a face turns toward her. "He's not the only person playing games today, of course, but they are mostly accounted for. Nothing like a dynastic rupture to flush out the false courtiers, what? Be not afraid: your loyalty is recognized. But you are not Our only priestess. I have other clergy, of considerable power but less reliability." The PM raises His left wrist, where a Rolex Daytona gleams incongruously. "One in particular is running late, but she should arrive any time now." He gestures at the far side of the summoning grid laid out before the altar. "If you would be so good as to anchor the southern axis? Only until our guests arrive."

Iris pauses. "Who is she?"

"My archpriestess. Vicky is the last of the anointed bloodline, unfortunately. I'm expecting her, along with her consorts, wife and husband." The PM turns to the altar. It's a plain slab of stone bearing certain ritual objects: a silver cup and an ivory wand with gold end caps. These are placed around an inlaid metal grid with a ribbon cable trailing toward a laptop on a cart nearby. The altar is centered on the patio inside a circle of steel inscribed with writing in an alien syllabary. The PM places a canvas roll on the altar, releases the ties that hold it closed, and unwraps a filleting knife; then he removes a fiber-tip pen that paints with silver conductive ink, and uses it to draw a diagram around the periphery of the summoning grid. "It is time for a reckoning! And then I shall assume my final form."

I'm off-balance, fighting my way back to awareness through a wall of brain fog. The corridor crackles with sorcerous static that sets my teeth on edge. I stumble forward, catch my balance, wondering where everybody went. Then I realize: Mike used my command code to trigger a buried macro, something he left in my head last time he activated my oath of office. I don't know what it was supposed to do, but it was obviously nothing good. Now he and Mo are missing and time has passed. I glance at my watch and see it's been three minutes, which is an eternity in a sorcerous firefight. I open my mind's eye wide and see eaters clustering outside the corridor. There's precious little left to feed on in here apart from me, and it'd be like minnows trying to take down a megalodon. But like calls to like.

The PM. This is all about the PM, of that I can be certain. And Continuity Operations. CO was the plan to preserve the Laundry and continue its core mission in event of a disastrous government initiative. It was CO—in the person of Mike Armstrong—that made a Faustian pact with the Black Pharaoh. So, obviously there was also a contingency plan to get rid of His Dread Majesty if things go too far, equally obviously Mike has now activated it . . . and the wheels are falling off, we're in the middle of a magical singularity, Pete is trying to raise the fucking Queen as a vampire because it's the lesser evil, and I last saw the PM evacuating in the direction of—

Oh shit.

I make my way through the Chapter House (currently hosting an undead dance party) and escape from the Abbey through a back entrance. The paving stones and neatly manicured lawn of St. Margaret's Churchyard are all churned up, graves gaping open like empty sockets in a mandible denuded by a demonic dentist. They all want to join in the danse macabre.

I hotfoot it in the direction of the Palace of Westminster, then hang a left past Parliament Square Garden and jog down Whitehall.

Everything is wrong. The helicopters have left. There's a plume of smoke rising from the South Bank, just visible over the gothic roofline of parliament. There were crowds lining the temporary barriers along the side of the road but they're taking a dirt nap. A skin-crawling sensation of being watched tells me all I need to know. I tap my earpiece again—and now that Mike isn't jamming it, it works. "Howard here, sitrep anybody."

"Sir? OCCULUS FOUR, Blue Three here—I have eyes on you. Sir, you need to get out of sight now, there's a General Activation Alert for SCORPION STARE on Whitehall and Westminster Abbey, three-minute warning. Uh, two minutes, forty-second warning and *mark*."

The rise and fall of air raid sirens bleeds through my earpiece. SCORPION STARE is the network of basilisk cameras that protects the center of our larger cities against incursions by Kaiju, Shoggoths, unicorns, and other legendary nightmares; also anti-N'yar Lat-Hotep demonstrations and attempts to overthrow the New Management by force. It's only been activated once before, during the *alfär* invasion that leveled the center of Leeds and killed twenty thousand civilians. Firing it up in Central London is a very bad sign: it means mass casualties are acceptable collateral damage in the face of whatever's about to hit us.

"Did the PM come this way?" I ask, with a catch in my breath—I'm not used to jogging.

"Principal was evac'd to Downing Street five minutes ago. You are six hundred meters away."

"Can you"—gasp—"notify SCORPION Commander that I'm on my way and need rolling cover?"

"On it."

The bodies behind the barriers to either side of Whitehall are stirring. A quick side-eye tells me that they're possessed. Behind me something unspeakable is awakening in Westminster Abbey, preparing to emerge into the daylight for the first time in over a thousand years. I pass a windrow of dead civilians, then I'm about halfway to Downing Street when a big red incident command truck rumbles up beside me and somebody throws the door open. "Agent HOWARD, your ride's here," says my earpiece.

I grab the proffered hand gratefully and a soldier in everything-old-is-new-again steel plate armor lifts me bodily into the front passenger seat. "Rolling," says the voice in my ear and we lurch into motion before I can grab my seat belt.

Less than a minute later we screech to a halt outside the security gates. I fumble the door open and jump down. "How long have I got?"

"SCORPION STARE goes live in thirty seconds but you are now outside the automatic engagement zone."

Thank fuck, I think. "Where is that?"

"Westminster Abbey, Parliament Square, and everything within a two-hundred-meter radius of the Abbey. It's all going to be a permissive fire area in . . . twenty seconds."

"Right, well I'll just"—the police on gate duty are opening the barrier and waving—"talk to the—" *Fuck.* And the gate is closing again. It only opened to allow a short figure clad from toe to helm in polished steel armor to step out in front of me. "What?"

"Bob." I still do a slight reflexive cringe at her more-in-sorrow-than-in-anger tone.

"Mhari? Sitrep?"

Mhari—my last ex, before I met Mo—is now Baroness Karnstein, chair of the House of Lords Select Committee on Sanguinary Affairs, vampire-in-chief to the New Management. And she clatters ominously as she walks. She's clad head to toe in new pattern fluted gothic plate armor (titanium is protective against basilisk weapons, unlike high-carbon steel). Worn over a silicone body stocking it's enough to keep a PHANG from cooking off in full daylight. Mind you, she's got to be melting in all that metal, even though it's a mild spring morning with a London overcast. "I'm Gold Commander today." She walks past me and opens the side door of the OCCULUS truck. "Get in the truck, His Majesty says this is the big one."

She gestures toward the park at the far end of the road and I hear a clattering and rattling as a couple of platoons of Harries do their herky-jerky march toward us, like a macabre reenactment of one of the Terminator movies. Behind them there's a rumble of diesel engines as a couple of Challenger 2s grind into position, tank crews buttoned up inside as their turrets traverse to enfilade Whitehall.

"The big what, exactly?" I follow Mhari to the back of the command truck, which is full of PHANGs in armor instead of the normal SAS headbangers. Hell, maybe the Artists Rifles are vampires these days, I mean, why not? They're all suited and booted in white plate, armed to the teeth and ready to rip arms and legs off whoever we're waiting for. The only reassuring thing is that they're not wearing *alfär*-pattern plate—and on second thought that's not very reassuring either. The *alfär* host are mostly posted overseas these days, but the New Management's pointy-eared version of the Wagner Group are all about occult firepower, and I would find a squadron of heavy equoid cavalry kind of reassuring right now.

"Off with the monkey suit, Bob." I shrug out of my jacket, pull off my tie, and a team of unarmored PHANGs in black silicone gimp suits close in and strip me down like a pit crew attacking a Formula One car during a tire stop.

"The big nemesis." Mhari shrugs—it's amazing how much expressive mobility there is in a well-fitted suit of armor. "We're up against a resurrected state level actor. Lecter bled the Queen's *mana* and spilled a load, thinning the walls of the world with a royal sacrifice, and it's given the oldest king in the crypt a jump start. Our job is to stop him biting the heads off what's left of the royal family and Parliament, while the boss gets on the hotline to his greater avatar, who is still stuck in the land of the dead, and diff-merges him so that he can adopt his final form."

"Whu—" I nearly swallow my tongue. "I thought this was a double cross op? By Mike?"

"Leave it for the after-action report." Someone hands me a great big sword with a squared-off point, sheathed in a fiberglass scabbard embossed with the portcullis-and-crown symbol of Parliament. "Sign there, Bob." Mhari points to a very official-looking form on a clipboard. "Not every day someone hands you a national treasure."

"The fuck." I sign. "It says this is Excalibur 2.0. But I thought that's what the Leader of the House was carrying? That giant skeleton-thing grabbed it—"

"Miracle of modern metallurgy." I swear I can hear Mhari grimace inside her tin can. "There wasn't enough of the original left uncorroded to forge a new sword so they melted it down and made two or three, or maybe a dozen, replacement Excaliburs. There's enough iron from the original in it to make a Minimum Viable Product—they're all entangled, so as long as only one is being wielded at a time it works, kind of like a preemptively multitasking magic sword—unlike the one in the Abbey this one is ultra-low carbon, made from high-grade maraging steel."

The penny drops as I take the sword. "The risen dead are proof against SCORPION STARE but Arthur's sword isn't . . ."

"Listen to me, Bob." Mhari briefs me while one of the other vampires shoves me legs-first into what feels like a wetsuit. There's a dress stand with a suit of armor waiting behind them and I'll bet it's my size. "The psychic shock would kill a human or a PHANG so you're our best shot at decapitating Arthur, King of the Britons. The rest of us are just along for the ride.

And to hold off the rampaging horde of eaters, of course, we don't have time for you to deal with them first."

"You want me to chop King Arthur's head off. With Excalibur."

"Yes, Bob, it's traditional. That is not dead which can eternal lie, and he's been down for more than a thousand years at this point. There's a linear feeding circuit embedded in the blade, you can suck his soul out through it like a blood smoothie. It's an executioner's sword, after all. Once you're armored up we'll get you into position outside the Banqueting House, then lure him along Whitehall so you can get the job done."

I shake my head and lift my other leg so they can get me strapped in. They beheaded Charles I outside the Banqueting House on Whitehall (it was part of the Palace of Whitehall, before it burned), so I suppose this is optimal for sorcerous sympathetic amplification. Best place to end a royal threat to Parliament. There's probably a summoning diagram buried under the tarmac, configured as a strange attractor for dead kings. The irony keeps me absorbed while my support crew strap on greaves and pauldrons and cuirass and gauntlets and a whole bunch of other bits with names I haven't learned. The helmet is opaque but once I get my head inside it one of my attendants switches on the high-resolution displays for each eye. "Testing, testing, can you hear me?" says Mhari.

"You're loud and clear."

"Okay, then we're good to go." I look round and Mhari gives me a thumbs-up as my attendant hooks Excalibur's scabbard to the back shell of my cuirass, and we move off down Whitehall for a minute or two. Then the truck stops and the door opens onto a scene from hell.

A stone door opens beneath a lintel of grinning skulls, framed by Doric columns of carefully bundled human femurs to either side. Their binding mortar is decorated with tiny, polished babies' teeth.

A face peers out from behind the door, flashlight raised: then the Archpriestess steps aside to make room for the Countess, who coughs delicately. Evidently nobody has dusted down here for decades.

"What is it?" buzzes the Professor, catching up from the rear.

"It appears to be"—Mrożek coughs again—"a dream of catacombs."

Behind her, a walking skeleton (which has no throat to clear) taps her shoulder for attention.

"What is—oh." It proffers a locked violin case; another skeleton offers her a bow. Their payloads delivered, both skeletons collapse. "Yes, all right."

"After me," Phibes grates, hunching past his two ladies. He enters the darkened tunnel and raises a hand to spill eldritch corpse-light across walls and floor.

The tunnel is dry and musty. Its roof is barrel-vaulted, rising just above head height at its middle; the walls consist of interlocking stacked bones, neatly organized by size. Anton's clockwork bandsmen wait to one side, their papier-mâché faces glowing faintly from the lich-light of the eaters that control them. Faint screams and wails of terror echo down the stairwell and through the crypts, attenuated by distance, but the charnel passageway itself is silent as a long-undisturbed grave.

"Our lord summons us yonder," Victoria intones, a trifle too portentously to be entirely serious (although as His Archpriestess it is her duty to issue overblown exhortations to the faithful). "Let us hasten to join Him!"

"Yes, let us!" Vulnavia rapturously assents, hamming it up a trifle excessively.

"Forward," buzzes the Professor. And together they hasten down the corridor of bones, the jazz band from hell marching behind: never looking back, inattentive to the rolling fogbank of unreality that laps at their heels.

(It is a good thing for the Phibes gang that they are traveling through the ghost roads—having entered via a summoning circle Phibes furtively inscribed inside one of the pipe cases of the Abbey's main organ and energized with *mana* bled from the souls of the congregation. Behind them the Abbey has descended into what disaster responders call a "non-survivable situation." Even practitioners of their caliber would be hard-pressed to escape the feral ghosts of the pre-Tudor kings that stalk the nave above them, but the energized circle enabled Phibes to punch a hole through the walls of the world and slither behind the scenes. So now they follow Victoria's inexorable draw toward the object of her veneration, the god who restored her to life nearly a century ago.)

They walk along the charnel passage for a subjective eternity, although in truth the journey takes less than a quarter of an hour. Vulnavia cradles the violin case nervously: it's lined with protective wards and thoroughly grounded with cold iron bands, but she can still feel the thing inside it banging against the walls like an angry hornet, eager to escape and sting the souls of any survivors. Doubtless Lecter will blame her for his confinement when he is released at their destination; she can only hope that the one who summons them is strong enough to restrain him. Ahead of her, Victoria hurries like a woman enthralled, eager to meet the Prime Minister again.

They pass side tunnels branching off into darkness and mist that seems to smoke as if reality itself is on fire.

They cross the floor of a great cavern overlaid in curiously rounded white cobbles that, after a minute, Vulnavia realizes are skulls; the pillars of long bones that support the ceiling are sheathed in rib cages. If she were more modern media literate she would draw comparisons to the work of H. R. Giger, but as things stand she merely sees it as gauche and excessively florid necromantic wealth signaling, using bones instead of gold plate.

The tunnel continues, then widens and arches over an underground river for a while. Its waters are turbid and barely seem to move. A punt is tied up alongside the wharf, its pole neatly laid atop it, and Vulnavia thinks she has seen its like before. "Our onward travel is assured," blats Anton, "for our appointment in Samarra."

Victoria chuckles mordantly. "None of us is going to die today, dear."

"Of course not." Professor Phibes pats her hand proprietorially, setting Vulnavia's teeth on edge with jealousy: "You already got that out of the way a century ago, my love."

The Countess holds her counsel. Lecter, imprisoned within her violin case, bangs against the interior in some agitation: perhaps his food coma is waning, or he apprehends what awaits him (if a necromantic instrument possessed by the hungry ghost of a monster can be said to apprehend much of anything except blood and pain).

The tunnel begins to slope upward, leaving behind the underground river. As it does so the floor evens out—it is now paved with close-set flags of limestone—and the curtain walls of bone disappear, replaced by mundane masonry. They finally come to an exit framed by stone pillars, doorless, beneath a nighttime sky dominated by a thin blue smoke-haze of stars.

The air here is dry and thin, as if they stand atop an ancient plateau on a dying world. Ahead of them rises a monstrous step pyramid. The platform on top is dominated by a windowless stone temple, not dissimilar to the Parthenon of Athens, only scaled for the use of giants. Behind them a circle of stakes bearing grisly human sacrifices surrounds the pyramid: mummified corpses that will provide the eaters that guard this sacred space with physical bodies to use when they awaken to defend it from the unworthy.

Victoria raises her left hand, rotates her wrist in a strange, circular motion, then utters a phrase in Old Enochian. The guardians show no sign of life, but Vulnavia feels their acknowledgment: they are recognized, and the Archpriestess and her retinue are permitted to approach the sanctuary unmolested.

Anton, characteristically, can't pass up an opportunity to hear his own voice. "Behold the temple of many doors, guarded by the Sleeper," he buzzes. "Let us ascend, my loves, and meet our Lord within."

The temple has many doors, although only one is manifest at any time—it connects the dream roads, or it can be connected elsewhere, depending on the rite and the elder god in whose name it is invoked. It's a giant gateway router serving nightmares as a service. They have been here before, when Phibes and Vulnavia ferried Victoria's crystal coffin along the sacred River of Life. But back in the 1920s, the walls between the worlds had been impenetrable. A lower population, no computers, and determined efforts to suppress public belief in magic had effectively locked His Dread Majesty out of the human world. You can't accommodate a tyrannosaur in a chicken coop, after all.

Things are different today, and the walls are nearly down. A minor avatar of the Black Pharaoh has been awake and at large for a couple of centuries, but until quite recently He could have been mistaken for just another prestidigitator, a music hall conjuror and magical fraud. Now He's the Prime Minister, gathering power to Himself in an exponentiating avalanche of necromantic puissance: but He's still barely the smallest sliver of His Dark Majesty, the eldritch trickster-god who reigned over predynastic Upper Egypt millennia before the pyramid-building pharaohs. He and His ilk are the human-recognizable incarnations of much older patterns, egregores that parasitize sophont species and metabolize their faith. The instance of the Black Pharaoh who reigns here is not in contact with the one who rules modern London—but has the full complement of knowledge and power, lacking only the *mana* to fully transmigrate into the human world.

It takes the soul-stuff reaped from millions of sacrifices to force open a dream road from this chilly plateau to the realm of human life of sufficient diameter to accommodate a god. And so Countess Mrożek cradles her unquiet instrument, engorged with the raw, distilled belief of sixty years of British monarchy, and walking between her wife and their sometime lover she makes her way up the staircase, nerving herself for the ritual to come.

THE MATTER OF BRITAIN

Mo is in the passage leading to the Cloisters when Dr. Armstrong touches his headset and utters a command that chills her to the bone: "Hello, Bob: Ruby—Seminole—Kriegspiel—Hatchet—execute Untergang."

When she glances round her husband is frozen in mid-stride, his mouth hanging gormlessly open, as if he was frozen in the act of speaking. A posse of breakdancing skeletons are also frozen in mid-caper behind him. They break apart for real as she channels her frustration through the borrowed violin and sucks the eaters right out of their bones. Then she turns back to the Senior Auditor: "What have you done?"

"Nothing irreversible," he says mildly. "We need to talk. In private."

He turns and walks through the doors of the Chapter House. Mo follows, warily.

The Chapter House is a large octagonal room, with a vaulted stone roof fanning out from a central pillar. Stained glass windows fill the upper half of each gothic arch above wooden wall panels painted with scenes of the apocalypse. The King's Great Council met here in the mid-thirteenth century, and a century later the House of Commons used it as a debating chamber. It is, to put it mildly, steeped in history.

The Senior Auditor has inscribed a great ward around the perimeter, loaded with power so concentrated that it makes Mo's skin crawl. The magic circle is guarded by a dozen Harries stationed around its perimeter, their chromed exoskeletons gleaming in the multicolored light from the windows. They bear an unsettling resemblance to gibbets, if gibbet cages were equipped with loudspeakers and marched around in public to proclaim the king's anger. And in the middle of the great circle Dr. Armstrong has installed a steel containment grid, much like the one around the royal sarcophagus in the nave.

"I suppose you're wondering what the big plan is, what I'm trying to achieve," he says. He looks slightly embarrassed, like a sixty-year-old schoolboy caught with his hand in the sweet jar. As he talks he crosses the room to stand behind the magic circle, next to a mobile equipment rack that is wired to the grid. Its blinkenlights are aflicker with the network activity of a cluster of computers harnessed to run his summoning firmware. "I honestly didn't bring you here to listen to me deliver a villain monologue. But I don't expect to survive long enough to explain myself to the inevitable board of inquiry and somebody needs to bear witness, so it might as well be you, Dominque."

"I suppose you know this is all going to end in tears? And it's no good telling you there's still time to repent?" Mo side-eyes the corners of the room, the hungry eaters trapped in their motorized steel cages, the carnage outside: "He'll call it treason, you know."

"Of course He will. And He'd be absolutely right." Dr. Armstrong smiles sadly. "I never expected the New Management to get this far when I cut the deal. Was it only last year? No, year before . . . ? Well, time flies. I only activated GOD GAME INDIGO and PLAN TITANIC because we were in desperate straits, the Sleeper's cult followers had got their teeth into the cabinet, we had been purged and the survivors were being hounded—"

"*I was there*, Michael," she interrupts him. "Why don't you get to the—"

"No, I need you to listen." Dr. Armstrong is never irate and seldom does vehement, but he's perilously close to both right now. "Bear witness to my testimony, all right? *Please?*"

Mo ostentatiously checks her watch. "I suppose so," she says through gritted teeth.

"We had Fabian on ice, thanks to you. We had Iris and most of his leading clergy in Camp Sunshine and other detention centers. But when you're fighting a war on multiple fronts you only have to lose a battle on one of them to eventually lose the entire war. And that's what happened in Leeds. Can't sweep losing a major city under the rug, so then the elected government got involved and thought they were in charge of things, and Schiller's mob moved in and you know the rest. Most of it, anyway."

Mo nods. *Keep talking*, she thinks, not daring to raise her violin or try to stiff him with a subtle *geas*—Mike is, or was, stronger than she is, Mike was the best of the best, and he probably still is, and he was always a planner with a counter-move at the ready—

"Are you sure you want to do this?" she asks. "I mean, you can still shut this down and let me arrange a deal."

"I don't think I can," he says sadly. "Once you let the camel's nose inside the tent it's only a matter of time before the rest of the camel follows. And we let the whole dromedary in. It's an institutional failure going all the way back to the 1920s. Over in the States the Nazgûl went the whole hog, enslaving nonhuman entities and using them as proxies for large-scale occult operations, but then they succumbed to regulatory capture. If you employ demons eventually you can't operate without them, and it's a short step to being run by them. We tried to avoid that—told ourselves we weren't that stupid—but we were kidding ourselves. Dr. Angleton, the previous Eater of Souls, should have been a red flag, but nobody upstairs was listening. What could one alien intelligence do? So we starved it and kept it chained up in the basement—and now look at us."

"Michael, you don't need to—"

"Oh, but I do." He rolls his shoulders as if shedding the weight of ages. "What do you think I'm trying to do here?" he asks, changing direction.

"You're trying to rug-pull the New Management," she says. "Obviously."

"Ah, but *how* am I going to rug-pull an elder god?"

"You—" Her eyes narrow as she adjusts her grip on the violin, her fingers slippery with fear-sweat. "You planned for this. Sooner or later N'yar Lat-Hotep was bound to make a move against the royal family, wasn't He? I mean, the Prime Minister is not the ultimate power in the kingdom, and He wouldn't put up with playing second string forever. He'd want to add the Crown's power to His own, use it to reunite with His greater avatar and become the first of the Elder Gods to successfully immanentize in our world. So you set up a plan to derail Him when the time came. Hence retrieving Lecter and feeding him the royal *mana* in return for . . . for what?"

(She's desperately afraid she knows the answer already, but she has to hear it from the horse's mouth.)

"Lecter is no friend of the Black Pharaoh," Dr. Armstrong comments. "Meanwhile, since he drained the Queen and the Church popped her in a warded box to save her, nobody in the agency is bound by their oath of allegiance to the Crown right now. Not me, not you, not Harry over there, not Bob—how does it feel to have free will again?"

"I don't feel any different, but then I'm not planning on bringing down the government!" she scolds him. "I mean, why are you doing this? You must have killed thousands! It goes against everything you stood for!"

He shakes his head. "We're at war. Worse, we already nearly *lost* the war: you just didn't notice. Look at the roster of Active Ops, never mind External Assets, and tell me, how many of us are still human?"

"Brains—"

"Doesn't count, he was badly injured two years ago and is sight-impaired: also, he was tech support."

"Derek? Pete? Mhari?" She racks her brain: "Yarisol? Vik?"

Dr. Armstrong gives her a slow clap: "Congratulations!

Vikram Choudhury *is* still human. Only he isn't engaged in Active Ops, is he? For the rest, you just named four PHANGs, and one of them is an *alfär* battle mage at that. You"—he points at her—"I'm afraid you don't count. You and your husband both remember being human, but *you* banish demons and turn invisible at will, and Bob is bound to the Eater of Souls the way Fabian Everyman is bound to the Black Pharaoh. The organization is the problem now, not the solution. We lost control the same way the Black Chamber lost control—one tiny and perfectly reasonable step at a time."

He gestures at the equipment rack, and Mo notices that his right hand is shaking slightly. "As of last month, 70 percent of Active Ops personnel had lost their humanity, one way or another. Even if you don't count Residual Human Resources, the figure is over 50 percent. If you include those *alfär* who we've bound to service then it's over 85 percent. Thanks to CASE NIGHTMARE GREEN thinning the walls, thaumic resonance is so much more efficient that it's trivial to accidentally wreak summoning algorithms or cast spells, as the ignorant put it, in the privacy of your skull. So more and more people are coming down with K syndrome, or metahuman associated dementia—same thing, different label. Those who don't generally go PHANG, with a handful of gorgons on the side: there's no coming back to humanity from that. Anyway, the writing has been crawling up the wall in flaming runes for months.

"If His Ghastliness succeeds in merging with His greater self, CASE NIGHTMARE GREEN will run to completion and humanity is doomed. We've got to put a stop to it in order to save humanity. But the PM will absolutely *not* allow that to happen if He can prevent it because it'll cripple Him."

Armstrong rests his hand, palm down, on the instrument rack. "So you see, it comes down to a matter of priorities: humanity, or duty? And I choose humanity."

Mo sends him a hard stare. "Even though you're dying of K syndrome?"

The Senior Auditor nods convulsively. "Correct! Especially now, because when better? As Dr. Johnson put it, if a man knows he is to be hanged in a fortnight, it concentrates his mind wonderfully. Speaking from experience, he was absolutely right. If the progression isn't stopped, if we arrive at the magical singularity, nobody's going to survive. Everyone will be infested with eaters, K syndrome parasites or V-symbionts or worse—rarer and deadlier species of extradimensional brain worm. Even the non-adept, the ignorant, the innumerate, the muggles as the young kids call them these days. We're facing a species-level extinction threat, and so"—he snaps the fingers of his left hand, twice—"it's time to dance or die."

He walks toward the summoning grid in the middle of the room, and Mo instinctively raises her borrowed violin. The eight Harries turn their skulls toward her, green-glowing spirals visible in their eye sockets. She should disengage, she knows, but her former director has just delivered a classic villain set-piece monologue. It's clearly a setup—he's setting her up to play her part in some scenario he hasn't fully briefed her on, which is infuriating. And while he's not completely wrong, he's misguided and possibly cognitively impaired from the eaters chewing on his gray matter. He seems to be ignoring the risk that the Black Pharaoh will take a grisly revenge on humanity if they foil His ascent to full godhood, or to the other threats from outside the UK—from the Mouthpiece of Cthulhu in the west, to the Servants of Chernobog in the east, the King in Yellow in lost Carcosa, and the other, more liminal horrors from which the Elder Gods themselves are fleeing.

Mo has witnessed an Ice Giant eating another version of Earth, orbited by a moon engraved with the likeness of Adolf Hitler. She's heard Bob's description of a temple on a pyramid on a dead planet in a galaxy where the stars are dying. She has no doubt that there are worse things than the Black Pharaoh; things like the entity at Nether Stowe House that threw down with Him and lost; like the Host, and the dreaming eggs, and the Sleeper in the Pyramid. And it's clear to her in this moment that the PM represents a ghastly, but lesser, evil.

So as Dr. Armstrong's grid opens a dream road to who-knows-where, and the Harries start advancing, Mo throws herself forward—and the chase is on.

The Reverend Peter Russell is having a very bad day.

This isn't the first time he's been dragged into a combat situation, but he's not really an active operations kind of guy. He's terrified half out of his skin—so scared, in fact, that his incisors keep dropping and retracting, alternately aroused by the scent of blood and so frightened they're crawling back into his skull. He's a vicar first and a vampire second, and he's so far outside his comfort zone right now that he'll need a passport stamp and a cavity search to get back in.

The choir are all dead or unconscious, bleeding from ears and eyes. Corpses clad in mostly decayed cerements clambered out of their graves and turned the nave into an undead mosh pit, but then Mo (who he has known since university, godmother to his daughter and so on) came over all uncanny and eldritch. He felt the wind of her malice pass him by, like a predatory tiger that has for some reason decided he is not her prey and has instead focused its attention on the lesser eaters ahead. And then there's Bob, who is not his normal amusingly cynical nerdish self but a grand beast out of Revelations, a full body Leatherface mask worn by some great and evil thing. Pete—a vampire, remember—feels very small and timid in their presence but does his best to conceal it. And then Bob and Mo make for the Chapter House.

Pete, who is still shaking with terror at his old friends' transformations, barely hesitates before he clambers over the bodies in the choir to check on the Queen's chrome and crystal coffin. Which is sealed safely shut with Her Maj inside, awaiting a dubious revival, and is there enough air for her? Is she even still breathing? Will he have to donate blood for her, or is she going to need less willing donors? There's no FAQ for this stuff and he's desperately afraid he may have skipped over a few vital steps in the middle of the chaos. "Fuck," he whispers under his breath, racking his brain for whatever he needs to remember about the protocol he's supposed to follow if present at a monarch's deathbed. It really calls for absolution, which is a job for the Archbishop, but if he's in the Abbey he's probably one of the walking dead by now. Pete may be the only ordained clergyman available to do the job.

He's trying to figure out how to work the controls on the coffin lift so that he can send Her Majesty down to the crypt when he feels a chill run up and down his spine. Without willing it, he turns to face the side door leading down to the catacombs. The door is open again, and something horrid is coming up the stairs.

Skeletons aren't just coat racks for flesh suits: in every human culture they serve as a symbol of mortality. They usually signify death (because *duh*), but are also frequently harbingers of doom, reapers of golden fields (black robe optional), and walking nightmares that portend starvation, war, horror, and revenge.

The thing crawling out of the crypt is one of the latter persuasion—most clearly related to the Japanese yokai known as Gashadokuro, a gigantic skeletonoid assembled from the crumbling bones of two score tyrants. A king is a hereditary military dictator, entitled to rule by the law of bloody-handed conquest, and the monarchs who lie below Westminster Abbey are some of the most brutal mass murderers in British history. Their ancient bones are gray and mold-encrusted, half-rotten and porous with age, but they jostle and cling together with a restless parody of life, grinding and meshing in a necromantic gear train.

The skeleton monster stretches up as it emerges from the

vault, then rises, first two, then three, then four meters, until only the nave of the church is tall enough to overtop it. It walks on femurs bundled together from the shanks of dead royalty, the stained glass windows casting bloodstained shadows across its many-bladed scapula. It has several arms of various lengths, some with as many as three elbows and two hands all tipped with yellowing talons, which it scrapes along the stone pillars, using them as a whetstone for its many claws.

The royal Gashadokuro looks in every direction at once, using a capital cluster of crania. Four dead monarchs surveil the quarters of the Abbey with their green-glowing death gaze while a fifth skull, rotted almost to a featureless lichen-encrusted stub, stares down at the sarcophagus of Queen Elizabeth the Second. Skulls have no musculature with which to convey expressions, but Pete senses a vast and airy malevolence emanating from the frontmost skull. This ancient head of state is puissant and bears absolutely *no* affection for his successors. Before the Norman conquest England was another realm, and before England became a nation it was a handful of precursor kingdoms. It was Sussex, and Essex, and Wessex, and the Danelaw, and other realms beside. Before any of these, before the Normans and the Vikings and the Saxons and Angles, it was the Roman province of Britannia. And it was Britannia that Arthur sought to reunite and rule, and fuck *all* those barbarian invaders who came later.

Pete finds himself staring up at the hostile personification of pre-Norman monarchy, illuminated by a malice so intense that it feels as if his skin is crisping in the noonday sun. The monster leans over the catafalque, extends a three-meter-long arm with talons like spearheads, pulls back momentarily, then stabs at him.

But Pete isn't there anymore. Pete has the reflexes and strength of a PHANG, unlike the undead tower of calcium that is still learning to coordinate its seven limbs and five heads. He leaps over the coffin, somersaults past the drooling revenant of a Lord Chief Justice, and dives under the cheap seats tapping his earpiece. "Dr. Russell here, Code Red, Code Red! A giant skeleton monster is loose in the Abbey! Help, anyone, what should I do?"

Time seems to slow as the monster slams into the royal seats with a crash. It turns, searching for him. Pete's hair is on end and emitting crackling blue sparks from the backwash of *mana* sloshing around in the Gashadokuro's wake. His earpiece crackles: "Dr. Russell, please respond."

"Still alive," he gasps, belly-crawling at speed beneath a row of seats occupied by corpses. "It came from the crypt where they store the royal bones and *it's hunting me*—"

There's a deafening crash as an oak pew older than the United States goes flying overhead. King Arthur (or the thing wearing his skull as a crown) is taking out his ire on the occupants of this heretic church led by a foreign queen.

"Still here," Pete adds, rolling under the next row of seats. "Can't go outside, it's daylight and this thing's between me and the crypt. Please advise—"

A new voice cuts in. "OCCULUS Four here, can you lure it toward the main entrance in the west front? We can take it from there."

"I'll try." Pete grits his teeth and crawls rapidly until he comes to a tangle of fallen bodies, soul-sucked vessels ridden by now-banished eaters. There are skeletons in the nave—they *were* skeletons, he realizes: they were attacking the survivors as they fled, but now they're fallen apart as piles of disarticulated bones, then joined together to form mounds and clumps that ooze toward Arthur's enormous rib cage like slime molds migrating toward a collective fruiting body. Arthur, Pete realizes, is a skeleton Katamari—every time he comes into contact with a bone it's absorbed into the growing Gashadokuro. God only knows what will happen if it gets out of the church and staggers across the burial ground outside.

Pete is still terrified but now he has a goal and, truth be told, he's more frightened of the thing with five heads than he is of the scorching daystar that waits outside. So he ducks out from beneath the chairs and dashes toward the columned vestibule.

"If you're wearing a robe or gown pull it over your head and hands as soon as you get outside, then turn left, take five steps, and crouch down facing the wall. Duck and cover like it's a nuclear attack. We'll get you out before you burn too badly to transfuse," says OCCULUS Four. Telling a vampire to step out into the noonday sunlight is madness and it's a symptom of how stressed Pete is that it doesn't register with him: Truck-kun could roar up and banish him to Isekai heaven right now and he'd just be grateful it's not the vengeful spirit of Arthur Pendragon, who is hot on his heels and gaining ground.

"What are you going to—" Pete is interrupted by another crash from the nave. A severed human head whizzes past his shoulder like a grisly cannonball, but he's close enough to the exit to see that the doors are open. Sunlight spills into the lobby, bright as a magnesium flare. It leaves afterimage trails across his retinas. He pulls his scapular up and wraps it around his face, pulls his hands back into his sleeves (*This is going to hurt*, he realizes distantly), and ducks out into the killing light. The last thing he sees before he screws his eyes shut is the blocky silhouette of the Challenger 2 main battle tank parked across the square, turret traversed so that he's staring straight down the barrel of its main gun.

One step to the left, then two. During the third step he can smell his hair burning. It's like walking in front of the open door of an electric arc furnace. OCCULUS Four is talking to someone else in his ear: "Main gun, three rounds rapid, shoot on my command—"

Four, Pete thinks, and his hands and his face are on fire as he takes another step and falls sideways with his face to the wall, thinking, *I'm not going to make it*. Then his earpiece says "Shoot" and the world explodes.

*

All guns are loud, really, really loud: but modern tank guns are something else again. High velocity artillery is so loud that window panes shatter nearby, so loud that without active noise-canceling suppressors you'll bleed from your ears. They're so loud that half a city away they sound like a door slamming in your back yard. The tank now firing into the nave of Westminster Abbey makes my eyes water all the way down Whitehall. It's firing APFSDS rounds, armor-piercing tungsten javelins that can punch through fifteen-centimeter-thick armor six kilometers away.

The tank crew are using a smaller propellant charge (otherwise they could end up accidentally punching a hole right through the Abbey and several buildings on the other side), but they're firing projectiles with a banishment circuit, which is a new twist. We have banishment rounds for pistol cartridges and rifles, but this is the first time I've heard of something that can banish a possessed battleship: I guess the powers that be wanted to have a solution ready for the next *alfär* invasion. One of those darts should put down even a high-end class four manifestation, by disrupting its summoning or by dumping as much energy into it as a shell from a First World War dreadnought, but—

—And this is a *big* but—

Gashadokuro King Arthur is *not* easily impressed.

"Oh fuck me," someone says over the radio. Meanwhile the tank recoils in a flare of smoke and flame, reloads and fires again, and the skeleton monster keeps on advancing. Stained glass rains down in all directions, followed by a trickle of slate roof tiles (the blast overpressure from twenty kilos of tungsten blowing through at Mach 5 doesn't do an architectural heritage site any favors). But the banishment doesn't work: whatever necromantic force animates that thing holds the bones together despite a shockwave that should liquidize it like a stick of chalk in a blender. Arthur is powered by the distilled *mana* of a dozen centuries of English monarchy, I realize: he's not exactly a pushover.

(It's then that I notice a small black hump lying on the ground a short distance from the doorway, smoking slightly. A pair of silver-armored figures have ducked behind the nearest buttress, and are working their way toward him in preparation to rush in once the tank finishes firing. *Good*, I think, *at least they're trying.* But it may be too little too late for Pete—)

The tank takes another shot, and Arthur *screams*. It's not sound as such, but a psychic blast of rage and hatred directed against everything that has come about since the fall of the Antonine Wall. He rises to his full height—he's as tall as the tank is long—and marches toward the Challenger, which rumbles into reverse gear and backs away from the giant yokai. Its turret traverses to engage the target at point-blank range. Which is very bad, because APFSDS darts fired with a full propellant charge shed their enclosing sabots as they leave the gun barrel with enough force to kill somebody a hundred meters off-bore from the line of flight.

"Blue One, pull back," I hear over my headset. Evidently the tank commander isn't going to argue because his driver hits the brakes, does the sort of funky turn-in-place you can do in a tank if you spin the tracks in opposite directions—the tank's firing computer counter-rotates the turret at the same time, so it stays locked on the target, now directly behind it—then the driver floors the accelerator up Whitehall. He's heading toward Parliament Square, which means the angry giant skeleton monster is now chasing a main battle tank toward me.

The tank fires once more, a thunderclap so loud it rattles my helmet. That's the third shot, and it doesn't work. Gashadokuro King Arthur has a teeny-tiny pen knife clutched in his monstrous eighteen-fingered right hand and I realize what it is just as the self-propelled ossuary leaps forward and chops at the arse end of the tank with another copy of BAe Systems' Excalibur. A large lump of composite armor falls off, and through the ringing in my ears I hear a grinding sound as the tank sheds its left track and rolls to a standstill, turned diagonally across Whitehall.

"OCCULUS Four to Blue One, your target is King Arthur and he's armed with an Excalibur which means *he cannot be defeated in battle—*"

Someone else talks over them: "SCORPION STARE is going hot." Things are now clearly going pear-shaped. The Challenger crew are immobilized, but they can't bail out even if someone else captures the monster's fancy. Then the snowdrifts of bodies along either side of the street catch fire and blaze like magnesium flares. While I'm blinking away the afterimages, Arthur casually walks toward the stricken tank (the turret of which is still traversing to keep a bead on him, although fuck knows what use it is if the heavy-duty banishment artillery isn't working) and raises his sword. It's sparkling with pinprick flashes as its high-carbon steel degrades, but that doesn't stop him bringing the blade down on the barrel of the Challenger's L30A1. Whereupon Excalibur slices through what is essentially a two-tonne pipe made of the same grade of steel as a nuclear reactor pressure vessel like it's a stick of butter.

"Fuck me," someone says over the radio in a slack-jawed tone of terror as the Gashadokuro bends down, grabs hold of the tank's hull, and lifts one-handed. Seventy-five tons of British Steel creaks and squeals, then crashes over onto its turret. An upside-down tank baking in the desert sun while a giant skeleton whacks on it with a magic sword is a sad and pathetic sight, and there's nobody waiting in the wings to give this Voight-Kampff tortoise a happy ending. And now a thin trail of smoke rises from the rear of the tank because—*yes*, Arthur has penetrated one of the fuel tanks, exposing over a ton of diesel fuel to SCORPION STARE, so that a couple of seconds later it explodes violently.

My view of what happens next is obscured for a few seconds because, firstly, the shockwave knocked me on my back and, secondly, Mhari's merry men—or women, it's hard to be sure when they're all wearing head-to-toe titanium plate—are rushing past me like infantry racing to storm an enemy strongpoint. (Which I suppose they are.) One of them pauses in passing to pick me up one-handed and puts me back on my feet like I'm a tin soldier that's toppled over. Then they race off to rejoin their team.

Everything around me—the pavement, the buildings, the curled-up incinerated bodies with protruding bones to either side—glitters with Cerenkov-blue speckles of light. (Turns out there are trace amounts of carbon in pretty much everything: Who knew? I remember to keep my sword in its scabbard until it's absolutely necessary to draw it.) My skin crawls from the thaum flux as I feel an awful hunger take hold.

I notice a couple of *alfär* suits taking up positions behind an infantry fighting vehicle that's clanked up from the direction of Scotland Yard and parked side-on to give them some cover. I can feel them doing something profoundly unpleasant and necromantic, but it's directed at Art so I'm okay with that. An Apache gunship hovers over the South Bank, across the river, then unleashes a white contrail that swoops and dives toward the slavering revenant and impacts in a cloud of smoke and fire. The Gashadokuro emerges basically unscathed. And that's the last of the artillery for now, because we're trying to defend the heart of government from the Matter of Britain, and if Art's proof against tank guns and Hellfire missiles it's not immediately obvious how to escalate without blowing up London.

Arthur rises to his full height and stretches. Judging by the wreckage of the tank, he's got to be eight to ten meters tall. A steady stream of decrepit skeletal resupply elements emerge from St. Margaret's Churchyard and lurch toward him. He keeps growing as he absorbs them. When he screams again I see that something glitters upon his frontmost skull—a crown, no, *fuck*, that's the Imperial State Crown (and why the hell none of its nearly three thousand diamonds have exploded is a mystery: personally I blame Excalibur and its mystical Invulnerability Shield), and of course the bastard has pulled off the first successful theft of the British crown jewels since Colonel Blood three hundred and fifty years ago. Which is just the icing on the cake, isn't it?

"OCCULUS Four to Howard, do you copy?"

I yawn: not with my jaw and my lungs but with my internal body image, the one that doesn't reflect anything human, the thing I became after the ritual in the chapel under Brookwood Cemetery. I work my imaginary mandible in preparation to masticate, and I take a step toward Arthur, then another. (Chances of him coming to meet me at the scaffold: negligible.) His crown of skulls is looking around, as if it can smell the aroma of filled underpants wafting up the mall from Downing Street.

"Howard here, moving in now," I say.

The PHANGs and their *alfär* support sorcerers are shooting at Arthur with no obvious effect, although it serves to get his attention. He swipes at them, but he, too, is ineffectual. PHANGs can move very fast indeed and they've got the advantage of range thanks to their L85 rifles. Arthur seems infuriated by the pinprick bullets, but other than walking toward them he doesn't seem to know what to do with these mayfly adversaries. An inkling comes to mind: He's not very smart, is he? He's acting more like a superpowered eater than one of the dangerously clever revenants we normally expect to find at the high end of the power spectrum. Maybe spending one and a half thousand years in a box rots your cognitive functioning. I mean, he was a war leader once upon a time, wasn't he? But he's not acting like one today. (As I walk forward I'm furiously second-guessing myself: if *I* were walking in his bones I'd be sending in all my other Harries first, a skeleton wave attack to divide my enemy's attention . . .)

"OCCULUS Four to Howard, head for the gates, we have you covered."

All of this has taken much longer to describe than it actually takes in real life. Arthur advances faster than I can run: he covers half the distance from Westminster Abbey to the Banqueting

Hall in less than five minutes, despite being under fire from all directions. Meanwhile I walk toward him, sword in hand. You'd think they could have found someone better suited to carry this thing, I've never held one of these pig-stickers before in my life. I feel oddly light-headed in the pink haze of gorgon light. Is my time up at last? There's some shit you don't get to walk away from. Finding myself carrying a sword to protect the ancient evil in Downing Street from the one foretold to return in Albion's hour of greatest need is so far beyond irony that you need to add a new row to the periodic table in order to see it.

So I do what comes naturally: I submerge my will beneath the dark and rising tide of the Eater of Souls, and fully embrace what I have become.

Michael Armstrong throws himself into the nightmarish tunnel between worlds, as if the hounds of hell are chasing him—and indeed, his squad of Harries is hot on his heels, with Dr. O'Brien trailing some way behind.

It has been more than two decades since the last time Mike took to the field on active duty. He was a lot younger and stupider—and fitter—back when he partnered with Bob's predecessor, Angleton. He has tried to keep in shape, but sixty years wears on a body even if you don't have any serious health problems: he's not sure he's fast enough to make it through this temporary ghost road before it dissolves into the chaos of the Other Side. It's vital that he succeeds, just as it's important that Mo also makes it—but he can't let her catch him before the end. And it all hinges on the other players making it to the rendezvous through their own tunnel. Timing is everything, and if Mike has miscalculated then it might set in train a series of events that could lead to the extinction of the human species.

(The trigger for this desperate gambit was the Black Pharaoh's little joke: naming the replacement for SOE Q-Division the Department for Existential Anthropic Threats. *We do not add the H*, He'd said, with a grisly little chuckle: *Don't want to frighten the flock.* Which is plausible. But equally plausible: it's because it's not about protecting Humanity at all. Humanity has run its course if CASE NIGHTMARE GREEN can't be averted; the thaumaturgic singularity is unavoidable. The Black Chamber in D.C. was taken over by the monsters decades ago, and Laundry active ops are clearly going the same way. Worst of all, the dutiful workers refuse to notice the smoke leaking around the door, or that the handle is too hot to touch. Mike is under no illusions: he'd be one of them, too, if he hadn't paid attention to the advancing tremors and the memory blackouts and forced himself to stop using his powers before it was too late. Sometimes he can hear V-symbionts in his dreams, pleading with him to let them in.)

So he rushes headlong through a tunnel walled in kaleidoscope patterns, like the intro sequence to an early episode of *Doctor Who*. It takes a sustained effort of will to keep his feet on the ground because gravity twists and shifts between surfaces erratically. He manages somehow, and also manages to keep control of his rebellious stomach, but it's hard to do all that and keep running. And the gang of robotic gibbet cages and their eater-possessed skeletons march in lockstep behind.

Dr. O'Brien—or whatever is wearing her skin these days—pounds after the peloton. But she's not a spring chicken either, and she has the added handicap of three-inch heels. (Mike swapped his Oxfords for trainers right before their little chat: he'd known what was coming.) Her eyes may not glow with eaters like extradimensional Leucochloridium parasites, and she's still carrying the spare violin (which is important to Mike: if they're both in time his plan might work), but she's hardly his friend right now. Her outrage at his betrayal was palpable, as it should be. She'll try to stop him unless she realizes what he's trying to do in time—but he couldn't tell her, lest the PM has implanted buried commands that will detonate like mines if something triggers them.

That's always been the problem with the Laundry's system of binding oaths: like the *alfär* web of *geases* it's a hierarchy of delegated authority, and Mahogany Row isn't even at the top. Once installed as Prime Minister, Fabian Everyman, the Black Pharaoh's flesh puppet, was very much in charge—senior enough to override the Auditors and the Board of Control, vulnerable only to the root authority wielded by an eighty-five-year-old woman with no understanding of necromantic bindings. Now that the monarchy is in an indeterminate state there's nothing to stop Him from performing a god-in-the-middle attack and swiping all the power of the Crown for Himself, rebinding the entire civil service and military to Him by oath, and assuming personal control of the nation. Then it's just a matter of acquiring enough *mana* to reconnect with His greater self, and bingo: job done. N'yar Lat-Hotep will be fully incarnate on Earth—and it's springtime for Elder Gods, winter for Humanity and Hope.

Time's up: the floor of the liminal tunnel between realities rises and then the roof disappears and he's wheezing up an incline on the floor of a desert plateau, ascending toward a picket fence of grisly crucifixes that circles an immense step pyramid.

"*Lift me*," he commands in Old Enochian, and just as his knees lock up Harry scoops him up in a bridal carry and jogs tirelessly toward the steps. Seven more undead soldiers in steel cages ring him as they pass between the crucified guardians, creaking and wheezing against their bonds as they struggle to reach him: long-dead soldiers, immobilized to watch over the temple of the Sleeper.

"*You and you*," he addresses the two rearmost Harries, "*delay but do not kill her*," indicating Dr. O'Brien, who is doggedly limping up the incline behind them. He doesn't expect the eaters to do more than mildly irritate Mo—he saw the video of what she did to Harry 61—but they might delay her for a minute. And meanwhile, he's gaining on her.

His bearers start up the steps to the top of the pyramid. If he's lucky, he'll find the Phibes gang waiting for him in the cella of the temple. Hopefully they'll have bought Lecter, now fully engorged with as much *mana* as could be drained from a million human souls. Even after wastefully spilling so much of it in Westminster Abbey, there should be plenty for the task ahead.

One more summoning, one more double cross, and his job will be over.

Ice-cold hunger descends on me, as tranquil as the grave and as inevitable as glaciers. *And I remember.*

Past lives: most people don't have 'em. You can usually expose people who say they can remember their previous incarnations as confidence tricksters or delusional by using this one logic trick called the principle of mediocrity. If reincarnation is real, then who you are a reincarnation of is essentially random: you don't get to choose your past life. So we can dismiss out of hand anyone who says they were Julius Caesar or Cleopatra. Famous people whose names have survived from antiquity are rare. The principle of mediocrity—the iron rule of statistics—dictates that in your past life you were probably a faceless agricultural laborer, factory worker, or domestic servant, and probably lived in China, India, or Africa during the nineteenth or twentieth century.

I, in contrast, know *exactly* who I used to be: I'm the Eater of Souls, and I'm starving, and I contain multitudes.

I was an English school master in the early twentieth century who faced the gallows for an abominable, horrific error of judgement—then was diverted by government order to face a sacrificial altar and hooded thaumaturges. He underwent plastic surgery somewhat more successful than Anton Phibes's, and found fulfillment after a fashion in public service.

Before I was the man renamed Angleton, I spent a few decades living in a village on the roof of the world. I was an herbalist and priestess of a secret faith, married to a peasant farmer who fathered six children on me and only occasionally beat me. It ended when a devil in human form rode into our village at the head of a column of Russian troops, hanged the hetman, and conscripted every young man who failed to flee in time. The rest of us he slaughtered—we would be reborn to serve his cause with the next turn of the great wheel, he declared, before he set his soldiers loose to rape and murder. I left him with my dying curse: and I died hard that time. The Baron's men had heard there was a witch, laid an occult trap, pinned me down, and shot me from a distance while my house burned with my youngest still inside—

What I remember the most about those early incarnations is the hunger. It was a constant through the ages, always there, always strong. I sucked the souls from those who threatened me but never achieved satiation.

That was the worst: the memories grow faint the further back I go, but I'm absolutely certain I wasn't Julius Caesar or Cleopatra. Most of my past lives were miserable, hungry, poor, and were ended prematurely by accident, disease, or violence. More recently I came to the attention of important people and immersed myself in service to the secret state. And I have walked the earth and learned what a hungry ghost can achieve, and I am no longer burdened by the principle of mediocrity. Honest.

Anyway, I know who and what I am now: I'm Bob Howard, and I'm not human. But I remember being human-Bob, just as I can remember those earlier hosts that bore the Eater of Souls, and I'm mostly trying to be a good person, I think.

Of course, memories of earlier lives may bring wisdom and abstract understanding but it doesn't bring muscle memory. I'm still Bob Howard, fortyish bureaucrat, and my right bicep aches fiercely where Iris Carpenter's hellspawn took a lump out of it then cooked and ate it about eight years ago. I am not some kind of historic European martial arts geek who can tell his hauberk from his hankyū and knows how to hold a longsword. Principle of mediocrity again: although one of my predecessors was a dab hand with a short-muzzle Lee-Enfield, none of them were knights in shining armor. So I need a plan, and the plan is—

Face a giant Gashadokuro monster with sword in hand, remember I'm the Eater of Souls and a power in my own right: and make Arthur Pendragon's vengeful ghost eat my fucking shorts.

I shout at Arthur, open my mind's mouth and bellow rage and hunger: then I snap at the animating presence, trying to bite off a chunk. It tastes disgusting, rubbery and dry and rotten as a long-dead thing, which is in fact exactly what it is. (Also, it's too big to swallow because Rule Two, *never try to eat anything bigger than your own head*, applies to extradimensional intruders as much as to double cheeseburgers.) Without waiting for his reply I turn and run toward Downing Street—or more accurately jog toward Downing Street, rattling like a dump truck full of empty beer kegs. Which, because the OCCULUS truck dropped me outside the Banqueting Hall, means I'm actually heading *toward* Arthur.

I'm closing in on the front gates when the armored vampires make contact with Arthur, who is now less than a hundred meters away. At which point everything goes sideways. Or rather, the soldiers go sideways: do not underestimate the strength of a seven-meter-tall Excalibur-wielding skeleton monster that's gotten high on the Queen's *mana* supply. He's already flipped a main battle tank upside down. A couple of PHANGs go flying, one unfortunate's upper and lower halves go flying in different directions, and Art *howls* at me, a stridulating shriek of loss and hatred that makes my eyes water. His heads turn, rotating full-circle atop whatever he has for a spine, so that all ten eye sockets get to leer at me in sequence—an indescribably creepy experience—and as I trot toward the gates of Downing Street he shambles after me.

My spur-of-the-moment plan, for what it's worth, is: get inside the gates, ideally inside Number Ten if possible—the fancy brickwork is a shell over steel and reinforced concrete, it's been rebuilt numerous times—and force him to come to me headsfirst in a cramped, defensible space. I will then hit him very hard with my sword, maybe nibble on his soul, and if that doesn't work I'll ask the PM to lend a hand. (See, this is why I'm not part of the army general staff, right?)

My earpiece buzzes. "Bob!" It's a familiar voice, vaguely female, though I'm not sure who: "Get in here!"

I see the gates to Downing Street opening. They're motorized and designed to stop truck suicide bombs, so they might keep Arthur out for a few seconds. I pick up my pace and bolt for the gap. Armor plate is nothing like as heavy as Victorian tall tales make out, but it's still hot, noisy, and cumbersome. I'm half winded as I scramble the last twenty meters to where a gaggle of cops in their own silverplate armor are waiting. As I dive between the gates two of them grab my arms and practically frog-march me toward the black-painted door of the Prime Minister's residence. "You're wanted in the back garden, sir," one of them says as the front door to Number Ten opens and I see Yarisol of the Host beaming a demented smile at my shoulder. She's unarmored: Downing Street is zoned no-look-no-kill for SCORPION STARE.

"Mister Howard! Oh yes yes, All-Highest's Highest wishes your obeisance! He's in the garden! Fun will now commence!" She retreats ahead of me, gaily throwing open doors as she goes.

"The Black Pharaoh?" I gasp, slightly breathless.

"Yes yes! He's expecting you!"

I recall the PM's measured retreat from the Abbey seconds ahead of the bloodbath, then note the presence of heavy armor equipped with banishment weapons outside Parliament, not to mention the whole preposterous poisoning plot—I still don't know exactly who administered the dimethyl mercury to Her Maj, only that they had an in with MI6—and a lot of things fall into place suddenly. N'yar Lat-Hotep doesn't merely play nine-dimensional chess: His board is mapped across the whole of Hilbert space. His adversary in this match wasn't Continuity Operations, or even the House of Windsor: He's fighting the Matter of Britain, the myths and legends upon which the identity of England and the other peoples of these isles are built.

Yarisol, the neurospicy *alfär* battle mage who does hatchetwork for Mhari, throws open the French windows onto the terrace overlooking the back garden. "Are no basilisk cameras here," she reassures me, "your head is safe!"

I flip my visor up and step into the garden. There's a stone altar (mounted on a wheeled trolley for convenience) and a bunch of other summoning affordances, along with a big circular grid embedded in the flagstones. And, of course, the obligatory robed figures chanting ominous verses in Old Enochian: that sort of thing goes with the territory.

"Ah, Mr. Howard." An avuncular void turns and smiles at me across the altar. "Are you enjoying yourself today?"

"You organized this, didn't you," I say, in the grip of a vast and chilly disappointment that isn't really my own. "*Why?*"

"Guess." His smile widens, and I see the shadows of His teeth for the first time ever. I wish I hadn't. (Ordinary Bob, the Bob I was before I remembered who I am, was human enough that he would be unable to apprehend such details. Perceiving the teeth of the eternal void is not compatible with human sanity.) "How does it feel to be you again?"

"Thanks, I hate it," I say sourly. "Going to answer my question? Or are you just here to set up a game of lets you and him fight?"

The Black Pharaoh makes a show of yawning. (Behind him, the other robed figure—Iris, I think—shudders. Serves her right.)

"Your greater half was here all along: mine is elsewhere. Perhaps you'd like to meet Him? Your wife should be getting acquainted with Him by now, I think. She might also be having a spot of difficultly with your former fearless leader: I assume you'd like to help her out? Unfortunately Lecter is a messy eater—him spilling his food across the bones is why you're here right now—but if you reap Pendragon's *mana* and feed it to Me I shall use it to open the dream roads and take you to her."

His tone is light, almost mocking. It takes an effort of will not to rise to His bait, but now I'm wholly me again I manage to contain Bob's inappropriate sarcasm. "I take it all other courses of action on my part will prove suboptimal."

"Exactly, Bob." I grit my teeth at His pharaonic familiarity. "Dr. Armstrong's Continuity Operation has been a charming Children's Crusade, but I feel it has run on for long enough. That, and his recovery of and bargain with Lecter is . . . sufficient unto the day, perhaps? So—"

A skeletal foot of brontosaurian proportions slams down on the lawn before me, sending turf flying.

I look straight up into a bone-jenga in the shape of a pelvic girdle: if the Gashadokuro had flesh I'd be getting an eyeball of his junk right now. Arthur's other leg comes flying over the garden wall and I realize he didn't bother coming through the gates. He stepped over them, or went around, or bulldozed a path through the government buildings to either side, kaiju-style.

"Time's up," the Black Pharaoh says laconically. "Fight or die, Mr. Howard." *Asshole*, I think.

I pull out Excalibur and bring my blade up overhead as Yarisol, Iris, and the Boss prep the altar and the electronics cage plugged into it as if nothing untoward is happening behind them. A ruined death's head peers down at me, then Arthur raises his own sword with an arm as long as a tank's gun barrel and swings it down at me. I brace myself for impact.

His blade slams down on my sword with the force of a car crash—then snaps off, close to the hilt. High carbon steel exposed to a basilisk field stops being high carbon steel when enough of the carbon atoms in it magically turn into silicon; instead it becomes a spongy iron mess riddled with radioactive hot spots. Whereas mine has stayed out of the SCORPION STARE fire zone. Both swords come from the same batch, both have the same undefeated-in-battle enchantment, but mine isn't degraded. *Take that, Art!* Well, maybe not. I don't successfully deliver a timely riposte while Albion's Revenge staggers off-balance above me because I'm not sure which way is up, my arms feel like they're on fire, and I'm dizzy, possibly concussed. Because even with a sword that's rotting to bits in his hands, Arthur hits like a tyrannosaur-sized skeleton monster.

After a few seconds I blink away a layer of brain fog and take two dizzy steps toward the giant skeleton's legs. He's no longer paying me any attention: he seems to be bending over the altar and swinging a giant arm toward Yarisol. While he's distracted my sword takes over and drags my arm up, so that I hack inexpertly at his patella. Excalibur slides into the knee joint as if it's a lump of jelly, and suddenly I'm drowning in a sea of soul-stuff. It seems that the two magic swords cancel each other out, but I'm still the Eater of Souls and now I'm trying to drink my way out of a *mana*-filled beer stein the size of an Olympic swimming pool while a castle of bones disintegrates overhead. I dimly recognize another presence in my head—it's the Black Pharaoh, for He now holds the ultimate source of authority for my oath of office—and He's soaking up the *mana* Arthur is leaking as fast as I can funnel it to Him. Meanwhile the roof of moldering bones is falling, and while I may be wearing armor it's not entirely proof against an avalanche of blunt impacts.

So, for the second time in about an hour, I check out in the middle of the action.

—

All the ghost roads now converge on the temple of the sleeper.

While the sleeper lies entombed in the temple—or lay entombed, or will lie entombed: time is malleable here—he isn't the only god to have used this node to enter our world. It's energetically favorable to crack the walls of reality in this place, but their thickness varies, and the amount of *mana* it takes to force an entry varies. The failed attempt by Raymond Schiller's congregation in Colorado Springs, and the more recent flailing attempts of the Mouthpiece of Cthulhu in D.C., have raised a callus on the face of reality. While small minds may scurry through a gap in the wainscoting of the world, the big beasts need a bigger door to come hither from yonder, which takes correspondingly more power.

The splinter of the Black Pharaoh that inserted itself into the human realm in centuries past seeks to reunite with His greater self, to regain in full His power and His glory. To do so He will expend only *mana* bled from His main rival for supremacy over the mortal kingdom He has taken as His own, rather than weakening Himself to open the connection.

At least, that is His intent.

While His Dark Majesty runs rings around the merely human, He is not the only being of His ilk contesting supremacy in our mortal realm. The riotous awakening of Arthur Pendragon, King of the ancient Britons, must have come as an unwelcome surprise (although not insurmountable, for N'yar Lat-Hotep is a state-level actor in our time). And while He clearly intended to use His coup against the Queen to lure His internal opposition out of hiding in order to execute a classic rug-pull, He can hardly have expected Dr. Armstrong to retrieve Lecter, the strongest and most self-aware instrument of the bone orchestra. Much less to have subverted His Archpriestess Victoria's lover Vulnavia, and to have convinced her—whether through bribery or lies—to strike up her soul-sucking solo on Lecter instead of the weaker and more passive instrument He supplied for the purpose of siphoning off the Queen's *mana*.

No plan of battle survives contact with the enemy . . .

*

One end of the temple building is walled off to form a cella. Within the cella a stone altar provides a setting for votive offerings, sacrifices, or—as now—a summoning. It is here that Anton, Victoria, and the Countess have gathered, along with a shipping trunk of equipment carried hither aboard the boat of a thousand years. The boat is currently moored at the wharf they passed in the tunnel, to expedite their retreat. Meanwhile the clockwork bandsmen are positioned around the altar, their trumpets and stringed instruments at the ready; the drummer holds a pair of tibia above his kettles.

Victoria and Vulnavia silently dress the altar and set up the summoning grid. Anton strides around the interior of the temple building, droning an impassioned if incomprehensible monologue about the necessary sacrifices to symbolize his devotion to the god-king undying. His gesticulations become increasingly dramatic as the appointed hour approaches: Vulnavia catches Victoria's gaze and rolls her eyes, but Victoria's brief chin-jerk puts an end to it.

"Is your violin ready?" Victoria finally asks.

"I believe so, yes." Vulnavia is reluctant to commit. The violin in her case is not the violin Victoria and Anton have been led to expect, or even the one supplied by the temple on behalf of their master. Lecter is certainly powerful enough for the job at hand, and he drank deeply from the well of royalty. Vulnavia's lack of confidence is directed not at the instrument but at her own ability to control it.

Finally everything is in place for the summoning. Victoria starts by getting Anton's attention. "Coo-ee darling!" she shouts across the temple, causing her husband to jump, startled. His cloak flaps like the wings of a nightmare-sized bat.

"What?" he grates.

"We are ready to begin!" Victoria elbows Vulnavia lightly: *"Violin,"* she hisses.

Anton strolls over to take his place as Vulnavia unslings her instrument case and withdraws Lecter. For an artifact of hard bleached bone he feels disturbingly warm and fleshy, almost moist to the touch: he pulses sluggishly between her fingertips.

They begin. The rite is much the same as any other opening of a new ghost road: the only differences are the location (in a place of power outside human space and time) and the source of the *mana* (Lecter's stolen soul-surfeit).

*** *Are you going to cooperate?* *** Vulnavia asks her instrument, as she touches bow to string.

*** *Of course.* *** Lecter's thoughts are full of an overweening smugness as he vomits up stolen lives.

Vulnavia can't hear her own thoughts. Her fingers move without her willing them to do so, and the bow likewise. Something not unlike music, if music were the food of death, floods out of the soundbox of her instrument. She can't quite grasp what's happening. Anton and Victoria stagger backward from the altar and there is a smell of burning hair and flesh, as of an electrocution in progress.

*** *Come join me,* *** Lecter taunts from unimaginably far away, and he's not talking to her, or to anyone human. The way is open but Vulnavia doesn't have enough vision left to see the new ghost road open, or the faceless presence racing toward them along a tunnel from the land of the dead.

Mo chases after Dr. Armstrong and his gang of Harries, running up the dusty ramp to a twilit plateau beneath a desolate, alien sky. She's panting by the time she gets to the top. He's left two of the eater-possessed skeletons to block her way forward. *Wonderful*, she thinks dismally.

She knows this place from Bob's descriptions: the step pyramid, the arid air, the ring of crucified watchers around it. (He wouldn't shut up about it, once he learned that she held the correct clearance to confess to.) She didn't tell him that she's been here herself, albeit speeding overhead at Mach 2. RAF

Squadron 666[1] still operates photoreconnaissance overflights of the plateau, and they need half a dozen practitioners on each mission to manage the gates for the overflights.

The plateau is a weak spot in reality, a node through which intelligences from other realms may intrude, if granted enough power. But why has Mike come here? Or rather, why has he led her here? She's under no illusions: this is a setup, and if Mike meant to kill her she'd already be dead.

The two inbound Harries leer gruesomely and reach for her with defleshed hands. Mo doesn't bother rolling her eyes: she utters the same deplorable word she used to put down the ghost of Harry 61 and the walking dead crumble before her. They're not the only thing that crumbles—whenever she uses that word, it feels as if a piece of her soul dies with it—but she doesn't stop, can't stop. She marches on, slowing now to a pace she can sustain, then pauses and takes off her shoes. She carries them along with the violin and fiddle as she starts up the seemingly infinite staircase.

There's no point in running. She can't catch up with Mike now that he's caught a ride: it's obviously a lure. She just needs to not be out of breath when she gets to the top.

It takes Mo almost fifteen minutes to climb the steps: there are more than five hundred of them, the air is thin, and she has to stop to gasp for breath a couple of times once she passes the halfway mark. But Mike doesn't waste any more Harries trying to slow her down. It was simply a message—follow, but don't get too close. (It leaves her wondering what exactly Dr. Armstrong was doing with Harry 61 before he released it for decommissioning. But now is not the time . . .)

Mo pauses for a few seconds outside the temple doors, taking

---

1. The Concordes fly at night, with a crew of thaumaturges and a rack of equipment in the back. The job of the sorcerers is to open the gate for the plane to fly through; the mission is to provide photographic proof that the Sleeper has not yet awakened.

stock of the situation. Mike must know she's about to enter: he'll have set a watch. Whatever he wants her to do, or to witness . . . it must be significant, and it's going to be aimed at the Black Pharaoh. So she prepares as best she can: puts her shoes on again, even though her feet ache (the confidence of three extra inches will help, and anyway, if it comes to a fistfight she's already lost). Then she gathers her grip on the violin. It squirms unhappily. *** *Behave, you,* *** she warns it, and it subsides. (If Lecter is a Bengal tiger, this one's an overweight tabby cat.)

Finally she steps inside the temple, just in time to see two ghost roads open and the end of the world approaching down one of them.

I awaken lying on my back to see Angleton leaning over me, glaring disapprovingly. "On your feet, boy, I don't have all day," he says. I blink and he's gone, replaced by Yarisol of the Host, beaming crazily: "Hello?" she asks.

Everything aches. "Ow," I say, and try to sit up, dislodging an implausibly large vertebral column that is hugging me like a boa constrictor. Sitting up doesn't work very well until Yarisol grabs my left arm and lifts, at which point a not insignificant number of bones cascade off my armor. I find I can move again, albeit creakily. My head aches like Royal Harry has used it as a piñata, which is not far from the truth, and—

"Back with us? Jolly good, come along now, old boy!" says the PM, with a leisurely wave in the direction of the hole in reality floating above the grid on the patio. "Step lightly!" And without any involvement on the part of my brain, my legs get to work and carry me into the ghost road He opened while I was fighting for my life.

Having your body remotely controlled like a Harry is profoundly bewildering, not to say alienating and disturbing and a whole bunch of other adjectives, so I'll spare you the angst and

THE REGICIDE REPORT 317

just briefly recap: Arthur is dead and the Black Pharaoh used the shitpile of *mana* Arthur's demise released to power up a path to the temple on the pyramid. Due to being on some sort of mystical access control list, He can neatly tether the other end of His road inside the temple itself, so at least I don't have to slog up that goddamn staircase again. So the dream road glides by around me like a hallucination while I struggle to pull myself together enough to function, and I'm still not quite done when we get to the far end and I find out that all hell is breaking loose.

We arrive in the quadrangle of the temple facing the central shrine. A rite is in progress within the shrine and it's unleashing an eye-watering amount of *mana*, of the same order as that released in Westminster Abbey an hour ago. I can hear a horribly familiar violin's triumphant cacophony, but I can't see what's going on because the door to the cella is blocked by a bunch of penguin-suited automata with papier-mâché heads. They're engaged in a pitched battle with a squad of Harries. It's absolute chaos, and that's before I notice the other fight in progress: Dr. Armstrong stands before the main arched entrance to the temple, facing off against—*oh, it's Mo*—then *fuck, she's got another violin?* To my horror, it appears that the past and future senior auditors are throwing down.

Five years ago, a very powerful PHANG called Old George got suckered into making a suicide run on the New Annex, our former temporary headquarters. He ran head first into Dr. Judith Carrol, then the second-ranking auditor within the department. I've seen the after-action report on their sorcerous duel: nearby metal fixtures melted, bone-deep burns were inflicted, thanotic anti-patterns got thrown around like confetti. Old George only prevailed by means of vampire super-strength, bludgeoning his enemy to death with her own traumatically amputated arm. Mike and Mo are both stronger—much stronger—than Judith ever was, Mo has a violin (not Lecter: some lesser instrument), and they're going at it hammer and tongs.

I can't watch. I mean, I physically *can't* watch: both auditors are wrapped in eye-hurting visual distortions like migraine scotoma. They don't seem to be entirely present in the same universe as everybody else. A numinous haze of eaters surrounds them, drawn by the massive dissipation of *mana* as they trigger combat macros and transient wards. Mo is playing the devil's fiddle and Dr. Armstrong has *a magic wand* for Cthulhu's sake—okay, it's a pointer made from somebody's ulna—and she's throwing angry colorless blue chords while he's relying on a noise cancellation algorithm re-implemented in Old Enochian by an impressive array of enslaved demons. I feel like I should wade in to help my wife but my feet won't move and my mouths won't open—my physical mandible and the jaws of my inner maw are both wired shut by another's will—and the Black Pharaoh giggles: "You can't fight in here, this is the War Room!"

I swear I have never hated the PM so much as the moment when, completely against my will, my legs start to carry me toward the cella and away from the doorway.

I manage to glance sideways at Iris, who is marching stiff-legged alongside me, looking as if she's on the way to the gallows. "What the hell?" I manage to ask, and her reply—a raised eyebrow—speaks volumes. We're just plastic soldiers from His toy box, and she's resigned to her fate. But then the PM makes a surprising announcement: "I'll deal with them," He tells me, a subtle whisper that I suspect nobody else can hear. And then we're walking through the rioting Harries and clockwork bandsmen and I'm unmuzzled but too busy to think. They're all class three summonings and if I don't focus on crunching them as they come at me they could conceivably take a nip out of my soul, which would be bad.

Don't look back. Don't look away. Here comes Jeeves (chomp), oh look it's another Terminator (chew). Then I'm through the mob and in the doorway of a darkened inner shrine. Anton and his women stand motionless around a stone altar that is lit up with eldritch magical lightning, erupting from the frozen spiral stormcloud of a dream road leading to the Other Side. It's warded to keep meddlesome intruders like me at a distance. The only sign of life in the triptych is Vulnavia's hands moving. Lecter is using her body (dead or alive makes no difference) to play his tune. He is the source of the surge of *mana* I felt from across the temple: it's like he's disgorging all the stored power he drained from Her Majesty, pumping it into—

"Stop him!" the Black Pharaoh snaps querulously: "This is blatant treachery!"

Crap. And now I see that the figure coming toward us through the path the Phibes ménage have opened inside their ward is not N'yar Lat-Hotep's greater avatar. It's someone—something—else: a gaunt figure floating in midair, its face veiled behind yellow lace.

Lecter always had an agenda of his own.

The instruments of Erich Zahn are amazingly good at storing and releasing sorcerous energy. It makes sense that the Black Pharaoh would want to use one as a capacitor, to soak up *mana* from the Queen and bring it here where he can open a road to His greater self. But it also makes sense that someone else—*Mike, dammit!*—would count on Lecter to fulfil his own goal and summon *his* greater self, the King in Yellow. Who is absolutely no friend of the Black Pharaoh.

I don't know who told the Countess to play the pale violin, but there are two instruments in the temple right now and the other one is notably weaker. I can recognize a bait-and-switch when I see one: someone is playing *lets you and him fight* with the gods, and Vulnavia—and Mo—are just pawns in their game.

That's the moment when I realize Mo is as unambiguously dead as I am—she died during the incident at Nether Stowe House. She stayed alive through it because she is entirely N'yar Lat-Hotep's creature, restored by His grace to serve His ends. I, of course, died when His servants sacrificed me under Brookwood Cemetery trying to bind the Eater of Souls into a new body. And now we're both stuck here, conscious and aware and compelled to serve Him. It's a subtle hell of His contriving.

There are no flames and no capering devils poking us with tridents: from a strictly human viewpoint, we *are* the devils.

The Black Pharaoh strides up to the altar, dragging Mike Armstrong along by physical force. "You utter, utter fool," He hisses, betraying the disbelieving anger of a minor god who has just discovered that he isn't the brightest bulb under the lampshade after all: "What have you *done*?"

A pair of Harries trail along behind, clearly attending to their monarch's desires because they carry Mo between them without making even the most cursory attempt to eat her soul. She's barely conscious, and blood drips from her fingertips where she gripped the bow. I look again and confirm that this instrument is definitely not Lecter. Seen through my inner eye it's gray and flaccid: if it were human it'd be wheezing into an oxygen mask in the high-dependency unit.

Dr. Armstrong makes a choking sound and the PM relaxes His grip somewhat. He gathers His poise. "Explain yourself," He demands, icily correct—an English gentleman is at his most dangerous when he resorts to civility after murderous fury, and the Black Pharaoh incarnated within Fabian Everyman's urbane shell is nothing if not murderously English.

Within the bubble around the altar, the King in Yellow is drawing close. He's soaking up all the *mana* Lecter spews at him. I don't think he'll keep us waiting much longer.

Mike draws a hacking breath, then chuckles. "Zugzwang," he says. It's a chess term for a situation in which the obligation to make a move inevitably puts the player at a disadvantage. "For humanity to survive You have to lose—"

"So do you," says the Black Pharaoh, in a voice like distant thunder: His mask of humanity is slipping.

"—I'm already dead."

Mo is stirring and I want to go to her but my feet are rooted in place. The Black Pharaoh's mask cracks for a moment, and instead of the blank whorl of amnesia that usually passes for His face I make eye contact with the distillate of rage and an ocean basin of heartbreak five thousand years in the filling. The Prime Minister snaps His fingers at me: "Sword," He demands.

I watch my arms hold out Excalibur hilt-first. He takes the sword as if it's as weightless as a toothpick, even though it's two-thirds the length of His human vessel and lifting it made my damaged arm ache like a motherfucker. For an instant the Senior Auditor flinches, but the Prime Minister's grip is inexorable. Excalibur reforged is a thirsty blade, craving bloody sustenance after all the lost centuries. As He slides it through Mike's neck the Black Pharaoh angles His victim's body so that bright arterial blood sprays across the surface of Phibes's warded altar, the droplets and the ejecta of his soul hanging in midair briefly before they sizzle through the barrier and splash across the necromancer and his wives.

The Black Pharaoh dances sideways around the collapsing body of the most powerful thaumaturge on Mahogany Row, then extends His left hand in Mo's direction. "Violin," He commands, in a tone that can compel reality and animate the dead.

The two Harries raise Mo almost upright. She's barely conscious, but her arm extends just like mine did, and the Black Pharaoh collects her violin with His left hand and for a moment strikes a pose, as if to play: but it's no bow He draws across the blue-glowing strings, and the bone fiddle screams despairingly as He draws Excalibur through its body.

The sacrifice of even a sickly and diseased lesser instrument releases far more *mana* than a mere sorcerer's death, and the ward around the altar is already cracked. The Black Pharaoh flourishes His sword at Countess Mrożek. "*Enough*," He snarls, and utters a single word in a tongue that predates Old Enochian, a word I can't quite hear. (For which selective deafness I am very glad, because to hear it is to die.) He blasts every shred of His stolen *mana* through the sword and into Lecter, and thence into His ancient rival, the King in Yellow, who has had bare seconds to react between Mike saying *I'm already dead* and the Black Pharaoh unleashing His black lightning.

(Five thousand years of planning His return: then the Black Pharaoh overturned His own chessboard in a heartbeat, with a series of sacrifices so dizzyingly fast I can barely parse them. All in response to Dr. Armstrong's dying move.)

Finally He brings the tip of Excalibur down on the altar, and *pushes*. The ghost road flickers to a vanishing point, taking the King in Yellow with it. He keeps pushing, then angles his blade, tilting it upright, stepping between Vulnavia and Victoria (who is slumped across the altar and the smoking body of the bone violin), angling the sword until it stands proudly vertical. Then He lets go, leaving the sword embedded in the stone slab. Never let it be said that He has no sense of humor.

EPILOGUE

They put Mike Armstrong up on Marble Arch today.

Excuse me. They mounted his head, torso, and limbs—amputated by the Home Office executioner—on spears on top of the Tzompantli. It's a revival of a custom that died out in the eighteenth century: a savage expression of the monarch's rage, a public display of the mutilated remains of the enemies of the Crown. Terrible public sanitation, but it makes a very pointed statement: His Nibs is furious.

I take comfort from the knowledge that Mike died more than a week before the grim ceremony, and he sacrificed his own life gladly. He was a true patriot, which is why he'll be remembered in the history books as a traitor—his kind always are.

As for the rest . . . listen, do you really want the infodump? Okay, here goes.

TLDR version: Mike won, even though he died in the end.

Longer version: we have averted CASE NIGHTMARE GREEN. The stored-up royal *mana* that the Black Pharaoh intended to use to call up his greater avatar got wasted on sidequests: the danse macabre in Westminster Abbey, the disastrous resurrection of King Arthur, the attempted summoning of the King in Yellow, and his final banishment (and the actual physical destruction of Lecter) by the Black Pharaoh.

It doesn't mean that the long emergency—too much magical pollution, too many idiots uncorking stoppered bottles saying DEMON INSIDE—is over. The repercussions will be with us for centuries, lingering like a stale fart in a rush hour tube carriage.

But at least it's not getting exponentially worse anymore. It's not going to continue until all life with nervous systems become extinct thanks to an invasion of mindless computational parasites. It's even safe to mine bitcoins for now: What's the worst that can happen, an HMRC audit?

I think it unlikely that the PM will make another attempt to invite his greater avatar into our universe. Each subsequent attempt to perform the ritual takes more power, and this time around he already splurged the accumulated faith of over a hundred million monarchists from two-thirds of a century. Any future attempt will be problematic. Never say never, but don't expect it to happen any time soon, either.

Mike anticipated that the Black Pharaoh would try to sideline the British monarchy in his own favor at some point, so he set things up well ahead of time. He manipulated the whole of Continuity Operations—which the Black Pharaoh knew about and had tolerated as a minor amusement until it became an obstacle, at which point he crushed it. He gaslit Mo, he tried to reprogram me, and he lied to the Phibes trio. He, and he alone, summoned Lecter—he had the security clearance to see how Mo's team at the Home Office had banished him—and he planned the shell game with the instruments to keep Mo from holding Lecter in check. Once the King in Yellow was in play, the Black Pharaoh had no real choice but to make it His overriding priority to slam the door on His rival: only one head can wear the crown, after all. But in getting rid of the ancient enemy from Carcosa the PM was forced to give up on His greater avatar, and in so doing weakened Himself grievously.

So what about everyone else?

Well, the Queen ain't dead yet, as Granny Weatherwax put it. She spends all but seven days a year in suspended animation in her crystal coffin in Balmoral: this keeps her need for donors under control—nobody wants another Bloody Mary in the palace. Mhari Murphy, Baroness Karnstein, organizes her blood meals and I gather that Her Majesty is, if not amused, then at least propitiated. In a decade or so we'll have to explain to the public at large why the Queen appears to be aging backward and no longer attends outdoor events, but by then it'll just be part of the new normal.

I don't remember the aftermath of the fight with the King in Yellow—there was some backlash from the deplorable word the Black Pharaoh uttered—but I know that Iris took control of the surviving Harries and had them carry Mo and myself back down the step pyramid behind the PM. Who, after permitting a single tightly controlled survey visit, has declared the pyramid off-limits, an infinite thaumaturgic hazard site. There are fresh guards stationed around it with standing orders to stop anyone trying to gain access to the temple. (Which is unsurprising: the only active instance of Excalibur is in the stone altar there, and He can't be happy about the prophecies associated with that damned sword.)

The survey expedition found no sign whatsoever of the Archpriestess, the Professor, and the Countess. Nor did it find the clockwork band, the crystal coffins, Phibes's Wurlitzer, or the boat that sails the River of Life. One can only assume that they made themselves scarce out of fear that the Black Pharaoh would hold them responsible for allowing themselves to be deceived by Mike Armstrong. They've got the means to check out for a few decades: I imagine we'll hear from them again . . . eventually.

We returned home to find London in absolute chaos. Half the royal family and cabinet have been transformed into zombies (some would call this an improvement). King Arthur ran rampaging through Whitehall, tens of thousands of bystanders died—so of course the PM invoked the less well-exercised sections of the Civil Contingencies Act and effectively imposed martial law. He seconded all former SOE personnel to DEAT and required us to swear our oath of allegiance immediately. This had the handy side effect of putting him at the top of our chain of command (DEAT is part of the Prime Ministerial portfolio, after all) and flushed the last remaining members of Continuity Operations out of hiding. The row of skulls on the Tzompantli is expanding, and I know a good third of them by name. I make a point of saying "Hi" whenever I go past: do as you would be done by, is my new watch word.

Spoiler time:

Pete survived. He was badly burned when he ran outside the Abbey, but he's a PHANG—they can heal from almost anything that doesn't kill them outright if they have enough victims to drain. Needless to say, he's not terribly chill about that—but Elinor still has her daddy, so I suspect he'll come around eventually.

Derek and the OCCULUS crew all survived, mainly by not getting trodden on by Gashadokuro Arthur. Unfortunately some of the police and soldiers deployed on Whitehall and defending Downing Street were less lucky.

Iris also survived, to my intense regret.

The Black Pharaoh . . . didn't I already imply He survived? Well yes, He did, and He was in an absolutely *foul* temper when He got home to Downing Street. When He gets mad He's *terrifying*. He doesn't foam at the mouth, scream, cry, and chew the carpet: He just goes very quiet and starts scribbling a little list of enemies while the sun turns black and a headsman's wind blows through the corridors of power. (Memo to self: try to avoid ever appearing on the PM's enemies list. Life insurance underwriters consider it grounds for denial of coverage.)

Mo recovered from her scorched fingertips, concussion, and borderline case of Krantzberg syndrome. (Eventually she cleared herself of eaters the same way I did, by digesting them before they could digest her.) But rather than transferring her to DEAT as a Senior Auditor, the PM put her on indefinite furlough and sent her to Birkbeck College, where she currently lectures on Arcane Musicology three days a week.

As for me . . .

The PM *did* assign me to DEAT, but I've been derated from active ops ever since we got home. I've been given two related

THE REGICIDE REPORT 327

jobs: to index and transcribe the contents of Angleton's Memex, and to compile a classified history of the Laundry, using my predecessor's and co-workers' journals.

Which is what you're reading right now.

Compiling a history of the former agency is a measuring-the-coastline-of-Great-Britain assignment. It's fractal, and the closer you look at it the more details come into view. The Laundry has roots all the way back to the time of Gloriana. I'm not a trained historian although I'm playing catch-up, and it could easily take me the rest of my working career. Which, thanks to the whole Eater of Souls lark, could be a very long time indeed. But I'm not discontent, because I'm out of the firing line for the time being—maybe forever. Besides, in the course of studying part-time for a degree in the field I've been reading a lot of history lately—my secret goal is to gain an understanding of how autocracies develop—and it seems to me that a quiet archival job where I'm no threat to anybody is a really good thing to have right now.

The PM owns me but He doesn't trust me. And the PM lives by the aphorism that one should keep one's friends close and one's enemies closer.

This is not a work of fiction, but a journeyman's work of history assembled from firsthand accounts. There are loose ends and ambiguities and contradictions because unlike fiction, reality is under no obligation to make sense. Reality doesn't deliver a sense of closure until everyone is dead and civilization has fallen. In fact, reality doesn't have an end state that can be encompassed within the human perception of time. So I can't tell you what happens next, or that everyone lives happily ever after (or dies unhappily ever after, for that matter) because it isn't over yet.

What I *can* say is that this is how SOE Q-Division ended: not with a bang but a crisis followed by a reorg and too many committee meetings.

And here I sit, working from home with a cat snoring on my

lap as I beat up a manual typewriter on the kitchen table and write these closing remarks. (By decree of the Prime Minister I am specifically forbidden from using any Turing-complete computing appliance, with the dubious exception of the Memex and a very old-fashioned cellphone: I think it's meant to be some sort of punishment, but I'm really not feeling the pain.)

I may be out of favor and untrusted, but I'm still here and so is Mo, and nothing is trying to eat us, which is very important. He never discards a tool which, having once been useful, may prove useful in the future. So, with regards to my retirement from active ops:

Never say never.

ACKNOWLEDGMENTS

This book marks the end of a twenty-five-year-long project. The Laundry Files (a name pinned on it by editorial fiat once it passed three books) was only ever intended to be a single short comedy novel back in 1999. During that time, innumerable people have worked on it, starting with Paul Fraser, whose magazine of Scottish science fiction, *Spectrum SF*, serialized that first short novel in 2002–2003. He was followed by Marty Halpern, of American small press publisher Golden Gryphon, who acquired an extended version of *The Atrocity Archives*—and a sequel, *The Jennifer Morgue*—and who has stayed on as copy editor ever since (lending invaluable continuity to the project). Subsequent editors have included Ginjer Buchanan at Ace, Patrick and Teresa Nielsen Hayden at Tordotcom, and in the UK, Darren Nash, Bella Pagan, and Jenni Hill at Orbit—and their highly competent assistants. The entire series has been repped since the beginning by my agent, Caitlin Blasdell of Liza Dawson Associates. There have also been a host of test readers (too many to credit by name here)—and this doesn't even scratch the surface of spin-off projects like the tabletop role-playing games and the various translations.

All errors, typos, continuity bloopers, and inconsistencies are of course mine—although I blame Bob for getting it wrong a lot of the time in the earlier books!

Thank you for reading.

ABOUT THE AUTHOR

Charles Stross is the author of the bestselling Merchant Princes series; the Laundry Files series; and several standalone novels, including *Glasshouse*, *Accelerando*, and *Saturn's Children*. He has won three Hugo Awards, including one for the Laundry Files novella *Equoid*, published by *Reactor*. Born and raised in Leeds, England, he lives with his spouse in Edinburgh, Scotland, in a flat that is slightly older than the state of Texas.

Find out more about Charles Stross and other Orbit authors by registering for the free monthly newsletter at orbit-books.co.uk.